*Synod of Sleuths: Essays on Judeo-Christian
Detective Fiction (editor with Martin H. Greenberg)*

*Loose Lips

*Murder Off the Rack: Critical Studies of Ten Paperback Masters
(editor with Martin H. Greenberg)*

Touch of the Past

Murder, California Style (editor with John Ball)

American Murders (editor with Rita A. Breen)

*Triple Crown

Novel Verdicts: A Guide to Courtroom Fiction

The Gathering Place

*Listen for the Click

Hair of the Sleuthhound: Parodies of Mystery Fiction

*What About Murder?: A Guide to Books About Mystery
and Detective Fiction*

*Jerry Brogan mysteries

HOT AIR

Jon L. Breen

SIMON & SCHUSTER

New York   London   Toronto   Sydney   Tokyo   Singapore

SIMON & SCHUSTER
Simon & Schuster Building
Rockefeller Center
1230 Avenue of the Americas
New York, New York 10020

Designed by Caroline Cunningham
Manufactured in the United States of America

1   3   5   7   9   10   8   6   4   2

Library of Congress Cataloging in Publication Data

Breen, Jon L., date.
Hot air / Jon L. Breen.
p.   cm.
I. Title.
PS3552.R3644H6   1992   91-3710
813'.54—dc20   CIP
ISBN 0-671-68105-2

To all my friends at
Rio Hondo College . . . and
the rest of you guys, too.

PROLOGUE

Manhattan, Sunday, May 4, 1958.

Will Wardell couldn't stay away from her. He knew enough not to get too closely involved with contestants, female ones specifically, and as long as she was on the show, he wouldn't. But after that, he couldn't stand the idea of not seeing her again.

He saw her in the greenroom before the show. He was doing his best to jolly along the very nervous grocer, a little bald man whose subject was American literature, but he couldn't stop watching her over the man's shoulder, sitting there, an old hand at it by now, looking not nervous but pensive.

She was twenty. Will was only thirty-five, not such a big difference in their ages. He probably seemed older to her because he'd been on TV for so long, nearly as long as there'd been TV. She was blond and blue-eyed with features that were classic in the girl-next-door rather than the Grecian sense. She had fabulous legs, shapely and bold in contrast to her innocent little-girl face. All that acrobatic leaping as a California high school and college cheerleader. He'd love to watch her do that some time.

9

PROLOGUE

As soon as he could extricate himself from the grocer, he walked over to her, trying to say hello in as friendly but casual a manner as he could. She looked up at him, and he was astonished to see tears in her eyes.

"What's the matter?" he said.

She tried to smile, shook her head in an it's-nothing-aren't-I-silly way.

"Silky Sullivan?" he said with a grin. It was all he could think of.

"Didn't run very well, did he?" The West Coast stretch-running flash had run twelfth to Tim Tam in the previous day's Kentucky Derby.

"Nothing to cry over. He'll get 'em in the Preakness."

She looked almost angry now. "I don't cry over horse races."

Will raised a placating hand. "I'm sorry. What is it then?"

"It's all this stuff they're saying about the quiz shows. You wouldn't believe what they're saying to me every week at school."

"Kids can be cruel," Will said.

"This is college, Mr. Wardell, not elementary school. They aren't being mindlessly cruel. If that were all it was, I wouldn't let it bother me. College students think about things. They read all these articles about the big quiz shows being fixed or controlled or—"

Will sat down next to her and put his hands on her shoulders. He was sorry she was upset, and the intensity of her feeling touched him, but he didn't like the topic she'd introduced for greenroom conversation and wished she'd lower her voice. That grocer was nervous enough already.

"Judy, you don't believe that, do you?"

"I don't know what to believe."

"It's all just rumor and innuendo. There's nothing to it. The big quizzes are all over the dial, making all sorts of money for all the sponsors and the smart people like you and the no-talent emcees like me, and a lot of people are just jealous, that's all. You're in the middle of it, Judy. You'd know if it was crooked."

PROLOGUE

"How would I know, Mr. Wardell?"

"Well, have you been given any answers?"

She drew her hand across her eyes, a childlike gesture. "No."

"So what you've won you've earned."

"But I knew the answers. What if I didn't and you wanted me to stay on the show? Or, what if I did, and you or your sponsor wanted me off?"

"That's not the way it works, Judy."

"Do you promise me that's true?"

"Yes, sure, I do."

"Because if you didn't, I might not even want to go on tonight. I don't want anything to do with anything crooked."

"Judy, I promise you: 'The Big Question' is an honest show. I'll bet the others are, too, but our show I can personally vouch for." He patted her knee. "Have to go now. We no-talent emcee types need lots of makeup, you know." He gave her his widest smile and forced himself to leave the greenroom.

The bald grocer was looking at him oddly. Suspiciously. He'd probably read all those articles, too, and if he lost in the first round he'd think he'd been jobbed to make more room for nubile cheerleaders who were probably sleeping with the host.

Will hated to contemplate such cynicism. He knew Judy wasn't sleeping with the host, and she seemed so sweet and innocent and unspoiled—so out of place in this jungle they called New York—he was willing to bet she wasn't sleeping with anybody. He hoped the network chaperones were doing enough to protect her from all the evils the big city could throw at a naive young beauty. To save her for the day she *would* sleep with the host.

1

Frances McIntosh hated Florida.

Backing through the sliding door of the balcony of their beachfront condo, she held her *National Enquirer* in one hand, Buller's can of beer in the other. She noisily lowered the beer to his little round wobbly table, making sure he knew it had arrived. Buller didn't even lower his binoculars or offer a word of thanks. The beach bunny on the other end must be something. Frances planted her widening rump in her own deck chair and gloomily looked out at the boring Atlantic.

It had seemed like a swell view when they bought the place. Even she had to admit that, and she'd hated Florida from the first minute of their retirement. But no matter how vast the view was, the balcony was small. As she'd grown larger over the years—and so had Buller, at least in his obscene beer belly; the rest of him was skinny as ever—the balcony and the whole condo had seemed to shrink.

Buller set down the binoculars, took a long drag on his beer, and grinned at her. It was the same grin that had knocked her for

13

a loop forty-five years before, and Buller appeared confident it still had the same reliable impact. Well, maybe it did. She hadn't ever left him, had she?

"Time we had a vacation," Buller said slyly.

It was an uncharacteristic remark, and Frances wondered what could be behind it. It was usually her role to broach the subject of a vacation, and in the past couple of years she'd virtually given up. Buller regarded his Florida dream home as a permanent vacation. His wants were small: beer, binoculars, and something to look at through them. Besides which, he was too damned cheap to spring for anything else.

"You won't get any argument from me," she replied cautiously.

"Didn't think I would. Got something interesting in the mail yesterday. Didn't mention it, because I wanted to give it some thought first."

Frances paid little attention to Buller's mail. For such a devout cheapskate, Buller managed to attract a world-class volume of junk mail. He was on every list going.

She had to ask, but she was careful not to sound excited. "So where are we doing?"

"California," he said.

Frances let the word hang there. What was he up to anyway? Did he just want to make her mad for the fun of it? Had she given him too few entertaining diatribes lately? She was determined not to play into his hands, to keep it low key.

"Buller," she said in a reasonable voice, "California is just like Florida."

"It isn't just like Florida. It's really very different."

"They got an ocean; we got an ocean. They got a Disneyland; we got a Disney World. They got sun all year round and no interesting weather. We got the same. They got a Hollywood. We got a Hollywood. They're both phony, just in different ways."

"Honey, you got it wrong. They got everything in California. Mountains, desert, forests, big cities and little towns, everything you could want."

HOT AIR

She looked over at him, still staying calm by force of will. "Don't mess with me, Buller. You know we're not going on any kind of vacation. And you also know I would not see California as a choice vacation spot even if we were. If we actually took a vacation, you know where I'd like to go. England, Scotland, places with some history and some class and some tradition."

"And some weather."

"Okay, and some weather. Or I'd settle for Canada. Quebec maybe or British Columbia. California's no vacation."

"What do I do then? Go without you?"

It was just starting to dawn on her he might be serious. He really seemed to be contemplating a trip to California. She took a deep breath and said, "Okay, I'll play your game, Buller. Just what part of California are we bound for? The mountains? The forests? San Francisco?"

"Surfside."

"Sounds like another beach town."

"Well, yeah."

"Sounds like the part of California that *is* just like Florida." The question of why crossed her mind, but it was quickly replaced by a continuing grievance. "I guess you wouldn't consider going anyplace you didn't have a bunch of naked young women to look at, huh? Going someplace civilized wouldn't give you your daily bikini fix, huh? You spend more time with those binoculars than watching TV or reading a book put together, Buller, and I don't like it. Oh, I put up with it—what choice do I have?—but I don't like it. Are you telling me all this time you haven't been cheap at all but couldn't stand leaving your personal skin show? And now you been brainwashed somehow and you wish they all could be California girls? Buller, if you dare let loose of a buck for once in your life to spend on a real vacation, and then you turn around and spend it going to California, and not just California but a California *beach* town, well then, that's it for you and me. I know I've said this before—"

"First time was 1949, I think."

15

"—but this time I mean it. And if I do take a walk, see if you can get one of those young chicks to do for you everything I do for you. Even if you opened your wallet for once, you don't have enough money for that, Buller."

Frances was about to cry, and for Buller it wasn't fun anymore. "Baby, relax and let me finish." He flashed the grin again with wavering confidence. "I'm just as cheap as I ever was, honest. The vacation's gonna be free. All expenses paid."

"Paid by who?"

"Surfside Meadows. That's a racetrack."

"A racetrack, huh? I might have known. What is this, one of those gambling junkets like the casinos do? I always said Calder and Gulfstream ought to send a limo for you, but I didn't know racetracks went in for that."

"I don't have to bet to get the trip. It's a surprise for my nephew."

"What nephew?"

"What nephew, she says! Brad Roark."

"We haven't seen him in twenty years, Buller. Why would he want to see you now?"

"He's quittin' the saddle, and they're having this special day for him. They're gathering the family to surprise him."

"Who else?" Frances demanded.

"Don't know. They haven't told me who else."

"I'm not going."

"Come on, baby—it'll only be for a few days, and we'll only have to spend a couple of hours with the relatives. It's a free vacation. It's a change of scene, even if it is another beach town. Let's take advantage of it, and if we don't like it, we can just turn around and come back home."

"Buller, you know how I feel."

"One thing I haven't told you yet," he said, the sly look returning. "You know who's putting this together? Just your all-time favorite, that's who."

"My all-time favorite what?"

HOT AIR

"TV personality. Reunion organizer. Of course, the guy never did much for me, but—"

"Is this going to be on TV, Buller?"

"Naw, I don't think so. He's on the board of the track."

"Who is?"

"Will Wardell." Buller drew out the syllables, knowing if that name didn't deliver his wife to California, nothing would.

Mo Roark loved New York. Despite potholes, crowds, crime, and hurry, Mo could think of nowhere he'd rather be. The truth, Maisie Cooper knew, was that he had rarely been anywhere else. Just to hold all the jobs Mo claimed he had held in his fifty-two years, he couldn't have spent very long out of the city.

In the years they'd lived together, Maisie seemed to know everything about Mo except what he was doing at the moment. When they rode in a cab, he talked about how he used to drive a cab and would have got them there faster. When they ate a meal out, he talked about how he used to be a waiter and would do the job better. When they watched *Miracle on 34th Street* on TV every Christmas, a movie that made Maisie all weepy and sentimental, he talked about how he used to be a department store Santa and what a messy job it was. Mo had held all the New York jobs, to hear him talk, from pushing racks of clothes through the garment district to selling peanuts in Yankee Stadium.

But what are you doing at the moment, Mo? Don't ask.

Maybe it was better not to know. Mo was a decent enough guy. He had his prejudices, against gays and feminists and minorities in groups, though not necessarily one by one. Maisie didn't share them, but she knew they weren't uncommon among people of Mo's generation—she was almost twenty years younger than he. She had learned to overlook a lot, to be truthful. Maybe if she knew what Mo actually did, it would give her more than she could ignore.

Lying by her side, on a hot Manhattan night with the open window letting in the noises of the city, Mo ran his palm along her bare thigh and said casually, "I'm flying out to California."

"Flying?" Maisie couldn't believe her ears. Mo had always liked to spring surprises on her after a bout of acrobatic lovemaking, but this bombshell set a new standard.

"In a plane."

"Sure, sure, I figured. But you never flew before, did you, Mo?"

"Occasion never came up. I guess that makes me unusual these days, huh? But who flies the distances I travel? Subway's more convenient."

"I flew to my mother's funeral in Cleveland," Maisie said, not enjoying the memory.

"Yeah, you told me. You didn't like flying."

"I didn't feel safe. It just didn't seem natural, a big heavy plane up in the air with nothing to hold it up. I mean, I can understand going into orbit and stuff like that. There's no gravity."

"God, you sure pick up a lot watching those public TV shows, Maisie."

That made her self-conscious. She wasn't sure if Mo was making fun of her or not, but it was true she knew a lot more than he did. About some things anyway.

"Why you gotta fly to California?"

"I don't gotta. I want to. It's to surprise my brother."

"The jockey? I guess you'll surprise him all right. You ain't seen him for . . . how long is it?"

"I saw him just last year, when he rode in the Met Mile at Belmont."

"So did lots of people. I mean to talk to."

"Who keeps track? I think Johnson was President."

"Will it cost you much?"

"It's all free. The track's paying for it."

Maisie lay there for a moment, watching the reflected lights from the street below flashing on the ceiling of their bedroom. Finally she said, "Is it just for you? Can you take somebody along?"

Mo didn't say anything for a minute, and Maisie knew the

question made him uncomfortable. "I didn't think you'd wanta go, Maisie. The way you feel about flying, I mean."

"Not go to California? Sure, I wanta go. But you haven't asked. I guess you must not want me to go, huh, Mo?"

"Sure I'd like you to go. I just didn't want to put you through flying—"

"I can deal with it, Mo, I can deal with it."

"You'll have to be my wife, then."

"I am your wife."

"I mean—"

"I am your wife in every way that matters, that's what you've always said."

"Not legally. And I wouldn't want to embarrass Brad."

"Why should you embarrass Brad? So I'm Maisie Roark and not Maisie Cooper. I'm his sister-in-law he never met. It shouldn't surprise him he has a sister-in-law. He didn't even call you when he was in New York, and you two guys never were exactly pen pals, were you? When are we leaving?"

She said it like it was a settled thing. She had the feeling he didn't really want her to go, but at the moment she didn't much care what Mo wanted apart from her body. And as long as he wanted that, she'd get what she was entitled to.

Naomi Burns tolerated Berkeley.

She'd been through a lot with the university town. For twenty years, she'd had a job waiting tables in one of the restaurants on Telegraph Avenue. When she'd first come to work there, the sixties student movement was still at its height, and it was an exciting place to be. But as the sixties turned into the seventies, a decade she could never quite peg with a handy tag the way you could the raging sixties or the Reagan eighties, the street had got more and more depressing, businesses closing right and left, and apolitical derelicts replacing the socially driven hippies.

Still, her employer had hung in there with Telegraph Avenue.

Jon L. Breen

"Hey, Naomi," he'd say, "I been here since the days of Stewart and Schorer and Lawrence and Ashwin, and I'll be damned if I won't outlast *these* creeps. Telegraph will come back, you'll see. You can't have Skid Row a stone's throw from Sather Gate." The boss talked like that. He was an unpublished poet.

He'd been right to some extent. Telegraph had come back, sort of. So here she was, a two-decade waitress in the same spot, pushing forty now. Not pushing it too hard. She knew when she looked in the mirror in the morning she looked at least as good as she had as a teenager, and though she'd never registered for a class at the University of California, her friends from the campus—they included students, teaching assistants, untenured professors, tenured professors, librarians, administrators, gardeners, security guards, custodians, you name it—had taught her more about the workings of the place on all levels than practically anybody else knew. People seemed to love telling her things. She had a hunch she'd talked to more Cal luminaries than anybody in Berkeley over the past twenty years—and maybe, she admitted ruefully, slept with more of them than anybody, too. But lately AIDS had made her more cautious and nervous about sex—San Francisco was just across the bay, and who knew which of her lovers might be bisexual or which condom would fail in the clutch?—and she'd begun to think that if her contribution to the city (and to the world) consisted in waiting tables, listening sympathetically, and going to bed with intellectuals, well, maybe it was time to reconsider her role in life.

Just a few years before, seeing her family again would have been the last thing she wanted to do. What would it be like if she ran into Uncle Buller, who'd initiated her sexually when she was sixteen? She'd come from an unhappy home to stay with people who really seemed to care for her for a change. But Uncle Buller had cared for her in a way she hadn't expected. The experience had led her to run off with that bastard Burns less than a year later.

20

HOT AIR

The prospect of seeing Uncle Buller again wasn't great, but after years of counseling to come to terms with it, it was nothing she couldn't handle. Aunt Frances might be another matter. Officially, Aunt Frances never knew what had happened between Naomi and Uncle Buller, but Naomi was convinced, from Aunt Frances's behavior to her afterward, that she must have known. And blamed Naomi for what had happened just as Naomi had blamed herself for years, thinking she must have done something to provoke him. Now she knew better.

As for seeing her older brothers again, that had its downside, too.

Still, Naomi knew it was time for a change of some kind. Any kind. Maybe if she went to this surprise reunion, she could meet somebody worthwhile, somebody in racing. She always had liked horses, nearly as much as Brad had.

So she went to the boss intending to ask for a few days off. She was almost as surprised as he was when she heard herself quit the job completely. He wanted to know if the most recent earthquake had scared her, said you always got unpredictable things to live with wherever you go. She laughed a little at that: some things in her life had made most earthquakes seem downright orderly by comparison.

The two weeks' notice she gave him would bring her right up to the day before she was expected in Surfside.

Brad Roark sipped his cognac and gazed at the wall of paintings facing his favorite chair.

This year, there would be no leaving them for rented apartments in Arcadia or Inglewood or Del Mar. This year, he could stay in Surfside right through the winter, enjoy his life full-time for once. His last worry about money had come years ago. He was smart and careful with his investments, had no romantic entanglements at the moment, and was, to put it simply, set for life. Soon his last worry about making the weight would be gone as well. His wine cellar and his culinary skills could be given free rein, while his books and his paintings permitted him to enjoy a life of the mind.

And what a fine way it was to go out. One last ride on a mount he thought could not just win, but win in dramatic fashion. He would go out, not exactly on top—he didn't kid himself he'd ever been in the class of a McCarron or a Pincay or a Cordero, though he'd had his measure of success here at Surfside—but he would go out when he wanted to, at a time of his choice, not hanging on till he could no longer do the job. His friends over at Surfside were doing a fine thing for him, and he was determined to cooperate with whatever promotional ploys they had in mind.

Brad Roark turned in his chair and hit the remote-control button to start up the videocassette of Jean Renoir's *Grand Illusion*. A lucky find. It was tough to get the real classics on video.

Thinking of the publicity machine surrounding his farewell to the saddle, Brad chuckled. They'd asked him if there were any friends he'd like brought in for the day in his honor. He had thought a bit and decided, no, most of his friends were right here, in the racing colony or in the local cultural and intellectual community. This was a Surfside occasion; it could stay that way.

And what about relatives? he was asked. Were there any members of his family he would like to have share this day? No, he'd said, I haven't seen most of them in years. My real family is right here—on the track, and in the town.

He was proud not to have reacted to the questions with hysterical laughter. Invite his family? What an utterly unappetizing idea. He hadn't any use for the lot of them. The farther away they stayed, the better.

2

The preparations for Brad Roark's last ride had been in full swing at Surfside Meadows since before the beginning of the meeting, and now the great event was only a day away. Still, on that Friday morning, the newly appointed general manager of the track seemed unconvinced.

"It's not worth all this hassle," Keene Axtell moaned to the much larger man seated across his desk.

"Believe me, it is," Jerry Brogan replied, tactfully not pointing out that he was absorbing much more of the hassle than his boss.

"I mean, who is this guy? A good jockey, sure, but he's no Arcaro. He's no Longden. He's no Shoemaker."

"For our purposes, he might as well be. He won five riding titles at Surfside, and he's a local resident. The fans here couldn't love him any more if he was Sunday Silence." Jerry felt sure he was pointing all this out for at least the fiftieth time. "And you remember what Shoemaker's people wanted in appearance money at his farewell tour, don't you?"

"They asked us fifteen at Conway," Axtell said, referring to the midwestern track he'd managed before Surfside's board of directors had lured him west. "We paid it and maybe broke even on the deal."

"Here they wanted fifty, and we didn't pay it. I kind of wished we had, but you know the old management. No vision. No creativity. But here's my point. What's Roark costing us? Nothing."

"Nothing?" Axtell squawked.

Jerry raised his hand to ward off a full accounting of just how much the Roark day was costing Surfside Meadows. "Nothing in appearance money, I mean."

"I should hope not. Why should he charge us appearance money? He lives here. He's riding here anyway. And he probably won't have to pay for a meal all week. And, Jerry, when we had the Shoe at Conway, all we had to do was pay him, make up some posters, take out some ads, and make sure he had a couple of live mounts on the card. We didn't have to shell out for some secret family reunion because a member of the board's into heartwarming. We didn't have to plan for some fuckin' hot-air balloon taking off from our infield."

"Can you imagine the visual impact, Keene? We'll have a picture in every paper in southern California. Front page maybe. Color."

"Yeah, yeah. What I want to know is, can that guy really get his balloon up high enough and quick enough to clear the plant? I can just see him coming down in the middle of the barns and scaring the horses, or in the grandstand and getting us a raft of lawsuits. I never should have agreed to it."

"Parker Fuentes knows what he's doing, Keene. It's not as if he had to *land* the thing in the infield—that would really be tough. The takeoff he can manage with no problem. And he's a friend to Surfside Meadows. We need all the friends we can get at the moment."

"Don't remind me, will you? And you think Roark has a chance to win on Fuentes's horse?"

HOT AIR

"I think he has a good shot. He won't be the favorite, but that'll make it a better story if he wins. And if he does win, it'll be from out of the clouds. That the horse is a photogenic gray doesn't hurt. He'll remind people of Vigors. Can't you see the coverage? Brad Roark's two final rides. Hot air, the balloon, and Hot Air, the horse."

Axtell wagged his head. "They brought Hot Air in for our main stakes at Conway last year. Crowd made him the favorite because he came out from California, and I think he ran eighth. Didn't impress me a bit."

"That was before they knew how to handle him. They don't even try him at middle distances anymore. The horse is a real good sprinter. He may turn out to be a great one."

"A sprinter? The way he runs from twenty miles out of it?"

"That's what fooled them into thinking he wanted to run farther. Silky Sullivan was basically a sprinter, too." Jerry took a breath and tried to bring the therapy session to closure. "Keene, it's gonna be a great day. Everything's in place. Everything's going smoothly. You just enjoy it."

"Yeah, yeah, enjoy it."

A moment later, Jerry Brogan was relievedly walking back toward his own office. These sessions of handholding with Keene Axtell were becoming more and more frequent. The new general manager had come to Surfside with a heavy reputation for having moved a minor track close to the big time, attracting better horses and stables while turning around its attendance and handle figures. And it was true that the aging Surfside management had been somewhat moribund in recent years, especially unfortunate in a climate where rising property values and the vulture eyes of developers threatened the track's continued existence. But Jerry was beginning to doubt that Keene Axtell was going to be that much help.

Jerry returned to his desk to find a stack of phone messages. If he returned all these calls before the races started, he might just have time to get up to the announcer's booth in time to begin his public-address duties. Doubling in publicity and public relations at the track afforded Jerry a year-round job, but some of the responsibilities could become burdensome during the days of the race meeting, especially when he was doing most of the coordinating for a special event like Brad Roark Day.

The name on the first message was one he hadn't seen or heard in years. It was the call that there was the least reason to return. Thus, if he didn't do it first, it probably wouldn't get done, and his curiosity got the better of him.

He heard the click of a recording device, followed by a bugler playing "Boots and Saddles." Then a frenzied voice said, "Hello, racing fan, you have reached Info Central. The call you've just made may change your life. Info Central holds the key to consistent winning. No complicated systems mired in higher math. No expensive personal computers and software to buy. No need to study the form for hours on end. Just the application of a few basic, simple principles can make you a winner in less than fifteen minutes a day. A limited number of racing fans will be offered this key to handicapping success, and you may be one of the lucky ones. Sound exciting? Then leave your name and number at the sound of the beep, and an Info Central representative will contact you to discuss our program."

Following the beep, not trying very hard to keep the annoyance out of his voice, Jerry said, "This is Jerry Brogan, returning the call of Stan Digby...."

A live voice, the same one but markedly less frenzied, came on the line. "Jerry, this is Stan. How ya been?"

"Okay, Stan, but I don't really have a lot of time. You're in the horse-tipping business now, are you?"

"Getting into it, yeah. Sorry about the recording. What do you think? Will that get me some clients? I might want to make it a little classier, give it a little more snob appeal. Think so? But it has to be believable, that's the important thing."

"Some people will believe it. What are these few basic principles that will make everybody a winner?"

"I haven't actually worked that part out yet. I'm concentrating on test marketing first. Once I go after clients in a serious way, I'll have something to offer them, you can be sure of that. I don't know if it's best to have a printed publication. Maybe that's passé. What do you think?"

"Well, the *Form* and the tip sheets they sell at the track still go that route."

"That's what I mean. There's so much competition. I thought maybe I should go on line with it, have a sort of computer bulletin board for my clients. Of course, I know diddly about computers, but I could learn. Or I could do it with a nine hundred number. A lot of people are doing very well with nine hundred numbers, I hear."

Jerry thought 900 numbers were the worst rip-off to appear on the commercial scene in decades, but he resisted giving Stan his potted lecture on the subject. It would probably only make the prospect sound more attractive.

"But anyway that's for later," Stan went on airily. "Right now the area I need to explore is getting some recognizable name in racing to become part of my organization, give the whole thing a touch of authenticity, you know what I mean?"

"Stan, I hope you're not asking me to—"

"To lend your name to Info Central? Jerry, I'd love to have you, it'd be great, but I know an employee of Surfside Meadows can't connect himself with something like that, however classy and legitimate it might be. But I was hoping you might get me to-gether with somebody who *could* help me."

Seriously doubting it, Jerry asked, "Who'd you have in mind?"

"This jockey who's riding his last race out there tomorrow, Brad Roark. I don't know what he's planning to do after he retires."

"Neither do I. He doesn't want to train, but he has plenty of other options. There's some talk he might run for office. Or maybe open up an art gallery or a wine shop."

"Sounds like he's open to a lot of possibilities. I'd like to have a chance to talk to him, offer him a proposition, but I don't know how to get ahold of the guy. I was hoping you might introduce us, give him some assurance I was on the level."

"On the level? You're kidding."

"Jerry, come on." Digby sounded convincingly hurt.

"Stan, the only contact we've had up to now is when you were running a con game on my Aunt Olivia, pretending to be a private detective."

"I can't believe what I'm hearing. Elton Maxwell and I helped you and the cops crack that case, Jerry, and I wasn't pretending. I was a private investigator duly and legitimately licensed by the state of California."

"And are you still?"

"I moved on to various other lines of work. Didn't keep up my license, but that's beside the point. I thought you and your family were grateful to me, and that I could rely on you for a little help when I needed it."

"Stan, if you were offering to ghostwrite some mystery novels and make Roark the American Dick Francis, I might play ball with you. But to draw him into some kind of a racing-information scam, taking in gullible horseplayers? You expect me to go along with that?"

"He doesn't have to throw in with me, Jerry. I just want a chance to make him the proposition, that's all."

"Stan, I can't help you, and I have to go."

"Okay, Jerry. Thanks for calling back anyway. And say hello to your Aunt Olivia for me." Though losing this round, Stan Digby continued to be ingratiating.

The next message was from Will Wardell. Jerry couldn't see the name on a slip of paper without picturing a gleaming set of teeth, surely twice the normal complement, straining the limits of a small black-and-white TV screen. Wardell hadn't been an on-the-air personality for years, now producing and packaging game shows instead of hosting them, but he'd kept up his classy set of enhanced choppers. He was the Surfside board member who had come up with the idea of bringing together members of Brad Roark's family, some of whom he hadn't seen for many years, for the retiring jockey's last ride. Jerry hoped the forced reunion was a good idea. Sometimes relatives who had avoided each other for that long a time had good reasons for their continued separation.

After getting through the grandmotherly secretary who'd been with Wardell for forty years, Jerry heard the familiar voice.

"Good morning, Jerry. Just wanted to let you know that Brad Roark's Aunt Frances and Uncle Buller have arrived from Florida and are safely ensconced at the Surfside Inn. We're expecting his brother to get in from New York midafternoon, and the sister should be coming down from San Francisco on a late flight tonight."

"Great. Need any help?"

"No, my gang will take care of it. I have people who used to handle this kind of thing all the time, when we did it for TV, and the fewer people who know, the better. At Surfside, it's still just you and Keene, right?"

"Right."

"He didn't seem too keen on the idea, did he?" Wardell paused for appreciation of his pun. Jerry groaned to accommodate him. "If your boss just understood how exhilarating it can be to make these happy events happen. Of course, when we were doing it on the show, it was always tough to ensure that the subject of the surprise didn't find out about it in advance. It's natural for a loving relative to want to contact the person as soon as he gets in town. We have to be especially careful in this case, because Surfside isn't exactly New York or L.A."

"Thank God for that."

"Oh, I agree. Why do you think I moved here?"

"What are the uncle and aunt like? Do they seem likely to want to throw their arms around Brad prematurely?"

"No, I think they understand what we want to do here. And usually people getting a free vacation aren't that anxious to cross the ones who are paying the bills." Wardell chuckled. "To be strictly truthful, Aunt Frances and Uncle Buller seemed a lot more interested in the amenities of the Surfside Inn than in anything to do with Brad Roark. The uncle was taking a long look at the swimming pool, not so much the body of water as the bodies surrounding it, and the aunt was more taken with the idea of the complimentary afternoon tea they pour than with being reunited with Brad. I don't think the tea will fully satisfy the uncle's needs, but we'll see to it he gets whatever he wants, too."

"Will, how many of these surprise reunions have you master-minded?"

"Gosh, in the days we were doing 'Hold Out Your Heart,' it must have been a hundred."

"And do they always work out? What if the reunitees aren't that anxious to see each other?"

"You'd be surprised, Jerry. It's almost always a warm, emotional, uplifting experience."

"It will be for Roark. He's going up in a balloon right after it's over." Jerry thought the line would appeal to a punster like Wardell, but it seemed to sail right past him.

"Even people who think they don't want to be reunited come to love it. The old hurts, if there are any, are usually healed, often magically."

Not reassured by the number of qualifying words Wardell felt obliged to throw in, Jerry asked, "For how long?"

"Well, we didn't do a follow-up study, so I don't know. I mean, this is show biz, not scholarly research. But the bottom line is, it's a nice thing to do for people. I'll tell you something, Jerry. It may not be very macho of me to admit this, but the main reason I quit doing 'Hold Out Your Heart' was that I couldn't stand up to the emotional requirements of the job anymore. The older I got, the more the reunions would get to me, really touch me. And you can't have the host of the show standing there and sobbing along with the relatives. If nothing else, the sponsors don't like it."

"Did the straight game shows give you the same problem?"

"Only once in a while. My sentimental nature wasn't the *only* reason I got off the air, but it was a factor. Believe me, Jerry, when that jockey steps out in front of that hot-air balloon tomorrow after the race and is greeted by his family, there won't be a dry eye at Surfside Meadows. Even Keene Axtell may come around. And since I won't have a TV audience to worry about, I can indulge myself and cry with everybody else."

"Sounds like it'll be a terrific experience," Jerry said, hoping so but not quite believing it. The surprise reunion was one aspect of Brad Roark Day he was deeply apprehensive about, though he couldn't pinpoint just why.

"Actually," Will added, "some of the other relatives will be having a reunion of their own tonight. I gather they haven't seen each other in quite a while either."

"Hope they get along."

"Why shouldn't they? I'll be having dinner with them this evening, along with a couple members of my staff to let them know what to expect tomorrow. I just wish PBS didn't have that documentary scheduled for tonight."

"Documentary?"

"On the quiz show scandals. They're dredging all that stuff up again. When their producer came to talk to me, I wanted to tell her to let it lie, leave it alone. Why bring back unhappy memories for people? But they were determined to do it, so naturally I cooperated with them. I just hope they got it right."

"What time's it on?"

"Nine o'clock, right after 'Wall Street Week.' I won't be back from dinner by that time, but Judy will tape it for me. I'm not exactly looking forward to seeing it, but I feel like I have to watch. They asked for a clip of Judy the night she answered the big question. I hope they use that—Judy'd get a kick out of seeing it again, and so would I. How many couples have a documentary record of the way they first met, huh? But they just better make it clear our show was on the level. They'll hear from my lawyers if they're the least bit ambiguous about it, I can tell you that."

"I believe you," Jerry assured him. Will Wardell was notoriously litigious.

"That's what was so unfair, Jerry. We were honest, and yet we got dragged down with the rest of them. In our case, it was a matter of ratings, along with network and sponsor distaste for big-money quiz shows generally. You remember who sponsored us, Jerry?"

Jerry's memory for TV trivia wasn't the greatest, but he could answer this one because it was a locally prominent company. "Purejoy Cosmetics, right?"

"Sure. They saw how well Revlon did with their show and they wanted to jump right in. But the slightest hint of trouble and they jumped right out again. I don't hold a grudge, Jerry, but, do you know, they do? Here they have their testing lab right here in Surfside, and I've offered to help them with some promotional things and they want nothing to do with me. They could use some friends, too, with the animal rights activists breathing down their necks. It's almost as if they thought our show was crooked."

"Maybe it isn't that. Maybe they have you confused with Bob Barker." The former "Truth or Consequences" host had become one of the most visible animal rights champions.

"Nice try, Jerry, but that isn't it. At the time it was on, there wasn't a hint our show was anything but on the level, not a hint. But with time, people's memories fade, and I sometimes think 'The Big Question' is indistinguishable in people's minds from 'The $64,000 Challenge' and 'Twenty-One.' "

"In that case, having this documentary on tonight may be a good thing."

"Maybe it is. Just so they get it right."

Jerry somehow managed to bring the conversation to a close,

reminding himself never to get on the wrong end of a lawsuit with Will Wardell. The deceptively lachrymose emcee-turned-entrepreneur was a notoriously bad man to cross in either business or society.

The next call was to Richard Henry Dana High School, merely to leave confirmation with Donna Melendez of their dinner date that evening. Jerry left a message with the principal's secretary.

Finally, there was Parker Fuentes to deal with. As always, a call to Fuentes Motors necessitated dealing with three other voices before he got to the boss. Before the personnel had come to know Jerry's voice, he'd had to halt several sales pitches before it finally sank in that he had business to discuss directly with Surfside's number one import car dealer. Jerry felt sure there was something wrong with the phone system at Fuentes Motors. If he had ever had to call himself at Surfside Meadows, he might have been more understanding.

"Jerry, good, good, *bueno.*"

Why, Jerry wondered, the *bueno* when he'd already said, "good, good"? Jerry would not have been so insensitive as to call anyone a professional Hispanic, but the evidence was clear over years of TV car commercials that the dealer's accent had become heavier and his pronunciation of Spanish names more pedantically correct. The Hispanic population of Surfside had grown with the Fuentes dealership, and Parker had once entertained political aspirations, running unsuccessfully for the City Council on a couple of occasions. He still entertained them, but not for himself.

"All is in readiness on my end, Jerry. Fuentes Motors Car Number One will be looking its best." Jerry wondered how calling the dealership's trademark hot-air balloon "Car Number One" helped the sale of cars with motors, but it seemed to have worked for Fuentes. "Yes, I am ready to carry our friend Roark from the dangerous world of race riding to the stimulating world of city politics."

"He's agreed to that?"

"No, but I think our time in the balloon together will give me a chance to bring him around. You know, it's getting serious, Jerry. If we don't get a friend of the track on the City Council in this next election, your area will be rezoned for commercial development and the owners will be pressured to sell at a price too high to refuse."

"There's been talk like that for years."

"Talk has a way of flaming into action. Believe me, Jerry, anybody who wants a future for Surfside Meadows had better get off the political sidelines. The next election is absolutely crucial."

"Donna says the big issue is going to be animal rights."

"What? Your girlfriend still thinks horse racing is cruelty to animals?"

"No, Parker, not at the moment anyway. She's talking about animal experimentation at the Purejoy Cosmetics lab."

"Oh, that." Fuentes didn't sound the least bit interested. Politically, he picked his issues, and obviously animal rights wasn't one of them. Jerry wished Parker could hear one of Donna's harangues on the subject. Preferably in place of Jerry's having to listen to it himself. "I don't know where Brad would stand on that. I don't even know how *I* stand on that. But we have to get somebody on the Council who's a friend of Surfside, Jerry, whatever his animal rights stance is." Fuentes sighed. "I have great hopes for our time in the balloon together."

"What are you going to do, Parker, threaten to dump him with the ballast if he doesn't agree to run?"

"Nothing so dramatic. But the view of Surfside Meadows from high above should emphasize to him how unfortunate it would be to lose our great local tradition to unfettered development. The beauty of the scene should make him want to run. I had hoped to treat our friend to breakfast tomorrow morning, make my proposition to him before his last ride, but alas he turned me down."

"He has to exercise horses in the morning."

"His last day as a jockey, and he has to exercise horses in the morning?"

"With a camera crew. It's a media event." In normal circumstances, Brad Roark had been a late riser for years.

"Oh, I understand."

"You of all people should."

Even Fuentes's throaty chuckle seemed to have a heightened shot of Latin ethnicity. "A little bit of show business, no? Someone has to provide it. I'm surprised Señor Guillermo Wardell doesn't have something special up his sleeve."

The car dealer had no idea Wardell was planning to upstage the balloon launching with a tearful family reunion. Wardell and Fuentes had had an uneasy relationship at meetings of the Surfside board, often falling on opposite sides of issues, besides having a general personality clash. Their most memorable battle had been over the use of conspicuously labeled Fuentes Motors vehicles to carry the placing judges to their posts before each race. Wardell had objected, not so much to the blatant commercialism as to the fact that they were foreign cars. Fuentes had been equally fervid in his efforts to obstruct Wardell's plan to give a special trophy to the leading U.S.-born rider of the meeting at a time when Latin American jockeys were dominant.

Still, Jerry doubted Fuentes would feel threatened by the reunion stunt. The visual impact of the balloon launching would take a lot of upstaging. And maybe the relatives could follow along in the tracking car and share the obligatory bottle of champagne when the balloon finally landed.

"Is Hot Air the horse ready to play his part in the scenario, Parker?"

"There is no writing scenarios for horse races," the car dealer said sententiously.

"It's been tried occasionally."

"But surely not at Surfside Meadows. My little horse will make a good account of himself, Jerry, and I will love him win or lose.

Jon L. Breen

My trainer is most hopeful. And I realize things could be much more dramatic should we win. Even more dramatic than you know."

The car dealer sounded as if he had more surprises up his sleeve, and Jerry's exploratory questions made it clear he had no intention of tipping them in advance. When Jerry hung up the phone a moment later, he glanced at his watch and got up to take a quick walk to his announcer's booth.

The short field for the first race, only five horses, was not the sort that endears itself either to bettors or racetrack management. But the essential details were quicker for a track announcer to memorize, and as Jerry trained his binoculars on the field heading toward the six-furlong chute on the backstretch, he had to admonish himself for feeling grateful. Hadn't he once called a Kentucky Derby on the radio that had a field of twenty? Didn't he want his talents as a track announcer to be fully challenged? Was he letting other duties make him lazy about his primary responsibility? Besides, many more five-horse fields in the first race on the card and an eventual surrender to the developers would look even more attractive to the track's stockholders.

"The horses are approaching the starting gate," Jerry intoned over the public-address system. That meant the outrider leading the field could now see the gate without his glasses.

Jerry trained his lenses on the inside horse, a four-year-old filly named Cosmic Swoop, carrying garish, easy-to-spot pink and green colors, worn by the soon-to-retire Brad Roark. These days, every Roark ride was making track management a bit edgy. What if he should suffer some injury before the day of his last ride, with all the preparations in place? At least he couldn't get in much trouble in a five-horse field. At 30–1, Cosmic Swoop didn't figure to be near the rest of the field for very long anyway.

"They're at the gate." That meant that the distance between the outrider's pony and the gate was about equal to Secretariat's margin of victory in the 1973 Belmont Stakes.

36

HOT AIR

By the time the five fillies and mares actually reached the gate, the tote board had a chance to adjust its odds a couple more times. The field were loaded without incident, and Jerry said, "The flag is up." This was the truth.

"They're off! Cosmic Swoop loses her rider at the start!" The crowd groaned as the filly leaped in the air and Brad Roark was pitched to the dirt. Jerry made one call of the leaders before pointing his glasses back toward the gate. He was relieved to see Roark on his feet and waving to the outrider he was okay. Then Jerry switched his attention back to the race. Cosmic Swoop, staying with the field around the far turn, was a danger to the other runners, as a riderless horse always is. With no one sitting on her back, she ran a much better race than her odds suggested, but still could manage no better than third. Not that any show bettor could collect.

As soon as the race was over, Keene Axtell was pounding on the door of Jerry's booth. Was nothing sacred?

"Did you see that?" Axtell demanded.

"If you mean the race, it's my job to see it."

"Jerry, we have to keep that fool Roark alive for his big day. A guy could get killed out there."

The tirade seemed to beg for sarcasm. Don't I do enough? Jerry wanted to ask. I can't ride the horses, too. (Given his bulk, the horses were very grateful.) Instead he just said, "Relax, Keene. Brad Roark will be alive for his last ride. I guarantee it."

3

Jerry met Donna for dinner at Guido's, a small Italian restaurant that was conveniently located between the track and the beach. They had a booth near the rear, where Jerry sat with his back to the rest of the room, giving Donna a chance to people-watch and Jerry a chance to Donna-watch, which was plenty for him. The walls of the room were lined with pictures of racehorses, some in action, others celebrating with their connections in the winner's circle. Some of the best-known horses ever to run at Surfside were here—John Henry, Vengeful, Native Diver, Vicar's Roses, T. V. Lark—along with one picture of a broadly smiling restaurateur holding the bridle of a 100–1 shot who had just won a $2,000 claimer in 1961. It was Guido's only victory in a frustrating career as an owner of thoroughbreds.

"So," Donna was saying, "this turkey Bosworth jumps all over me in the school cafeteria for having a hamburger."

"What's Bosworth teach?"

"Woodshop and social studies. So there he is haranguing me about how if I believe in animal rights, I should be a vegetarian."

"Is he a vegetarian?"

"No, he's a hunter and a fisherman and eats raw steak for breakfast. He's not on me for eating animal flesh; he's on me for being a hypocrite. I tell him I never said people shouldn't eat meat, and I never said people shouldn't use animals in legitimate, necessary medical experimentation. Of course, there have to be controls on it to protect the animals from unnecessary cruelty, but if we *Homo sapiens* are at the top of the food chain and at the top of the scientific chain, I have no problem with that, but it gives us a certain amount of responsibility to go with the perks. All I'm saying, I told him, is that our arrogant vanity isn't so important that we should be blinding rabbits to develop products that won't make us live longer or better but might make us look prettier."

"Impossible," said Jerry. The compliment got him nothing but an impatient scowl.

"That turkey can even hunt and fish if he wants to, for all I care, just as long as he eats whatever he kills. And if the Eskimos and Laplanders wear animal fur to stay warm, that's okay with me, too, but I'll be damned if I need to have an animal killed to make me a coat when I live in a culture that can keep me warm other ways."

"I can keep you warm other ways," Jerry said, gazing into the fiery brown eyes. Jerry had learned long ago he wasn't supposed to tell Donna she was beautiful when she was angry. But she was.

"I know you can. So can Bosworth." The comical sight of Jerry's face falling at that remark finally managed to put a slight crack in Donna's mood. "Come on, Brogan," she said with a grin, "there are different ways to keep warm, and some of them are more fun than others."

"Then you'd rather cuddle with me than yell at Bosworth?"

Her grin became wider. "Sure, on the whole. But to be a well-balanced person, I probably need both. How was your day?"

"No great moral dilemmas. Just the demands of commerce. I'll be glad when tomorrow's over." Between finishing the antipasto tray and the arrival of their entrees, Jerry filled her in on the day's activities. Not until the generous pasta dishes arrived did their conversation level fall enough for them to be conscious of anyone in the restaurant except each other.

It was one of those tantalizing overheard conversations. Jerry could hear the voices coming from the booth behind him, but he couldn't see the speakers without turning around and looking over the seat, a maneuver no one over the age of four could pull off.

The female voice, low and throaty, said, "He'd never get away with it."

The male voice, high and nasal, said, "Don't be too sure about that."

"How could he do it?"

"Plenty of ways."

"People would know, wouldn't they? How could they not know?"

"Not if he used his Purejoy connection. Don't you get it?"

"No, I don't. What Purejoy connection? And how—?"

The woman's voice cut itself off as abruptly as a plug on a radio being pulled out of the wall, and at that instant Guido appeared at Donna and Jerry's table, asking them how they were enjoying the meal, asking for a tip on tomorrow's card at Surfside, the usual customer small talk. Apparently the approach of Guido had been what had caused the conversation behind Jerry to be broken off. It sounded like the kind of conversation they wouldn't want anyone to hear, and they hadn't taken into account the booth-to-booth acoustics.

"Should I put some money on Hot Air, Jerry? Roark's last ride?"

Jerry shook his head sagely. "He'll be a shorter price than he should be because of the sentimental angle. That'll bring up every other horse's price. The field will be full of overlays. Pick one of them. Remember Shoemaker's last ride on Patchy Groundfog—

he was odds-on, and Exemplary Leader with Eddie Delahoussaye beat him at a nice price."

"And Ms. Melendez?" Guido said. "What do you think about tomorrow's race?"

"I don't think there'll be any fog," Donna said.

"She likes to pretend she knows nothing about racing," Jerry said.

"Caught me at it again. Guido, you just have to figure out which overlay is a transparency."

"What are you talking about?" Jerry asked.

"Jerry likes to pretend he knows nothing about AV equipment."

Sufficiently confused, Guido smiled and moved on. Jerry heard him greeting the couple at the booth behind him. It didn't sound as if they were regulars.

"Oh, this is just marvelous," the woman's voice said.

"Yeah, great," said the man. They both sounded as if they wished Guido would go away so they could get back to their cryptic conversation. Jerry felt the same way.

"You watch. He'll file," the man's voice said a moment later.

"Not with all that hanging over him," the woman insisted.

"You wait and see. They'd never use it against him."

"Don't underestimate them. They might do anything."

Jerry didn't have the slightest idea who or what they were talking about, but the urgency in their voices made an impression on him. And the only substantive clues were the reference to Purejoy and the reference to filing. Something to do with the upcoming City Council election? And if so, which candidate were they referring to? And, forget Purejoy, where did this candidate stand on the development of Surfside Meadows' property? He wanted to turn around and ask questions, but he just couldn't do that.

"Let's go," said the woman.

"Yeah, okay."

The couple must have rushed their meal. Jerry was sure that

booth had been empty when he and Donna had come in. But Jerry was only halfway through his linguini. Across the table, Donna was almost finished and was looking at him oddly. It was unusual for her to empty a plate faster than Jerry.

"Aren't you hungry?" she asked.

Jerry made a face and tried to gesture to the booth behind him with his shoulder. It only made him look as if he'd developed a twitch.

"What's the matter?"

He leaned across the table. "Did you get a look at the couple in the booth behind us?"

She shook her head and looked up to see the man and woman rising. She watched them walk out of the restaurant.

"Do you recognize them?"

"No," she said. "Why?"

"Did you hear what they were talking about?"

"No. Is that why you've been so distracted tonight? You've been eavesdropping on the next booth? Your companion of the evening doesn't provide sufficient diversion?"

"Come on, Donna, cut it out. Would you know them if you saw them again?"

"Guido keeps it dark in here, but it's not that dark."

"Describe them to me."

She sighed long-sufferingly. "The guy is about five foot nine, balding on top and maybe fifteen pounds heavier than he should be. Snazzy dresser. Expensive metallic-gray suit. Tailored. Blond hair, about forty, probably good-looking when he was younger in a Troy Donahue sort of way but nothing special now. Pink complexion. Should stay out of the sun. The woman should, too, but doesn't. Has the kind of tan a lot of people would kill for, but it could kill her. Okay, okay, don't look at me that way—I'll skip the skin cancer lecture. Nice brown hair, down to the shoulders. Didn't see her face very well. She's probably fortyish too but thinks she has the legs for a short skirt. She doesn't, even with the tan. They're too heavy. Good figure otherwise. In pants, she'd be terrific."

Jerry looked at her admiringly. "Charlie Chan mustache?"

Donna grinned. "He doesn't. Not sure about her." She knew without asking he was complimenting her on her powers of observation, comparing her account to bookseller Dorothy Malone's description of Arthur Gwynn Geiger to Bogart's Philip Marlowe in *The Big Sleep*. "Now that I've done my party trick, tell me what they were talking about that was so interesting."

"A candidate for City Council that has something to do with Purejoy Cosmetics."

"I just remembered some more details. He had a forked tail hanging out under his suit coat, and she had that great brown hair combed over her horns. Now I know I'll recognize them if I see them again."

"Don't be too hasty. They may be on your side." He didn't say anything about wondering where the candidate stood on the really important issue of the campaign. You could only tease Donna so far.

At another and posher Surfside restaurant, Will Wardell had reserved a private room with a table for seven where he and two of his longtime staffers were doing a reasonably successful job of entertaining the Roark relatives. Wardell was well practiced at turning on the charm, and an observer would have had no idea what things were going through his mind about his table mates.

Frances McIntosh was clearly having the time of her life. Dolled up to the maximum and seeming content to emphasize the contrast with the ingrained seediness of her husband, she couldn't stop talking about the elegance of their accommodations and the generosity of their host.

"Will—I just have to get used to calling you that after all these years of watching you on TV, and I never missed 'Hold Out Your Heart,' did I, Buller?" Her husband nodded humoring acquiescence. "Will, this place is lovely. Such elegant and attentive service, nothing like the fast-food places Buller takes me to in Florida. I can't imagine how much this must be costing you. It's so sweet of you to do this for us. And for Brad, of course. I always love to see someone with a real concern for his fellow man. And woman. And I can't tell you how much I appreciate staying at the Inn. It's so nice to see such class, such hospitality. I mean, an afternoon tea, with scones and things—is that a California tradition? We just don't have that kind of thing in Florida. It's just so civilized here, nothing like you'd think from TV. I'd love to see Great Britain, but Buller normally won't travel, will you, Buller? This is the first vacation we've had in I don't know how long, but being able to meet you, Mr. Wardell, Will, and have dinner with you, well, it's been worth waiting for. It truly has. You're handsomer in person, do you know that? And younger, too."

Since Will Wardell had been off the TV screen for all practical purposes for a decade, this last testimonial hardly seemed to hold water, but he knew how selectively sighted fans could be. Ordinarily Wardell would have been uneasy faced with such a naked display of adoration from a woman, even one in her sixties, whose husband was also present at the table. But Buller McIntosh was too busy ogling Maisie, introduced as his nephew's wife, to notice or care how much fascination his wife drew from the host's gleaming teeth.

Maisie was a gorgeous woman, dark-haired and classic-featured, on the small side everywhere but in the bust line. Her voice, an odd combination of Midwest and New York, should have sounded more cultured to go with her beauty, but the contrast was rather charming. She and Frances seemed to have found a common interest in the British upper-class dramas on public television. Mo and Buller seemed to find no great excitement in being reunited with each other, but they found common ground in various sports interests with Phil Botts, the male half of Will's staff team.

Thus the dinner was going reasonably well, and Will had no

need to take extraordinary measures to keep the conversation going, something he had feared with this oddly assorted group. But there were tensions at the table, no doubt about it. Maisie periodically cast a distasteful glance at Buller, who sat next to her—was the old goat trying to play kneesies with her under the table? And then there was Mo, who stared sardonically and knowingly at his host much of the time. It was damned unsettling.

At a rare lull in the conversation, Will asked the group for their memories of Brad Roark. Surprisingly, it seemed to be one topic they had little to say about.

"Well, we're real proud of him," Buller McIntosh offered after an awkward pause. "Aren't we, Frances?"

"Oh, sure. I never really knew Brad very well. As well as I'd like to, I mean."

"What was Brad like as a kid, Mo?" Will asked. "Crazy about horses, I guess."

"Brad had lots of interests," Mo said vaguely. "He was always a guy with lots of interests, that's for sure." He paused, as if trying to recall some of them. "It's funny, you know, we were never all that close, Brad and me. We both got out of the house as soon as we could. Nothing against our folks, but they were ..." he trailed off.

"My sister did her best to be a good mother to those kids," Buller said. "But she was sick a lot. Died too young. And old Roark, well, he had his problems, too. I guess he did his best."

"What a shame they couldn't have lived to be here for tomorrow," Will said.

"Sure," said Mo Roark, and Will thought he and Buller McIntosh exchanged a meaningful glance. It appeared the late Roark parents were not really that sorely missed by anyone.

"You know," said Mo after another lull in the conversation, "Naomi was a lot closer to Brad than I was growing up. She was closer to him than anybody."

"Then it's too bad she isn't here," Maisie said.

"Oh, but she's coming," Will said. "She'll be in from San Francisco tonight. Too late to join us for dinner, but you'll all see her tomorrow."

"Won't that be nice?" Frances McIntosh said. Will couldn't decide if the woman was trying to sound sincere, but if so, she definitely wasn't succeeding.

At that moment, the waiter entered with their elaborate desserts, and that seemed to be all it took to lower tension and restore enthusiasm. Mo took one bite of his cheesecake and offered the ultimate encomium. "This has been almost like eating in New York, Mr. Wardell."

Maisie shook her head. "The waiters are too polite."

"I guess you know how to find the good East Coast–type places, huh?" Mo went on. "You sure worked in New York a lot of years, didn't you, Mr. Wardell?"

"It's so much nicer out here," Frances McIntosh said. "You know, I've lived on the East Coast all my life, and I'm starting to realize I really hate it."

Mo shook his head as if he couldn't understand what he was hearing. "There's no place like New York."

"How do you feel about that, Will?" Frances asked with a simper. "You've lived back there and out here."

"I could never criticize New York," Will said, flashing his teeth. "After all, I met my wife there."

"Why didn't we get to meet her tonight?"

"She had another engagement. Charity thing. She's looking forward to meeting you tomorrow." The truth was, Judy had always begged off the pre-reunion dinners, even back in the "Hold Out Your Heart" days. Either she saw them as boring business meetings or, as Will preferred to think, she didn't like to have the drama of the live reunion spoiled for her by a behind-the-scenes preview. Judy was a sentimentalist at heart—just the right girl for a guy like Will Wardell.

"Hey, this was a terrific meal," said Maisie. "I can't eat like this too often. I'm getting too fat." She said it with the confidence of one who knew all visible evidence contradicted the statement. Then she shot a look of disgust at Buller McIntosh, who a second later appeared to wince with pain. If he was giving her a body-fat test under the table, it was clear she'd retaliated. It didn't seem anyone at the table could have missed the significance of her glare, but she went on as if nothing had happened. "I could use some exercise to work off some of this food. We should have a nice walk, shouldn't we, Mo?"

Mo Roark shrugged without enthusiasm.

"Come on, Mo. Out here we can probably have a walk after dinner without carrying two guns and a can of mace, huh?"

"Everybody puts the knock on the Big Apple. You're a traitor, Maisie, you really are. Okay, okay, let's go for a walk."

"I wish you wouldn't," said Will Wardell.

"Why not?"

"As I told you, this is not a big town, and I don't want to risk anybody seeing you on the street who might get word back to Brad. We want to surprise him tomorrow, don't we?"

Maisie sighed. "So we gotta keep playing cloak-and-dagger, huh? Oh well, I can have a walk anytime. Not a safe one, but a walk. We don't want to argue with the man that's paying the bills, do we, honey?"

"No, I guess not. I guarantee you, Mr. Wardell, I want to surprise Brad just as much as you do."

4

Jerry and Donna got back to Jerry's beachfront apartment just in time to microwave some popcorn and turn on the quiz-show documentary on PBS. It was a smooth and enthralling production, leading to the obvious comment from Donna.

"British import, right?" she said.

"The narrator doesn't sound British to me."

"They buy stuff from the BBC and ITV and replace the voice-over with an American. They do it all the time."

"But it's such an American subject," Jerry protested.

"Doesn't matter. Some of the best documentaries on American subjects are done by the British. Look at that series on silent movies they showed a few years ago. Hollywood subject, British production. If it weren't for British imports, PBS would be out of business."

"Come on, Donna, *all* good TV isn't British. And why would they be interested in our quiz-show scandals?"

"You wait till the closing credits and see."

"There's a lot of good stuff on American TV, Donna. There's—"

"Shhh! Isn't that your friend Wardell?"

Sure enough, Will Wardell, thirty years younger but easily recognizable by his elaborate pompadour and gleaming teeth, was looking out at them from an old black-and-white kinescope. He turned to a typical fifties quiz-show isolation booth where a cute young blonde was smiling back bravely but anxiously.

"Judy Constable, you've decided to go for The Big Question—your topic, horse racing. We're all rooting for you, Judy. Just take it easy, relax, and don't even think about the hundred thousand dollars that are riding on your answer." He grinned, she giggled, and a little of the tension seemed to be dissipated. "Judy, we're going to show you three pieces of newsreel film, each depicting a unique and well-remembered horse-racing event. Watch them carefully, and then we'll ask you The Big Question."

The first newsreel clip appeared to date from early in the century. A large field of horses was seen jerkily rounding a turn. A figure in a long Victorian dress rushed onto the track and was felled by the oncoming horses. Donna gasped.

"Jerry, what in the world—?"

The second clip, somewhat longer but not much more recent, showed two horses side by side charging down the homestretch, with their jockeys having a virtual wrestling match. The third clip, less grainy than the others, showed a horse running by himself and suddenly collapsing on all fours. It drew a nervous titter from the quiz show's studio audience.

"Those are the clips, Judy. Now, here is The Big Question. The first clip showed the running of the English Derby—" Wardell gave the word the proper British pronunciation: Darby—"in which a suffragette grasped the bridle of the king's horse and died. Judy, we want you to tell us the year this took place, the name of the winning horse and jockey, the name of the king's horse who was interfered with, and finally the name of the unfortunate suffragette."

The blond Judy Constable looked very worried in her booth.

"How could anybody possibly know all that?" Donna scoffed. "Do you know the answers, Jerry?"

"I think the year might have been 1913," Jerry offered.

"Your question on the second clip," said Will Wardell. "Name the race, the year, the winner, the second finisher, and finally the two battling jockeys."

"I could answer that one," Jerry said. "I think."

"And on the third clip, name the race, the year, the unfortunate horse, his rider, and the horse and rider who won the race. Judy, you have fifteen seconds to think about your answer."

While the suspenseful music played, and the camera concentrated on Judy's worried features, Donna said, "How could they expect anybody to know all that stuff if the whole thing wasn't fixed? They really were all crooked, weren't they, Jerry? How could people be fooled?"

"Will claims his show was on the level. And when you meet Judy Wardell, you'll see she really is encyclopedic on racing."

Donna grunted unconvincedly.

"Judy," Will Wardell said, "are you ready with your answer?"

"I think so, Mr. Wardell," she said, her high voice full of girlish pluck and determination.

"Very well. I shall repeat the first part of the question."

With a breathless headlong speed, occasionally interrupted by lip-biting pauses, Judy delivered her answers. "The Suffragette Derby was 1913. The suffragette was named Emily Wilding Davison. She ran onto the course at Tottenham Corner and snatched the bridle of the King's horse, who was named Amner. The winner was Aboyeur, ridden by A. B. Cunliffe."

"You're right!"

"The second clip shows the 1933 Kentucky Derby. The winner was Broker's Tip, ridden by Don Meade, by a nose over Head Play, ridden by Herb Fisher."

"You're right, Judy! Just one part to go!"

"The third clip is much more recent. It shows Devon Loch, owned by the Queen Mother, leading the 1956 Grand National into the stretch when he collapsed—no one was sure just what happened to him. His jockey is Dick Francis. The winner was E.S.B., and the jockey's name was Mr. Dick. Not sure of his first name. Not Dick Francis . . ."

There was a seemingly unnecessary pause, and the young woman in the isolation booth looked a bit uncertain of herself for an instant. But her discomfort was brief.

"Judy, you are right for one hundred thousand dollars!" Will Wardell shouted. She came out of the booth, and he threw his arms around her. Had the romance already started then or was this just standard show biz?

The program went on to show scenes from the other big quiz shows of the period, including Charles Van Doren's well-orchestrated exploits on "Twenty-One." Late in the program came an interview with Will Wardell.

"Our show was completely on the level. I've been happily married to Judy Constable for over thirty years now, and she's as cute today as she was then. She also still has her absolute recall on horse racing. What pains me is that someone, somewhere, may be thinking we were as dishonest as some others, that my lovely wife is a fraud." Quite genuine-looking tears were coming to the eyes of Will Wardell, and the camera moved in closer. "To have my integrity questioned or, much worse, to have hers questioned—well, it just isn't fair. And I'm glad for the chance to say so. I've done nothing in broadcasting of which I can't be proud."

That was all of Will Wardell. The narrator didn't comment on his claim of innocence. The show closed with some comments from people who admittedly had been involved in deception, either as contestants or producers, and a final assessment by the faceless narrator of what it all meant in American media history. The final credits showed it had been an American-produced documentary, a fact Donna didn't dwell on, and Jerry wisely chose not to, either.

After they'd turned off the program, Donna scooped up a last handful of popcorn and said, "He seemed sincere, didn't he? Do you really think 'The Big Question' was on the level?"

"As long as Will Wardell is on the board of Surfside Meadows, Donna, I think it was on the level."

"No, seriously."

"I am serious. And you could tell from what we just saw there were gradations of dishonesty even on the shows that are known to have been rigged. I mean, it's one thing to actually give the questions and answers in advance, and that was sometimes done. But what about finding out in interviews what areas the contestant was shaky in? There was a jockey named Billy Pearson on one of the shows as an expert on art. He said his knowledge of Chinese art was weak, and when he was on the show, questions on Chinese art never seemed to come up. If you wanted a contestant to stay on the show, you could avoid those weak areas in doing the questions."

"Or emphasize those areas if you wanted to dump the contestant."

"Well, yes, there was that possibility, too. So maybe they knew enough about Judy Constable's horse-racing knowledge to know what areas she was solid in and in what areas they could trip her up. That's the kind of thing that could be done by the producer or some staff member. It wouldn't be in the host's domain at all."

"So you're saying Wardell could be telling the truth as he knew it, and the show could still be crooked."

"I don't know if I'd call it crooked if they didn't actually give the answers."

"It's crooked, Jerry. Maybe not as crooked, but crooked just the same. You say we're likely to see Wardell and his wife tomorrow?"

"I'd think so, at the party for Brad Roark after the races. Oh, and you'll see them sooner than that. You'll have a seat in their box for the races."

"Hey, that's convenient. I'll have a chance to talk to Judy Wardell and find out how pure and untainted that show really was."

"Donna, I kind of wish you wouldn't get into that with her."

"How come?"

"You can see Will's very sensitive about it all, and . . ."

"Come on, Brogan, I don't have to get into it when he's around."

"Sure, but if you upset her—"

"I can have a sisterly conversation with another woman without putting on my spikes. What do you think I'm going to do, interrogate her like a district attorney? I can find out all kinds of stuff without asking a single inflammatory question."

Jerry shrugged. "I can't stop you."

"I'm so glad you know that."

Maisie Cooper pulled back a corner of the curtain and peered out at the Pacific Ocean. Their room at the Surfside Inn was dark except for the illumination of the TV set. Here they were in far-off California and Mo had somehow found a New York Knicks game to watch.

"I'd sure like a walk," she said plaintively.

"You heard what Mr. Wardell said."

"Mo, it's ten o'clock at night. We have a little walk along the beach, who we gonna meet who's gonna spill the beans to your brother? You don't think Wardell posted a guard or something, do you?"

"After tomorrow, we can walk all we want."

She strolled over to the foot of the bed where Mo was lying in his shorts, peering at the screen, mesmerized by ten guys also in shorts running up and down the court. Maisie was naked, and she had a realistic idea of what effect she should be able to count on, but she couldn't distract his eyes from the guys in shorts. She was feeling taken for granted. Still, he'd brought her to California—lot of good it was doing her at the moment.

"That uncle of yours is something, you know? If we have to eat with them again, I'd just as soon not sit next to him."

"Uncle Buller's harmless. Probably can't even get it up anymore."

"He can get his fingers up, I'll tell you that."

"Let him have his fun."

"He's had all the fun he's having out of me. Can't you see my bruises?"

That got him to look, and she knew there were no bruises to see. Mo reached out for her, started to pay her some attention. It was okay, but no better and no worse than in New York.

The centerpiece of the Wardell bedroom was a huge circular water bed, facing a giant-screen TV built into the wall. It was a large enough room to keep these oversize fixtures from dwarfing everything else. The big screen hadn't helped the old kinescope clips from the quiz-show documentary as taped on the Wardell VCR. It made them seem even grainier.

Will, propped up in bed in his yellow silk pajamas, stared at the screen. Judy, whose sneaking desire to sleep nude had been quelled early in their marriage, was also wearing proper pajamas out of a forties movie. She looked at her husband anxiously. He hadn't spoken since the documentary ended, and now the screen was filled with snow.

"It wasn't so bad, was it?" she ventured. "I mean, you had your say."

Will turned to her as if he'd just remembered he wasn't alone in the massive bed. Tears were running down his cheeks. This in itself was not so alarming. Will was the most lachrymose man she had ever known, and she found his ability to cry rather an endearing trait. She couldn't even remember the last time she'd shed tears herself.

"You were lovely, you know," he said. "You still are. More so than ever, now. But we were so young then, weren't we?"

"We'll always be young, Will." It was the kind of sentiment she knew would appeal to him.

He reached over and grasped her hand. "Those creeps who

ruined it all, they should have put them away forever. People who saw you tonight for the first time—I just hope they know it was all for real. You didn't need any help."

"Don't worry about it, Will. Who cares what people think?"

He smiled. "I guess I do when it comes to you. I want everybody to love you like I do."

"I hope you don't mean that, Will," she said kiddingly. "That's really a shocking statement when you analyze it."

Will Wardell hit the remote control and shut off the snow. It was a relief. He also turned off the bedside light before he moved toward her, his eyes bright, and took her in his arms, his hand sliding under the waistband of her pajama bottoms. "Who was Horse of the Year in 1951?" he murmured.

"Counterpoint."

"That's my girl!"

"You mean we'll miss the afternoon tea, Buller?" said Frances McIntosh.

"We have to go to the track and see Brad's last race, honey. It's part of the deal."

"I suppose so."

"You can probably get some tea at the track."

"That's not the same, and you know it. It's not the tea. There's tea everywhere. It's so elegant having it poured for you, and tomorrow the lady said she'd be serving a raspberry-and-cream-filled sponge cake. She does a different cake or pastry every day of the week, you know that? That and civilized talk. I'll bet you can't get that at any racetrack."

"Your friend Will Wardell won't be coming for tea, though. He'll be at the track."

"He's such a fine man, Buller, just as nice in person as on TV. But I don't look forward to spending more time with those relatives of yours."

"You've only had to spend time with Mo so far, and he's not such a bad guy."

"I didn't know you even noticed Mo was there with all the attention you were paying that wife of his."

"Just trying to be a good mixer, that's all. She's a cute one, isn't she? Wardell's assistant isn't bad either."

"They should be complimented. Those girls are thirty-five if they're a day. Back home, you usually aren't interested in watching anything older than twenty through those binoculars of yours."

"With those girls on the beach, what you get through the binoculars is the best you can get."

"The best *you* can ever hope to get, yeah. And what do you think you'll ever get out of those two dames at that table tonight?"

Buller McIntosh grinned. "Why do you wanta be so crude, Frances? I finally get you into some interesting society, and all you can do is make dirty remarks. Your mind's in the gutter, you know that?"

Suddenly Frances dropped the bantering tone, and turned her indignation up a notch. "It's not *my* mind that's in the gutter, it's yours. You look through those binoculars back home, and all you're doing is showing me what kind of a lowlife you are, but you get in a situation like tonight and you're showing everybody what you are and humiliating me into the bargain."

"You should talk, the way you were kissing up to Wardell tonight. At least I admit I like to have a look once in a while at whatever's around. I'm not a hypocrite about it."

"Sure I look, Buller. But I don't look through binoculars. And I don't touch. And it seems to me you were doing some touching tonight."

"What, my nephew's wife? She's practically family. I sometimes don't know what to say to you, Frances."

"Then why don't you just get lost for a while, Buller? Go have a swim or something."

"You know I never swim."

"Never far enough from the water to miss your bikini fix, and yet you never swim. If you never swim, how can you expect to drown?''

''Huh?''

''Just get out of here!''

Buller McIntosh decided that was not such a bad idea. Frances had gone from the usual nagging and harping to a full-fledged shout in record time. There had been a special edge to her mood ever since they'd decided to make the trip. When the glamorous Will Wardell was around, it melted away, but the rest of the time it was industrial strength. Buller couldn't understand it. She was way too old to be having a mid-life crisis.

Their room was on the second floor of the Surfside Inn. He decided to walk downstairs and try to find the bar.

As he got to the lobby desk, he noticed a familiar figure. It was Phil Botts, Will Wardell's gofer, the guy who'd met him and Frances at the John Wayne airport, driven them down to Surfside, and talked baseball and basketball with Mo at dinner. After a polite ''Hi,'' Buller made an immediate decision to ignore the guy and concentrate his attention on the newly arrived guest he was carrying bags for, a woman in a short skirt and sandals. Following his standard procedure, he looked at the body first, bare toes to knees to flat tummy to bust (no bra), finding it intriguing enough to hope she'd display it more definitely around the pool. After a suitable interval, he got to her face. A nice face that hadn't changed that much since he'd last seen it years and years ago.

''Well, hi, Naomi.''

She didn't look all that thrilled to see him, he had to admit, but she managed a tiny smile. ''Hello, Uncle Buller.''

Brad Roark hadn't expected to have trouble sleeping the night before his final ride. He'd always been noted as a cool head, an image he had cultivated so carefully he had almost come to believe it himself. The other jocks called him the Iceman, a label previously applied to oldtime California jockey George Woolf.

The most dangerous thing he would do would be to ride Hot Air, but it would be only one ride instead of five or six as on a normal day, and the extra responsibilities dealing with the media didn't faze him, nor did making a speech to the crowd—he'd given a lot of thought to what he was going to say. The balloon ride would be a new experience, but he had the feeling he would be glad to get away and leave Surfside Meadows behind when the time came. There was Parker Fuentes to listen to, but the car dealer couldn't make him do anything he didn't really want to. And maybe he did want to run for office after all. It was good to have options available.

He wasn't having trouble sleeping, either. But after his umpteenth viewing of Olivier's *Henry* V, he'd started reading the new John Updike novel, and that had kept him awake until well after midnight. The ringing of the phone still irritated him. How was the caller to know he wasn't already asleep? After all, he had to work horses in the morning.

"Hello," he said, with a weary testiness, ready to give the caller a piece of his mind.

"Roark?" said a faint, muffled, unidentifiable voice.

"Yes, this is Brad Roark."

"No . . . hot . . . air." The words were carefully spaced.

"What do you mean? Who is this?"

"You heard me. No . . . hot . . . air."

The caller had hung up. Roark had the distinct feeling he'd been threatened, but with what? And what did the caller want him to do? Stay off the horse? Stay out of the balloon? Or keep out of politics?

5

In all the years she'd known Jerry, Donna Melendez had rarely attended the races at Surfside Meadows, even though the track was less than three miles from her house. Basically she was a Jerry fan rather than a racing fan, and it wasn't that much fun sitting and watching the races while Jerry was working up in his booth. Accompanying Jerry to races at farther distant tracks like Santa Anita or Hollywood Park or Del Mar, where he could be a spectator rather than an announcer, was another matter.

Still, Jerry had convinced her the last ride of Brad Roark was not to be missed, and though she could take the race or leave it alone, she was looking forward to seeing that orange-and-white-striped hot-air balloon soar aloft after it was over. It sat a few yards from the stretch turn, on the edge of one of the track's infield lakes. Half a dozen people were working on it—there seemed to be a lot more jobs than just to inflate and go. She'd have to get Jerry to take a balloon ride sometime.

Jerry had been thoughtful enough to provide her with company for the races—or maybe the idea was to keep her away from any company she might find on her own—so today she found herself in a director's box in the Turf Club, with the best view in the house of the finish line and winner's circle.

Donna vaguely remembered Will Wardell on TV, but he meant relatively little to her generation. He was sort of a living historical monument, along the lines of Art Linkletter or Bert Parks. He was proving a gracious and attentive host, but the gesture she was most grateful for was his frequent absence from the box to deal with the unspecified business of Roark Day. That gave Donna a chance at what she really wanted to do: get to know Mrs. Wardell.

Donna had done the requisite math. If Judy Wardell was a college student of about twenty in 1958, that would put her age today at past the half-century mark. It was hard to believe. She might have gone for a remarkably well-preserved forty, but fifty seemed out of the question. The woman's rich blond hair, un-weathered face, trim figure, and ready smile seemed still to go with pom-poms and acrobatics.

Wardell, by similar mathematical applications, would have to be in his late sixties at least. With the right TV makeup and lighting he might have seemed astonishingly youthful himself. In person, though, Donna could well believe he was pushing seventy, even with obviously artificial enhancements to his trademark teeth and pompadour. He treated Donna with courtly friendliness and Judy with the deference due a fragile house-plant. You'd have thought they were newlyweds instead of thirty years married. It was difficult to get any kind of meaningful conversation going as long as he was in the box.

When Wardell did leave them for the first time, about half an hour before the first race, Donna knew she wasn't going to jump in and start throwing questions at Judy like an old-movie cop applying the third degree. Her hidden agenda had to be approached subtly. But her first comment surprised her as soon as she heard herself say it.

"It's great to see two people who are so much in love."

HOT AIR

Judy smiled. "It's great to *be*. He is sweet, isn't he? I've been very lucky." Donna didn't have a doubt Mrs. Wardell meant what she said. "Will said you teach at Dana High, Donna. What subject?"

"Drama."

"That must be fun."

"It can be. It can be a lot of hard work and frustration, too."

"What's the last play you put on?"

"Last spring we did *You Can't Take It with You*. But right now we're working on *Cat on a Hot Tin Roof*," Donna said with pride. The selection had been one of her major victories in play selection over the conservative principal. ("Tennessee Williams is an American classic," she'd proclaimed. "It's like doing Shakespeare!")

"Mmmm. You found a high school girl who could handle Maggie the Cat?"

"Plenty of them actually. You'd be surprised at the competition."

"And Big Daddy?"

Donna nodded confidently. "I got that covered, too. The kid has a voice like Orson Welles and looks middle-aged before makeup. I expect to get accused of using a ringer, but he's only seventeen."

"I was in a play in high school. I didn't have any talent, but I was uninhibited."

"What was the play?"

"It was called *Time Out for Ginger*."

Donna made a face. "We did that at Dana just a few years ago. Some show. My principal loved it."

Judy laughed. "I didn't like it much, either. Of course, the fact that I didn't get to play Ginger might have had something to do with that. They told me I just wouldn't be believable as a girl who wanted to play football. As one of the other empty-headed daughters, I'd be fine. Not very complimentary, huh?"

"To some girls it would be. To the ones nobody would ever think of picking, I mean."

"I suppose. I got my revenge in a way while I was on 'The Big Question.' The girl who played Ginger never got offered a screen test."

"Did you really?"

"Oh, yeah, some producer saw me on 'The Big Question' and thought I could develop into another Grace Kelly. He said I was a perfect Hitchcock blonde."

"An ice maiden, huh?"

Judy paused a moment before she answered. "Somebody did call me an Ice Queen once. Not the producer, though. And my stage experience was enough to convince me I'm no actress. But I really love the theater, and I always did. That was one of the great things about flying to New York every week to do 'The Big Question.' I really love New York."

Donna nodded. "Me, too. Jerry and I were back there a couple years ago when he was calling the Belmont on the radio. It's a wonderful place."

"Will, for some reason, hates the city with a passion—he says the only good thing that ever happened to him there was meeting me—so I don't get there very often these days. But back then it was great. Every weekend I'd get met at the airport by a representative of the producer, and usually I'd get to go to a Broadway play or two, courtesy of the network. With a network chaperone, of course," she added, somewhat ruefully. "I remember one weekend I saw Ralph Bellamy playing President Roosevelt in *Sunrise at Campobello*. And another time I saw Laurence Olivier in *The Entertainer*, and Alfred Lunt and Lynn Fontanne in *The Visit*. When I'd see Will on Sunday in the greenroom before the show, I'd be nervous and he'd do his best to relax me. He'd ask me if I was having a good time in New York, and I'd tell him about what plays I'd been seeing. And you know what he'd say?"

"Let me guess. That Broadway wasn't what it used to be, and you should have been there when it was really great."

"How'd you know?"

"Everybody always says that. They were probably saying it in 1890. Will must have been pleased to have a contestant to talk about the theater with."

"He could talk about anything. I was very attracted to him from the first, had a real crush, but I had no idea he felt the same way."

"Did the network pay for everything?"

"Oh, sure, meals and hotel, of course, and they did a lot of other things to keep the contestants occupied. They kept a close watch on us, too, didn't want us to get in any trouble, especially somebody like me. It was almost like being a prisoner sometimes. You know it's funny: my subject on the show was horse racing. It was something I knew a lot about. A lot of girls love horses, but I loved them to the point of memorizing all kinds of facts and names and dates. They liked to have contestants with unexpected specialties. Did you know Dr. Joyce Brothers did 'The $64,000 Question' as an expert on boxing?"

"You have to be kidding."

"No, it's true. It was the same thing that made my subject an easy sell: the fact that it was so incongruous. This white-bread young cheerleader knowing so much about a wicked gambling sport was what made me interesting as a contestant. But do you think they ever took me to the races while I was in New York, or offered to? No, sir. I'd have loved to go to Belmont, or Jamaica before they tore it down. But regardless of my book learning, I symbolized unspoiled American youth, and an actual trip to the racetrack wouldn't have fit in with my innocent image."

"And weren't you innocent?" Donna asked kiddingly.

"I guess I was pretty innocent, but I wasn't all *that* innocent. I mean, I liked to go to the track with my parents and watch the horses run, but I don't think I ever placed a bet before I was married. But aside from that, I was a healthy twenty-year-old and very much attracted to young men of my own age. I got into older men later." She laughed again. "One older man, I mean, not a series of them."

"Was there a disappointed boyfriend waiting for you back home?"

Judy shook her head. "Disappointed maybe, but not really waiting. Just a week before I went back for the show the first time, I broke up with my high school sweetheart. Mark was his name. I guess I was pretty innocent at that. Oh, I wasn't a virgin or anything that drastic—he'd broken down my defenses the first time when we were sixteen, but he was the only one I'd been to bed with before New York and that not too regularly." She grinned. "I was a true fifties girl. I kept putting the defenses back up. Everything Mark got he had to work for. Over and over again."

"I guess you must have watched the documentary last night on PBS."

"Yes. I got a kick out of it the first time around, but then we had to watch the tape again when Will got home. He found it pretty upsetting."

"I thought his statement on the program was very moving."

"I guess so. He's always been sensitive about that, thinking all the stink about the other quiz shows somehow casts my accomplishment under a cloud. And, of course, puts his own integrity in question. I don't really think people take it all that seriously, do you?"

"Did you ever have an inkling that 'The Big Question' wasn't on the up-and-up?"

Judy glanced at her a big sharply. "Never." But then she relaxed, smiled somewhat apologetically. "But what does it really matter after all this time?"

"It certainly matters to Will."

She nodded. "He still tests me on racing trivia, you know that? To reassure me or to reassure himself, I don't know. Fortunately he sticks to pre-1960, and I'm still pretty good on that. If he asked me who won last year's Breeder's Cup races, I might stub my toe." She sighed. "To Will, I haven't changed in any essential way since the day we met. I'm still the wide-eyed innocent he wants to protect from the world's realities. But I'm not all that naive. I know life isn't a storybook, and horse racing isn't all *National Velvet*. Back at the time I was on 'The Big Question,' I was fiercely defensive anytime you suggested to me anything about horse racing might not be aboveboard. Now I recognize that sometimes there have been fixed races and betting coups, and that just makes the game more colorful."

"Can you apply the same thinking to the quiz shows?"

"Sure. Oh, I do believe Will's shows were essentially on the level, and I'd be disappointed if somebody showed me otherwise. But it wouldn't make me want to kill myself or leave Will or throw away everything we've had together. In an era where men are underprotective of their women, Will goes the other way. I have to admit I find it refreshing, but it really isn't necessary."

At that point, Will Wardell rejoined them in the box and they turned their attention to the eleven runners for the first race.

Brad Roark's reunited family were brought to the track in an unmarked VW van under a cloak of secrecy. Buller McIntosh sat next to his wife and behind the driver, Phil Botts, not seeming to notice the other two women were staying as far away from him as possible.

"Your pal Wardell thinks he's planning the D-Day invasion," Buller McIntosh said. Frances didn't respond, and no one else in the van even smiled. She had turned a notch cooler, if that was possible, when Naomi Burns arrived on the scene, and none of the family members seemed to have much to say to each other. The mood was not as festive as the reunion organizer might have preferred.

"Will we get there for the first race?" Buller asked Botts.

"No, I'm afraid not."

Buller looked at the *Racing Form* he'd purchased at the Surfside Inn's desk. "Just as well, I guess. I got one I like in the second, though. Are we allowed to go to the windows by any chance?" he added sarcastically.

"I'm afraid not, but you can send any bets you have with me."

"Hey, do we even get to watch the races?"

"There's a closed-circuit monitor in the room we'll be taking you to."

"Some outing, huh? I was hoping for a little sun, weren't you, Mo?"

"Yeah, well, those are the breaks," said his nephew, who was so pale he obviously had been avoiding direct sunlight for years.

The van parked in the stable area, and the Roark relatives were hustled into the same tunnel the horses would take to go under the infield to the receiving barn and walking ring. But the party made a left turn midway along a narrower, human-proportioned tunnel and finally emerged in a large cavernous room that had obviously been spruced up for the occasion. There were vases of flowers, tables, and armchairs, and, as promised, a closed-circuit TV monitor on which the odds for the second race were flashing.

"Anything you want to drink, just say the word," said Phil Botts. "And as I said, I'll be glad to carry any bets."

"Where are we exactly?" Naomi Burns asked.

"We're in the infield, just behind one of the tote boards. These walls are removable, and normally this would be an open-air group picnic area. We're only a few yards from where you'll be reunited with Brad, right after the fifth race."

"He leaves in a balloon then?" Naomi said.

"That's right."

"Then what do we do?"

"There's a big celebration honoring Brad tonight, where of course you'll all be honored guests."

"I think my niece wants to know," said Buller McIntosh, "if we can get out and look around the track a little bit. Once Brad has had his surprise, I mean."

"Oh, certainly. There'll undoubtedly be some newspaper and TV people who will want to talk to you after the ceremony, though. You folks will probably be on the news tonight."

"Hey, that'll be great," said Maisie. "Do you think we can get a videotape of it? I'd love to show my friends Mr. and Mrs. Mo Roark on TV." Mo threw her a warning look.

Frances McIntosh established herself in one of the armchairs. "And how long till all this happens?" she asked a bit sourly. The young assistant had not had the same mellowing effect on her as Will Wardell.

"Well, we're coming up on the second race. It should be about an hour and a half."

Frances sighed heavily. She'd already spent more time with Buller's family than she'd wanted for the rest of her life.

Keene Axtell came back from circulating in the Turf Club and entered the press box, trying to keep his festive smile frozen in place.

"Great day, isn't it, guys?" he said.

"You look worried, Keene."

"Well, this is a big day. I'll be relieved when it's over."

He made it along press row without having to say anything substantive and tapped on the door of Jerry's announcing booth. It was only moments after Jerry had announced the result of the second race as official.

"Let me in," Axtell said urgently.

Jerry opened the door. "Let you in? Did you bring your shoe-horn? There's barely room for me in here."

"I have to talk to you privately," said Axtell, speaking like a ventriloquist through his fixed smile. "And I *don't* want the media to suspect anything."

"Why should they suspect anything?" Jerry said. "The general manager always visits the track announcer in his booth between races. It's an old racing tradition. Helps the announcer concentrate on his job."

"Just get out of the way and let me in."

Jerry reluctantly made room. Axtell crouched in a corner, like a hiding fugitive. "Are you sure your mike isn't live?" he demanded.

Jerry looked at the mike. "Gee, no, I'm never sure whether it's on or not." In his announcer voice, he intoned, "The third race is a six-furlong boat race for fillies and mares. Throw your money away early." In a normal tone, he said, "No, it's not on."

"Jerry, this is serious. Brad Roark's getting threats."

"What do you mean?"

"He got an anonymous call last night. The caller said, 'No Hot Air.' He reported it to track security this morning, and they told me."

"Is *he* taking it seriously?"

"Not as seriously as I think he should. According to security, he almost didn't report it."

"What do you want him to do? Not ride in the race? Not go up in the balloon? It's probably just a joke."

"Well, I don't think it's very funny."

Jerry didn't either, but the humorless general manager's analysis meant nothing one way or the other. "Okay, what else?"

"What do you mean, what else? Isn't that enough?"

"Well, I don't know, but you did say 'threats.'"

"That's the only one. So far."

"Keene, don't worry about it. Our security is good to begin with, and they'll be keeping an extra watch on Brad today. Unless you want to alter the program, which would be just terrific for our public relations, just let everybody do their jobs. Okay?"

And get your anxiety out of my booth? Okay?

Brad Roark heard the applause as he crossed from the jockey room to the walking ring to get his final instructions as a rider. The fans were ten deep around the ring, with parents holding small children aloft to give them a look at the retiring reinsman. Some people were snapping pictures, unusual in a racing crowd. Even the owners and trainers of the other seven runners in the race were joining in the ovation, and he shook hands and exchanged greetings with several of them before he got to Parker Fuentes, who was dressed in the ten-gallon hat and white, black-trimmed cowboy regalia he always wore to sell cars in his TV commercials. The Fuentes orange-and-white silks were colorful enough, but you could always rely on the owner to outshine them in the walking ring, even today. The guy looked like a frustrated movie star.

"Congratulations, *amigo*," Fuentes said. "I am very, very proud today to have you on my horse."

Brad turned to the bland and inconspicuous Fuentes trainer. "How do you want me to ride him, Carl?"

"Take him to the front," the trainer said, deadpan. The owner and jockey laughed.

"If I can do that, I better not quit after all. Anybody who can take Hot Air to the front is too good to retire."

"*Amigo*," said Fuentes, "Carl meant at the *end* of the race."

"If I lose, do I still get a balloon ride?"

"Yes, but it won't make nearly as good a story on the evening news."

The call came for riders up, and Carl gave Brad a leg up on Hot Air, precipitating another cheer from the fans. Brad glanced over at the odds board and saw that he was even money. Even money? That was all wrong. He'd been 5–2 on the morning line, and Valley Moon was the logical favorite. He hoped these people would still be cheering if he didn't manage to get the big gray home in front. If Bill Shoemaker and Fernando Toro couldn't do the trick with their farewell mounts, why should it be expected of him?

Because this was Surfside, his hometown track, that's why. He patted Hot Air's silver neck. They'd get the job done.

The red-jacketed blower of the hunting horn—no simple bugle would do at Surfside Meadows—did an especially impressive "Boots and Saddles," with a few extra flourishes, and the field for Brad Roark's last ride began to come onto the track. Hot Air was number four, and the first surge of applause from the grandstand came as soon as his gray head showed out of the tunnel between the walking ring and the track. As the field turned left and began their parade past the stands, the ovation grew. It rippled through the large crowd as Roark and the horse passed each section of seats. Jerry Brogan's voice over the public address introduced each horse and jockey in turn, as dramatically as if this were the Kentucky Derby—or at least the Surfside Handicap. As the tote board flashed the changes in odds, Hot Air went from even money down to 4–5.

Donna watched the field through her binoculars, reflecting how dramatically valid it was for the focus of attention to be a light gray, almost white horse, when all the other runners were bays and chestnuts. Hot Air was a beauty all right, and she supposed she should put a bet on him, just for the sake of the occasion. She lowered the glasses and glanced at her program. As little as she followed racing, she was surprised to find one of the other horses was a familiar name.

"Valley Moon," she said. "I remember that horse. I saw him run at Santa Anita."

Will Wardell, put through an emotional wringer by the post parade, now seemed distracted, and was clearly ready to run off again on reunion business. But he said politely, "Very fast horse. Should have the lead early."

Judy Wardell said, "You might want to bet on him, Donna. He's all the way up to three to one. He was eight to five on the morning line. And Hot Air is odds-on now."

"Jerry said there'd be transparencies in the race," Donna said thoughtfully.

"What did he mean by that?" Judy Wardell asked.

"Overlays, I mean. That's it, overlays. A horse that's longer odds than he should be, right?"

"That's the whole field except Hot Air at the moment," said Judy. "Dana Point's gone from four up to six, Rickety Split from six to ten. The field's full of bargains."

"Don't tell me you ladies are going to bet against Brad Roark in his last ride," Will Wardell said. The outrage in his voice was put on, but Donna had the sense he was no more than half joking.

"Sentimental bettors never make a profit, Will," Judy said.

"I'm shocked, that's all I can say. Well, I gotta go visit the relatives. We'll be having the reunion inside of half an hour. You girls do what you like, but Brad Roark's going to win this. I can feel it." And the emcee was gone again.

Donna shook her head. "I'm not betting on Valley Moon. I remember now. The race I saw him in, he led from the start and didn't have anything left at the end."

"But I think I know the race you mean," Judy said. "The San Antonio Handicap, against Glad Tidings and Loose Lips. At a mile and an eighth, right?"

"Wow, you really are encyclopedic, aren't you?"

"He won't stop at six furlongs. He's practically unbeatable sprinting. Hot Air has to come from way out of it, and if none of the others can keep up with Valley Moon, he'll never be able to catch him."

"How are you betting?" Donna asked.

"Oh, I don't bet that much. But if I *were* betting, it'd be Valley Moon."

Maisie Cooper watched the Roark relatives watch Brad in the post parade. It wasn't very edifying. None of them seemed to be getting unduly sentimental about things. She'd been all prepared to get choked up, but she sure wasn't going to do it alone. Maybe the Roarks and the McIntoshes were one of those dysfunctional families she'd heard about on PBS.

"You betting this one, Unc?" Mo asked, not sounding all that interested.

"I can't figure this California form. Only one horse in here ever ran in Florida."

"What's that?"

"Golly Molly. And she's up to twenty to one." Buller McIntosh sounded insulted by the odds.

"Was she any good in Florida?"

"Not that bad."

"Good enough to beat these?"

"Could be."

Frances McIntosh said peevishly, "Buller, if you're gonna bet, bet. But don't keep talking about it."

"Talking about it's half the fun, baby," Buller McIntosh said.

Maisie turned to Naomi Burns, who'd had practically nothing to say since they'd been locked up together in this plush holding cell. "Did Brad always want to be a jockey?"

Naomi smiled weakly. "Gee, I don't think so. We all thought he was a brain as a kid. Never figured him for an athlete. I thought he'd be a college professor or something by now."

Mo Roark snorted at that. "Oh, yeah, sure. Instead he got the kind of education that counts. Same as me."

"School of hard knocks, Mo?" Maisie said.

"Come to think of it, he may not be as well educated as I am at that."

Maisie tried to read Mo's face and couldn't. She'd thought he really wanted to be here, but he sure didn't seem to have any feeling for his brother.

"Anybody sending any bets?" Botts inquired.

Buller McIntosh reached for his wallet. "Ten to win on Golly Molly."

Mo Roark said, "Ten-dollar exacta box, Valley Moon, Dana Point, and Rickety Split." He handed the runner sixty dollars in twenties.

Maisie said disgustedly, "I think I'll take a flyer on Hot Air. Two bucks to show."

"Want to split it?" Naomi said. Maisie thought she looked grateful.

The horses had disappeared to the other side of the track and were approaching the six-furlong gate. Donna lowered her binoculars to pan the crowd. Surely there'd be some celebrities in attendance.

The local celebrity she finally spotted impressed her not at all: Parker Fuentes, the car dealer and owner of Hot Air. Easy to spot in his overdone cowboy regalia, he was in his box several rows down receiving good wishes from the people seated near him. One conversation went a big longer and seemed a bit more serious, and Donna suddenly realized the man talking to him was the snappily dressed blond she'd seen in the restaurant the night before. Jerry had seemed so interested, she wished she had developed a facility for lip reading so she could report on their conversation. Ah, well. Chances are what they were talking about had nothing to do with politics or Purejoy Cosmetics.

"They're at the gate," Jerry's voice announced.

Training his binoculars on the field, Jerry considered how to approach this race. "Like any other" was the obvious answer, but clearly Brad Roark's last ride was something special, and in recent years the local fashion in race-calling had shifted from the purely factual description of past icons Harry Henson and Joe Hernandez to the more colorful and editorial style of Trevor Denman. Jerry had adjusted his approach somewhat but had balked at developing a South African accent.

One thing was certain: the early fractions would be crucial. The faster Valley Moon and his companions ran the first part, the better the chances for Hot Air to come charging from behind at the end.

A last click of the tote board saw Hot Air holding at 4–5 and Valley Moon at a generous 5–2. Dana Point was 6–1, every other entry in double figures, with Fault Line the longest shot of the eight at 50–1.

The eight starters were all seasoned older horses, and if the unusual level of crowd excitement during the post parade had discommoded any of them, they had left their nervousness on the front side. They loaded quickly and efficiently, and Jerry said, "The flag is up."

The start came almost immediately. "And they're off in Roark's last ride!" Jerry roared into the mike. Valley Moon shot to the front from his inside post with the Floridian Golly Molly in closest attendance. Hot Air dropped four lengths behind the others almost before the field had cleared the flagman, and Jerry thought he heard a slight moan of disappointment from the crowd. Not the knowledgeable part of the crowd, however. Didn't they know what to expect of the gray stretch runner?

"Down the backstretch, it's Valley Moon by a half length; Golly Molly is second by two; then it's Rickety Split third along the inside by a head over Dana Point fourth, half a length back to Mustachio between those two in fifth; another length back to El Perfecto sixth, Fault Line seventh, and Hot Air with Brad Roark is far back in eighth place, about twenty lengths off the lead. They did the first quarter in twenty-one and two!" Yes, that was fast enough, but how could Roark's mount make up twenty lengths in a six-furlong sprint?

"He'll never make it, will he?" Maisie Cooper said.

"Looka my exacta," Mo Roark chanted. "Looka my exacta."

"Hang in there, Molly!" Buller McIntosh was shouting. His wife wasn't even watching the race.

Maisie shook her head. There was something very wrong here.

Donna kept her glasses fixed on Hot Air. Whatever Judy said, she was sure Valley Moon wouldn't be there at the end, and if Roark's last ride was the attraction, Roark's last ride was what she'd watch. In the middle of the stretch turn, she realized the slow-starting gray had actually caught up with one of the other horses.

"The half in forty-three and three!" Jerry's voice roared over the public address. Donna decided if he was that excited about it, it must mean something.

"Turning into the stretch, it's Valley Moon now clear of Golly

Molly. The filly is dropping back fast. Dana Point is now second by a half over Rickety Split but not gaining. Then it's El Perfecto, Mustachio, and here comes Hot Air on the outside!"

Donna lowered the glasses now so she could see the whole field. Hot Air was striding long, eating up the ground, moving past most of the field as if they were standing still. Most of them, but it was still Valley Moon clear of the rest with a daylight lead.

"At the eighth pole, it's Valley Moon by four, Hot Air now second out in the middle of the track. Can Brad Roark get him there? It's Valley Moon, but the margin's diminishing. Valley Moon by a length but Hot Air gaining with every stride. Coming to the finish, it's going to be close!"

The public address, per Surfside policy, didn't call a winner, and though Donna was right on the finish line, she wouldn't have liked to call one either. The gray horse's last ground-eating burst might have got him there, but Valley Moon could just as easily have held on.

Donna turned to Judy and demanded over the cheers, "Who won?"

Judy wagged her blond head. "Don't know. Could be a dead heat. But look at that time. A new track record." The tote board said they'd finished in 1:07⅖.

The photo-finish sign came up, and Jerry hoarsely and unnecessarily advised the crowd to hold all tickets. Donna wished she knew what horse he'd called the winner for the radio and TV replays. It didn't seem fair that he didn't have to commit himself to the in-person crowd, but she supposed there was probably a good (if chickenhearted) reason for the policy.

Judy Wardell was doing some figuring on a blank page of her program. "This is amazing," she said.

"What is?" Donna asked, thinking her students would find the spectacle of somebody doing math without a calculator amazing enough.

"Hot Air's fractional times. Whether he won the race or not, that was one of the most incredible displays of speed in racing history. Look, I figured he was about twenty lengths off the lead at the quarter. So if Valley Moon went in twenty-one and one, Hot Air went in twenty-five and one. Of course, that's figuring one length to a fifth of a second."

"Of course," Donna said agreeably.

"By the half, let's say he'd made up half the deficit and was ten lengths off the pace. He'd have to have done the second quarter in twenty and two. Horses just don't run that fast, Donna. His last quarter would be almost as amazing, twenty-two flat, while Valley Moon was doing twenty-three and four, which would be remarkable in itself as fast as he ran the first part. We just saw something very special."

Donna trained her binoculars on the horses returning to the front side. Hot Air came back around the clubhouse turn last of all to a roar of approval from the grandstand. This crowd loved Roark and Hot Air whether they'd won their race or not. She saw Parker Fuentes down at the edge of the winner's circle, smiling and shaking people's hands while looking nervously at the tote board, waiting for the result of the photo to be flashed. Presumably the owners of Valley Moon were down there, too, ready to accept the victory but a little shellshocked at how hard-fought the race turned out to be.

The photo sign came down, the winning number came up, and the crowd that seemed it couldn't get any louder suddenly did. Hot Air had won Brad Roark's last ride by the hair of a nostril.

Naomi Burns had been screaming like a banshee as the TV monitor showed the stretch run, and Maisie was happy for an excuse to join in. When the race was over, the two women threw their arms around each other, and when the winner was announced, they did it again. There wasn't much other activity among the gathered relatives.

Buller McIntosh said to his wife, "The kid's a good rider, no doubt about it. Sorry about that exacta, Mo," he added with just a touch of malice.

*   *   *

In his booth, Jerry joyfully announced the details of owner, trainer, and breeder to the roaring crowd and hoped he could get his voice back for the next race.

Then he thought of the threat Axtell had reported, and he noted the extra security personnel surrounding Parker Fuentes's balloon. Brad Roark's last ride on the track had gone beautifully, and Jerry hoped his first ride *off* the track would do as well.

Hot Air, paying $3.60 to win, had won by an official nose over Valley Moon, with the 25–1 long shot El Perfecto eight lengths farther back in third place, and the rest staggering. The sentiment of the occasion aside, the spectators were buzzing over the finest performance by two sprinters they'd ever seen, and the most amazing display of stretch-running speed since the best and most improbable days of Silky Sullivan.

In the winner's circle, a TV starlet presented the winning owner's trophy to Parker Fuentes. There were louder cheers and a few more pictures than usual, plus an impromptu press conference limited to five minutes after Roark had weighed out. The reporters always loved Brad Roark, who punctuated his post-race comments with quotations and literary allusions. They all amounted, though, to what everybody at the track already knew: Hot Air had run a remarkable race.

His duty to the media done, Brad Roark belted back to the jockey room to change his clothes for the balloon takeoff. Normally jockeys at Surfside go among the spectators quite freely between track and tackroom sanctuary, but this time he was accompanied by security guards on both sides.

Minutes later, Roark was back on the track, being given a ride in a hackney pony carriage the length of the stretch, until debarking to walk across the turf course to the waiting balloon.

"Ladies and gentlemen," Jerry announced, "Brad Roark will shortly bid farewell to his riding career at Surfside Meadows in Surfside Meadows Director Parker Fuentes's balloon. But first, to make one final presentation, let me turn you over to another member of the Surfside Meadows Board of Directors, Mr. Will Wardell."

Wardell stood on a raised platform a few feet from the balloon. Fuentes stood there beside him, looking at the emcee suspiciously and wondering what this toothy has-been had to do with the occasion. Wardell was always trying to upstage the other members of the Board.

"Ladies and gentlemen, on behalf of the management of Surfside Meadows, let me add my congratulations to Brad Roark on the success of his final ride. Brad, would you like to step up here with me, er, us, and say a few words?"

Brad Roark, dressed now in a stylish blue jumpsuit that seemed appropriate to aeronautical adventures, stepped up to the platform to another resounding ovation.

"Thank you, Mr. Wardell. I don't know which makes me shakier, the prospect of emulating Phileas Fogg or the ordeal of making a speech." That drew a laugh. Even to his closest observers, Roark didn't look shaky at all. "I want to express my gratitude to everyone at Surfside Meadows for all you've done today. And thanks to you, Mr. Fuentes, for the opportunity to ride this wonderful horse Hot Air one last time. I'm certainly going to miss him.

"Horse racing is not war. It's quite a civilized pursuit, actually, and one honored by years of tradition. And these other jockeys have not precisely been my comrades in battle so much as my competitors in business. And my withdrawal from battle *or* business is not a great event that will be talked about for decades to come in the context of a great feast day. Hot Air may be remembered far longer than I am—and should be.

"But still, I ask you to indulge me for a few moments. When I have sat in the jockey room with my fellow gladiators, ready to do battle on the turf—or the dirt—I often have thought of some lines from *Henry the Fifth*, Act Four, Scene Three, and I thought of them again today.

> "Rather proclaim it, Westmoreland, through my host,
> That he which have no stomach to this fight,
> Let him depart. His passport shall be made,
> And crowns for convoy put into his purse.
> We would not die in that man's company
> That fears his fellowship to die with us."

Roark spoke the lines well and with feeling, if not in a class to threaten Kenneth Branagh. He had been dry-eyed all day, but reciting the words caused his eyes to mist over, though his voice was not affected.

The whole crowd was surprised to hear the retiring jockey quoting Shakespeare, but all the talk of dying had a particular reverberation for the security guards. Truthfully, somebody could take a shot at this guy, and there was precious little they'd be able to do about it.

> "This day is called the Feast of Crispian.
> He that outlives this day and comes safe home,
> Will stand a tip-toe when this day is named,
> And rouse him at the name of Crispian.
> He that shall live this day, and see old age,
> Will yearly on the vigil feast his neighbors,
> And say, 'To-morrow is St. Crispian.'
> Then will he strip his sleeve and show his scars,
> And say, 'These wounds I had on Crispian's day.' "

Upstairs Jerry Brogan, who had left his cramped booth to watch the ceremonies from the press box, was having the same uneasy thoughts as the security guards about the kind of target Roark was presenting. Keene Axtell stood beside him, almost literally wringing his hands.

"He's talking too long," Axtell said out of the corner of his mouth.

"Don't worry, Keene, nobody's going to take a shot at him."

"That's not what I mean. If he talks much longer, he's going to delay the next race. We still have to hear from Wardell. And Fuentes will probably have a few well-chosen words, too."

Jerry shook his head. Now it seemed Axtell wished somebody *would* take a shot at the retiring jockey.

"This story shall the good man teach his son;
And Crispin Crispian shall ne'er go by,
From this day to the ending of the world,
But we in it shall be remember'd,
We few, we happy few, we band of brothers. . . ."

"That'll be it," Jerry assured Keene Axtell. "Nice dramatic finish, now in the balloon and outa here."

"After the family reunion," Axtell reminded him.

"Right."

"And to my fellow riders, that is the way I will always think of you: 'We band of brothers.' For me, this is a special day, but this will always be a special place, a special town. Surfside is a racing shrine."

Parker Fuentes was bobbing his head in agreement. Surely, Roark would do all he could to preserve a sacred shrine.

"Surfside Meadows means quality racing, as surely as Dom Perignon, Remy Martin, Beluga, Rolls-Royce, Harvey's Bristol Cream, and Stephen Sondheim spell the very best in their respective areas."

The crowd kept interrupting Roark's remarks with applause, as if he were a President. Most of them probably didn't recognize all the literary, artistic, and culinary allusions he was making, but they were intrigued by a jockey who could sling the elegant talk like Alistair Cooke.

In the director's box, Donna Melendez was less impressed. "He should have stopped with *Henry the Fifth*," she whispered to Judy Wardell. "He's milking this too much."

"Let me just conclude with a few lines from a favorite poem," Brad Roark said.

Donna groaned. "Pretentious bastard," she muttered.

A smallish man appeared on Jerry's other side, saying, "Hey, this guy is good. He'd really give my tipping service some class. Why didn't you tell me he was literate, Jerry?"

Jerry just scowled and wondered by what series of shady machinations Stan Digby had got into the press box.

When Roark had drawn his remarks to a definitive conclusion, Parker Fuentes made a move toward the mike, but Will Wardell beat him to it.

"Thank you, Brad. They ought to call you Brad the Bard down in the jockey's room. That was one of the best speeches I ever heard. But your special day isn't over yet, Brad. We have some more surprises. Did you ever happen to see a television program called 'Hold Out Your Heart'?"

Brad nodded politely but without enthusiasm. Some of the crowd managed another, somewhat halfhearted cheer. But now that the guest of honor's entertaining oration was concluded, they were anxious to see the balloon take to the air and the track be cleared for the next race.

"Well, today we have what might be called a special, live, in-person edition of 'Hold Out Your Heart.' We've brought here for your special day some people who have been very special in your life. And we'll start with a girl who once put her bubble gum in your toy truck, someone you haven't seen for fifteen years, your sister, Naomi Burns."

Everybody in the crowd saw Brad Roark take a jerking step

backward as his sister appeared, seemingly from out of nowhere, on the little makeshift stage, and those closer to him saw an almost horrified expression on his face. But he collected himself, stepped forward, and briefly embraced the woman. The smile she gave him was kind of sad and wistful, even apologetic. He nodded to reassure her, mouthed, "It's okay."

Will Wardell was aware this first reunion hadn't had quite the dramatic impact he'd hoped for, but maybe the cumulation of relatives would give the event some heartwarming momentum. He willed his teeth to gleam and pressed on.

"And now, Brad, the man who took you on your first trip to the racetrack and the woman whose chocolate-chip cookies you always loved, flown here especially from their retirement home in Florida, two folks you haven't seen for twenty years, your aunt and uncle, Frances and Buller McIntosh."

The couple came surging onto the platform. Frances, as always seduced by the Wardell magic, seemed to have convinced herself this would be just like TV, or if it wasn't, they were duty-bound to pretend it was. Brad returned her bubbling embrace even less enthusiastically than Naomi's, and he managed only a polite handshake with his uncle.

"And finally, Brad, the management of Surfside Meadows has brought from New York the closest pal of your boyhood days, whom you have not seen for twenty-three years, here with his lovely wife, Maisie, your brother, Mo Roark!"

Mo came out with the swagger of a New York street kid and grasped his brother's hand. The handshake seemed grudging on both sides. Brad shook hands equally formally with his brother's unsuspected wife, who started to smile and aborted the effort. Since the first shock of seeing Naomi, Brad had registered all the delight and animation of a wax figure. There wasn't a wet eye in the house, not even Will Wardell's.

Dispirited at how his event had turned out, Wardell carried on regardless. "Well, I know you folks all have a lot to talk about, and there'll be plenty of time for that at a special celebration to be held tonight in your honor at the Surfside Inn. But now it's time for the balloon ride."

Brad Roark was already being helped into the wicker basket under the balloon, which was ringed by wary-looking security guards, and it clearly could not begin its rise too soon for him. His shoulders slumping with the letdown, Will Wardell made a move to unplug the hand-held mike, but Parker Fuentes tapped him on the arm and took it from him with a withering glare. Wardell retreated and the car dealer began his contribution to the festivities.

"Ladies and gentlemen, *señoras y caballeros*, Brad Roark and I will be leaving Surfside Meadows in a moment in this rather exciting and surprisingly reliable form of transportation, though perhaps not as practical for most journeys as one of my cars. I am especially proud of the race today, proud of my horse, proud of my jockey. Not since Johnny Longden on George Royal has a jockey had such an amazing final ride. Before we go"— now there were audible groans from the impatient horseplayers—"I have a special presentation to make to Brad on behalf of myself, a gift to express my congratulations and gratitude. Ah, you say, Parker Fuentes is going to give the great jockey a car. Very nice. Is it not an appropriate gesture? Is he not the leading import car dealer on the West Coast? But, you say, athletes are always being given cars. The Most Valuable Player in the tiddly-winks All-Star Game gets a car. This is boring. Get on with the races." Here there was a derisive cheer. "But I am not going to give Brad Roark a car. As you may know, jockeys are prohibited by the rules of racing from owning racehorses. They may breed but not own. There are good reasons for this, related to the protection of the public, which is always the primary concern of racetrack management." That line got some catcalls. "However, today Brad Roark is no longer a jockey. He is retired. Thus, I asked myself, what gift could be more appropriate than the one I am about to bestow? Brad Roark, here is my gift to you. You are now the *owner* of Hot Air."

That regained the crowd's attention. As Parker Fuentes climbed into the gondola, Roark shook hands with more enthusiasm than he had accorded any of his long-lost relatives.

Down below the platform, Will Wardell was reflecting that "Hold Out Your Heart" had been driven off the air by merchandise-related shows like "Let's Make a Deal" and "The Price Is Right." And they haunted him still. Classy sentiment was losing out to crass commercialism once again.

A mariachi band began playing the Fifth Dimension's "Up, Up and Away," not part of their regular repertoire, as Fuentes Motors' orange-and-white-striped Car Number One lifted heavenward with Parker Fuentes waving his cowboy hat dramatically. The crowd couldn't even see Brad Roark now, but the spectacle was impressive.

"Can't you just see tomorrow's papers? Tonight's eleven o'clock news?" Jerry enthused.

Keene Axtell was still gloomy. "Can't you just see the handle for the next race? The crowd is going to watch that damned thing till it disappears, and they won't bet any money."

"Horseplayers aren't that easily discouraged," Jerry said. "Are they, Stan?" he added, recognizing that Digby was still standing on the other side of him.

"I don't think we've met," said Axtell, with a nervous public-relations smile at who he thought was an unfamiliar journalist.

"I don't think you want to," Jerry said. "When I find out how this guy got into the press box, I'm going to give those security guards something else to do."

Stan Digby was nothing if not thick-skinned. "Thanks for the invitation to tonight's party," he said.

"What do you mean?" Jerry demanded.

"They gave me my invitation as soon as I got here. All the working press are invited."

"Why would that include you?"

"You know I do some free-lancing, Jerry. I got credentials up the kazoo. I'll bet I can even sell an article on Brad Roark, the literate jock."

"Why don't you write about somebody who's still riding?" Keene Axtell suggested. "Or do something on a trainer?"

"Keene, we want to keep this clown off the backside or all the horses'll have needles in *their* backsides. This guy is not to be trusted."

Stan Digby's hurt look was unconvincing. "Jerry, I never fixed a race in my life."

"It's only because you never got the chance."

"Always kidding, huh, Jerry? Thanks for agreeing to introduce me to Brad Roark. You're a real pal. Give my love to your Aunt Olivia. I gotta go now."

"Yeah, go file your story."

When Digby had left them, Jerry said, "He's relatively harmless, really. But I'm not sure I want him turning up at that party tonight."

Axtell shook his head. "I don't want to offend anybody in the media."

"I tell you, he isn't *in* the media. He's a con man."

Axtell was still staring at the rising balloon, now almost disappearing into the clouds over the backstretch. One problem the new general manager had, Jerry decided, was his refusal to worry about things he really *should* worry about.

"Did you know Fuentes was going to give Roark the horse?" Axtell asked.

Jerry shook his head. "Maybe Parker didn't even know it himself until he got swept up in the occasion. Wanted to upstage Will Wardell in a big way, as if the balloon weren't enough. That reunion looked kind of tense, didn't it? I always thought relatives who hadn't seen each other in twenty years must have their reasons."

"Is it legal?"

"Is what legal? Surprise family reunions? Maybe they shouldn't be."

HOT AIR

"Fuentes giving Roark the horse."

"I don't know why not. It's his horse. I'm sure it has some tax ramifications for both of them, but let them worry about that. For Surfside Meadows, it's more good copy."

"You think so?"

"Sure. Suppose Hot Air and Valley Moon have a rematch in our big sprint next month? Today's race made that a drawing card anyway—with Brad Roark making his debut as an owner, it'll be all the bigger."

"Okay, okay, I guess we might as well try to salvage something out of this." Axtell trudged toward the door of the press box, leaving Jerry to return to his public-address duties. Jerry looked down at the huge crowd and reflected that his boss would never be satisfied.

Jerry had no sooner completed some routine announcements regarding the sixth race than Keene Axtell was pounding on the door of his booth again.

7

From the moment the balloon started to rise, Brad Roark was fascinated. As his gathered relatives, only Naomi essaying a shy wave, grew smaller on the ground below, his embarrassment grew smaller with them, and he was able to relax and enjoy the spectacle. He was aware that Parker Fuentes was doing a major hammy farewell, but he was too intrigued by his first experience of ballooning to join in.

Only when it became clear the balloon would safely clear the surrounding obstacles—trees, light poles, grandstand—did Fuentes say anything. "How do you like that, *amigo?*" he asked over the roar of the gas burners.

Brad looked down at the racetrack and the surrounding city with such awe he couldn't even think of a poem to quote. It was a cloudless day with an eastward breeze, and the gradually revealed coastline looked postcard-perfect. "This is amazing, Parker, really amazing."

"A beautiful city, yes. But what would it be like, my friend, with another unsightly condominium development instead of the racetrack?"

"I think the ocean would still look pretty nice," Brad said mildly. "I guess you were lucky we had such great weather. On a day with no wind, we wouldn't even get off the ground, would we?"

"You can always get vertical thrust with the gas burners," Fuentes said, tolerating a neophyte's ignorance. "On takeoff, too much wind would be a hindrance. We usually take our flights in the early morning or late afternoon because there is *less* wind then. How far you will go and in which direction is dependent on the wind—I have some control, you understand, but less than God does. This breeze should give us a fine ride. Though perhaps not so fine a ride as you gave your horse."

"You're really giving him to me?"

"Would I tell the world that for a joke? I'm part of history today. I'm grateful to you. And I'm hoping there are even finer things ahead for you."

"Was the horse a campaign contribution?"

"There can't be a campaign contribution until there is a campaign."

"A bribe, then?" Brad said, less than half kidding.

Fuentes chose to smile at the lesser half. "Will there be a campaign, Brad? Will you run?"

Roark shook his head. "Only from my relatives."

Fuentes wagged his head companionably. "That was not a good idea, eh? This reunion of Wardell's? They told me nothing about it, so don't blame me. You weren't happy to see them?"

Brad concentrated on the ground below and considered an answer. If Fuentes didn't insist on bringing up subjects he really did not want to talk about, the balloon experience might prove as serene yet exhilarating as advertised. He didn't want to discuss his family, and he didn't want to talk about politics either. He'd have to get Fuentes to give him a thorough lecture on hot-air ballooning—surely he'd have one at his fingertips.

"Oh, I wouldn't say I wasn't happy to see them." Fuentes looked at him skeptically. "I guess I don't *have* to say it, huh? We just don't have a lot in common, that's all there is to it. They're from a world I left behind me—or tried to. And I know they didn't come here to honor me—they just couldn't pass up a free vacation. Except maybe for my sister Naomi. I don't have anything against her."

"That Wardell." Fuentes shook his head. "All misguided flash and showmanship."

Brad Roark looked at the cowboy-clad car dealer who had just taken him aloft with all the reserved dignity of the Wizard of Oz and nearly laughed.

To change the subject, Brad offered what he thought was an intelligent question. "Why no ballast? I was expecting sandbags or something."

"Not needed in a hot-air balloon. We rise or descend by heating and cooling the air in the envelope. It was in the gas balloons they used ballast."

"Oh. How far can we expect to go today?"

"With this breeze, as long as the nylon holds out, as far as we want. You, too, can go as far as you want, *amigo*."

Brad sighed to himself. Fuentes was making his segue as blatantly as Marlin Perkins used to shift into his Mutual of Omaha commercials.

"Horse racing is a most important industry in the state of California, my friend. It seems healthy, but there are threats everywhere. Sports betting. The lottery. The inflated value of real estate. Most of those threats can't be dealt with anywhere but the political arena, state, county, and perhaps most important, local. Without friends on the City Council, Surfside Meadows will not survive, Brad."

"I'm sure you're right, Parker, but I don't think I'm cut out for politics."

"Look below you, my friend! Houses and condominiums where there used to be only orange groves."

"And an occasional oil well."

"Do you want the sport we love to disappear from Surfside just as the last orange was squeezed out of Orange County? Is that what you want, my friend?"

"Growth and development are inevitable. They can be slowed but not stopped. If people want horse racing, horse racing will survive. If they don't—well, we can remember Hot Air. They can't take him away from us, can they?"

Fuentes abruptly downshifted his approach and paused to wallow in the sentiment offered. "No, that is quite true. And I am being unfair to you, my friend. You have come to the end of a dangerous career. You have been brave. But to ask for more acts of courage, it may be too much. A man has the right to withdraw from battle, put his valor on the shelf, make a demonstration of his courage and then withdraw into comfort. You are so right. We can remember Hot Air and quote Shakespeare on long-forgotten battles."

Brad didn't like the way this was going. "You consider running for political office an act of courage?"

"In some cases, it is."

"That doesn't fit with most of the politicians I've seen. Avarice and ambition, yes, but courage?"

"Most politicians don't have the kind of enemies a candidate to the Surfside City Council might have. Some of our developer friends would do anything to influence a key vote their way. I don't blame you, *amigo*, not one bit. Enjoy our ride—it was unfair of me even to bring any of this up on a day that you should remember only with pleasure."

Now Fuentes seemed ripe to deliver the ballooning lecture, but Brad had a perverse impulse to keep worrying the subject he'd wanted to avoid. He had reported the threatening phone call, but it hadn't really concerned him that much. He wasn't even sure it had anything to do with politics. Would his decision not to run for office be taken as a demonstration of cowardice?

Moving into his instructional mode, Fuentes gave Brad a rundown of the equipment in the basket, starting with the instruments on the dashboard.

"This is the variometer, which shows our rate of ascent and descent. The thermister measures the temperature of the balloon's crown. And the altimeter tells us our height above sea level, *not* from the ground below. These are the propane tanks that power the burner."

"And where's the champagne bottle? Or is that just folklore?"

"No, the tradition truly exists, for very practical reasons. Often you must placate that farmer or businessperson whose property you happen to land on."

Fuentes opened a wicker compartment under the seat to show Brad the champagne bottle. But the other object he saw caused him to draw back with a fearful expression. Brad followed his eyes.

"What the hell is that?" he asked. He was hoping his eyes deceived him. It was a small and compact package of what looked like coin rolls bound together with wire and attached to a small alarm clock. There was a deceptively festive touch: a tiny plastic figure of a jockey in the orange-and-white Fuentes colors standing on what (on second thought) undoubtedly were not coin rolls. To the plastic jockey was affixed a small card with the words NO HOT AIR in block capitals.

"It looks very much to me like a bomb, my friend," said Fuentes, his voice shaking. "A bomb with a timing device." The car dealer drew a deep breath, as if struggling to collect himself. He managed a nervous smile. "You have proven you are well-read, but do I guess right that you share my ignorance of how to dismantle such devices?"

"You guess right," said Brad.

"Then short of throwing the thing out of the balloon, which would not endear us to the innocent citizens below, I fear our only alternative is to make an emergency landing."

Fuentes got on the radio to the tracking car following them on the highways below and announced his intent to land immediately. He admonished the driver to alert the Surfside police, the county sheriff, and the Surfside Meadows management.

"That looks like our best chance, my friend," he said, pointing to a wide green playing field surrounded by buildings and houses. "Forgive me for what may be a rough landing." Pulling a cord, he said, "I'm opening a vent in the envelope to help us descend somewhat more quickly than usual." The message Brad's stomach gave him made the last phrase superfluous. He had the sensation of going down in an express elevator. "As soon as we touch the ground, I'll pull the rip panel, and the balloon envelope will deflate quickly—that will keep us from being dragged on the ground until we run into something that stops us. We may still hit rather hard, I fear."

Brad swallowed. "I've had a few hard landings in my time."

"You are well prepared then." Fuentes cast a nervous look at the compartment that held the bomb. "I hope we have enough time." With gallows humor, he concluded, "This may be the first time I share my bottle of champagne with the bomb squad!"

Jerry found the news of the balloon's problems distressing, but he was especially aggravated by Keene Axtell's unspoken assumption that he should (or could) do something about it.

"If they called the police, they made the right moves," he said. "They're off Surfside property, I assume, unless they come down in our parking lot, and we have a racing card to finish here. I have four more races to call."

Axtell seemed frozen into inactivity. "What do I tell the reporters?"

"Do they know about it?" Jerry paused. "How the hell did they get a bomb into the balloon gondola without anybody seeing it? Parker's people were surrounding it all afternoon."

"So were our security people."

"Did they search the inside of the gondola?"

"I don't know."

"Parker's people would have found it. Unless it was one of them who planted it."

"Or one of *our* people."

"What would be the point?" Jerry wondered. Then he wagged his head to shake out the cobwebs. "Keene, unless you're postponing the rest of the program to wait for the explosion, I have to get to work here!"

Jerry arrived at Donna's apartment to pick her up for the Brad Roark party a little after seven o'clock. She'd been home long enough to ride her bicycle through the streets of Surfside, have a shower, watch the local news, and change into a party outfit—sarong-style silk skirt with electric blue top—that would necessitate extra effort on Jerry's part to concentrate on his driving. He came straight from the track, where being questioned by the Surfside police had been added to his usual duties and Roark Day special duties, but he was now high enough in the track management pecking order that he could clean up and change at his place of work. A few days before, this had shaped up as a fun evening, but recent events made Jerry more than a little apprehensive.

"They had some terrific balloon footage on the news," Donna said. "Great publicity for one of our major local sports venues."

The grin fighting to overtake her face gave Jerry an inkling of what was coming, but he decided to give her the straight line she wanted. "You mean the balloon taking off from Surfside Meadows?"

"No, the balloon landing on the Dana High football field. It was pretty dramatic. The basket went on its side and Roark and Fuentes sort of spilled out of it. They were okay, though. I guess somebody must have alerted the network outlets in time to get the word out to their mobile units."

"They were already at the track. Did they have *any*thing about Roark's last ride?"

"I think they did mention he was a jockey." She paused and studied his profile for signs of humor. "Oh, of course they did, Jerry. It just made the last-ride story bigger."

"How did they handle the balloon incident?" Jerry inquired casually. "Like it was really a major threat, or a big joke?"

"Somewhere in between, I guess."

Jerry smacked the steering wheel. "Big joke! I should have known."

"Well, Jerry, they did land safely, and the bomb was a dud."

"Less than a dud. It was a dummy. They weren't in any danger at all, unless they'd crashed into a power line or something during their panic landing."

"I don't know if panic is an appropriate word. Apparently Parker Fuentes handled the whole thing like a hero. And *he* didn't know it was a fake bomb."

"I just hope they don't think it was a Surfside Meadows publicity stunt. Did they interview Parker on TV?"

"Sure. It was a nice free commercial for his car lot. He was smooth as ever—opened his champagne bottle and said he hoped he wouldn't get in trouble for bringing alcohol onto school grounds. He was kidding, but if the principal had been there, he might have. He got serious, too. He was outraged, said someone was using his balloon for a deadly attack on Roark, maybe to prevent him from running for City Council. I think that was before they'd announced the bomb wasn't real."

"And did they talk to Brad Roark?"

"That pompous windbag."

HOT AIR

Jerry looked over at her, amused. "You don't like the guy, do you?"

"I don't know the guy. But I don't like his public persona, you're right. He had a smirk on his face, and when they asked him to comment on Fuentes's heroism, he came up with another inappropriate Shakespeare quote." With stilted gestures, Donna declaimed, " 'I have scaped by a miracle. I am eight times thrust through the doublet, four through the hose; my buckler cut through and through . . .' *Henry the Fourth* this time—he sure likes the Henrys, doesn't he? Okay, maybe you can excuse him babbling a little bit after a scary experience like that. But, Jerry, that spectacle he made today at the track was ridiculous."

"I thought you'd be impressed by a retiring jockey quoting Shakespeare."

"Quoting Shakespeare is one thing. Doing a whole audition is something else. I mean the lines didn't even fit the occasion; he as much as admitted it himself. Here we have a commander trying to make his troops celebrate the fact that they're terribly outmanned. What does *that* have to do with jockeys? But he had to get up there and show us what a literate, superior being he is."

"I better not introduce you to this guy."

"No, no, I want to meet him. And I won't embarrass you, Jerry. I know how to act in polite society. And sometimes people are very different in person."

"Sure. I hear Andrew Dice Clay is a sweetheart."

The low-slung, two-story Surfside Inn was a larger operation than its small lobby would indicate. On the ocean side were a series of meeting rooms and a larger one called (with only slight hyperbole) the ballroom. Quite a few of the long list of invited guests (and, Jerry suspected, a few uninvited) were already standing in groups and quaffing champagne from a fountain when Jerry and Donna arrived. The room was decorated with miniature hot-air balloons straining toward the ceiling from long ribbons. A pianist was running through the "easy listening" play list. On one side of the ballroom an elaborate buffet table was set out, highlighted by a horse-and-jockey ice sculpture, and next to it, in the corner farthest from the entrance, was another table with a display of Brad Roark memorabilia.

Backed into that corner was the principal item of memorabilia, guest of honor Roark himself in white dinner jacket and black trousers, and, Jerry was chagrined to see, backing him there was none other than would-be turf adviser Stan Digby, wearing Damon Runyon plaid. Waving to others in the room as they passed, Jerry swiftly guided Donna toward the two men.

Roark looked relieved to see someone coming to his rescue. Digby turned, and his face lit up as if greeting long-lost friends. "Well, what do you know?" He pumped Jerry's hand. He leaned toward Donna with a social kiss in mind but had the good sense to abort in mid-swoop when it became clear she was only offering a cool handshake. Jerry introduced Donna to Brad, something he'd been looking forward to doing, but before they could exchange any social pleasantries, Digby made it clear he would not give up the conversational impetus easily.

"I was just talking to Brad about what happened today, with the balloon and everything. I think it was gutsy of him even to show up tonight, don't you?"

Roark shrugged. "I'm not taking that very seriously. Just somebody's idea of a joke."

Digby shook his head, his brow furrowed in elaborate sympathy. "I don't know if I could be that calm about it. Look, I was about to say—well, Jerry can tell you that I'm a licensed private investigator, and I've done quite a bit of bodyguard work in my time." He grinned ingratiatingly. "I'm small, but I'm wiry. If I can help out in any way, look into what happened maybe, or bolster your protection, you just say so. I'd do it for nothing."

"Gratis?" Brad asked, raising an eyebrow.

"Sure, as a courtesy to a business associate."

"Oh, are you business associates?" Donna said brightly.

"Not exactly," said Brad.

"We're in the early stages," Digby allowed. "Having what you might call exploratory talks."

"We're in the early stages, Stan, if we're Plautus and Terence and our end goal is David Mamet."

Stan shook his head admiringly. "Isn't he something, Donna? Isn't this guy something? Donna teaches drama, you know, so she'd appreciate that kind of thing more than most people."

"Sure," Donna said, "I love people who try to talk like characters in Amanda Cross novels."

Jerry thought she was getting a little acerbic, but Roark seemed to take it as a compliment.

Jerry said to Stan Digby, "Could we have a word, Stan?"

"Sure, Jerry," Stan said, nodding apologetically to the others with the air of a man who has just been consulted by the President on matters of state. They stepped to one side.

"Renewed your license this afternoon, did you, Stan?" Jerry said between clenched teeth.

"Well, I—I could very easily. I'm just offering to help the guy out."

"I don't think he's interested in joining your information service, Stan."

"Oh, I don't know about that. We had quite a nice conversation about it before you came."

"If I understand his dramatic allusion right—"

"I didn't quite get that, to tell you the truth. It sounded real classy, though, didn't it? The guy's amazing."

"If I understand it, you have about as much chance of getting Brad Roark as a business partner as Plautus has of having a new play on Broadway next year. And there's no need for you to join the security force. We've got Brad Roark well protected."

Stan Digby smirked. "Oh, I believe that, Jerry, even if you're the whole security force yourself. See you around, big guy. I don't want to monopolize the guest of honor." The ex-private eye drifted away, and Jerry turned back to Donna and Brad Roark.

Brad was giving her a guided tour of the display table. The items on exhibit weren't under glass museum-style, but most of them were too large to be easily stolen.

"Those are the colors I wore when I won the Surfside Handicap in 1985," he said, pointing to one of three sets of silks, this one composed of a black-and-white checkerboard pattern. "That was one of my biggest wins, my biggest here anyway. The orange and white are the Fuentes colors I wore today, and I won the Hollywood Gold Cup in that sickly lime outfit. And here's a whip I've carried in a lot of races."

Donna looked at it distastefully. "Did you use that very much?"

Roark shook his head. "I'm known as a hand-rider. Only go to the stick when I have to. I think most jocks use the whip way too much."

Jerry didn't have to be told Donna's opinion of Brad Roark was rising.

"You know, Trevor Denman—he's the track announcer at Santa Anita—"

"Yes, I know," said Donna, with a sidelong glance at Jerry.

"Trevor told me they have a rule in England you can only hit a horse so many times in the last quarter of a mile. I think we should have a rule like that here. Most horses will do their best without being excessively punished."

"I'm so pleased to hear you say that."

"It may surprise you, but there are quite a few people on the racetrack who belong to animal rights groups."

"Really?"

"Most of the people who work in racing really like horses. And we as a highly developed species have a responsibility to other species, not just those in the wild, but domesticated ones, ones that serve us in one way or another. I really feel strongly about that."

Afraid this was going to develop into a discussion of Purejoy Cosmetics and their testing labs in no time, Jerry said, "What are these other things, Brad?"

"Oh, various stuff. Everybody wanted to give me a poster or a plaque or a proclamation today. That one's from the mayor of Surfside, that one's from the governor." He pointed to an onyx-based statue of a horse and rider. "That's the winning jockey's trophy for today's race."

"And what's that?" Donna asked, with only slightly less distaste than had greeted the whip. "Looks like an ice pick."

Roark picked it up by its gleaming silver handle. "That's just what it is, but I'm not going to pick any ice with it. Silver-plated. The other jockeys gave it to me." He turned it over to show Donna and Jerry the inscription on the handle: WHEN THE MONEY'S ON THE LINE, THE ICEMAN COMETH.

"And you're the Iceman?" Donna said.

"That's what they called me. Ice water in the veins, you see. I'd love to know who came up with that inscription. I'd have sworn nobody in that jocks' room ever heard of Eugene O'Neill."

"Why would you assume that?" Donna said. Jerry caught the undercurrent of exasperation in her voice and sensed she wanted to withdraw the impulsive question as soon as she said it.

Brad shrugged. "I guess you're right. There's more to all of us than what you see in the locker room. Or any other one place." He put the ice pick back on the table.

A wave of new arrivals was closing in on Brad Roark, so Jerry and Donna moved away toward the buffet table. Donna said under her breath, "Eugene O'Neill's Iceman was Death."

Great, Jerry thought, just the kind of thought I need to help me enjoy the festivities.

As Donna and Jerry filled plates with shrimp, pâté, oysters, raspberries, quiche, a variety of cheeses, and other items from the buffet, Jerry looked over at a pair of gaunt young men standing nearby and reflected on how cruel it was to invite jockeys to an event like this. At least now Brad Roark could eat what he wanted.

While Jerry had no problem with eating on his feet (or in any other position), Donna usually wanted a surface if one was available, so they grabbed vacant seats at one of the insufficient number of tables in the room. Jerry went off to fill a couple of glasses from the champagne fountain, exchanging hurried greetings with a dozen or so racing people along the way. By the time he returned—it hadn't seemed all that long—Donna was in deep conversation with the youthful-looking but silver-haired man they'd joined at the table. Trust Donna to make friends fast.

She politely acknowledged the champagne and turned back to her companion. Jerry groaned inwardly when he realized what the subject under discussion was.

"I have sympathy for your position, believe me. You seem to be a very reasonable young woman, unlike some."

Terrific, Jerry thought. Donna just loves to be patronized. This should be good.

"It's one thing to say you have sympathy for my position. But when are you going to do something about it?"

"What we do first and foremost is in the interest of consumer safety. Isn't it more important to create a first-rate product for human beings than to worry about a few lab animals?"

"There are plenty of other ways to test products," Donna said heatedly. "Use computer simulations. Use in vitro testing."

"The new methods aren't proven. Animal testing is. We have to worry about liability suits, you know, if we put out a product that proves harmful. We have to be able to show our testing methods are thorough and reliable."

"Purejoy is one of the few major cosmetics firms that still finds it necessary to do animal experimentation."

"That's not strictly true—"

"I don't know how strict you want to be. But I find it unacceptable that in the very city I live in, small defenseless animals are being tortured and sometimes sacrificed, not to cure cancer or AIDS or something important, but in the name of beauty. Beauty!"

The man smiled suavely and said, "Have some understanding. Not every woman is as naturally gifted in that department as you are."

Great. Donna loved flattery, too, especially in lieu of reasoned argument. Jerry decided he'd better intervene before this smoothy wound up with a lapful of hors d'oeuvres. "Hi, I don't think we've met. My name's Jerry Brogan." He extended a hand across the table.

The man shook it. "How do you do? I'm Myron Gilhousen."

Donna looked a little sheepish. "We haven't actually met, either. My name is Donna Melendez. Hi."

"You guys started in fighting before you even heard the referee's instructions?" Jerry kidded.

Gilhousen laughed. "I'm used to it. When I meet someone in a social situation in this town, I very rarely tell them I work for Purejoy. Cowardly on my part, I suppose. Just how did you know, Ms. Melendez?"

"Your tiepin and your cuff links both have the company logo."

"What do you do at Purejoy, Mr. Gilhousen?" Jerry asked.

"Call me Myron. Dreadful name, but I'm stuck with it. I'm Vice President for Research and Development." Knowing that could bring on another onslaught from Donna, he hurried on. "You don't have to tell me what you do, Jerry. I've enjoyed your work for years. And I guess Donna's a detective."

Donna shook her head smugly—that was one piece of flattery she seemed to receive with pleasure. "Jerry's the detective. I teach drama at Dana High."

"Are you involved in racing, Myron?" Jerry asked. He was

frankly wondering how Gilhousen had happened to be invited.

"Only as a fan so far. But I'd really like to get into the sport as an owner. A member of your board was kind enough to send me an invitation to this event."

"Will Wardell?"

Gilhousen looked surprised. "How'd you know that?"

"Just a guess. I know Purejoy used to sponsor one of his TV shows."

"Well, yes, but he hasn't had any direct connection with the company in years. He calls periodically, but most of our promotional activities are directed into other channels these days."

Donna said, "I have an idea for you. Halt animal experimentation and promote *that*."

"We'd be too late on the bandwagon," Gilhousen said good-humoredly. "If we change our policies, Donna, and I hope it will be possible, we will do it for the right reasons, not for public advantage and not to give in to pressures from special interest groups. Don't think Purejoy doesn't listen, though. One of the main parts of my job at the moment is developing a practical and humane policy on animal experimentation. Now, if you two will excuse me, I think I'll grab a bit more to eat."

Gilhousen rose to a leanly impressive height of about six four and strode away from the table.

"Don't you just love that?" Donna said. "If they quit maiming animals, it won't be from public pressure or political action. Just like the Vietnam War ended and the lunch counters got integrated and people got paid a living wage because the powers that be had a sudden attack of niceness."

"He doesn't seem like such a bad guy," Jerry said mildly.

Donna shrugged. "I suppose not. Maybe I got through to him a little, huh? You know, I hope Brad Roark does decide to run for City Council."

"You think he'll be sound on the cosmetics-testing issue, right?"

"Could be. He better not overdo the Shakespeare quoting in his political speeches, though." Jerry saw Donna's eyes widen slightly at something she saw over his shoulder. "Well, look who's here."

Jerry half turned in his chair and looked across the room at the entrance. "Yeah, Will and Judy Wardell."

"I don't mean them. Look a few degrees farther and you'll see our two friends from Guido's."

Jerry clicked off the description she'd given him and immediately knew the couple she meant. The guy was blond, balding, and chubby, the woman alarmingly suntanned, and both were dressed to kill. He had on a dark blue suit with a blue-and-red bow tie and a gardenia in his lapel. She had a very short white linen dress that showed off her tan, but—Donna was right—bad legs.

"I meant to tell you: I saw him talking to Parker Fuentes today at the track," Donna said. "I wasn't close enough to hear what they were talking about."

"I have to have a word with those people," Jerry said. "Give me a clever social ploy I can use."

Donna stood up. "You'll think of something. Maybe they sell cars and can give you a test drive. You go pump them, and I'll say hi to Will and Judy."

No time like the present, Jerry agreed. Not even waiting to enjoy the sight of Donna's retreat, he strode across the room toward the restaurant couple, determined to play it by ear.

He would not have been so crude as to stage a collision as an icebreaker, but the woman, making a sudden and unexpected turn toward the buffet table, did it for him.

"Oh, excuse me!" she said. "I'm so sorry."

Jerry was treated to a close-up view of her impressive cleavage. He couldn't help wondering where the suntan stopped.

"My fault entirely," Jerry said. "It's great to see you again."

"Again? I'm sorry—do I know you?" That low, sexy Lauren Bacall voice he remembered from the restaurant.

"Didn't I see you at Parker Fuentes's place?" Jerry was proud of the neutral word. Place could mean Fuentes's home or his car dealership.

"Oh, yes, of course," she said uncertainly. "What was your name again?"

"Jerry Brogan. And you're—oh, it's on the tip of my tongue."

She was looking at him suspiciously now. "Is it really? You know, Mr. Brogan, if I'd ever met you before, I think I'd remember. You're really kind of memorable."

"Well, thank you, I could say the same," Jerry said, but he knew his ploy hadn't worked. It was true. Men of his bulk didn't exactly disappear into the wallpaper. "Maybe I saw you from a distance and just *thought* I knew you. Some kind of political fund-raiser maybe?"

Her companion, who'd been deep in conversation with his back turned to them, now turned around and said, "Hi." It was the kind of friendly greeting given invaders on one's territory. He'd have managed it better if his nasal voice had been lower than his girlfriend's."

"Hi," Jerry said brightly. "We've just been trying to figure out where we know each other from. I'm Jerry Brogan."

"Ohhh," the man said, gratifyingly. Jerry would have hated to be really famous, but minor celebrity had its benefits. "I'm Larry Halvorsen. Glad to know you. Enjoy your work. And I guess you've met ..."

"Esme Flint." The woman extended her hand. "You know, it could have been at a fund-raiser at that. We managed Parker's last campaign for Council."

"Not one of our triumphs," Halvorsen said ruefully. "I never understood why he couldn't get the votes in this town. Everybody knows him from his TV commercials. Had it over every other candidate in name recognition. Can't figure it."

Esme said, "That kind of name recognition can work against you sometimes."

"And what do you think about the current Council race?" Jerry asked casually.

Halvorsen shrugged. "Too soon to tell till the filing deadline. Of course, I guess you know who Parker would *like* to have on the ballot. Doubt he'll go for it after that incident today, though. These people play hardball."

Jerry shrugged. "A phony bomb? Could be just a joke."

"Well, it's not that damned funny if you're the target of it, I can tell you that," Halvorsen said heatedly. "I wouldn't blame Roark if he backed off running because of it."

"You're assuming he'd made the decision to run?"

"I don't know for sure. I don't know how far Parker got with him. But I don't think I'd run if people were threatening me that way, sending me letters and making anonymous phone calls. If you can plant a phony bomb, you can plant a real one just as easily." Halvorsen smiled perfunctorily. "Of course, you don't see me riding racehorses or going up in hot-air balloons, either. I keep my feet on the ground."

"Firmly," Esme Flint agreed, and Halvorsen glanced at her as if unsure whether he was being needled.

"You understand, I hope Roark does run, because I think he's needed, and Parker's decided he's unelectable, for whatever reason. I'd love a chance to manage Roark's campaign. You know better than anybody how popular he is in Surfside."

Jerry said, "Don't be so sure about that. I don't know what percentage of the actual city population goes to the races. Roark has a lot of fans in the area, but how many of them are within the city limits?"

"Enough," Halvorsen said with unconvincing confidence.

"Any idea of who else might run?"

Halvorsen waved a hand. "The usual hacks. Nobody really formidable that I've heard anything about."

"No dark horses on the scene, huh?"

"It's the light horses that win the big races. You saw that

today." Halvorsen beamed at his own cleverness. For him, that was probably quite a bon mot. Jerry wasn't impressed, but the guy must have something going for him as a political manager. Or maybe Esme was the brains of the pair.

As he weaved his way through the rapidly filling ballroom in an effort to rejoin Donna, Jerry replayed the conversation he'd heard at Guido's. Somebody was going to file for election, but it couldn't have been Brad Roark. It seemed Fuentes's candidate was their candidate, and they'd been talking about somebody they didn't expect to file and presumably didn't *want* to see file. Somebody with a "Purejoy connection," somebody with things hanging over him that somebody else may or may not be prepared to use against him. Jerry hadn't been nimble enough to squeeze a reference to Purejoy Cosmetics into the conversation—Donna might have helped him on that—but at least he now knew who the people were and had laid some groundwork for future conversations.

Jerry found he had covered the whole room without finding either Donna or the Wardells. Some of the party had spilled out of the ballroom into the corridors and even a couple of the adjacent meeting rooms. He'd find them later. Replenish his champagne first.

Brad Roark, he noticed, was still in the corner by the display table. He hoped the retiring jockey would have a chance to get something to eat at his own party. Now an elderly couple was monopolizing him, and Brad, whose patient friendliness had stayed steady up to now, was showing signs of strain. The man's attire was casual to the point of seediness, and the woman was decidedly overdressed, in a hat and lace-underlaid silk dress appropriate to a wedding party. Moving slightly closer, Jerry realized they were Brad's uncle and aunt from Florida. They were going on, noisily enough for all around to hear them, about how doggone proud they were of their nephew, and the best term for Brad's expression was one usually reserved for teenage girls: mortified.

HOT AIR

It was clear enough that Will Wardell's reunion had not been a good idea.

And something else was clear. Glancing at the display table from a distance, Jerry did a mental inventory of the exhibits. The silver-handled ice pick was gone.

9

Standing in a small group in the corridor outside the ballroom, Donna reflected what a beautiful crowd this was, with stunning women and impressive men in abundance. But only two had that larger-than-life quality bred by years of work before the TV cameras: Parker Fuentes and Will Wardell. And it seemed only appropriate for Fuentes the commercial to interrupt Wardell the show.

Will thought a tuxedo proper for any evening occasion, and on him it never seemed excessive. His wife, Judy, in a black St. John's knitted dress with a string of pearls, and a black pillbox hat with a short veil, was enviably elegant, while Naomi Burns, in a long floral-patterned dress with rampant cabbage roses, was slightly outclassed.

Will was regaling Judy, Donna, and Naomi with a long anecdote about his early days as a teenage radio announcer during World War II when Fuentes strode down the hall, singing-cowboy regalia gleaming.

"Guillermo," Fuentes intoned, throwing an arm around Wardell's shoulder and pumping his hand vigorously. He knew just how irritating Wardell found the latinized version of his name and used it whenever they met in the presence of other people. "How are you, my friend? I guess neither of us had our plans for Brad Roark Day turn out *quite* as we might have wished, eh?"

Wardell flashed his teeth bravely. "I don't know what you mean, Parker. Sorry about that mishap with your balloon, though. We were concerned about you, weren't we, Judy?"

"Mishap you call it? My balloon performed perfectly. I am undefeated. And when I find you, Guillermo, surrounded by three such beautiful women, I see you have salvaged something, too, eh? *Señora* Wardell, it is a delight to see you again. And ladies . . . ?"

Will Wardell introduced Donna and Naomi. Donna thought Fuentes's manner had hand-kisser written all over it, and she was relieved he didn't carry the act quite that far.

"Ms. Burns," Fuentes said, "your brother was so pleased to see you today. He has told me a great deal about you."

Naomi Burns smiled. "My brother Brad, you mean?"

"Yes, certainly. I have not had the pleasure of meeting your other brother."

"I don't know what Brad could have told you, we haven't seen each other for so long. But I was certainly proud of him today, the way he won with your horse."

"Now *his* horse," Fuentes said. "We have a great deal to talk about, Ms. Burns. If your friends will excuse us, perhaps you will join me for a bite."

After polite bows had been exchanged and the pair had walked into the ballroom together, Will Wardell muttered, "She better be careful. He just might bite her at that."

"I think Naomi can take care of herself," Judy observed. "She's been around the block a few times."

"I'd hate to see her hurt by Fuentes," Wardell said. Donna was struck again by the way Wardell seemed to idealize women, as if he imagined them all as innocent and needful of protection as he imagined his own wife.

"Don't feel responsible, Will," Judy said, clutching her husband's arm. "You brought her here, but she *is* an adult." She threw Donna a very subtle wink. The two of them seemed to have built a happy marriage on treating each other like children. Well, whatever works.

"She's the only one who really seemed glad to see Brad Roark," Wardell said, something he hadn't admitted out loud since the reunion fiasco.

"Maybe Fuentes thinks she'd have some kind of influence with him," Donna offered.

"What do you mean?"

"Well, he's trying to get Brad to run for City Council, isn't he?"

"Oh. I never thought of that."

Maisie Cooper, wearing an extremely low-cut, short-hemmed, and high-waisted outfit with long white kidskin boots, came striding down the hall, male heads turning to follow her as if choreographed.

"Hi, Will!" she said. "Hey, this is really nice."

"Donna, Judy, this is Maisie Roark, Brad's sister-in-law," Will said. "Where's Mo?"

"Still down in the room. We're just down the hall, real handy. He'll be along later. He and Brad still haven't had any time together, and I know they have a lot to talk about."

"I hope they do."

"Oh, sure, they do. Men can be so exasperating sometimes, just can't show their true feelings. You girls know what I mean. I mean these guys are brothers. Brothers. They love each other. But can they say so? Can they throw their arms around each other and give each other a big hug when they haven't seen each other all these years? No. Gotta be cool. Gotta be macho. Gotta be Mr. New York Streetkid and the Iceman. I think they found the reunion so overwhelming, both of them, they just couldn't cope with it. That's what I think."

"They couldn't handle the emotion, so they didn't show any?" Donna said.

HOT AIR

"That's what I think. You did a real nice thing bringing everybody together, Will. And we all appreciate it. I want you to know that."

"Well, thank you," Will said, with a solemn bow of his head. Donna was surprised that he seemed to be buying it.

"Mo wants to talk to you, too, Will. In private, he says. Probably to tell you just what I've been telling you, and if it doesn't come out quite right when Mo says it, just know that's what's behind it, okay? If you want to drop down to our room, it's one-oh-nine. Just down the hall on the right, and the door's wide open."

Will nodded. "I'll do that." Donna wondered why the need for a private meeting in Mo's room, but Wardell seemed to accept the idea unquestioningly.

Back in the ballroom, Jerry had been buttonholed by racing writer Jack Morgan, who was already looking forward to the following month's Surfside Sprint Championship. The veteran of many freeloading sports buffets, Jack could eat on his feet as comfortably as Jerry and talk a blue streak at the same time—tolerable if you didn't watch his mouth or stand too close.

"It'll be the sprint of the decade, Jerry, the sprint of the century."

"Well, I don't know about that. But I'm excited about it, I'll admit. At seven furlongs, you'd think the stretch runner would have the edge, but—"

"Not necessarily. Valley Moon can get seven panels. He's done it plenty of times. And it's just possible that extra furlong is more than Hot Air wants. Out of the clouds or not, he's basically a speed horse, Jerry."

"That's just what I was going to say."

"Ah, but I obviously know something you don't. This will be no two-horse race. There's a third runner on the horizon that will really make it something special." Morgan lowered his voice as if pronouncing the unspeakable name of a deity. "Craven Clay."

Jon L. Breen

"You're putting me on," Jerry said. Craven Clay, a fragile five-year-old who had won the Belmont and Breeder's Cup Classic at three and had been the unanimous choice for horse of the year, had missed his four-year-old season with injuries. He'd come back brilliant as ever in a couple of tuneup races the previous winter at Santa Anita before going on the sidelines with another minor injury. "They wouldn't bring him back in that spot."

"He's ready to run, I tell you, and they have to run him somewhere."

"Has the horse ever sprinted in his life? His best distance is a mile and a quarter."

"He can do anything he wants, Jerry. He's a fast stayer. And he runs great when he's fresh, you know that. And middle-distance horses who'd be outrun at six furlongs win at seven all the time. It's a tough distance on the pure sprinter. You know that."

Everything Morgan said about past form and the peculiar nature of the seven-furlong race was true, and Jerry hoped his information on Craven Clay was correct. That really could make the Surfside Sprint Championship the race of the year—he still didn't buy decade or century—at whatever distance.

"What a story," Morgan chortled. "That and the new ownership of Hot Air—"

"Right. Roark the gentleman owner, huh?"

Morgan looked smug. "Once again, Jerry, your information may be a trifle out of date."

"What do you mean?"

Morgan lowered his voice dramatically. "Not fifteen minutes ago I heard Brad Roark offer to sell Hot Air."

"What did you say?" roared a voice from behind Jerry's head. Morgan clearly had not lowered his voice enough. Jerry turned to see Parker Fuentes, a glass of champagne in each hand.

Jerry said, "How are you, Parker? Jack here was just spreading an unlikely rumor."

Jerry expected the reporter to put on his interviewing cap and ask Fuentes how he felt about his gift horse being looked so promptly in the wallet. But Morgan disappointed him. "You misunderstood me," he said.

"How do you know I misunderstood you, Mr. Morgan?" Fuentes demanded.

"What did you think I said?"

Now Fuentes lowered his voice, for once not determined to be heard by the whole room. "That Roark offered to sell Hot Air."

"Now I understand. I said he offered to *spell* Hot Air. Give him some time off for a rest. Turn him out."

"That doesn't make sense. The horse is in the peak of his form."

"Well, you know Roark. Always real considerate of horses. I guess that'll be true as an owner, too."

Fuentes shook his head in bafflement and moved on. Jerry noticed he was delivering the second glass to Naomi Burns. There was an intriguing alliance.

Turning back to Morgan, Jerry said, "And who did Roark offer to 'spell' Hot Air to?"

"I said too much already," Morgan said. So he resorted to nonverbal communication, making a slight motion of his head in the direction of the exhibit table, where Roark was deep in conversation with Myron Gilhousen, the Purejoy vice-president.

Norgan looked at his empty plate in dismay. "This is great food, Jerry, but I'm eating too much."

"Me, too," Jerry agreed, and they both marched back to the buffet table.

Jerry and Donna were finally reunited about an hour after they had separated. They stepped out onto the ocean side of the Inn to compare notes.

"I told Brad the ice pick was gone, and he just said don't worry, he knew where it was."

"They borrowed it for the kitchen?" Donna speculated.

"Who knows? Maybe he'll tell me later. Not that it matters, but when a guy's been getting threats, I'd think the whereabouts of something that sharp would be a matter of concern to him."

"It probably doesn't mean a thing," Donna said.

"Mmm. When you saw that news report today, did they say anything about *other* threats to Brad? Or did they just talk about the bomb?"

"Just the bomb. And they didn't mention that little plastic jockey or the warning on the bomb you told me about."

"The police like to keep those details to themselves if they can. They certainly weren't volunteering any information when they talked to me, and some of those guys are friends of mine. But Larry Halvorsen seemed to know all about a *series* of threats to Roark. He mentioned phone calls and anonymous letters, which is more than I know about."

"Fuentes could have told him."

"I don't know if *he* even knew about any earlier threats."

"He could have heard it from Brad. Brad might even have said it to somebody from one of the other channels—I only saw one, and I'll bet the other stations were there, too. Not to mention radio and print people."

"True," Jerry said. "Just my suspicious nature."

"So you didn't find out what candidate Halvorsen and—what's her name?—"

"Esme Flint."

"—were talking about?"

"Nope."

"You could have just asked them."

"What, and told them I'd been eavesdropping on their restaurant conversation?"

"No, just tell them, since they are political types, you wondered if they'd heard a rumor somebody with a Purejoy connection . . ." She trailed off. "Okay, I admit it'd be tough to bring off."

"You can try it if you want. Be my guest."

Jerry and Donna wandered along the ocean walk, glad to leave most of the party behind them. Occasionally they saw some of

HOT AIR

their fellow celebrants reeling along, champagne glasses in hand, or sitting along the benches by the beach. It was a warm autumn evening, and it was good to have the option of going outside.

On one of the benches were a flowered dress and a cowboy shirt, oblivious to the passing parade, in the kind of passionate embrace that makes onlookers feel like voyeurs.

As they walked past, Jerry and Donna just looked at each other. At a safe distance, she remarked she had no idea Parker Fuentes and Naomi Burns would hit it off so well so quickly.

A couple of hours later, Jerry decided it hadn't been such a bad party after all. Donna had lured him onto the dance floor to fake it to the music of a small combo that could handle rock, jazz, country, and even big-band music with competence. Everyone he'd talked to earlier in the evening seemed to have stuck around and loosened up to one degree or another.

Keene Axtell early on had been his worried self, fretting about the efficiency of the private security force assigned to guard Brad Roark. He claimed they were inconspicuous to the vanishing point, while Jerry assured him that was just what they were supposed to be. By eleven o'clock, Axtell was performing an unlikely tango with a surprisingly graceful Frances McIntosh, while Buller enjoyed the free-flowing booze and undulating bodies.

Stan Digby had not attempted to approach Brad Roark again. The guest of honor had managed to get out of his corner, eat something, and circulate throughout the room in relaxed and cordial fashion. As long as he didn't come into contact with any of his relatives, he seemed to enjoy the evening.

Mo Roark was the least seen of the relatives, appearing in the ballroom only sporadically in a floral print shirt worn outside his trousers—he still looked more like a Dead End Kid than a Californian. Once Jerry spotted him talking to Will and Judy Wardell and overheard a snatch of their conversation.

"Thanks for the great accommodations, Mr. Wardell," Roark

117

was saying. "Room one-oh-nine is so terrific, I could hardly tear myself away for the party."

"I'm glad you're enjoying yourself," Will Wardell told him.

The body language belied the polite words. Mo Roark was staring at Judy as if he were undressing her; Judy was receiving his ocular attention with noticeable embarrassment; and Will was straining to remain civil.

Jerry reflected it was just as well Mo didn't spend that much time in the ballroom. Certainly Maisie seemed to be enjoying herself without him. She also had a dance with Keene Axtell. Jerry was glad to see his boss so at home on the dance floor and reflected he would probably run an Arthur Murray studio better than he did a racetrack.

Larry Halvorsen and Esme Flint were doing a lot of circulating, together and separately, and around eleven-fifteen, Parker Fuentes and Naomi Burns, seemingly joined for life like Siamese twins, reappeared in the ballroom.

At eleven-thirty, Jerry and Donna crossed paths with Myron Gilhousen for the second time. The Purejoy vice-president smiled and raised his hands in a conciliatory gesture.

Having gotten in her polemical shots the first time around, Donna just gave him a friendly grin and inquired, "Having a good time?"

"Very much so."

"Making any progress in your efforts?" Jerry asked.

Donna said, "Come on, Jerry, even I don't expect Myron here to write his revised and more humane animal experimentation policy in the middle of a party. Tomorrow morning's soon enough."

"No," Jerry said. "I meant any progress in getting into race-horse ownership."

"You'll need a humane policy there, too," Donna said. "No whips."

"As a matter of fact," Gilhousen said confidentially, "I just may become the owner of a rather well-known thoroughbred. I'm afraid I can't say any more about it, though."

It was around midnight that Jerry and Donna decided to call it a night. Jerry felt very mellow, and he hadn't really had all that much to drink, just enough to be grateful the lightly imbibing Donna had nominated herself "designated driver" at the beginning of the evening.

They were on their way out of the building when a piercing scream from down the hall destroyed the mood.

Maisie was running toward them, crying hysterically, "Help me! Help me!"

Jerry dashed down the corridor after her. As they walked through the door of Room 109, he knew there was precious little help he'd be able to give. Mo Roark lay nude on his back in the bed, covered in blood, a silver handle protruding from his chest. He didn't look alive.

1O

Jerry put his arm around Maisie's shoulders, turning her away from the bed and supporting her in the event of a faint. His stomach was giving him uneasy messages, but there was no time to give in to that. He turned to a frightened-looking hotel waiter, who had followed them down the hall at a trot but had left his heroism in the doorway. The guy was looking at the bed with his mouth hanging open, his freckled face pale. Jerry propelled Maisie out the door and told the waiter, "Don't let anybody in here unless I find a doctor," knowing as he said it that the only doctor who might have any business with the blindly staring Mo Roark would be a pathologist.

He had given his instructions just in time. Now the corridor was filling with people who had spilled down from the ballroom. Donna was there to take charge of the sobbing Maisie, and he turned her over to Donna, mouthing grateful thanks. Jerry looked at the group and said, not as articulately as he might have hoped, "Is there? A doctor, I mean?"

In a party full of horse owners, there was bound to be at least one physician on hand. Jerry hoped the white-faced and portly man who reluctantly stepped through the door of Room 109 to look at the body wasn't some specialist who rarely saw any blood.

By the time the medical volunteer came out the door, the house physician was bustling along the corridor, on a broken-field run through the gawking partygoers, carrying his bag. The chunky guest shook his head at his colleague. "Nothing we can do for him."

"Then nobody enters the room," Jerry said authoritatively.

"Are you a cop?" someone asked.

"Ah, no. Has anybody called them?" The sound of an approaching siren answered his question. The waiter was still manning his post and looking a little further from keeling over than he had. Jerry decided he had done his duty—let the pros take it from here. A little while before, his stomach had been demanding a receptacle, but the moment had passed.

As he walked down the corridor toward the ballroom, most of the faces he saw were only vaguely familiar. No Brad Roark. None of Brad's relatives. Jerry was thankful. Jack Morgan cut him off before he returned to the ballroom.

"I got a look through the door, Jerry, before you decided to get all heavy-handed. Was the guy stabbed?"

Jerry nodded.

"Who was he?"

"Mo Roark. Brad's brother." He wondered if he should have told Morgan. But what difference did it make?

Morgan went dashing for a phone, looking like a character out of *The Front Page*. When Jerry reentered the ballroom, he saw three other turf writers standing around incuriously with drinks in their hands, presumably discussing tomorrow's pick-six. It was good to know at least one handicapper had enough journalistic instinct to venture off his beat for an exclusive.

Jerry soon found there would have been no point to keeping the identity of the dead man confidential. The buzz of conversation already was focused on what had happened to Mo Roark. Most of the guests were standing around in stunned groups, while others tried to make their way to the exits. The first arriving police were turning them back, saying they couldn't go home just yet. The little hot-air balloons still strained at their ribbons, the champagne fountain still bubbled away, the buffet was still in business, and the ice sculpture had not completely melted, but most of the festiveness had gone out of it all. After a whispered word from a worried-looking man who might have been on the hotel's management staff, the musical combo had abruptly stopped playing.

Jerry looked for Donna and Maisie but didn't see them. He assumed Donna had taken her somewhere private, maybe sought some help from the house doctor. In one corner, Parker Fuentes was comforting Naomi Burns. Judy Wardell, sobbing on her husband's shoulder, seemed even more upset than Roark's sister.

The police had cleared the corridor and funneled the rest of the guests back into the ballroom. Out of the corner of his eye, Jerry saw Keene Axtell striding toward him but pretended not to, and took evasive action to avoid him. Whatever the track manager had to say about the death of Mo Roark probably wouldn't be very helpful.

Jerry scanned the room for familiar faces. Frances and Buller McIntosh were together again. She had found Brad Roark and was gabbling to him. This time he looked not mortified but stony-faced and stunned. Buller managed to look a little somber but not really distressed. Jerry was only half conscious of what he was doing: searching the room for a face that looked like it had recently committed murder. An empty hope, probably.

More and more police were in evidence, and Jerry could imagine a small army of technical personnel swarming over Room 109. He wasn't sorry not to be there, but he'd give a lot to get in on some of the interrogations to come. Maybe he'd have a chance if his old acquaintance Lieutenant Wilmer Friend was on the case—and on the relatively small Surfside police force, who else would be in charge of a major homicide?

Wilmer Friend had been rousted out of bed almost immediately after the murder of Mo Roark had been reported, and he arrived at the scene within an hour. He felt like snarling at the dispatcher who'd awakened him—and his wife—from an unusually deep and satisfactory sleep, but how could he do that? The department had standing orders to call him immediately on anything really big, and this looked like the first major murder case in Surfside—major meaning involving the rich and powerful, and not boringly open-and-shut—since the death of jockey Hector Gates several years before.

On arrival at the Surfside Inn, he was filled in by the patrol team who had been first on the scene. He instructed them to start getting names and addresses of the people at the party and to let them leave unless they seemed to have some direct connection with Mo Roark. Then he asked the manager if there was a room or an office he could use as an investigative command post. He was offered one of the meeting rooms adjacent to the ballroom.

"Who found the body?" Friend asked the patrol cop.

"The wife, sir. She's in pretty bad shape—"

"Who was next on the scene?"

"Guy named Jerry Brogan. He's the public-address announcer at—"

"Yeah, I know," Friend said. He'd known Brogan since the Gates murder, and they'd had occasional contact since. Brogan fancied himself an amateur detective, and Friend had talked to several cops from other jurisdictions who'd been irritated by his interference in their investigations. True, they had occasionally benefited, too, but not as much as Brogan imagined. Friend was sure all the cases he'd been involved in would have been solved anyway—and just as fast—by solid police work.

"Okay," Friend said. "Bring me Brogan first."

Jon L. Breen

When Jerry walked into the meeting room, he didn't look cheerful, but there was a certain eagerness about him. If the track announcer wanted to play detective, Friend would have to put a damper on it and fast. But first he had to find out what he knew.

After getting Jerry's account of the evening up to the finding of Mo Roark's body, Friend said, "We have plenty of people to get the names and addresses of all the guests, but I want to talk to everybody at the party who had a direct connection to Mo Roark. And tonight." He looked ruefully at his watch. "This morning. Who should I talk to, Jerry?"

"His brother Brad, certainly. The aunt and uncle. His sister Naomi. She may be alibied, though—she and Parker Fuentes were inseparable through the evening. You'd also want to talk to Will Wardell. He's the one who brought all the relatives here. There aren't any other people I know of with direct connections to Mo. Why do you think he was nude?"

"Let me ask the questions, will you, Jerry? I don't want to hold these people here all night."

"I just think it's an important point."

"And it's one we would naturally think of," said Friend, with strained patience. "Now, you say the weapon had been on the exhibit table earlier in the evening?"

"Right, and when I noticed it was missing, I pointed it out to Brad, and he said he knew where it was. If he can tell you who took it from the table—"

"Another key point, I agree. I guarantee we'll ask."

"It was Brad who was getting the death threats, not Mo. You don't suppose someone could have killed Mo thinking he was killing Brad? Of course, they didn't look that much alike, but . . ."

"Jerry, just facts, not theories." The guy was on another planet with all his convoluted reasoning. Friend was still optimistic this would turn out to be a straightforward, uncomplicated killing, easily solved, and he'd explore the traditional possibilities before he started looking for tontines, family curses, and identical

124

twin brothers from Australia. "When Roark's wife came screaming down the hall, and you followed her—"

"She didn't have any bloodstains on her clothes, and I think she would have if she'd stabbed him."

"Unless she stabbed him wearing something else, or nude, then got dressed and came screaming for help. Now you've got me doing it, damn you. I started to ask, when she came down the hall and you followed her, did you see anybody else?"

"Not a soul."

"Did you see anybody go in the direction of Roark's room earlier in the evening?"

"Oh, sure. It was only a few doors down from where the party was, and people were spilling out of the ballroom in all directions. I think almost anybody could have visited his room."

"He came to the party, too, though, didn't he?"

"Sure, he was there. Not constantly, though."

"Do you remember the last time you saw him during the evening?"

Jerry considered. "Maybe an hour before Maisie found the body. About eleven o'clock. So anybody who wasn't alibied between eleven and twelve could have been the killer."

"You don't say."

"Why are you so sarcastic, Wilmer? I just want to help. In fact, I'd be glad to sit in on the interviews if you want."

"Why would I want you to do that?"

"Well, you've said before, cases that involve horse racing—"

"I don't know that this case involves horse racing directly."

"It could."

"And anyway, it's not kosher to have a civilian sitting in on a murder investigation. If I have questions for you, I'll be in touch."

"Okay." Jerry felt as deflated as Parker Fuentes's balloon.

As he left the questioning room, he passed Brad Roark, who was being escorted in by one of the police team. He gave the retired jockey a sympathetic nod and walked back to the ballroom. If there had been any vestige of festiveness left, it was gone now, and the people remaining were standing in small groups, speaking in hushed and funereal tones.

Donna found him. She looked drawn and tired, drained of her usual energy.

Jerry gave her a sympathetic hug and said, "How's Maisie?"

"Naomi's with her now. I think she'll be okay. Can we get out of here?"

"Soon as they'll let us. You're terrific, you know that?"

Keene Axtell appeared too suddenly for Jerry to take any evasive action. "So our security is fine, huh?" he said.

Jerry wondered how long he could keep working for a guy whose every statement begged for sarcasm. "Yes, our security is fine. But we didn't have anybody guarding Mo Roark. There didn't seem to be any reason to, did there?"

"I think somebody killed Mo Roark, mistaking him for his brother."

"What would Brad have been doing in Room one-oh-nine, Keene?" Jerry said, not pointing out he'd advanced the same theory to Wilmer Friend moments before. Hearing Axtell say it made him realize what an absurd idea it was.

"This won't take too long, Mr. Roark, but if we're going to find out who killed your brother, we'll need to find out as much as we can as fast as we can."

"Sure, that's okay. I'm glad to cooperate." Brad Roark was somber but obviously not grief-stricken.

"When was the last time you saw your brother? Before today, I mean?"

"I'm not exactly sure. Late sixties, I think."

"You weren't close?"

"That's putting it mildly."

"I'm told you weren't very glad to see him today."

Brad shrugged. "Well, for one thing, I don't particularly like surprises. I think the track should have told me they intended to bring my relatives out here, so I could have vetoed the idea. Mo and I grew in different directions, you could say. The friends I've made in Surfside, in the community, I mean, have the same kinds of interests I do in art, literature, cultural things. I was having a great day, a day for the local community. And up turns my brother, like a character out of *Guys and Dolls*—or maybe I mean *West Side Story*. And Mo knew how little we got along as kids. He knew damn well how little anxious I would be to see him again. And yet he couldn't turn down a free trip to California."

When Brad wound down, Friend didn't ask another question, just let silence hang between them. Brad smiled grimly. "Am I talking myself into a noose here? Seriously, I hope you don't think I murdered my brother out of embarrassment. It was annoying to have him around, but not such a big deal. I was actually having quite a good time this evening. And I'm sorry for his wife. She seems like a nice enough person."

"Did you talk to your brother during the evening?"

"Oh, sure. I was civil to him. To do anything else would just have made things worse."

"What time did you see him last?"

"The *only* time I saw him was, oh, about nine o'clock, I guess. I'd spent most of the evening down in the far corner of the room where they had an exhibit table of some of my stuff. I was spending most of my time explaining to people what the different things were—silks and trophies and presentations, things like that. Mo came by and we talked a little."

"About what?"

"Well, our childhood was off-limits, so there wasn't that much we *could* talk about. I guess we talked about the race. Mo probably never sat on a horse in his life, but he was a horseplayer. Yeah, we talked about Hot Air and Valley Moon a little bit."

"What did your brother do for a living, Mr. Roark?"

Brad shrugged. "Damned if I know. He never did seem to hold a job for long. As a kid, he worked for a while as an usher or something. That's what he was doing when I started riding. And I think he drove a cab at one point. We weren't in touch very much."

"Was he your older brother or younger?"

"Two years older."

"And how old was that?"

"Let's see. I just turned fifty a month ago—which is one of the reasons I decided to quit the saddle—so that would make Mo fifty-two."

"How long had he been married?"

"I didn't know he *was* married until today. I never got my announcement in the mail. If you want to find out much about Mo Roark, I'm afraid I'm not the guy to ask."

"So you didn't see him between nine o'clock and midnight?"

"Not to talk to. I mean, I was aware that he was around off and on, but I can't remember any specific sightings."

"Mr. Roark, I understand one of the items on display tonight was an ice pick you'd been given by the other jockeys."

Brad nodded. "Right."

"And the ice pick was removed from the table sometime during the evening."

Brad's eyes widened. "Hey, you're not going to tell me that was what Mo was stabbed with."

Friend nodded. "What happened to the ice pick, Mr. Roark?"

"This won't help you much, I'm afraid. Mo took it."

"You gave it to your brother?"

"I didn't give it to him. He borrowed it."

"Why?"

"He said he wanted to show it to somebody."

"And you let him?"

"Look, Lieutenant, whatever I did tonight, I was *not* going to create some kind of scene with Mo. He might have enjoyed it. But he'd humiliated me enough just by showing up. I wasn't going to do anything to draw attention to him. I was just going to grin and bear it, that's all. He wants to borrow my ice pick, I let him borrow it. You don't suppose he stabbed himself with the idea of implicating me, do you?"

Friend shook his head. "Doesn't seem likely. Maybe not even possible, given the wound."

"Oh, well. Mo never seemed the suicidal type anyway."

"Did you ever go to your brother's room during the evening?"

"I don't even know where his room was."

"Were you alone at any time between eleven and twelve?"

"I don't think I was ever alone all evening." Roark shrugged. "Except when I went to the men's room. I'd have a tough time giving myself an alibi for the hour, but I could probably reconstruct it if it's necessary."

"Just think about it. Mr. Roark, there was some fear *you* might be the target of something tonight."

"Not fear on my part."

"That incident in the balloon this afternoon must have been frightening."

"That's not too strong a word for the forced landing, I'll admit. But the bomb was a phony. It was all a joke, I'm sure of it. And I'm sure it had nothing to do with my brother's death. Just a coincidence."

"How can you be so sure?"

"Just that the threats against me were a joke, and murder isn't. By definition."

"You also received a telephone threat?"

"Yes. I reported it to Surfside Meadows security."

"Not to the police?"

"I think I was being overcautious to report it to anyone, to tell you the truth. As I say, it was a joke."

"Were there also some threats by mail?"

"One, yes. I received it after I got to the track today."

"What did it say."

"Same message as the phone call and the bomb: NO HOT AIR. Block capitals, unremarkable stationery, Surfside postmark."

"You kept the letter?"

"Yes."

"Can you let our people examine it, please?"

"Certainly, if you want to waste your time."

"Whether the threat against you was serious or not, Mr. Roark, whoever planted that phony bomb in the balloon could probably be charged with something. Malicious mischief, maybe. We don't appreciate having the bomb-disposal unit's time wasted on hoaxes."

"I understand."

"Mr. Roark, do you know who was the author of these threats against you?"

"No idea," said Brad Roark, and Wilmer Friend was almost certain he was lying.

"It's good of you to talk to me, Mrs. Roark. I'm so sorry about your husband."

"Yeah, sure, thanks, I'm okay now." Her voice still shook, and her emotional state seemed precarious, but Maisie was determined to talk. She'd changed from her party outfit into jeans and a T-shirt. "First of all, I'm not Mrs. Roark. Mo and I lived together for years, but we never got married. My name's Maisie Cooper. I might as well have been Maisie Roark, but I don't want to start off lying to you." She paused. "That sounds funny. I don't want to finish up lying to you, either. I want to tell you the truth."

"When did you last see Mo Roark alive, Ms. Cooper?"

She drew a sharp breath. "I don't know. A little before eleven maybe. We had a dance. One dance, and off he went back to our room. I didn't go back there till I found him."

"Did he say why he was going back to the room?"

"Mo liked to be mysterious. If I asked, he wouldn't tell me. Mo always had things going on. Big deals, big projects, stuff he wouldn't tell me about."

"What did he do for a living?"

"I honest to God don't know." She reacted to Friend's skeptical expression. "I don't! He brought home money, and that's all he owed me. I knew things he *used* to do: cabdriver, peanut vendor, bartender, you name it. But never what he was doing at the moment."

"What did you think he did? Something illegal?"

"I never thought about it." She read his face again. "Okay, okay, I thought about it a lot. And I decided it was probably better *not* to know, okay? You can understand that, can't you?"

"Why do you think he came to California?"

"I didn't come in here to bullshit you. It wasn't to see his brother again and make things up with him. I wanted to think it was that, but I know it wasn't. And it wasn't because he liked the idea of a free vacation so much, either. Mo was no great traveler. I don't know if he ever left New York before. No, Mo was up to something."

"What?"

"I don't know. And I'd tell you if I did, believe me. Mo's gone." Her voice faltered and her eyes filled with tears, but she went on. "I can't do anything now to protect him. And I'd like to know who killed him and over what. He was no Prince Charming, but I loved him. I'll do anything I can to help you."

"Do you know what Mo spent the evening doing? I mean, who he talked to or anything like that?"

"He asked me to stay away from the room. And he asked me to tell Will Wardell he wanted to talk to him. In the room. And no, I don't think it was just to thank him for throwing the great family reunion."

"But you don't know what his business with Wardell was?"

"No."

"Did Mo bring anything with him outside of clothes and the usual traveling things?"

She nodded. "A little attaché case. I don't know what's in it. I don't even know if it was still in the room when I found him, but I guess it was. Go ahead and have a look at it if you think it might help you. You'll get no argument from me."

"What was Mo's relationship with his relatives?"

"He didn't have one. He hadn't seen his aunt and uncle or his sister for almost as long as Brad. That uncle—" She broke off.

"Yeah, what about him?"

"Nothing. Forget it. It's got nothing to do with what happened."

"How can you be sure? What did you start to say?"

"Just that he's a dirty old man, that's all. We had dinner, and he's feeling me up under the table all evening. Hey, though, it's nothing to do with this, and I wouldn't want to embarrass his wife."

"She probably knows what he's like, don't you think?"

"Yeah, I suppose she does."

"What was Mo's attitude toward them?"

"No attitude. Mo and his uncle seemed to get along okay, though. They had racing to talk about. But neither one of them seemed to have any interest in seeing Brad again. Mo and his sister didn't have much to say to each other."

"Did Mo resent his brother's success?"

"No, he seemed pretty casual about it. To tell you the truth, I don't think Mo cared one way or the other about any of his relatives, and they felt the same way about him. That's all I can tell you."

"Ms. Cooper, your—uh, Mo Roark's body was nude when you found it. Did he commonly sleep in the nude?"

"Always. No exceptions. You think he was asleep when—?"

"We don't know."

"If he was asleep, how did the person who killed him—? I guess he could have left the door unlocked, huh?"

"They lock automatically. But he could have left it ajar, or the killer could have gotten a key somehow. Had you ever seen the weapon before?"

"I haven't seen it yet. I mean, I saw it, but—I saw the blood mostly. I didn't notice what the weapon was."

"It was an ice pick with a silver handle."

"Oh, Brad's award from the other jockeys, you mean? Mo

showed it to me. So that was it? It was sitting right there on the bedstand where anybody could pick it up."

"Did Mo tell you why he had the ice pick?"

"No, he didn't," she said thoughtfully. "Doesn't make much sense, does it? Why would he be showing off his brother's award?"

"I hope this won't take long," Will Wardell said. "My wife is terribly upset, and I really want to get her home. I hate to expose her to something like this. She's not used to it."

"I can't say I'm used to murder myself, but I have to do my job. I'll make this as brief as I can, though. Did you visit Mo Roark in his room, Mr. Wardell?"

"Yes," said Will Wardell. "Shortly after his wife told me he wanted to see me."

"Why did you think he wanted you to come to his room?"

"That does seem odd, doesn't it?" Will said, as if considering the strangeness of the request for the first time. "I don't know."

"What did you talk about when you got there?"

"Mo Roark was a New Yorker, and I used to live there. He wanted to talk about New York."

"Did you like Mo Roark?"

Wardell offered a tentative version of his famous toothy grin. "No, I didn't. His kind of person was one of the reasons I left New York in the first place. I know it's not fair to stereotype a whole city, but why should I let that stop me? Living there over a period of years—oh, and I guess in other big cities, too—has an unfortunate effect on people, especially those who don't enjoy great financial or social success. Roark had the kind of ingrained rudeness people in service occupations tend to develop when they're frustrated by their jobs and by the city they have to cope with every day."

Friend thought Wardell was enjoying his sociological disquisition too much and tried to get him back on the subject. "What specifically about New York did you talk about?"

"I don't remember in detail. I just wanted to get away from him as quickly as I could without being rude."

"Were you angry at Roark because he ruined the family reunion?"

"Oh, I wouldn't say he ruined it. You never know how those things are going to turn out. Surprises come with the territory."

"You were disappointed, though, weren't you?"

"Well, sure. I like them to turn out well. Actually, it may have turned out better than it appeared at first. There was one thing Roark said to me that kind of stuck in my mind. When I asked him why he was staying in his room and not joining the party, he said he was planning a family outing."

"Those were his exact words?"

"Yes, I remember distinctly."

"What do you think he meant by that?"

"Oh, maybe that he was unhappy about the coldness of the reunion, and he wanted to make it up to his family by all going out somewhere as a group. Before they dispersed in a couple of days. In fact, maybe he really called me to his room to apologize for the disappointing reunion. He didn't actually say that, but maybe that was what he had in mind. Some people have a hard time apologizing."

"Was Mo Roark fully clothed when you visited his room?"

Wardell looked puzzled. "Yes, certainly."

"And you left him at what time?"

Wardell shrugged. "Perhaps nine o'clock."

"Did you see him again that evening?"

"Yes. About an hour later, he was out on the floor of the ballroom. He came sauntering up in that Bowery Boy way of his—and the guy must have been forty-five or fifty, so you can imagine how ludicrous it seemed. My wife, Judy, hadn't met him before. I introduced them. The way he stared at her was really—almost obscene. She was disturbed by it, I could tell. We got away from them as quickly as we could. That was the last time I saw him face to face, though I was conscious of his presence as the evening went on. Enough to avoid running into him again."

"Mr. Wardell, did you happen to see a silver dagger that the other jockeys had presented to Brad Roark?"

"No, I don't think so. Was it on the exhibit table?"

"It started out on the exhibit table, yes." And found its way into Mo Roark's chest. Wilmer Friend knew Wardell wasn't telling him everything he knew, and he was starting to wonder if anybody was.

11

Jerry and Donna hadn't left the scene of the aborted Roark party until almost 3 A.M., and the designated driver decreed they would both spend the night at her place. Not that either was in the mood for anything beyond comforting talk, followed, they hoped, by sleep. For Donna, sleep had come readily as it always seemed to. For Jerry, it hadn't. He estimated that he may have dropped off for a total of forty-five minutes, and now at six-thirty Sunday morning, he was sitting in the middle of her living room figuring he wouldn't see Donna for hours and contemplating making some coffee.

He looked around the room and reflected that they were compatible in their housekeeping habits. Not slobs, but not compulsively neat either, and given to too large an accumulation of soon-to-be-read magazines on the coffee tables. If they ever married—and surely that was their eventual fate, though Donna resisted the idea more than he did—he was confident that her Swedish modern furniture, theatrical posters, and buckling shelves of plays and drama histories could learn to coexist with his motel Gothic, winner's circle photos, and racing references.

HOT AIR

He couldn't have moved into her place, though, any more than she could into his, and it had nothing to do with square footage. They'd need to establish neutral ground.

He sighed and lowered himself carefully into a comfortable but fragile-looking chair. He was always afraid he'd break it. Nine more races to call in a few hours, and he was in no shape for it. Well, at least Donna was able to sleep late.

No sooner was that thought completed than the bedroom door opened. "Morning, Jerry," Donna said brightly. She was dressed for action: a bright yellow tank top and skintight black bicycle shorts.

"What are you doing up?" he asked.

"Couldn't sleep."

"What do you mean? You were snoring like a freight train."

"You're a sweet-talking son of a gun, Brogan. I didn't say I couldn't *ever* sleep, just not since I woke up about twenty minutes ago. I'm going to put in a few miles. Want to join me?"

"Gee, I'd love to, but I didn't bring my bike. And I doubt yours would hold us both." In truth, Jerry had made it through his childhood and adolescence without learning to ride a bicycle, and he wasn't about to start training for the Tour de France now.

"Make us some breakfast then, and I'll see you in an hour."

"You're not actually going out in the street in that getup, are you?"

"Sure, why not?"

"Those shorts are so tight . . . well, I don't see how they can be comfortable."

"No, really, they are. You'd be surprised."

"Donna, that outfit outlines your, uh . . ."

"Is my butt something to be ashamed of, Brogan?"

"No, and it's not your butt I'm talking about."

"Don't worry. Guys like you whose minds are in the gutter are never up this early on a Sunday morning."

Jerry smiled and watched her go. He wasn't really prudish enough to be shocked by her bicycle shorts. But they were a symbol of what always stood between them: exercise. Donna did everything: running, swimming, cycling, skiing, tennis, aerobics. True, Jerry had played football in high school and wrestled in college, but he had no inclination to be a lifelong jock. They'd once tried golf together, but it was too slow and sedentary a game for Donna. She still beat him at it, though. In a down mood, he sometimes reflected she was just tolerating him until she got a call from Arnold Schwarzenegger. But he was rarely in a down mood about Donna. He could share her with exercise happily enough, but she always wanted him to share exercise with her—not quite the same thing.

Jerry Brogan was a slow man in the kitchen, so an hour was about right to prepare a breakfast of coffee, fruit, French toast, and muffins. At the same time, he was putting together some breakfast conversation that he started to lay on Donna as soon as she walked in the door.

"Wilmer's going about this all wrong, Donna. He's going to miss something important."

"Sure, Jerry." Her tone said she'd heard it all before.

He followed her into the bedroom and kept talking as she peeled off the biking outfit. "There's so much going on here, and all he's doing is concentrating on the other Roark relatives. They don't strike me as potential murderers, Donna." He followed her toward the shower. "I think it has something to do with something closer to home. I don't think it's any imported murder. I think it's a *local* murder. With all this other stuff going on, the election, the threats on Brad Roark, it would be too big a coincidence for it all to be unconnected. Don't you think so?"

Being overdressed for the shower, he didn't follow her into the stall but kept talking over the running water. "It may even have something to do with Purejoy Cosmetics, you know that? What was that VP doing there, and why was Brad trying to sell him Hot Air, a horse he probably hadn't even taken formal title to yet?"

Donna didn't answer until she'd shut off the water and grabbed the towel that was hanging over the shower door. "Jerry," she said, "you've overdosed on party conversation. What did *any* of that have to do with Mo Roark?"

"I don't know. But I'd like to find out. I think I'll go talk to the Roark relatives before they leave town."

"A minute ago you said it had nothing to do with the relatives."

"I don't think it does, directly. But I'd like to find out more about Mo and Brad's background. Everybody else will presumably be around for a while, but if I were those relatives I'd want to be out of here as soon as the police would let me go. Besides, somebody should touch base with them on behalf of the track. We are their hosts, after all. I can talk to them legitimately, as a representative of Surfside Meadows, without it looking like I'm involving myself in a police investigation."

"Though you are." Donna emerged from the shower, the gigantic towel wrapped around her to conceal as much as a Victorian gown.

"Surfside Meadows is in trouble, Donna. My job's in danger."

"Don't be silly."

"I'm not being silly. If the track is torn down for condos, what do I do? Take up gardening?"

"Gardeners will probably be in heavy demand. I could use some help around here."

"This is serious. I have to find out what's going on."

"Mo Roark's death probably has nothing to do with Surfside Meadows," Donna said, marching into the bedroom. "Is breakfast ready?"

"When you are."

"You going to try to see the relatives before the races today?"

"If I can."

"And then what?" Donna whipped off the bath towel and tossed it on the bed. "Well? And then what?"

"I, uh, lost my train of thought."

Donna smiled broadly. "Well, good. I thought I was losing all my charm. You want to eat or—?"

Jon L. Breen

*　　*　　*

Jerry found Buller McIntosh reclining by the pool at the Surfside Inn. His thin, aged face was weathered and brown, his skinny legs pale as alabaster. Clearly he didn't wear shorts that much at home in Florida. It looked as if it would be a warm day, but McIntosh had the area to himself and was looking bored despite the massive Los Angeles *Times* on the table next to him. He was looking desultorily at the sports section, which he laid aside when he saw Jerry approaching him.

"Good morning, Mr. McIntosh. Can I join you for a minute?"

"Yeah, sure, pull up a chair. How are you? Jerry Brogan, right?"

"Yes. I wanted to see how you and Mrs. McIntosh are doing. Last night must have been a terrible experience for you."

"Yeah, yeah, terrible." Buller McIntosh obviously was weathering it well. "The wife'll probably sleep till teatime, but me, I'm a morning person." He winked. "Don't want to miss any of the local talent."

"Uh, right. I wanted to reassure you on behalf of the management of Surfside Meadows that you can stay here as guests of the track until the police say it's all right to go home."

"Well, that's nice, but the original deal was through Tuesday night, fly back Wednesday morning. And I don't think they'll want to keep us any longer than that, do you? I mean, we told that detective all we knew last night. I don't think he'll suspect Frances or me of bumping off Mo, do you? Not that we're in any hurry to leave, though. This is our vacation, and we're gonna enjoy it."

"That's fine. I hope you do. If you want to come out to the races again this afternoon, of course, you'll be our guests."

"Thanks. I might come out early and put some bets down, but to make the wife happy, I have to be back here for teatime." He made a face. "Maybe you understand women, Jerry. I don't claim to. Every afternoon about three-thirty, they have this old lady in their little library room here pouring tea. Oh, and she does some kind of pastry every day, too, dainty little cakes or muffins or something—you gotta go back three times to get one healthy serving. But the tea's the thing. How can women get so excited over tea anyway? Coffee, I can almost see—at least it's got some kick to it—or beer or booze or even wine. But tea? Anyway, to keep the peace, I gotta be here for the tea and the genteel conversation. I swear Frances is picking up a British accent in this place. She's gonna be the first person ever to vacation in California and come back sounding like a Limey."

On the other side of the pool, a young woman in a short white terry-cloth robe had appeared and was adjusting one of the lounges. Jerry sensed he no longer had McIntosh's full attention. One of the older man's hands absentmindedly reached for something on the table before realizing it wasn't there. Jerry wondered what McIntosh was looking for.

The woman removed the robe, revealing a very brown body in the briefest of string bikinis. Not until she was stretched out on the recliner did Buller McIntosh speak again.

" 'Bout an eight-point-five, you think?" he said in a low voice.

"Er, at least."

"Little short up top, but boobs are overrated, I think. Handful's all you need."

If the man on the lounge hadn't been over seventy and looking every day of it, Jerry would have sworn he was back in a high school locker room.

Wondering if McIntosh was lost for the morning, Jerry tried to bring him back to what he wanted to talk about. "It was a shame Brad Roark's special day had to end the way it did," he said.

"Oh, yeah, terrible. But I guess you know him and Mo weren't really that close. Brad was tickled to death to see Frances and me and his sister Naomi, but him and Mo never really hit it off."

"Why was that, Mr. McIntosh?"

"Well, they didn't have the very happiest home life. Their mother was my sister, Grace. Great girl, pretty girl, but lousy taste in men. I was born down South—guess you could tell from my good ol' boy name, Buller, huh?—but the family came north and lived in New York for quite a few years. My father had a good job in the subway system—this was the thirties, you understand, when even a bad job was a good job—but still and all, goin' to New York was a bad move, 'cause Grace got mixed up with the Roarks. Big mistake. Not one of 'em worth a damn, and Fred, that was Brad and Mo's father, was the worst of the lot. Drunk all the time, abusive, terrible husband, terrible father, couldn't hold a job. I don't know how she stood it. Well, she didn't, really. It killed her finally."

"Mo was the older brother, right?"

"Yeah, he was born in . . . 'thirty-eight, I guess, and Brad came along in 'forty or maybe 'forty-one. I know it was before the war. Come Pearl Harbor I joined up right away, spent some time in the South Pacific. Fred did, too, I think 'cause I shamed him into it. Grace was probably her happiest when the kids were little and Fred away overseas. But Fred, damn his soul, survived the Normandy landing and came back to continue their happy family life. The two boys hated him."

"But hating their father didn't bring them any closer together?"

"No, there were other things. They were different. Had different kinds of interests. Different in just about every way you could mention. I mean *every* way. Neither grew very big—Fred was a scrawny little runt, too—but Mo was a tough kid, always getting in scrapes, afraid of nothing. If you'd asked me which one of these guys was going to take up a dangerous job like race riding, I'd've said Mo. For Brad, hell, a merry-go-round would be more action than his little fluttering heart could stand. I think Mo terrorized his little brother. I don't know if you had an older brother, Jerry, but I did, and they can be like that. It was tough on me, and I wasn't any—I wasn't like Brad. They both hated Fred and the way he abused their mother, and Brad hated Mo 'cause to him Mo was just like another Fred."

"When you say Fred abused their mother, do you mean physically?"

"I think he slapped her around once in a while, yeah."

142

"You were her brother. Where were you when all this was going on?" Jerry sensed he'd just endangered his standing as a public-relations representative of the track, but he didn't really care.

Buller McIntosh didn't take offense. "I wasn't that close most of the time. I met Frances toward the end of the war—she was a pretty little thing those days herself, take my word for it—and when it was over we got hitched and settled in Maryland where I got me a job in a car dealership. Wound up sales manager, made a good living for a lot of years."

"So you didn't see your sister and brother-in-law in those years?"

"We'd get together once in a while. Look, if you think I ought to have got involved in my sister's marriage, rescued her or some damn thing, there are a few things you have to understand. First off, she never asked me to. She didn't badmouth Fred Roark. She never said a word against him, no matter how bad things got. And most guys who are like that can be nice as pie some of the time, and they get their women to forgive them, give 'em another chance. You met Fred at a party or something, you'd be charmed outa your socks. You'd have no idea what a bad 'un he was. I knew, but I don't think it's right to interfere in somebody else's marriage. Married people have certain ways of getting through life, and it's no outsider's business."

"Even if it includes physical abuse?"

"Sure. She didn't have to stay with him, and I wish she hadn't, but she did by choice, so there we are."

"Naomi is a lot younger than her brothers."

"Oh, yeah, and she looks even younger than she is. She was a late child all right, came along in—what?—'fifty-one or 'fifty-two, I guess. Big surprise to Grace and Fred, I'll tell you that. By the time she was four or five, the boys were out of the house, but they did some watching over her, Brad at least. Grace died in 'sixty, barely forty years old, and Fred got some other poor dame to marry him. They didn't care for having the little girl around

143

much, though she was a sweet little thing, let me tell you. They commenced sending Naomi out to stay with us summers for a few years. We took good care of her. We were more truly her parents than Fred and his second wife ever were. When she was seventeen, she up and run off with some wild kid named Al Burns. Couldn't pick men no better than her mother could. That didn't last long, lucky for her. We never heard from her again 'cept maybe a Christmas card until we saw her at the track yesterday. Growed into a pretty lady, huh? Took good care of herself." Buller McIntosh paused for a moment and stared across the pool pensively. " 'Bout a nine-point-one."

Jerry thought the old fart was rating his own niece until he looked up and realized a willowy redhead was poised to plunge into the pool.

"Just out of curiosity, Mr. McIntosh, what do you think happened to your nephew last night?"

"I think he died."

"But how and why? And who killed him?"

"I didn't know him that well, you know. We got along okay, but maybe that's why, 'cause I didn't know him any better. If he acted toward that little wife of his the way Fred did toward Grace, I wouldn't put it past her to have stuck him. And, of course, he and Brad didn't ever hit it off."

"Would Brad have had a motive for killing him, though?"

"Brad's not the same guy he was as a kid. He's so smooth and confident, got it all together. He wasn't glad to see Mo. It was like another part of his life, a worse part, coming back to haunt him. Maybe Mo knew things about Brad he didn't want to have known out here."

"What?"

"I wouldn't know what. But there might have been something."

"Did you see anything last night that might help the police solve the case?"

"I'd tell them if I did."

"I'm sure you would. I'm just curious."

McIntosh shook his head. "Hey, I was just havin' a good time. Couldn't give 'em an alibi worth a damn. Between the last time Mo was in the ballroom and the time that little Maisie started in screechin', most of the time I was by myself, just sort of people-watching. I wasn't out on the dance floor makin' a damn fool of myself like Frances was. That your boss she was dancing with?"

Jerry nodded.

"He looks too dumb to run a racetrack, but I guess appearances are deceiving, huh? I don't mind Frances having a dance, you understand. I'm glad to see her havin' a good time in her way, while I had one in mine. But I didn't have anything useful to tell the cops."

Jerry decided that was all he was going to get out of Buller McIntosh, and he'd had enough of the guy's company in any case. Jerry was proud of his ability to get along with almost anybody, but this particular Roark relative irritated him in a big way. To make him want to leap to the defense of Keene Axtell, McIntosh would have to have industrial-strength abrasiveness.

Jerry walked back toward the lobby desk, hoping for a chance to talk to either Naomi Burns, Maisie Roark, or the to-be-pitied Mrs. Buller McIntosh. He was surprised to find the first two standing at the desk, with packed bags on either side of them.

"Good morning," he said.

They turned and greeted them. Both attractive faces seemed to have aged overnight, partly accounted for by the difference in the light between a flatteringly dim ballroom and a brightly lit lobby, and partly by the effects of a stressful night.

"Are you, ah, checking out?"

Maisie nodded. "I couldn't stand to stay here any longer. They gave me another room for last night, of course, but ..." She trailed off. "Oh, don't worry, the police know all about it. We're not skipping town or anything."

"Well if you go to another hotel, be sure to have them send the bill to Surfside Meadows. You're still our guests." Keene Axtell would have wanted to know which hotel before making such a sweeping promise, but Jerry didn't feel like being a fiscal guardian at the moment.

"I will, don't you worry," said Maisie.

"And you, too, Mrs. Burns."

Naomi shook her head with a little smile. "I've been asked to stay with a friend."

"That's fine. On behalf of the track, there's not much I can say but offer condolences to you both on your loss."

Maisie nodded her thanks, and Naomi put a comforting hand on her arm.

"Do you have time for a cup of coffee before you leave?" Jerry asked. Maisie shook her head, gesturing to a cab pulling up outside the doors of the lobby, but Naomi accepted the offer. Jerry was just as glad. He wanted to talk to them both, but he believed he could get more information from them separately than together. After helping the cabdriver stow Maisie's luggage, he escorted Naomi to the Surfside Inn's coffee shop.

"Have you had breakfast?" he asked.

"No, but I've got a brunch invitation for later, and I'm not hungry anyway. Coffee's fine."

Looking across at her sad face, Jerry was reminded of an old friend who was a film historian—not just your everyday movie buff but a guy who got his greatest pleasure from pictures where no dialogue was spoken. His greatest compliment to women, though they didn't always know how to take it, was, "Your face was made for silent movies." Naomi Burns had a face like that. Boundlessly expressive. There was something in the lines in her forehead and around her eyes that radiated empathy. It was a face you could tell anything to, with the kind of complex beauty few women attain before the age of forty.

"I guess you had a tough day yesterday, too, huh?" she said. It was just the sort of thing Jerry would expect that face to say.

"None of us wanted to see things turn out as they did," he said carefully. "We wanted a great day for Brad."

She nodded. "Poor Brad. I'm not used to having people look at me the way he did when he saw me come out of that hole in the tote board yesterday. It broke my heart."

"I guess the reunion was a bad idea."

"It sure was, but that's not your fault. Or Mr. Wardell's, either. We all bought into it, and we all should have known how it would turn out."

"You mean you should have known Mo would be murdered?"

"Oh, no, not that. Just that it wouldn't be a happy occasion. We were probably all just selfish." She smiled wistfully—the woman was amazing; she had a different smile for every nuance. "Gee, that was a great race, though, wasn't it? I loved how that little horse Hot Air got it done for Brad. You should have heard me and Maisie screaming and yelling when they were coming down the stretch. Seems funny to come to a racetrack to watch the race in a closed-in room on a TV monitor, but it sure was exciting. I wouldn't have missed it. And then Brad quoting Shakespeare." She shook her head fondly. "Just like him, showing off like that. But it was his day. He deserved it. He should have just finished his speech and gone off in the balloon and forgot the damned reunion."

"Did you really put your bubble gum in his toy truck?"

Now she laughed. It was a nice sound. "Jerry, do your arithmetic. He's eleven years older than I am. By the time I got to bubble gum, he was well past toy trucks. Actually, he put the bubble gum in *my* toy truck. Wardell's scriptwriters got it wrong. Maybe they thought a little girl wouldn't play with toy trucks, but I loved them. Guess I was ahead of my time, huh?"

"I guess so."

"Actually, I guess they were my brothers' toy trucks really. Hand-me-downs."

Jerry looked out the window toward the ocean, momentarily at a loss for what to say next. "Beautiful day."

"Yeah. A swim would have been nice this morning. But not with old Uncle Buller stretched out like a lizard undressing everybody."

At least there was one person Naomi didn't have complete sympathy for. Jerry found himself liking her even more.

"I had a chat with your uncle this morning."

"Sweetheart, isn't he? Maisie said they had dinner the other night and he couldn't keep his hands off her. Little subtle grabs and pokes under the table."

"He says he and his wife were responsible for a lot of your upbringing."

"Oh, he was responsible all right." She raised her eyebrows in comic exasperation. "Want to hear the story of my life?"

"Sure, that's why I asked you for coffee."

"No," she said, shaking her head. "I better not. You know something, Jerry, I make friends very easily. Too easily. I'm friendly to a fault, that's my problem. And you're the kind of person people tell things to, aren't you? Come on, admit it."

"Uh, well, you know the old saying . . ."

"Which one's that? I know all the old sayings."

"It takes one to know one. I've been sitting here thinking *you're* the kind of person people take one look at and want to tell their deepest secrets to. You should be a psychotherapist or something. You'd be great at it."

"You think so? I went with a clinical psychologist for a while up in Berkeley. He didn't get tenure, poor guy. But it's a little late for me. To get an education, I mean."

"What do you mean? You're still young."

"Almost forty. It's time to do something with my life, but I don't think I'll go back to school. If I hung around Cal for twenty years without taking a class, I don't think I'm going to go enroll someplace now."

Naomi had the knack of talking to somebody as if he were the only person in the world and time didn't matter. But Jerry was conscious of the minutes ticking by, not just because he had to report to the racetrack in a couple of hours, but because he didn't know when her friend, presumably Parker Fuentes, though this lady would never lack for a lot of friends, was coming for her. He willed himself to quit fooling around, and he put on his amateur-detective hat.

"Naomi, do you have any idea who might have killed Mo?"

"It wasn't Maisie, I know that. That girl was blown away by his death. Some people cry gracefully. Like they're sort of soothed by it, you know? It's painful to watch somebody cry who isn't used to doing it. If she wasn't shocked to her soul by his death, she oughta be in the movies, that's all I can say."

"I'm sure you're right. But there has to be a motive somewhere. And you folks just arrived in Surfside the day before yesterday."

"I don't know what Mo might have been up to. Maisie didn't either. We talked about it. He had something funny going on, and I think it involved somebody outside the family." She grinned suddenly. "Listen to me. Why should I care if it involves the family? I mean, we're really not a family at all, are we? Nobody's fault in particular—that's just the way it is."

Jerry sensed she'd be asking about *his* family next, and he felt an inclination to indulge himself and talk about them—his parents had died when he was young, too, though they'd been happier in the years before than the Roarks. He made himself stick to the subject, however. "What were Brad and Mo like as kids?"

"Mo I didn't know very well at all. He was in a hurry to get out of the house. As soon as he was old enough, he was gone. I was just a little kid then. Brad was the same, but he was still at home a few years after Mo left, and when Brad went, he'd come back and visit me, so I knew him better. He'd bring me things. He seemed to know just what a little girl would like. When he started as a jockey, though, he couldn't break in at the New York tracks, so he went on to the Midwest. Later, of course, he came out here. I didn't see much of him after that."

"What were your parents like?"

Her eyes were sad. "They did their best, I guess. How can you blame people when you don't really know what they suffered? What's that Indian saying about walking a mile in somebody's moccasins?" Her face brightened again, and she gave a little wave to somebody. Jerry turned to see Parker Fuentes, dressed in a comparatively inconspicuous gray shirt and bolo tie in preference to the Roy Rogers outfit, walking toward their table.

"Good morning," he said, "*Buenos días.*" Jerry felt a tiny pang of jealousy as Fuentes gave Naomi a proprietary peck on the cheek and pulled up a chair between them.

"Hi," Jerry said. "Don't I know you from TV?"

"If you watch movies all night."

"That's how I knew my brothers," Naomi said, as if discovering a sudden insight.

"What do you mean?" Jerry said.

"From TV. I remember times in the sixties, when Brad was starting to make it big as a rider, there'd be a big race on TV and sometimes he'd have a mount. That's all I'd see of him in those years."

"Sure," Jerry said carefully, "but you said your 'brothers.'"

"That's right, you did," Parker Fuentes said. "Was Mo on TV, too?"

"No, he wasn't *on* TV. He was an usher at one of the networks. I remember when I was seven or eight, in the late fifties, watching some show and saying, 'My brother works there!'" Her companions stared at her with blank expressions. "Well, it impressed the kids at school."

12

Normally the Sunday card at Surfside Meadows would be better than the Saturday card, but the racing for the day after Brad Roark's final ride was only average. Jerry sat in his cramped booth studying the program, wishing he could go home and go to bed and reflecting that today's races would be a test of his professionalism.

The day would not be a total bore. He'd learned when he arrived at the track that there would be one extra attraction that would outshine all the races on the card: former horse of the year Craven Clay was scheduled for a workout between the second and third races. When Jerry made the announcement over the public address, there was an excited buzzing in the crowd. And when the five-year-old stepped out onto the track, his chestnut coat gleaming in the sun, there were louder cheers than Jerry had heard since the day before.

The jury was still out on where Craven Clay stood among the top horses of recent years. Was he really in a class with Sunday Silence or Easy Goer as some observers insisted or was he more along the lines of Lost Code or Shabu Shabu? But there was no question the chestnut had star quality. If he really did go next in the Surfside Sprint Championship—and what a sporting gesture that would be by his owners—he and Hot Air would provide such a brilliant display of dueling charismas, Jerry would need to wear sunglasses.

"Craven Clay will start at the finish line and work one mile," Jerry announced. The jockey brought Craven Clay past the grandstand and up to the finish line in a gallop, then gave him the message to do some serious running. To the first turn they went, to whoops from the crowd.

"Craven Clay ran the first quarter in twenty-two and four-fifths seconds," Jerry reported. And later, "The half mile in forty-six seconds flat. . . . The three-quarters in one-ten and two."

This was a serious work. Craven Clay was going in race time. The point of a public workout in the afternoon is either to provide hype for the track or to give a horse the experience of running in front of a big crowd. The latter was nothing new to Craven Clay, but the roar the fans made as he charged down the stretch may have surprised even him. He rose to the occasion.

"Craven Clay worked the mile in one thirty-four and four!" Jerry told the crowd, and the cheers grew louder. By the time the jockey had managed to pull him up on the backstretch, Craven Clay had finished out a mile and an eighth in 1:47⅘. If the horse could go that fast with only hand urging and no other runners to compete with, how fast could he have gone in a real race?

When Jerry climbed out of his booth for a break after the third race, he heard a couple of turf writers arguing about whether the Surfside track was souped up. One, a New York visitor, was claiming it had to be, while one of the California regulars was insisting it wasn't by comparing the unimpressive times of most of the races to the speedy heroics of Hot Air and Valley Moon the day before and the eye-opening work of Craven Clay. "You have to face it," the Californian said. "These are just some of the fastest horses you can ever hope to see, that's all."

HOT AIR

General manager Keene Axtell was ecstatic. "Wasn't that something, Jerry? That horse is ready for a race."

"I hear he may go after Hot Air and Valley Moon in the sprint."

Axtell shook his head. "I know he's nominated but . . . naw, the sprint's small potatoes for this horse. They're after the Surfside Handicap. But they'll need a race for him before that, and I don't see anything in the condition book. We should write something just for him, a sixty-thousand-dollar overnighter maybe, at a mile and a sixteenth. With the fans he'll bring in,' it'll be worth the money, don't you think?"

Jerry shrugged. "I wouldn't do anything to discourage them from running him in the sprint. With that speed he showed today, who knows what he might do?"

"But if he should lose the sprint, it'll detract from the Surfside Handicap," Axtell whined.

Jerry just shook his head. Shortsighted as ever.

If Jerry had thought events on the track could distract him from the problem of Mo Roark's murder—and he hadn't—a between-race visit from Wilmer Friend later in the afternoon would have changed his view.

"Anything to report?" Wilmer asked.

"What do you mean?" said Jerry.

"You were questioning the relatives this morning, weren't you? I just wondered if you found out anything we didn't."

"Wilmer, I was just checking in with the relatives as a representative of the track. We're their hosts, after all. I wasn't usurping any police functions."

"I know you too well, Jerry. You aren't going to just forget about this. You're going to have to find out what really happened. You wouldn't have made a bad cop, actually."

That grudging statement coming Wilmer Friend was equal to a serious buttering up from somebody else. Jerry magnanimously decided that would do as an apology for the detective's withering sarcasm of the night before.

"One of the people I questioned the other night said Mo Roark was planning a 'family outing' for today," Friend said. "Did any of the relatives say anything to you about anything like that?"

Jerry shook his head. "Means nothing to me, but I did find out one thing that was kind of interesting. I don't know what it's worth, though. In the late fifties, Mo Roark worked for one of the TV networks."

Friend nodded. "Oh, we knew that."

Jerry tried not to look put out. "Well, sure, you could trace his work history easily enough I guess. I'm surprised you could do it so fast, though. On the weekend, I mean."

"We found out from other sources. Is Will Wardell at the track today, do you know?"

"He usually is." Jerry paused. "Did he have some connection with Mo Roark in his New York days? Is that what you found out?"

"You think I could borrow an office?"

"Wilmer, I'll be glad to tell you what I know. Why can't you be as straight with me?"

"Because I'm the cop and you're the helpful citizen, that's why."

Wilmer Friend used an empty office in Surfside Meadows' administrative wing for further interrogation of Will Wardell. Ten minutes into the interview, Wardell was sobbing and Friend was feeling most uncomfortable.

"Mr. Wardell, try to pull yourself together. You're not being charged with anything. I'm not reading you your rights. What we talk about here isn't going to be on the front page of the L.A. *Times* tomorrow morning. Nobody has to know. I just want the truth. What did you talk to Mo Roark about last night?"

Wardell wiped his eyes. "Shall I start at the beginning?"

"Start wherever you want." Friend tried to keep the impatience out of his voice and was pretty sure he'd failed.

"No, no, I won't start at the beginning. I'll start at the end. I'll put the bottom line at the top. I did *not* kill Mo Roark. I first knew what Roark had when I brought him here for the reunion. He'd written to me, alluding to his relationship with Brad Roark and telling me he'd worked at the network the same time I was there. Looking back at it, it looks like he was making some kind of veiled threat, but I didn't really suspect that at the time."

"You're telling me Roark gave you the idea to do the reunion in the first place?"

"Yes. And once I got started making the arrangements, I got caught up in it, just like in the old days. But the bottom line is, I did not kill him. He was alive when I left him. You have to believe that."

No, I don't, Friend told himself, but to Wardell he said, "Okay, you've said that. *Now* start at the beginning."

"Right. In the 'fifty-seven–'fifty-eight TV season, there were more quiz shows on the air than any time before or since. They were big business, and our show was one of the biggest. Our ratings were great, we were leading our time slot, and more important than that, Purejoy Cosmetics was showing record sales. Everybody wanted our show to stay on the air and be just as exciting and suspenseful as it had been up to that point. The network wanted that, the sponsor wanted that, and we who were making big money out of it wanted it, too."

"Sounds too important to leave to chance, huh?" Friend ventured.

"I didn't think so myself. Understand that my whole career is built on reality. Real people—their hopes, their dreams, their accomplishments. Faking things is not my way. All those reunions you saw on 'Hold Out Your Heart' "—

Friend tried to remember if he'd ever seen the show.

—"were genuine. We never faked anything. We didn't have to. Real human drama will beat some contrived soap opera every time. This reunion we did yesterday for Brad Roark was handled the same way. We really did surprise him. You take chances when you do that, but—"

"Mr. Wardell," said Friend gently, "you were talking about the quiz shows. In 'fifty-seven–'fifty-eight."

"Sorry. Forgive the digression. The shit didn't really start to hit the fans, so to speak"— Wardell looked up, as if to see if Friend had caught the mild pun—"until the summer of 1958, but by spring, there were already plenty of questioning articles and rumors around. A couple of contestants from other quiz shows had tried to blow the whistle on the fixes before that, but they found it was like talking to a stone wall, as if the media had chosen not to listen to them and that was that. Herbert Stempel and Stoney Jackson were their names. Honest men. I admire their courage now. Wish they could have loaned some of it to me, but I had a hell of a lot to lose. I spent a lot of that spring reassuring contestants—my wife, Judy, was one of them, as you know—that it was all just blowing smoke, all just jealousy, that everything was lovely in the quiz-show garden. Well, it wasn't. And by that time, I had personal knowledge that it wasn't.

"I wish I could express to you what a blow it was to me when I found out that 'The Big Question' was not always completely on the level. It was like being hit in the face from out of nowhere. I was stunned. I stomped around my partner's office and ranted and raved and cried." Wardell smiled sadly. "That may not seem such a big deal. They used to say I could give points to Jack Paar in a tear-shedding contest. I've proven that today, huh? It's always been a weakness of mine. But I was devastated."

"How did you find out?"

"From one of the contestants. Can you imagine that? I was coproducer of the show, and I found out from one of the damned contestants that she'd been given help on some of the answers. She mentioned it casually, assumed I already knew what was going on. But I didn't."

"Who was that contestant, Mr. Wardell?"

"It wasn't Judy, if that's what you're thinking. It was a retired English teacher whose expertise was the history of automobiles.

Great angle, huh? She was old enough to know her subject from the very beginning, and she had an amazing memory. She knew all the various models and specifications of Duryeas, Stanley Steamers, and some cars I never even *heard* of. She's been dead for years, of course. I hope it won't be necessary to pursue it with her family or anything. If they didn't know, why tarnish her memory?"

Friend said, "I see no reason why she should come into it if she's dead."

"Good. At first, my partner claimed some of the assistants on the show had been trying to manipulate things without *his* knowledge. It didn't take long for that lie to fall to pieces, so he changed his tune, said he approved everything that had gone on but kept it from me because he knew it would trouble me from an ethical standpoint, and because he knew I had a heart condition and he was afraid it might endanger my health. That was really a good one. I've had heart trouble all my life, but you notice I'm still alive. Finally, he claimed he didn't think I could be as convincing a host if I knew some of the contestants had had help. I'm sorry to say I proved him wrong on that last point.

"Our show wasn't as crooked as some, you understand. My partner told me they kept it as honest as they could, just tipping the scales subtly when there was a contestant they wanted to keep. Or sometimes when there was one they wanted to lose and they could get into an area of the subject where they knew the contestant was weak. The car lady was great, and her knowledge was genuine. She got to be a big drawing card, the biggest we had before Judy came along. Women contestants were always in short supply, so they were cultivated like rare orchids. The car lady was going to quit, take the money and run, and my partner didn't want her to, so he guaranteed her the answers to the next week's question if she'd just stay on for one more program, get us one more big rating. She had a slight attack of the scruples, but he convinced her it wasn't really a game, it was just entertainment, and she was a well-paid performer who should just relax and enjoy it. I don't think she really quite bought it, and that was why she brought it up to me in the greenroom one day, looking for reassurance that she was doing the right thing." With self-disgust, Wardell said, "After I talked to my partner, I gave her the reassurance she wanted."

"What was your partner's name, Mr. Wardell?"

Wardell fluttered his hands and shook his head. "Abner Birnbaum, but don't go looking for him. He's dead, too. Shot himself in the mouth in 1962, I think it was. Nothing to do with 'The Big Question,' though. Inoperable cancer. He has a family, too—"

"Mr. Wardell, I'm investigating a murder, not doing a whole reopening of the quiz-show scandals. Believe me."

"Okay, good. When I found out what was going on, I could have blown the whistle myself on the spot. But there was a lot of money involved for everybody, not just the contestants. No matter which way I moved, my career was in danger. If I blew the whistle, I might never work in network TV again. If I played along and the whole thing came out, I'm branded as a cheat for life. Well, I decided to go along with it. At the time, I told myself, it was for the good of the contestants, like Judy, who really were honest. I was kidding myself, I know that now." Wardell's voice cracked again. "Judy never was given an answer. Her part of 'The Big Question' was strictly, absolutely on the level."

Friend nodded as if to reassure Wardell he believed him.

"Roark had documentary proof that 'The Big Question' was rigged and that I knew about it. You saw it. You opened that attaché case of his, didn't you, and that's why we're having this conversation? How he could manage it as a network usher isn't that hard for me to figure, looking back—those guys were sometimes almost invisible. Like Chesterton's postman, you know? And he was a sneaky little bastard, always out for the main chance."

"So you actually do remember him from those days?"

"I never knew his name then. He was just another usher. But

I remembered his face when I saw him. He was sort of a good-looking kid in those days, in a punkish kind of way. We had some rather impressionable young women on our staff, women who had access to some delicate information if they were to put two and two together—what an introduction to the world of television we were giving to them, huh? I suppose he could have gotten in with one of them, gotten into our offices to photograph the documents."

Friend knew from documents in Roark's attaché case that Wardell apparently had not seen—letters to Roark from his network contact—that this scenario was close to the truth.

"Why do you think he waited all these years to blackmail you over this, Mr. Wardell?"

"I've asked myself that. He may have been planning to do something at the time but backed off for some reason. I've given quite a few interviews in the last few years about the quiz scandals. Maybe he read those and decided the material he'd gathered would still have some value for blackmail purposes."

"Why have you been giving so many interviews on the subject, Mr. Wardell, if you had such good reasons to want it forgotten?"

"I couldn't help myself. I couldn't stop talking about it. It's bothered me more and more that memories, both the public's collective memory—very unreliable—and the recollections of those actually involved, have blurred over the years, and there's a tendency to obscure the line between the guilty and the innocent. Any suggestion, any thought that someone might believe Judy Constable, my Judy, was among the tainted money-winners would eat away at me like an ulcer. If you can understand, my own guilty secret made me all the more sensitive about it. I really believed everything I said about honesty and ethics, you know."

"Sure."

"If I hadn't gone on to marry Judy, it wouldn't matter so much. I was older than she, of course. She was just an innocent kid, no experience. I couldn't make a serious move on her in New York, but we wrote to each other after she left the show. We arranged to meet when I came out to the West Coast. Things went on from there. I'd give anything to protect her from this." He looked at Friend imploringly. "She must not know about this. I'll do everything I can to assist your investigation, Lieutenant Friend, but you must promise me to keep this away from the media."

"Mr. Wardell, if it turns out you killed Roark, there's no way this can be kept quiet."

"But I didn't kill him."

"You know whether you did or not. I have to keep asking questions. If you didn't kill him, well, I have no desire to cause a man trouble with his wife."

"Thank you for that. I don't know what else I can tell you that would help. I visited Roark's room just the one time early in the evening, and he was alive when I left him. I agreed to pay him what he was asking and did my best to avoid him for the rest of the evening. What he had couldn't have hurt me now, as far as criminal liability is concerned, I mean, but I couldn't stand having Judy know. Was there anything *else* in that attaché case, by the way?"

"What do you mean?"

"If Roark was doing that to me, who knows what else he might have been up to?"

"Mr. Wardell, if I'm going to keep your secrets, you can't expect me to—"

"No, of course not. Forgive me. What else do you want to ask me? I'm ready to help any way I can."

"What else did you lie to me about when we talked before?"

"I don't like to think of myself as an adept liar, Lieutenant Friend, but I do know enough about lying to understand the importance of insulating the lie with as much of the truth as possible. When we first met, I told you everything about my meeting with Mo Roark and about my actions for the rest of the evening." He grinned very weakly. "Except the few details we've just been discussing."

* * *

HOT AIR

Judy Wardell greeted her husband at the door, lovely and serene as ever. He felt relieved. He'd been worried about her the night before.

"Good day at the track, dear?" she asked.

He clung to her as if they'd been separated a year instead of a day. "No, not really. I ought to have stayed home with you. How are you feeling?"

"Fine, dear, really."

"You seemed so upset last night."

"Well, it was a terrible thing to have happen. But I'm okay now."

Will followed Judy into the kitchen, reluctant to let go of her. "I don't think Mo Roark was any great loss to humanity," he said.

"No, maybe not, but still it was a shocking thing."

"I'm sorry."

"It wasn't *your* fault, Will."

"You're not used to things like that."

"Are you saying you are?"

"No, of course not, but I just hate to put you in situations where . . . you know what I mean. I think that was my last reunion, Judy. In fact, I think it's high time I *really* retired. Sell my share of the production company. Get off the track board. Get out of public life completely."

"Will, what would you do with yourself?"

"Enjoy myself. Enjoy you."

"Well, you just think about it before you do anything too drastic. Go out on the patio. I'll bring you a drink."

Will wouldn't let go. "What did you do today?"

"Not very much. Read the paper. Oh, I had a call from Donna Melendez. She asked us to come to the opening of her play at Dana High."

"What are they putting on?"

"*Cat on a Hot Tin Roof.*"

"That sounds like strong stuff for high school kids."

"Donna says her kids know all about guilty secrets and men-

Jon L. Breen

dacity." Will pulled her to him again. "Will, is something wrong?"

"No, no, everything's fine. Who was the only horse to beat Citation as a three-year-old?"

"Saggy, in the Chesapeke Trial at Havre de Grace. April 12, 1948."

"That's my girl!"

162

13

Surfside Meadows was dark on Mondays. Jerry sometimes thought it should be the best day of his week, but it usually wasn't. For one thing, he liked his job. For another, the person he'd most like to spend a day off with inconveniently occupied her Mondays at Richard Henry Dana High teaching young thespians. This week, he couldn't even see Donna at night: she'd be holding rehearsals for her production of *Cat on a Hot Tin Roof* all week.

And this particular Monday, the death of Mo Roark was obsessing him. There were connections to be made, he was convinced, that would never occur to Wilmer Friend. After Friend had talked to Will Wardell the day before, Jerry had tried to get some more information from the detective and had been definitely rebuffed. It seemed odd because before Wilmer had borrowed the office to question Wardell, he had seemed much more willing to compare notes with Jerry, at least in a limited way.

Jerry started the day in Surfside's backstretch café. The coffee would only satisfy an undiscriminating caffeine addict—he liked it—and the quality of the food fit right in with the rundown truckstop decor, but it was always a key place to pick up race-track gossip.

"Oh, sure, Jerry," said Hortense, the tall sixtyish waitress who was a fixture of the place, "that rumor's all over the backside. They say Brad Roark couldn't wait to unload Hot Air. What do you think he could get for him?"

Jerry shrugged. "He's five years old and a gelding, but as far as I know he's sound, and he seems just to be coming into his own. Could race for years. Half a million? Or maybe that's conservative."

"Quite a gift to be handing somebody, huh? Either Parker Fuentes has got more money than he knows what to do with or he's running a few quarts low. What's your guess?"

"I know he was trying to get Brad to run for City Council, and we all know Parker's given to grand gestures. But it's a bigger mystery to me why Brad would turn right around and try to sell the horse the same night Parker gave it to him."

Hortense shook her head. "Downright unmannerly, isn't it?"

"There must be some theories around, Hortense. Come on, give."

She thought a minute, as if unwilling to admit she didn't have any insights on the subject. What she finally came up with had all the earmarks of an improvisation. "Well, you know Brad. Always wants to be different. Maybe he could use some extra money to finance him in his antique shop or whatever it was he was going to open up."

Jerry nodded politely. Nothing there. "Who do you like in the Sprint Championship next month, Hortense? Should be quite a race."

"Everybody seems to think Craven Clay's gonna run. He's got the class. And Valley Moon's got the early speed." She grinned. "But I sure do like gray horses, Jerry. Remember Vigors? And Pink Pigeon? And how about The Searcher?"

The Searcher? Jerry scratched his head. Hortense really did go back a long way.

Thumbing through the telephone book in his frontside office, Jerry reflected on what a desultory way this was to run an investigation. The gifted amateur didn't have to be well-organized or thorough like Wilmer. He could just nibble around the edges, pick his spots. It might be that the political intrigues swirling around Surfside had nothing to do with Mo Roark's death, but he was determined to sort them out anyway.

He could have tried to talk to Parker Fuentes directly. But somehow he thought he had a better chance to find out something from one of those two political managers. The directory had no listing for a Larry Halvorsen. Nor was there an Esme Flint. But there was one Flint, E. Worth a try. He dialed the number.

Sure enough, he got a recording, and the woman didn't identify herself by name, just repeated the number he had reached and asked him to leave a message. The throaty voice assured him he had the right Flint, though.

Jerry never could get used to talking to answering machines, but he plunged ahead. "Uh, Ms. Flint, this is Jerry Brogan. We met Saturday night. I have a question on the Purejoy connection. If you'd call me back, you can reach me at—"

"Yes, hello, Jerry." A live voice broke in on him. He was half relieved at not having to finish his stilted message and half irritated at people who used answering machines to screen their calls. "How are you? And what in the world are you talking about?" Jerry tried to decide if there was a worried edge in her voice, or just amusement.

"Is there any chance we could get together?"

"If you think it's important. I'm in the middle of planning a campaign kickoff event for City Council and I'm swamped at the moment."

"Oh? Who's the candidate?"

"I don't know. But Parker says he has one, and Parker is paying the bills. I don't think it's Brad Roark."

"I would like a few minutes of your time, if you could possibly spare it."

"All right. I work at home." She gave him her address and quick directions. "Come around to the back of the house. I'll leave the side gate unlocked for you."

Esme Flint was lying on her patio in full sunlight, propped up on her elbows and talking into a cassette recorder, when Jerry ventured into the yard. Her deeply tanned body was exposed except for a perfunctory bikini bottom.

Jerry waited until she had finished her current dictation and switched off the recorder. "Uh, hi," he said.

She turned her head, startled, and he briefly got an answer to how far the tan went before she reached for and put on her bikini top.

"Excuse me, I guess I'm a little informally dressed to be receiving visitors."

But you knew I was coming, didn't you? Jerry decided not to say it out loud. "Thanks for talking to me. I know you're busy."

"What was this stuff about a Purejoy connection?"

Jerry sat down in a patio chair and said, "I'll level with you. You must know I'm a friend to whatever campaign you're planning. I have as much interest as Parker in protecting Surfside Meadows from the developers, and I know how important it is to have friends on the City Council."

"Okay," Esme said, "so level with me."

"Naturally I'm concerned about all this talk of a Purejoy connection."

"What talk is that?" Her voice was flat and businesslike. Jerry wasn't finding this lady any easier to con than she'd been at the party.

"Well," Jerry said expansively, trying to sound like a political pundit, "as you know, to some people, the animal testing at Purejoy Cosmetics is as big an issue as development."

She waved the statement off like a fly. "Don't be silly. Animal experimentation is only the concern of a few zealots. Development is the concern of everybody. Animal experimentation at Purejoy has nothing to do with money, you see, and development has everything to do with money, both for those who are for it and those who are against it."

"Political issues don't always have to do with money. Uh, flag-burning wasn't a money issue, was it?"

"There's a difference between national and local politics, Mr. Brogan." She was starting to sound downright testy, and Jerry could sense her abruptly drawing back from it, realizing she might be offending a political ally. "Look, don't get me wrong. I appreciate your support, and I know Parker will. But this animal rights business is not going to be a major area of concern in the campaign. Believe me."

"Lots of people in Surfside have pets, you know."

"That doesn't matter. Most people regard animal rights as a crank issue."

"Then why all these rumors—?"

"Look, Jerry, the rumors are a crock. My partner may have taken them seriously, but I don't. Will Wardell is *not* going to run for City Council."

Jerry tried not to let his face show what a new idea that was. Wardell run for Council? After a slightly elongated pause, he said, "My informant seemed pretty sure of it."

"I've looked into it. Just this morning I made several phone calls on that very subject. There's nothing to it."

They both heard the creak of the gate. Larry Halvorsen strode into the yard, saw them sitting there, and stopped short. The balding blond looked back and forth between Jerry's face and Esme's brown navel. Jerry half expected a light bulb to appear over his head.

"I didn't know you had company," he said in his high, irritating voice. He seemed like a guy who would always come up with the appropriate cliché.

"I think Mr. Brogan was just leaving," Esme said, matching him banality for banality.

"If you're so sure Wardell isn't a candidate," Jerry said casually, getting to his feet and studying Halvorsen's face.

"What have you heard?" Halvorsen demanded.

"Just what we've heard, Larry," Esme Flint said carefully. "And it isn't true. I checked it out."

Jerry was experiencing the exquisite frustration of looking for a way to find out what he supposedly already knew. He tried to project a knowingness as he said, "A lot of people don't remember he was virtually an employee of Purejoy, back in the fifties when he was doing 'The Big Question.'"

"That's what I thought," said Halvorsen eagerly. "He could run on the Purejoy issue and use his inside knowledge of the company to make his campaign more credible. Just think how much mileage he could get out of his horror and disappointment that his old company was continuing with their disgraceful experimentation on animals. He could do a real number on how it distressed him to have people connect him in their minds with an outfit like that. He would low-key the racetrack issue, and everybody would assume he had a vested interest in keeping the track going. But as a major stockholder, as well as a member of the board, he might see an even bigger profit if the land got rezoned and they wound up selling out to the developers. If he gets elected, he becomes the swing vote against the track. It makes perfect sense to me."

Esme shook her head. "That he should identify himself with Purejoy? You're conveniently forgetting people connect Purejoy and 'The Big Question' with the quiz-show scandals, and you know how hard Wardell works to distance himself from that. If Wardell was foolish enough to run, quiz fixing would get to be a bigger issue in the campaign than animal rights."

"But Wardell always claimed 'The Big Question' was honest," Jerry said. "They never proved anything against it."

"And you assume there was nothing there to prove? You think he wants it all reopened in a local Council campaign? Wardell doesn't need that." She turned to her partner. "I did my homework on this, Larry. There's nothing to it. According to the people I talked to, Wardell isn't hurting for money and has no interest in a political career."

"Okay, I guess if you've checked it out . . . but Parker seemed so sure of himself."

Esme said, "You have to take Parker with a grain of salt. He's always been suspicious of Wardell. They don't like each other." Jerry saw the truth in that statement. "He'd believe anything to discredit Wardell. But we've got no reason to think Wardell's any more anxious for Surfside Meadows to be paved over than Parker would be."

A few minutes later, Jerry left the two political managers with the feeling he'd cleared a little more brush but still couldn't find the trail.

By late afternoon, Jerry had decided he had at least one reason to talk to Brad Roark. He'd phoned Brad, who, sounding surprisingly upbeat and hospitable, invited him to come over for a drink that evening. Moments after he accepted the invitation, a call from Donna gave him another reason.

"Jerry," she said sheepishly, "I think I've been a little dense."

"Impossible."

"No, really. We were reading *Henry* IV, Part I, in class today, and we got to that passage Brad Roark quoted on the TV news, and I think it explains a lot. I should have figured it out before."

When Donna had finished her explanation, Jerry was dubious.

"You really think—?"

"Just ask him," she said.

14

"I'm going to keep Hot Air," Brad Roark said. "He'll run in my name."

Jerry sat in the retired jockey's book-lined study with a brandy snifter cradled in his large palm. "But it's true you tried to sell him the night of the party?"

"Yes. I might still take in a partner in my stable, you understand, but trying to sell the horse outright was a silly, impulsive thing to do. At least something good came of it, though." Brad smiled with a sort of smug secretiveness, and Jerry wondered what he meant. "So tell me, Jerry. Do you have Surfside politics all figured out yet?"

"Politics is never something you *all* figure out. I know if you don't file for City Council, Parker Fuentes will have to find another candidate."

"Let him. At the risk of looking a gift horse in the mouth, Parker's a jerk. He doesn't play fair. First he tries to bribe me, then he tries something really underhanded."

"What was that?" Jerry asked casually, beginning to think Donna's idea may have been right.

"He was trying to use reverse psychology on me to get me to run. He thought I was such a macho character that I'd run if I thought somebody was trying to scare me into *not* running. So it was, 'Ah, *bueno*, *amigo*, no sense in your endangering yourself. You must withdraw into a stress-free retirement. You have been brave in the ring, *sí, sí*. Retire to your study and enter the imitation Hemingway contest and tell about the bulls and the horses and how they were brave.' And I was supposed to say, 'Nobody scares Brad Roark. If people are so determined I not run, then by pucky, I'm gonna run!' " Brad laughed. "Maybe I should be complimented he thinks I'm such a courageous person, but instead I choose to be insulted he thinks I could be that dumb. The damnedest thing about it was, Jerry, it was starting to work!"

"Was it?"

"Oh, sure, up there in that balloon, looking down at that toy countryside, where everything looks so quaint and simple. First he gave me the pitch about saving the track from the mean old developers, then he got into the macho thing. And it was working. For a while there, I was as tractable and suggestible as he could possibly have hoped for. But then he overplayed his hand. Can I pour you a little more?"

Jerry surrendered his glass with only token resistance, and Roark provided a generous refill.

Refilling his own almost as generously, Roark said, "I don't have to be so sparing with myself now that I don't have to make a hundred and seventeen pounds anymore. What was I telling you? Oh, yeah. That whole balloon landing was *so* damned phony. B-movie stuff. Fuentes must have thought I was an idiot. How did the TV crews get there so fast if they didn't have some kind of pre-warning? Fuentes had the whole thing orchestrated, the phony bomb and everything. It was probably his toady Halvorsen who delivered the threat over the phone. 'No . . . Hot . . . Air.' " Roark gave the words the spooky hollowness of a Halloween storyteller. "On the other hand, if Fuentes had miscalculated, he actually *could* have got us hurt or killed in that dramatic emergency landing of his. That's why I started shopping around Hot Air that same evening, as a way of showing him what I thought of his idiotic games."

"You could have just told the reporters on the scene you thought the whole thing was faked by Fuentes."

"Why test the slander laws? Anyway I *did* tell anybody with half a brain who was listening carefully."

Jerry nodded. "That *Henry* IV quote. Falstaff lying about his adventures."

" 'I have scaped by a miracle,' " Roark declaimed. " 'I am eight times thrust through the doublet, four through the hose; my buckler cut through and through. . . .' If quoting that old fraud Falstaff isn't enough to tell the world the whole thing was a bunch of playacting, I don't know what would be."

"Donna picked up on it, but not right away."

"That's an elegant lady. I like her."

"You and she hit it off so well, I was afraid you'd be asking her for a date."

Roark shook his head with a faint smile. "Don't have any worries on that score. Sharp as she is, I'd have thought she'd realize immediately what I was saying."

Jerry shrugged apologetically. "Well, I'm afraid she didn't expect anything quite so pointed. Based on your earlier speech, she thought your Shakespeare quoting was just a way of showing off your erudition."

Roark didn't take offense, just nodded. "There's probably something in that, now that you mention it. Maybe she's an even sharper lady than I thought."

"I think she'd support you for City Council if you decided to run."

"No way. Not after Parker Fuentes's wild west show."

"Have you told Wilmer Friend about your suspicions of Fuentes?"

"No. It's just my opinion, after all. I don't actually *know* anything. I'll volunteer the information if you think he needs to know, though."

"That's up to you. But I don't think you should give up running for Council. Look at it this way: Why should you deprive the city of a good councilman just because one overenthusiastic booster did something to upset you?"

"That's not what's happening. I don't want public office, Jerry. Probably I'm just using Fuentes as an excuse for not running, and if he hadn't pulled what he did, I'd find another one."

Jerry raised a hand. "Okay. I give up. But it would sure make things easier for me if there was a candidate who was on the side of the angels on *both* development and animal testing."

"I don't recall taking a public position on animal testing. I'll have my aides put together a forthright ambiguous position paper and distribute it to the press."

Jerry was surprised to see Roark in such a relaxed and playful mood, and wondered exactly what it all meant.

"I think there'll probably be a sound candidate or two cropping up," Roark said judiciously. "I'd prefer they were independent of Parker Fuentes and his bunch, though. And I think you and Donna can weather a little political difference anyway, can't you?"

"I hope I don't have to find out. Who's running? Have you heard any rumors?"

"I know a guy who *started* one about Will Wardell."

"Why?"

"Just 'cause he's a bullshitter. It was so ridiculous, though, I'm sure nobody'd be dumb enough to believe it."

"Was that by any chance the one about campaigning against Purejoy and then winding up selling out to the developers?"

"That's the one."

"Who started it?"

Roark shook his head. "Sorry. I have to protect certain confidences."

"Fair enough. So what are you planning to do with your retirement besides race Hot Air? Still weighing the wine shop or art gallery?"

"Leaning toward the art gallery. As an owner of thoroughbreds I think I'll pass on getting into the racing-information business. Your friend Digby is surely persistent, though."

Jerry wanted to get off that subject as quickly as he could. Besides which, he hadn't broached that other point he'd come to see Roark about. "Brad, you strike me as somebody who's pretty honest with himself."

"I hope so."

"Why were you so shocked when you saw your relatives Saturday? Your sister Naomi told me the look on your face broke her heart."

Roark sobered. "Yeah, I'm sorry about that. I didn't really mean that look for her, but I think she understands. If they brought Naomi down for the big day, it figured the rest of them would follow."

"And you just had no use for any of them?"

"Mo was a poisonous character, and I guess you can see I haven't been thrown into deep mourning by his death. Uncle Buller makes me sick. He fucked Naomi when she was sixteen. Nobody in the family is supposed to know that, but all of us do."

Jerry had figured Buller for a dirty old man, but this revelation still stunned him. Naomi's kind and sympathetic face flashed in his mind, along with her rueful reaction to Buller's statement that he had been responsible for her upbringing, and he felt angry and a little sick himself. "You mean he raped her?"

Brad Roark considered that. "Given her age, legally, yeah, he raped her. I think it's more precise to say he took advantage of her innocence and, when she consented once, put pressure on her to do it again. Who did she have to turn to if she didn't give in? Not Aunt Frances. She'd just blame Naomi for seducing Buller. That's typical of how victims get treated, isn't it?"

"Sometimes."

"It is, in sexual matters. There was nothing for her to do but run off with that skunk Al Burns."

"And what did *he* do to her?" Jerry asked, adding to the list of people he wanted to kill.

Brad sighed. "Just used her, lived off her, beat her up a couple times, landed in other people's beds when he felt like it. Not much different from our father, if you want to know the truth. Unlike our mother, at least Naomi was smart enough to dump him after a couple of years."

"What happened to Burns?"

"I don't know. I never met the creep. Heard all about him secondhand, and not from my sister. She never saw fit to keep in touch with me. I guess she wanted to put the whole family behind her. Who can blame her? Oh, I've been mad at her, too, over the years, don't get me wrong, but she's turned out to be a sweetheart, really. You can be mad at her from a distance of miles, but you can't look at her and stay mad at her."

"I know what you mean. And I suppose you were embarrassed at your Surfside friends seeing what ordinary uncultured common folk your family were."

Roark refused to take offense, saying mildly, "Jerry, if you want me to admit I'm an elitist snob, okay, you got it. I'll stipulate to that, as the lawyers say."

Jerry shook his head. "I can't believe that's all there was to your reaction. There has to be more to it."

The jockey sighed. "What are you getting at?"

"One of the people who talked to your brother Mo that night said he was planning a family outing for the next day. Do you have any idea what that was all about?"

"Oh, I see. A family outing." Brad Roark repeated the words slowly, as if tasting an obscure vintage.

"Does that term 'outing' have any special significance for you?"

Brad threw back his head and laughed. "Think you're smart,

don't you?" he said, unrancorously. "The cops know the word, too, you know."

"Has Wilmer Friend already talked to you about this?"

"No, but I'm sure he will. 'A family outing,' huh? That's real cute. Doesn't sound like Mo, though. A wordsmith he was not. Yes, outing has a special significance to me. It refers to a certain controversial practice in the homosexual community: revealing the sexual preferences of closeted gay people in print, thus in effect forcing them out of the closet. On the face of it, an invasion of privacy and to be deplored. But, some would argue, if a closeted gay man or lesbian is doing active harm to homosexuals, say as a legislator who consistently votes against gay interests, doesn't that person's hypocrisy deserve to be exposed? But leaving aside the moral and ethical questions, let's get down to the nitty-gritty and consider your scenario."

"I don't have any scenario," said Jerry innocently.

"Everybody's got a scenario. Don't let it get around you don't have a scenario."

Now the jockey was doing a Groucho Marx imitation. Jerry sensed Roark was high on something other than the brandy—or any other artificial stimulus for that matter. Whatever delicate topics Jerry could bring up weren't going to stop Roark from feeling good.

"What you're thinking is something like this: Brad Roark is gay, but has kept his lifestyle a secret throughout his riding career. There would be good reasons for that. Sports generally have not been anxious to admit to the validity or even the existence of alternative sexual lifestyles, and surely horse racing, a bedrock conservative bastion, can't be expected to be particularly avant-garde in that respect. Much the opposite, in fact."

Brad Roark stopped as if thinking about what came next. He had a swallow of his brandy and continued like someone making up a story as he went along. "My brother and sister know I'm gay, have known it almost from childhood. My brother hates queers and fags and pansies, and that's one reason we never got along too well as kids. My sister isn't given to hating, but instead she feels sorry for me for having embraced something that, in her mind, is so unnatural and abnormal and disgusting. However, well-intended, that kind of sympathy can be even worse than outright hatred.

"But back to our story. Whatever my plans for after retirement, the unexpected appearance of my relatives, whom I've been well rid of all these many years, presents the danger that I am going to be revealed in my 'gaiety' before the time of my own choosing. I realize that 'outing' his own brother is just the sort of cruel act that would appeal to Mo. This accounts for my exaggerated reaction to the unexpected appearance of my long-lost kinfolk.

"To protect my secret, I take my souvenir ice pick, given to me by those valued fellow professionals who I'd give anything to keep from finding out I'm a pervert, and I run my brother through with it. Thus, I'm safe in the closet for another day. Is that a fair summary of the scenario you *don't* have, Jerry?"

"That's about it," Jerry agreed. "And are you going to tell me I'm wrong?"

Brad shook his head slowly. "Not entirely. Most of it is all too accurate. The people in Surfside who know what I am are people I can trust. But on the biggest day of my career, from out of nowhere come a bunch of people who know, and who I can't trust. I'll say it was a shock. There are a few small differences, though. Mo did *not* threaten me with outing. I did *not* go to his room. I did *not* kill him. And there are several points to suggest I'm telling the truth about that. Number one, Mo himself removed the ice pick from my display of memorabilia. With my knowledge. You saw yourself that it was gone when I was still at the table."

"You could have taken it and hidden it from view until it was time to use it."

"Why would I call attention to myself that way if I was planning to kill my brother? Why would I use a weapon so directly associated with me at all, in fact? Number two, how much security would I really gain by killing Mo? I could not hope to continue concealing my sexual identity after Mo's death, could I? If that was my intention, it's clear from your visit tonight I've failed. And my sister knew. Would she stay silent if she thought there was murder involved? And what about my friends in Surfside who know the truth about me and have been so discreet about it? Would *they* continue to keep my secret if they thought that to do so was to protect a murderer? Members of the gay community can be surprisingly conservative and law-abiding, you know. We're not all drag queens and child molesters. We're really very conventional, and AIDS has made many of us even more so."

"You still could have killed Mo in a rage. You had plenty of reason to hate him. You wouldn't necessarily have thought everything out logically before you did it."

"All right, I'll give you that point. But—where was I?—number three, I don't believe Mo came up with that 'family outing' line. I knew him well enough to know he just wouldn't even be aware of such an expression. And that he would not have used the phrase suggests the possibility of malice from another quarter. He might have let slip something about my sexual orientation, or a Surfside person could have found out about it through local channels, discreet though my friends have tried to be. The person who came up with that very clever 'family outing' phrase could have been trying to cast suspicion my way, and perhaps divert suspicion from himself—or herself—at the same time.

"Let's see now. I can play amateur detective, too. It would presumably be someone who had had direct contact with Mo. It would help if it were someone who had reason for animus against me. And it would be a lover of puns. Will Wardell, maybe?"

Jerry said, "I don't know who it was."

"How about it? Do you think I killed my brother? Am I your number one suspect?"

Jerry shook his head. "No, you're not."

It occurred to Jerry again how much Brad Roark seemed to be

enjoying himself. It was as if all the cares of the world had been lifted from his shoulders. He didn't have to ride horses for a living anymore. He was spared the prospect of running for public office. And what else?

"You're coming out of that closet, aren't you, Brad? You can hardly wait."

The jockey nodded gleefully. "You know it. I'll be calling the members of the press tomorrow, a chosen few I have reason to expect sympathetic treatment from. I hated hiding for so many years. When I started out, it would never even have occurred to me an openly gay jockey would have a chance to succeed any more than an openly gay anything else. About ten years ago, the climate seemed to be changing a little bit, and I considered making my move. Then along came AIDS. That's what set us back just when we were on the edge of gaining acceptance. I knew anytime we got in close quarters in a race, the other jocks would start thinking they'd catch it from me. Not that I had it, but you see what I mean. It could have helped open up a few holes for me and get me some extra winners, of course, but that could only happen if the owners and trainers let me ride their horses in the first place. And I had no confidence that they would. There was no way around it: I couldn't be an admitted homosexual— vile phrase!—and a jockey.

"So I stayed in the damn closet till I thought I'd suffocate. Over thirty years, Jerry. Imagine it. Thirty years of denying who I am so I could make a living in my chosen profession. But now there's nothing stopping me. I found a group of friends in Surf- side who'd support me, and they'll support me out of the closet more enthusiastically than they did in. Maybe the jockey colony will even come around, at least some of them. I don't expect to lose *all* my straight friends. Of course, I couldn't expect the voters in this conservative little town to elect a self-proclaimed sod- omite to the City Council, and I'm not about to stay in the closet for a political career, no matter what kind of a macho trip Parker Fuentes laid on me. More brandy?"

Truthfully, Jerry had had enough, but now he wanted to avoid any impression that the open revelation of Roark's sexual identity made any difference to him. So he accepted another refill, and proposed a toast. "Here's to the empty closet."

Roark touched glasses with him and said, "Thank you very much. You know, I'm glad I'm hanging on to Hot Air. I'm still in racing. I'm an owner. Parker Fuentes with his damned grand gesture did me a big favor."

The doorbell rang, and Roark got up from his chair to answer it.

Jerry heard a vaguely familiar voice saying, "You've got company? I can—"

"No, no, come on in. We're celebrating."

Roark came back into the room with his arm around a slender man who was about a foot taller than he. "Jerry, do you know Myron Gilhousen?"

Jerry stood up to shake hands. "Sure, hi. Donna would be shocked to see you two guys together."

Gilhousen look startled. "What do you mean?"

Jerry realized the remark had been anything but tactful. "I just meant she thinks you're on opposite sides of the animal experimentation issue."

"Uh, not necessarily," Gilhousen said.

"Myron's quitting that Purejoy outfit, aren't you? We aren't experimenting on animals. Just on each other."

Now Gilhousen looked really flustered. "Brad, come on...."

"It's okay, Myron. Relax. Jerry's a friend. He's going to help us pick our racing colors."

Gilhousen managed a weak smile. "Anything but lavender."

15

Brad Roark made good his promise to come out of the closet in a big, splashy, public way, and it got him a large amount of publicity, mostly sympathetic. He did a few TV and radio interviews and could have done more. The coming out of a major jockey was something new in thoroughbred racing, and the quotes from his colleagues in the turf world were hearteningly measured and tolerant, though no one kidded himself there was not a good measure of prejudice and hostility under the surface.

With the exception of Naomi Burns, who stayed on to be with Parker Fuentes, the people gathered for the Brad Roark reunion returned to their home bases, the McIntoshes to Florida and Maisie Cooper to Manhattan, their fifteen minutes of fame seemingly over.

Both the murder of Mo and the sexual identity of Brad remained topics of interest in TV and newspapers, longer locally than nationally. They were generally treated as separate stories.

As those two stories gradually faded on the news pages, the upcoming Surfside Sprint Championship became bigger and bigger news on the sports pages. Craven Clay was announced as a definite starter, along with Valley Moon, and Hot Air would run his first race under the new Roark/Gilhousen colors.

Two weeks after the murder, and one before the big sprint, Jerry Brogan paid Wilmer Friend a visit at the shiny new Surfside police station, which would probably look like a corporate office for another year or so before taking on its true coloration. Friend, who didn't seem at home in the unmarked, crisp-smelling surroundings, could hardly wait for the transition.

"Who killed him, Wilmer?" Jerry demanded.

"I don't know."

"The threats to Brad Roark have stopped, haven't they?"

"You know all about those threats. Your friend Donna's department, a bunch of theater."

"But what's left? Who killed Mo? One of his relatives? They've scattered to the four winds."

"I can get any of them back here in a day if I find any evidence." Friend scowled at him. "Jerry, do you have something helpful to suggest, or did you just come here to torment me?"

"Neither one, I'm afraid. But something struck me funny. I've seen two articles about Will Wardell in the last week—"

"What about Wardell?" Suddenly Friend seemed more interested than Jerry had anticipated.

"One of them intimates he had planned to run for City Council and sell out the racetrack."

"Yeah, I know that rumor, and it's a bunch of crap. So what?"

"The other one suggests 'The Big Question' might not have been on the level."

"That's old news, too."

"Is it really?"

Friend waved a hand impatiently. "The accusation, I mean. What are you getting at?"

"He hasn't responded to either one with a letter to the editor. He hasn't filed suit, and everybody knows Will sues at the drop of a hat. Why isn't he reacting like the old Will? It's like waiting for the other shoe to drop."

"Jerry, it's nice of you to drop in, but why don't you just drop out, huh?"

Jerry left, hoping when the police station stopped smelling so new Friend would turn a bit more mellow. Sure, the odd omissions of Will Wardell might amount to nothing, but at this stage Friend shouldn't be above clutching at straws.

On the balcony of his Florida condo, Buller McIntosh had set his binoculars aside and was perusing the morning paper with more than customary interest. It had been three weeks since the murder of Mo Roark, and the national coverage had tailed off to almost nothing. But today there was a substantial article in the sports section.

"I wanna see that when you're done, Buller," Frances said, looking up from the society page.

"You never read the sports, baby," her husband said.

"Come on. Read it to me, why don't you?"

With annoying slowness, Buller began, " 'With the death of Mo Roark still unsolved, his brother Brad will make his debut as an owner in today's Surfside Sprint Championship.' "

"Buller, that's pronounced 'day-byoo,' not 'dee-butt.' " Buller read like a first-grader just to irritate her. She knew he could read better than that.

" 'A field of ten will start, but most observers consider it a three-horse race, matching former horse of the year Craven Clay, brilliant speedster Valley Moon, and electrifying stretch runner Hot Air.' "

"I don't care about that part. Isn't there anything in the article about *people*?"

"Not a mention of your precious Will Wardell, no. Or that track manager you got along so good with."

"Well, aren't there any new developments in the murder case?"

"Nothin' we don't already know, baby."

"I wish we could be there for the race."

"What do you mean? I thought you couldn't wait to leave. Next time we gotta go someplace with a little class, a little history."

"Oh, and you're planning our next vacation, are you, Buller?" she said with broad sarcasm. "Where we going? When do we leave? I had a good time out there. We could go again, stay at the Surfside Inn and have the tea and everything. We could afford it since we didn't even have to pay for this trip. Go again and we're getting two vacations for the price of one."

"Dumbest thing we could do would be to turn up for that race, Frances."

"Why?"

"You ever heard of the criminal returning to the scene of the crime?"

"Buller, they didn't suspect either of us."

"If we turned up out of the blue again, they just might. It would be out of character."

"That's the *first* thing you've said I've agreed with. For you to spring for a trip out of your own pocket would sure be out of character. What's wrong with goin' back to California? Don't those California bimbos give you a good enough skin show? Aren't they just as good as Florida butts and boobs? And if you think you'll get withdrawal on the plane, I'll buy you a *Playboy* to look at. How's that?"

"You're not bein' fair to me, baby. Anyway, it's too late to get out there for the race."

"I know it's too late, Buller. The race is today. I was just thinking how nice it would have been."

"I don't want to expose you to any more of that stuff. I was relieved they let us leave. Last place I'd want to go back to is Surfside. Besides, how would it look to go out there to be close to a nephew who didn't really want to see us in the first place—"

"Oh, sure he did, Buller. He was just a little shy."

"—and now is disgracing the family. I knew when he was a little kid Brad was queer."

"Did you? I never noticed."

"All the signs were there, if you just read 'em right. Look, I ain't ignorant. I know that stuff exists. I s'pose those people can't help it. They'd be normal if they could. Old cousin Joey Bob was queer er'n a three-dollar bill, and we all knew it, and that was okay, but damn it, you keep that stuff *quiet*. You don't go paradin' it in the street."

Buller tossed the sports section over to Frances and picked up his binoculars.

"Speaking of paradin' it in the street," his wife muttered.

Maisie Cooper had kept the apartment. At first she thought it would hurt too much, but apartments aren't that easy to find in Manhattan, and she found it easier to cope with what memories there were than to look for another place to live. She was surprised she'd managed to live so happily with Mo Roark—well, reasonably happily—and miss him so little. He was lots better in person than he was as a memory. It's better for a guy to have a little mystery to him than to be an out-and-out sleazeball, and that was how Mo was looking in retrospect.

She'd got the attaché case back from the Surfside cops. It wasn't what she'd call a happy souvenir of their relationship, but there it sat in the closet, waiting for some appropriate disposition. She had not been told what they'd found in it and she had pretty well decided Mo had gone out to California to blackmail his brother because of his sexual preference. What a bastard Mo had been, no kidding. She'd known he disliked homosexuals along with all his other middle-aged male prejudices, but that was talk and attitude. Blackmail was action. She knew a lot of gay people and liked them, and she was glad to read that Brad had come out with colors blazing. Good joke on you, Mo.

She saw an item on the morning news about the Surfside

Sprint Championship. It would have been fun to stay out there for it, maybe get some kind of job. There hadn't really been that much to draw her back to New York, but this was her home and that was that.

The Surfside race had enough angles that there was sure to be plenty of coverage—she could catch up on what happened when she got back from work that evening. A letter had come the day before from Naomi Burns—they'd got to be pretty good friends in the days immediately after Mo had died. Naomi gave Maisie some tips about her new waitressing job, assuming there wasn't that much difference between waiting table in Berkeley and New York. She'd also promised to put a two-dollar bet down on Hot Air in the big sprint and split the winnings with Maisie. "We'll bet to win this time," she said. That was a nice sentimental gesture.

She also had something to say about men: "They're always keeping secrets from us. Why do they do that? Don't they realize we're stronger than they are at coping with things? I've heard the deepest, darkest secrets from people I hardly know, but once I get really close to somebody, I can feel him holding back. Take Parker, for example. (Only you can't have him!) He got called in by that police lieutenant and really raked over the coals about something. He came back pale as that brown face of his will get. But would he tell me what it was? No. I asked him point-blank if the cops thought he was the one who killed Mo. I didn't think he could have been, because he was with me just about all the time, but I wondered if that was what they thought. He said no, it was something else, and they weren't going to charge him with anything, and he wanted to forget about it. I think he was telling me the truth. But what was the 'something else'? He wouldn't say. One thing I love about Parker, though, is how he's reacted to Brad's 'coming out.' I mean, what kind of reaction to a homosexual would you expect from a macho Hispanic man? But you can't stereotype people. I ought to know that from my Berkeley days. He's been real understanding. He was mad at Brad about something for a while, something about Brad trying to sell Hot Air, but he got over it and forgave him for not running for office. He'll be pulling for Hot Air as much as anybody on Saturday. Brad is still kind of cool to Parker, and I don't know what Parker could have done to him to make him that way—but men will guard their secrets, won't they? It took me a while to convince Brad I accept the way he is. I don't think I supported him the way I could have when we were growing up and knew he was not like everybody else. We all hurt him a lot in those days without meaning to. I've learned a lot about those things up in the Bay area. Well, that's about all from this end. Hope you're doing good, and if you ever want to come out to visit, the coast is clear. I don't think Uncle Buller will ever leave Florida again."

She signed it "Love, Naomi." Maisie wasn't much of a letter writer, but she'd be sure to write back. And send a dollar to cover her half of the bet on Hot Air.

Donna was back in the Wardell box for the Surfside Sprint Championship. The Wardells were as hospitable as ever, but both seemed to have aged ten years in those few weeks. That just meant Judy was starting to look within five years of her age, but Will didn't look well at all.

Donna had invited them to join her and Jerry at a performance of *Cat on a Hot Tin Roof* that evening, determined not to be disappointed if they begged off at the last moment. Her kids were terrific, but after all, a high school production was a high school production. Judy seemed enthusiastic about the idea, but Donna could tell Will viewed it as an ordeal to be dodged if possible.

"Who's it going to be, Judy?" she asked, looking at the field for the big race in her program.

"I should probably stick with Valley Moon," Judy said. "He practically did it for me last time, and look at those odds."

Valley Moon, 5–2 on the morning line, was up to 5–1. Craven Clay had dropped from 8–5 to 6–5, while Hot Air had gone from 5–2 to 9–5. The rest of the field were all 10–1 and up.

Jon L. Breen

"So Valley Moon's an overlay again?" Donna said, remembering her turf vocabulary.

Will Wardell shook his head. "The bettors are just being smart, in my opinion. He's fast as a rocket, but there's that extra furlong to run. And he'll have more challenge on the front end this time from Graceland and Knockemdeadpadre. Those are two very fast horses. Sure to soften him up."

"Is that horse owned by a religious order?" Donna wondered.

"Nope. A San Diego baseball fan. The horse was supposed to be named Knockemdeadpadres, but the owner made a mistake on the form."

Donna wondered about that. She'd heard stories like that before and couldn't understand why if they misspelled a horse's name they didn't just change it.

"I think I'll just bet on Hot Air," she decided.

In the press box, Jack Morgan was visiting the freeloader's buffet and explaining at length to a group of colleagues why the class of Craven Clay was sure to tell, regardless of the distance. "At six, I'll admit he might not be able to get up with these, but at seven, it's a piece of cake."

One of his companions shook his head. "I picked Groupie."

"You're kidding."

"My best bet of the day."

"What paper did you say you were with now?" one of the other reporters asked. Morgan, who had known Groupie's champion for a long time, wondered what answer he'd come up with.

"I, uh, free-lance. And I run a telephone information service," said Stan Digby.

"When did they start letting you guys in the press box?"

"Connections. Jerry Brogan's a very dear friend of mine."

The others drifted away. Morgan refilled his plate and continued his conversation with Digby. "This is Groupie, not Groovy. He's moved up the class ladder, won a lot of races, but he's never beat this kind. He's in tough."

"Yeah, I know. He's also twenty-five to one."

"By the time they get off, he may be fifty, and I think that's more like it." Morgan looked at Digby with narrowed eyes. "Tell me something. Do you really *know* something or what?"

Stan shrugged. "Just call it a hunch."

"Sure. Should I get a bet down on him?"

"Please don't. You might jinx me."

"How much are you betting, yourself?"

"I'm skipping the race."

"He's your best bet of the day, and you're skipping the race?" Morgan often ignored his own newspaper selections when he got what he considered a reliable inside tip, but he wasn't in the habit of making 25–1 shots his best bet of the day. "That doesn't sound ethical to me."

Stan decided he needed to counter that. "You remember an old play called *Three Men on a Horse*? The guy's a genius picking winners, but if he bets real money on them, he starts losing. Psychological thing. If I started betting on my own selections, it wouldn't be fair to my customers."

"And I shouldn't bet him either?"

"I'd appreciate it if you didn't." Stan licked his lips nervously. "If Groupie wins, I'll be a racetrack legend tomorrow. Word'll get around. I'll get more calls than I ever have."

"What if he loses?"

"I'll go into another line of work. I haven't been picking a lot of winners, and my client base is eroding. This race is make or break for Info Central."

When Brad Roark entered the walking ring for the first time as an owner, Myron Gilhousen at his side, he didn't hear the loud cheers that had greeted his final appearance as a jockey. But there was some supportive applause and (better yet) no negative cracks, though surely everybody here must know of his well-publicized coming out. While the racing game was undeniably hidebound and conservative, there was an easy tolerance about racing fans—at least on matters not directly related to their wallets—and Surfside fans were even more easygoing than most.

Brad shook hands with Parker Fuentes and gave his sister Naomi a hug. He'd invited them to see Hot Air saddled, not because he had any use for the car dealer but because it would mean something to Naomi.

Fuentes was wondering why he'd let Naomi drag him there. It was rubbing his face in it to be asked to watch a horse saddled that he'd given away. When he'd got the first verifiable report that Roark actually was talking about selling Hot Air, Fuentes had gone straight to his lawyer, who had assured him he could rescind the gift before the transfer of paperwork was completed. Since there was no consideration involved on Roark's side, the announcement of the gift didn't amount to an enforceable oral contract. But Fuentes knew that to take back the gift would have damaged his public image, and nothing was more important to him than that.

He suspected Roark had tipped off the police that he'd been responsible for the phony bomb in the hot-air balloon. There was no reason for him and Brad Roark to like each other, but he'd be civil for Naomi's sake. There was something about her that made people want to please her, and it was more than just sex. Parker Fuentes could go plenty of places for that.

Brad had kept Carl Felix on as trainer of Hot Air, which meant the gray was still stabled with Fuentes's other horses. They were also using a jockey who frequently rode for the Fuentes stable, but the silks were not the familiar orange and white. The newly registered Roark-Gilhousen colors were bright red, with a yellow artist's palette on the back, and a yellow cap.

Carl Felix gave the instructions—no jokes this time about taking Hot Air to the front—but the owner added a footnote. "Let him run his own race," Brad said. "This is a professional. He knows what he's doing out there. And he won't need much stick. Hand-ride him and he'll get it done for you."

*   *   *

"They're at the gate," Jerry announced a few minutes later. The ten horses would load into the seven-furlong chute on the backstretch, far to the right of the turn and almost out of view of the grandstand. Jerry could see the gate well enough to call the break, but soon after the start the horses would briefly disappear behind some trees.

He lowered his binoculars and took a last look at the tote board. Craven Clay was now even money, but Hot Air was holding at 9–5. Valley Moon had gone all the way up to an absurd 7–1, with two other quality sprinters who would be a short price against most fields, Knockemdeadpadre and Graceland, at 12–1 and 15–1 respectively. The rest were at boxcars. Jerry was surprised that El Perfecto and Dana Point, so badly beaten by Hot Air and Valley Moon last time, were in there again, but presumably their connections were hoping for fourth or fifth money. Of the other newcomers, the reformed claimer Groupie was the most interesting, having climbed the class ladder throughout the meeting, but Jerry was sure he was overmatched with this particular group.

"The flag is up. . . . And they're off in the Surfside Sprint Championship!" The field was away well, and this time Hot Air, who broke from the inside post position, only lagged behind two lengths when they passed the flagman and cleared the trees. Knockemdeadpadre and Graceland showed the most early speed, moving off from the others as a pair. Valley Moon settled in third, with Dana Point and Groupie outside of him.

Jerry was astonished. Either Valley Moon wasn't right today or his handlers had miraculously figured out a way to rate him off the front end.

"Down the backstretch, it's Knockemdeadpadre in front on the outside by a head; Graceland is second by two; then it's Groupie on the outside in third, Valley Moon along the rail fourth, Dana Point between them fifth, those three heads apart; back a length to Craven Clay in sixth place by himself. Then it's Vintage Port, Philanthropist, El Perfecto, and Hot Air trails, fifteen lengths off the pace." The gray laggard was closer up this time, acting less like Silky Sullivan than just a garden-variety stretch runner. Jerry wondered what that could mean.

"They did the quarter in twenty-one and four. Into the far turn, the field is tightening up. It's now Graceland along the rail by a half length; Knockemdeadpadre is second by a head; Valley Moon looms up between them, third by a head; Groupie moving with him on the outside fourth; Craven Clay making his move on the outside of Dana Point, those two with less than two lengths to make up. A length back to Vintage Port, El Perfecto, and Philanthropist. Hot Air is beginning to move, still about nine lengths off the leaders."

Knockemdeadpadre started to fade, but Graceland hung tough, battling it out with Valley Moon. As the two of them got clear of the others, Dana Point and Groupie fading, Craven Clay moved into third on the outside, but he was being carried very wide. "The half in forty-four and four," Jerry announced.

As they turned into the stretch, Valley Moon inched ahead of Graceland, but Craven Clay was full of run on the outside. Hot Air was beginning to pass horses, but he was doing his running on the rail where he'd started. It began to appear he was in danger of getting trapped down there. The jockey was taking a large gamble.

"Coming down the stretch, it's still Valley Moon in front a half length; Craven Clay is moving boldly on the outside; Graceland is third; and Hot Air finds a hole on the inside!" Jerry could hear the amazement in his own voice. The gray gelding had shot through past the tired bunch behind the leaders and now moved ahead of Graceland into third. He was going like a rocket, but Jerry wondered if he could make it. There might not be room inside of Valley Moon, and if he had to change course for the outside, he would not get there in time.

"It's Valley Moon and Craven Clay; they're head and head; and Hot Air is moving up on the rail. Hot Air is getting through!"

Donna was amazed. It was close again, but this time there was no doubt in the mind of anyone with a finish-line seat that he'd won by a good head, though there would be a *pro forma* photo. Whether Craven Clay had managed to nip Valley Moon for second was less clear.

Parker Fuentes shook his head at an offer to pose in the winner's circle with Hot Air. "This belongs to Brad and Myron," he said to Naomi. She thought it was sweet.

"I'm glad I didn't have to come through a hole like that last time," was Brad Roark's comment to his winning jockey, who replied, "I'd rather go through that hole ten times than go up in Fuentes's damned balloon."

Donna walked down to collect her win bet. Hot Air had paid $5.80, a bit more than for Brad Roark's last ride. She saw Naomi Burns in the line. Brad Roark's sister held up her winning ticket and waved, and Donna smiled back at her.

When she got back to her seat, Judy said, "I don't think we'll make the play tonight after all, Donna. Will's not feeling well."

Donna looked over at Wardell and saw it was not just a social lie. He looked terrible. But he managed to smile and say, "I've just seen enough of mendacity."

16

Driving home from the Richard Henry Dana High School auditorium that night, Jerry was more enthusiastic than he'd ever been after one of Donna's productions.

"They were terrific!" he said.

"They were good," Donna agreed, but without her usual ebullience. "I'm really proud of them all."

"Big Daddy was great. And that girl who did Maggie the Cat—are you sure she's a high school student?"

Donna smiled faintly. "Kids are a lot older than we were at that age, Brogan. Older and more knowing. They can't write an English sentence or add a column of figures, but about the kind of things Tennessee Williams was writing about—sex and money and stuff like that—they're way ahead of us."

Jerry could tell Donna was in a funk about something, but he didn't know what. He couldn't imagine she was so disappointed that the Wardells hadn't joined them for the play. Personally, he was relieved not to have to spend an evening with Will Wardell. Hearing Brad Roark's guess that Wardell had come up with that

194

"family outing" phrase to divert suspicion to Brad hadn't made him think any better of the old game-show emcee.

He switched on the car radio to a news station, and they rode a couple of miles in silence listening to pro basketball scores and weather reports. Then an item gripped their attention.

"Television personality Will Wardell, emcee of such programs as 'The Big Question' and 'Hold Out Your Heart,' died tonight at the age of seventy-one. The cause of death is believed to be a massive heart attack. More details when available."

"God," Jerry said, "I was just—"

"Thinking about them?" Donna said. "Me, too. He really did look awful today. I don't suppose it's such a surprise." She turned her face toward the window, and Jerry looked straight ahead. Donna shed tears very grudgingly and liked to keep it private.

A few minutes later, when he'd pulled up in front of her apartment, he walked around to let her out, and she, uncharacteristically, waited for him. She was dry-eyed but still very solemn.

"I wonder if I should go to her," Donna said, still sitting in the car. "It's hard to know. We were together just today. We weren't exactly close friends, but I wouldn't want her to be alone." Donna didn't seem like herself. It was as if her usual energy and confidence had been drained out of her. If she wanted to go to Judy Wardell, Jerry would be glad to drive her there, but he wasn't used to her being so indecisive. He just stood there by the car and listened to her talk. "Will had been under a lot of stress since Mo Roark was murdered. Anybody could tell how much he'd changed."

Jerry was reluctant to say it, but if Donna was thinking what he was, it might account for her acting so weirdly. "Donna, do you think Will killed Mo Roark?"

She looked up at him, her face expressionless. "No," she said simply.

"Maybe we'll never know the truth now, but he had some kind of a connection to Mo. Something to do with the time Roark worked as a network usher. Wilmer Friend knew but wouldn't tell me about it, really clammed up. Roark had asked Will to come to his room. You were there when it happened. Why come to his room? That never did make sense to me. And Will might have been the one who diverted suspicion to Brad Roark, with that thing about a 'family outing.' If he killed Mo, it would explain a lot."

She shook her head. "No, Will didn't kill him."

Donna finally got out of the car, and they walked into the apartment. Donna went to the phone in her office while Jerry sank onto the couch in the living room to await further instructions. He could hear her voice on the phone, low and soothing, but he couldn't hear what she was saying. When she came back, he looked up inquiringly.

"I was surprised somebody else didn't answer the phone," Donna said softly. "She's there alone. And she's in bad shape, Jerry. She says she killed her husband. I did my best to reassure her it was just a heart attack."

"Could she have killed him?"

"No," Donna said. "But she killed Mo Roark."

<h1 style="text-align: center">17</h1>

"Let's go," said Jerry.

"I can drive myself over there, Jerry. You don't need to come."

"Hey, look, you just told me you're going to visit a murderess—"

"Murderer," Donna corrected automatically. " 'Murderess' is one of those demeaning feminized words, like 'poetess.' Or 'actress,' for that matter. I hate words like that."

"Even 'actress'?" Jerry almost laughed, but Donna looked too serious. "Whatever you call her, you're not visiting her alone."

Donna just shrugged, and moments later they were back on the road. Jerry had been to the Wardell house once before and remembered how to get there. It was in the part of Surfside called the Bluffs, where the rich had built their massive residences to overlook the town half a century before. The neighborhood had never lost any of its fashionableness, primarily because it had never lost its view.

"Did she say she killed Mo Roark?" Jerry asked casually, as he began the ascent to the Bluffs on a narrow two-lane road.

"No."

"Then why do you think she did?"

Donna wagged her head like a horse discouraging a fly. "A bunch of silly things."

"And are you going to tell me what they are?"

"If I turned out to be wrong, I'd feel ridiculous."

"Then you have your doubts?"

"Not really. Not now. Though I wasn't really sure until I talked to Judy tonight. I think Will found out or suspected something about Judy's involvement with Mo. That brought on his heart attack, and that's why she thinks she killed him."

Donna sighed and went on. "First of all, Judy knew Mo. Everybody remarked on how uncomfortable the scene was when Will introduced her to him. You said yourself Mo stared at her in a very obvious way, and she was discomfited by it. Did Mo do that to anybody else we know of? And was that the reaction you'd expect from a cool and collected person like Judy? Any reasonably good-looking woman half her age has plenty of experience being stared at. It may irritate her, but she doesn't get thrown by it so noticeably. And Judy's breakdown *after* the murder seemed out of character, too.

"Assuming Will Wardell and Mo Roark worked at the same network at the same time in New York, who else might well have been there at the same time? Judy, that's who. And Will and Judy didn't become a romantic item until months after she was last on the show. But she said something interesting to me when we talked on Brad Roark Day. She said her only sexual experience had been with her high school boyfriend 'before New York.' That implies something happened *in* New York, doesn't it? And if it didn't happen with Will, whom did it happen with?

"Mo was nude when he died. It must have been by his own choice. If the killer had undressed him for whatever crazy reason in the short time available, the police would have found signs, wouldn't they? Why would Mo be nude? Because he expected to engage in sex. Unless he shared his brother's gay proclivities, the killer must have been a woman."

"It could have been Maisie."

"It could, but it wasn't."

As he pulled up in front of the Wardell house, Jerry said, "I don't think that's much of a case, Donna."

"Fortunately, I am *not* the district attorney. I don't have to make a case." Softening her tone a bit, she added, "Besides, there was the ice pick."

"The ice pick?" Jerry said.

Before Jerry could get any further explanation of the remark, Donna was out of the car. He followed her up to the door.

Jerry seemed to remember the Wardells' having a live-in housekeeper, but Judy answered the doorbell herself. Donna was right. She was in bad shape. Her composure seemed very fragile. She embraced Donna and, including them both, said, "It's so good of you to come."

She seated them in the living room, insisting on bringing them tea. Jerry was about to decline, spare her the trouble, but Donna accepted, quelling him with a touch on the arm and a subtle shake of the head.

Okay. It was probably good for the widow to be doing something. But when Judy poured the tea, her hand shook dangerously. Jerry was relieved when she completed her hosting duties and sat down in a chair opposite them.

In a monotone, she gave them the obligatory account of Will's death. When they'd got to their car, Will was feeling even worse. He said if he just went home and went to bed, he'd be fine. But she insisted on driving him to the emergency room of the hospital. She thought he'd died sitting in the passenger seat while she went inside for help. All the heroic measures of the emergency team were done after he was already dead.

"I'll always know I killed him," she said.

"No," Donna insisted. "You didn't. You did everything you could. You can't blame yourself for a heart attack."

"Oh, yes, I can."

"Did he have a prior history?"

"He'd had heart trouble for years. Not very many people knew about it, but we both knew something like this could happen at any time."

"Then how can you blame yourself? The past few weeks must have been very stressful for him."

"They were. One way I could tell was, he gave me more and more impromptu racing quizzes. That was some kind of safety valve for him. I never used to understand why he did that, but I do now. I just wanted to save him pain, not cause him more." Her voice cracked, and Jerry could sense her dragging herself back from the edge of hysteria. "More tea?" Not waiting for an answer, she refilled their cups, her hand still shaking.

When Judy spoke again, her voice was faint and distant, as if she'd forgotten they were in the room. "I hated being called the Ice Queen. It's stuck with me all these years, and I've wondered if it was really the truth."

Jerry felt Donna stiffen at the words "Ice Queen," but her face remained expressionless.

"Mo called me that. He said I belonged in an ice show he'd ushered at Madison Square Garden before he got his network job. He didn't just mean I'd look graceful on skates, either. He meant I was a cold person."

"When did you meet Mo?" Donna asked casually. It wasn't the voice of an interrogator but of someone who knew it would comfort the widow to keep talking.

"When I was on 'The Big Question.' I didn't know him as Mo Roark. He never told me his last name. So when Will told me who was coming to the reunion, I had no reason to connect it to him. I was quite resentful a lot of the time I was in New York because I couldn't get out and have any fun. They wouldn't even let me go to the races, can you imagine that? And horse racing was my subject. Mo was a real charmer in those days—a hunk, they'd call him now. Not a big guy but plenty of charisma. He helped me sneak out on the network chaperone a couple of evenings, and we had a good time. I wound up in his bed.

"I didn't recognize Mo when I saw him at the track. He was too far away. But when Will introduced us the night of the party, I knew him immediately, even if he wasn't quite the Adonis I remembered. Mo stared at me as if he'd just discovered a gold mine. That fixed look was his way of taunting me. He knew he'd be seeing me that evening. I found out later, he'd already made his preparations. It was so obvious to everybody—that he was staring, I mean, not what it meant. I wanted to crawl into a crack in the floor and disappear. Will knew I was upset, but he thought it was just a reaction to being stared at so rudely. Will was always ready to credit a Victorian explanation for female behavior." Judy's fond smile appeared for only a moment, jerked back as she remembered her grief and her guilt.

"Mo managed to mention his room number in the trite party conversation we were having. He said something like, 'It's so nice in Room one-oh-nine, I almost didn't get to the party'—and I knew he meant it as a message to me. When I got a chance, I told Will I was going to the rest room, and I went to see Mo in his room. He was stretched out on the bed, wearing a bathrobe. He told me how much Will was concerned about me, how I was his innocent flower, how Will wanted to protect me from any guilty knowledge.

"Mo made it clear he was blackmailing Will about 'The Big Question.' He said he would have used what he knew years before, but he had held back because of what he'd felt for me. He said he'd really been in love with me and hadn't wanted to spoil my happiness. He seemed to find it funny now that he ever could have felt that way.

"It didn't shock me that there had been some irregularities with the show. I'm not so dumb as to suppose there couldn't have been. It didn't even bother me that Will had concealed it from me. I knew he lived in the real world and liked to pretend I didn't. It was kind of touching, really.

"Mo said, 'How are you, Ice Queen? Look, I brought something along to chip away at your defenses.' And he held up that ice pick the other jockeys had given Brad Roark."

Jerry couldn't stop himself. He burst out, "It was self-defense. He tried to kill *you* with the ice pick."

Judy's laugh was jarring and hopeless. "No. He had nothing like that in mind. He wanted money from Will, and one last screw from me, but he didn't intend to kill anybody. And he wouldn't believe I was going to kill him."

"Did you plan to?" Donna asked softly. "Is that why you went to his room?"

"No," Judy said faintly. "I didn't think of killing him before I went to see him. He said he'd told Maisie not to come back to the room before midnight. We were alone, he said. Our privacy was secure. If I'd have a little party with him, he *wouldn't* tell Will where he knew me from. When he tossed off the robe and was naked on the bed, I knew I had to kill him. He wasn't very big, and I'm a pretty strong woman, but I knew I couldn't just pick up the ice pick and lunge at him. He'd overpower me easily enough. I had to pretend I was going to do what he wanted. I took off my dress. I had a slip on underneath. That was as far as I wanted to go. I picked up the ice pick off the bedside table and started fondling it in a suggestive manner. I held it in a handkerchief so the handle wouldn't get my fingerprints on it, but he was too mesmerized to notice. 'Ice Queen, huh?' I said. 'I'll show you who's an Ice Queen.' I lay down beside him on the bed, still holding the ice pick in my hand. He started to roll toward me, reaching out for me, and I shoved the point into his heart.

"The blood spurted out at me. I mopped off those few spatters my dress wouldn't cover, then got out of there to rejoin Will. I hadn't been gone all that long. No longer than the average visit to the powder room. I was a little shaky, but Will thought I was still upset from the way Mo acted earlier. After the murder was discovered, I could let myself go a little, break down. Nobody suspected anything, least of all Will. I don't think it ever crossed his mind I might have killed Mo. Until last night. He found the bloody slip."

"You hadn't washed it?" Donna said.

"By hand, and in a hurry. I missed a spot. Will saw it. The weeks since had been hard enough on him. I knew last night he was starting to wonder about me and Mo Roark for the first time. I couldn't tell him the truth."

Jerry said, "You could claim self-defense. You could say Mo tried to rape you, that you didn't tell anybody about it out of fear and shame. You could probably beat the charge in court."

"I'm not going to court. What would be the point? I killed Mo Roark. And I'm not sorry I did it. I may have done the world a favor. He was talking about a family outing the next day. I didn't know what he meant, but I could tell by the way he said it, it would be miserable for somebody."

Jerry said, "Brad Roark said that didn't sound like something his brother would say with that special meaning."

"Maybe he didn't know his brother very well. Cruel jokes were one of Mo's specialties. Like Ice Queen." For an instant, Jerry found himself mourning Will Wardell more than he had up to that point.

"I'm *not* sorry I killed Mo," Judy repeated. "But I killed my husband, too."

Judy's voice cracked, and again she seemed to be holding hysteria at bay by the most tenuous thread. Donna started to reach out to her, but Judy put both hands out in front of her as if to ward off the sympathy. "No," she said. She reached for an object under a magazine on the coffee table next to her. "Will's gun," she said, hefting it in her hand.

For one silly moment, Jerry thought she intended to kill them to guard her secret. But it was clear a few seconds later, she didn't intend the weapon for anyone but herself.

Donna and Jerry never asked each other if they regretted not being able to stop her in time. They thought they both knew the answer.

18

Life went on at Surfside Meadows.

It had taken Parker Fuentes years to figure out Hot Air was a sprinter. Brad Roark, the owner, forgot everything he'd learned as a jockey about Hot Air and tried him against Craven Clay in the mile-and-a-quarter Surfside Handicap. Craven Clay won by four lengths, Hot Air managing a slight dramatic bid on the far turn before flattening out to finish ninth of eleven starters. There was some criticism in the papers of the jockey's failure to whip the gray more vigorously.

Purejoy Cosmetics bit the bullet on animal experimentation and milked what goodwill they could from the decision. They inquired about sponsoring the big sprint for the following year, wanting to call it the Purejoy Sprint Championship. Jerry hoped they realized it wasn't always as exciting, and never as nationally publicized, as it had been this year.

On the day of the filing deadline for City Council, Jerry received an announcement in his mail at the track from Brad Roark. It had nothing to do with politics, though. Roark and Gilhousen were announcing the opening of their art gallery.

There was also a phone message from Stan Digby, whose Info Central had gone out of business following the sprint performance of Groupie. Jerry dialed him with a combination of irritation and curiosity.

"Hello. You have reached the headquarters of the Stan Digby for City Council Campaign Committee. You are cordially invited to the kickoff of the Stan Digby campaign at Fuentes Motors this Saturday: enjoy a gourmet brunch, celebrities, free-flowing champagne, and complimentary hot-air balloon rides for only $600 per couple. Or make a contribution, in whatever amount, to the people's candidate. We honor Visa and MasterCard. Leave your name and number at the sound of the tone."

SUNSET AND THE MAJOR

SUNSET AND THE MAJOR

Julian Jay Savarin

This first world edition published in Great Britain 2006 by
SEVERN HOUSE PUBLISHERS LTD of
9–15 High Street, Sutton, Surrey SM1 1DF.
This first world edition published in the USA 2007 by
SEVERN HOUSE PUBLISHERS INC of
595 Madison Avenue, New York, N.Y. 10022.

British Library Cataloguing in Publication Data

Savarin, Julian Jay
    Sunset and the major
    1.   Muller, Jens, Hauptkommissar (Fictitious character) - Fiction
    2.   Pappenheim, Oberkommissar (Fictitious character) - Fiction
    3.   Police - Germany - Berlin - Fiction
    4.   Suspense fiction
    I.   Title
    823.9'14 [F]

    ISBN-13: 978-0-7278-6418-5

All Severn House titles are printed on acid-free paper.

Typeset by Palimpsest Book Production Ltd.,
Grangemouth, Stirlingshire, Scotland.
Printed and bound in Great Britain by
MPG Books Ltd., Bodmin, Cornwall.

Prologue

August 1940. Nazi Germany. Berlin outskirts

A group of thirty freshlyminted young Waffen SS officers were listening with rapt attention to a guest speaker. The large, classic building in whose vast salon they sat, once belonged to a Jew. The red-backed chairs had been arranged in a semicircle in the elegantly furnished room, with the speaker sitting at its centre. This gave a sense of intimacy, making the young officers feel highly privileged; which was the intention.

'And so, my young gentlemen,' the handsome speaker said, coming to the end of his address, 'you belong to a very special organization. History is before you. Go out there and make it!'

As one, they sprang to their feet, snapped rigidly to attention, and thirty right arms shot out.

'*Heil Hitler!*' they barked in concert.

The speaker rose languidly to his feet. His arm did not shoot out in response. Instead, he smiled at them, nodding in satisfaction. He shook hands with each as they filed out.

He touched one on the shoulder. 'Von Mappus. Wait.'

To glances of barely suppressed envy from his comrades, the young von Mappus stood to one side to wait.

When the others had gone, two Waffen SS troopers looked enquiringly at the speaker.

'Wait for me,' he said to them.

They clicked their heels smartly, and left.

'Now, my dear von Mappus,' the guest speaker continued, 'please take a seat. Here.'

He indicated a chair closest to the one he'd been using.

1

He waited until von Mappus had sat down, before doing so himself.

He glanced around as he took his seat. 'You've got to hand it to the Jews. They knew how to live.' He smiled at the expression on von Mappus' face. 'You are surprised to hear me say that?'

'*Herr Doktor Untersturmführer . . .*' von Mappus began.

'Please. No formalities while we're here. There is no contradiction in what I have said. One can live well on stolen goods.' The doctor smiled, eyes angelic.

Von Mappus smiled in return. 'Yes. Yes.'

'I have heard excellent things about you,' the doctor continued. 'You are one of the elites of the elite. Much is expected of you.'

'I will do my best.'

'I am certain you will. What did you think of my talk?'

'I believe you are one of our most important pioneers,' von Mappus replied. He meant it.

The angelic eyes smiled, clearly pleased. 'You do me an honour.'

'The honour is mine.'

The doctor gave a slight nod of acceptance. 'Mark my words, von Mappus, what we are doing may not – for now – be fully understood by the outside world . . . but one day, everyone will be playing in what we seek to achieve. Eugenics, von Mappus. That is the key. One day, we shall not need wars to exterminate the subhumans. Nor will we need them for experimentation. We will be able to create specific laboratory specimens. Eugenics will do it . . . once we have all the keys we need, to unlock its secrets. *Then* we shall be free to create . . .'

The doctor paused, dreaming of the possibilities.

'They simply do not understand,' he went on. It was more to himself than to von Mappus. Then he was back from wherever his dreaming had taken him. 'You're off to Warsaw, I believe.'

'Yes.'

2

'I will also be there. Research to be done. Perhaps we shall see each other again. If not, do your own good work. Make us proud.'

'I shall!'

'Good. That is good to hear. I know you will. You have a bright future with the Waffen SS. I shall follow your progress. And remember, von Mappus, whatever the eventual outcome . . .'

'If I may interrupt . . .'

'Please do.'

'The outcome is uncertain? Victory will be ours, surely.'

The angel's eyes smiled again. 'One should always be ready to adapt to whatever the future may bring. It is what Nature does . . . adapt to survive . . . and eugenics is the primary key. Never forget.'

Von Mappus never would.

Among the 'great' things he did was wipe out an entire village, isolated and defenceless in the Russian snow. At the head of the starving remnants of an SS unit, he had repaid the offer of food by killing almost all the inhabitants. The two survivors were a hidden young boy watching it all, and his even younger sister. She had been saved by an SS sergeant with a conscience, the SS man using his body as a shield when the enraged von Mappus had coldbloodedly fired. Von Mappus had fired so many shots into the sergeant, he mistakenly believed the child had also died.

Decades later, the boy, Zima Rachko, then with the KGB and nurturing a burning desire for revenge, had one winter killed the wrong man on Germany's Baltic island of Rügen, believing him to be von Mappus. But it was Carey Bloomfield who had eventually got von Mappus.

Finishing the war a highly decorated SS general, von Mappus had vanished into the DDR, and became one of the founders of the inimical, shadowy crime organization, the Semper, which would eventually be responsible for the murder of Müller's parents, in order to silence them.

3

But von Mappus was also responsible for the one thing that would have gladdened the heart of the man with the angel's eyes: the development of one of the most fearsome weapons ever created.

One

Cape Leveque, Western Australia

The surrealistic red beauty of the pindan rock formations, the bright white of the empty beach, the deep blue of the cloudless sky, and the unworldly green of the ocean, was like a postcard from an alien planet.

Some distance offshore, beneath the green of the ocean, two divers headed for the depths. One had spotted something small and white on the bottom. As his partner kept an eye out for patrolling sharks, he glided just above the seabed, towards the white thing. When he saw what it was, he almost stopped completely in his astonishment, and felt a thrill of horror.

He trod water, staring at what he had found. It was a hand; a small, right hand, jaggedly severed at the wrist. It seemed to be closed about something.

Cautiously, the diver went forward again, and reached for the hand. It opened like a flower as soon as he touched it, as if it had been waiting for him to do just that.

The diver almost gasped in surprise when he saw what the hand had been holding, and remembered just in time that his jaws were clamped about his life-sustaining mouthpiece.

In the palm of the hand was a small, blue shell.

The diver picked up the shell, and concentrated upon putting it in a pouch hanging from his diving belt. When he looked up again, the hand was gone. He did a complete three-sixty degree turn. All he saw was the beautiful undersea landscape, open water, some fish, and his diving partner. The hand was nowhere to be seen.

5

He assumed it had drifted away on a current.

Even so, he felt a slight shiver as he signalled his partner for the return to the surface.

'Sunset, old boy,' the major said. 'Feel it approaching. Won't be long now.'

It was midday, and bright daylight.

Müller stared at him. 'Are you sure?'

'Oh, yes. Quite. My implacable friend – or should that be fiend – of many years, has finally succeeded in doing me in. Gave me quite a fair run of the leash, actually, if one thinks of it.' The major paused. 'Won't forget your promise, will you, old son?'

'I won't,' Müller assured him. 'Have you told Aunt Isolde?'

The major sighed. 'Dear, dear Isolde. Haven't said a word to her about this . . . yet. But she knows. She knows. Woman's intuition. Beats us Neanderthals hands down, that intuition.'

Müller had long become accustomed to the major's idio-syncratic way of speaking. A mixture of quirky fifties rhythms, slang, modern insertions and cadences from the various countries where he had spent most of his adult life; his English owed much to an era long vanished.

A Sandhurst graduate, Major the Honourable Timothy Charles Wilton-Greville had vanished without trace whilst carrying out dangerous and clandestine work for his country on a mission in the Middle East. Presumed dead for over two decades, he had suddenly appeared in the gardens of the Schlosshotel Derrenberg, causing Aunt Isolde to faint, upon seeing the living figure of her supposedly dead husband standing before her.

Having married again in the interim, and again become a widow, it was small wonder that she had.

But Greville had been at death's door for all of those years. It had simply taken some time to get round to opening it for him.

Death had extended the invitation in a laboratory in a Middle Eastern nation. The laboratory had not belonged to that nation. Greville's task, with others, had been to destroy it completely, and anything that was being cultivated there. He had also been instructed to remove one particular item. He had found it, and had been surprised by a guard who was not supposed to be there. In the exchange of fire the guard had been killed, Greville had been hit in a way he could never have expected in his worst nightmare.

The guard had lost the contest and no bullets had struck Greville per se; but one stray had hit the vial in a pocket. The vial had contained the nightmare from the laboratory. It had shattered, spilling its deadly contents, and thoroughly contaminating Greville – though he did not know it at the time. The laboratory had been successfully destroyed.

It was only later that he had discovered what had happened to him. The knowledge had so shaken him that he had decided then that he would vanish from the radar. Until one day when he had suddenly appeared before Aunt Isolde.

'When . . . when do you expect this to happen?' Müller asked after a long silence. It was obvious he did not enjoy asking.

'At any time. Right at this moment or not for some time, measured in weeks . . . not months, and certainly not years. It's a feeling. In me bones, if you like. And don't look so stricken. I've been waiting for years for this moment. Expected it. It was just a matter of time and, as I've said, I've had a fair run of it.'

'But you don't look . . .'

'As if I'm suddenly at death's door? That's the beauty of this monster, dear boy. When I look in the mirror, I actually do seem younger. Rejuvenates the system, and at the same time kills it. Clinical monster.'

Not knowing what to say, Müller remained silent.

Like Greville, he knew this would happen one day. Unlike Greville, he had dared hope for a stay of execution. The DNA poison, invented as a weapon, was implacable. During the years it had spent within Greville, it had evolved, seeming to purge his system of impurities, so that the appearance of abundant health conned the unknowing into believing that it was in fact a life-enhancing mutation. The cold reality was that it was feeding upon the host it appeared to nurture.

As if reading Müller's thoughts, Greville said, 'Its true nature is to kill. All the rest is a façade. That's the malevolent beauty of it.' A tiny laugh, strangely full of humour, escaped Greville. 'It's done things its inventors never expected.' Greville turned piercing eyes upon Müller. 'They must never get their hands on my remains. Cremation as long planned, old boy. Cremation, the ashes scattered to the winds.'

'You have my word,' Müller promised.

Greville suddenly appeared to be overcome by an uncharacteristic bout of shyness. 'Er . . . one other thing,' he eventually said. The words seemed to sneak out of him. ' "Stardust" . . . do you know it?'

Müller nodded. 'Hoagy Carmichael.'

'My word! Who'd have thought it? Young feller like you. Long, long before your time. How come?'

'I have a varied taste in music and my . . . father . . . was given an original recording by *his* father. He liked it, and used to play it to me. I even played it on the piano when I was younger.'

Greville nodded. 'Of course. Keyboard man. I remember Isolde telling me about your prowess with the ivories. Seen those two big Hammonds at your home in Berlin. Kept it up, eh?' Before Müller could comment, Greville went on. 'My favourite recording is the Glenn Miller version. Glenn Miller was before my time, of course.' He gave a short bark of a laugh. 'But liked it enough to play it to Isolde when I was at Sandhurst. She loved it. It became our "signature" tune, if you like. Special, if you see what I mean.'

Müller nodded slowly, but said nothing.

'Play it . . . play it for me, won't you, dear boy . . . on that last journey?'

'I will,' Müller promised again.

'And I shall hear.'

A long silence descended, broken only by the soft murmur of flowing water.

They were at their favourite spot for such get-togethers: at the bank of the stream that coursed through the vast, well-kept grounds of the Schlosshotel Derrenberg in the Saale Valley. A tiny tributary of the river Saale, it could sometimes become ferocious after heavy rain. Today, its barely perceptible motion made it seem as still as glass.

A former home belonging to Aunt Isolde's family and appropriated by the Party hacks in the days of the DDR, the elegant building that had subsequently become the Schlosshotel had been left a ruin. Lucky enough to have found its shell still intact after the DDR's collapse, she had rebuilt it with love. It now earned its highly successful keep as part luxury hotel, and part private residence for Aunt Isolde. Having brought him up as her own son after the death of his parents, she had long ago decreed that it was also Müller's home. The greater section of the winged building had been refurbished as the hotel.

The major broke the silence to remark in a voice almost as quiet as the stream itself, 'You've been back from Oz for what . . . two weeks?'

'Yes.'

'You've been noticeably reticent. Perhaps I should amend that – noticeably reticent to me. What did you find out there?'

'Things I did not expect.'

'Are you ready to tell?'

Müller shook his head. 'No.'

Greville looked at him for a long moment. 'As you wish. If I can help, you need but ask.'

'I know. Thank you. I'll tell you when the time comes.'

'Not too long, old boy, eh? Remember my nemesis. Kismet, and all that.'

Müller nodded. 'I know. I just need to . . .'

'Think it through.'

'Yes.'

9

Greville still kept up his piercing scrutiny of Müller. 'As you wish,' he repeated.

Three hours later. The Pentagon, Washington

The general stood up as a tall, hard-faced man entered his office unannounced.

'General,' he greeted. His voice gave nothing away.

'General,' the hard-faced man responded. His blond hair was cropped so close to his skull, he appeared bald.

Both were in civilian dress.

'To what do I owe—?'

'The pleasure?' the hard-faced general interrupted. 'Not sure it's a pleasure. That remains to be seen. I am here to speak with your colonel.'

The general was surprised. 'Lieutenant-Colonel Bloomfield? I'll go get her.'

'Don't you have enough people under your command to run your errands for you?'

'I need the walk.'

The general left his office before his unwelcome guest could interrupt again. He strode the few metres to Carey Bloomfield's small office, and poked his head through.

'Someone to see you, Colonel,' he began in a neutral voice, and loud enough to be heard by his uninvited guest. 'My office.'

Carey Bloomfield had risen to her feet. She thought she had spotted a warning in the general's eyes.

'Yes, sir.'

The general went back to his own office. 'She'll be here,' he said to the general whom he wished had chosen to annoy someone else.

'I heard.'

In her office – and like her superiors, in civilian dress – Carey Bloomfield composed herself. *I guess he was warning me of minefields,* she concluded.

She went out to face whatever it was the general had warned her about.

10

'Ah, Colonel,' the general began as soon as she entered. 'This is—'

'No need for formal introductions,' the hard-faced man interrupted for a second time. He fixed a baleful stare upon Carey Bloomfield. 'I'll come straight to the point, Colonel. How's the mission coming along?'

She glanced at her commanding general. He gave a barely perceptible nod.

'In what context, sir?' she asked.

'In what context?' he repeated, as if testing the remark for poison. 'You've been spending too much time with that limey-speaking kraut, Colonel. What does he call himself . . . the Graf von Röhnen?'

'He does not *call* himself . . . he *is* the Graf von Röhnen.'

'Defensive. Not good, Colonel. And what did you bring back from Australia? Seems nothing much more than a tan.'

Annoyed by the unpleasant visitor's deliberate goading, she gave her commanding officer a furious look. 'Do I have to take this kind of crap, sir?'

'You have to take this kind of crap, Colonel,' the general replied, straight-faced. 'And watch your step.'

His last comment had two possible meanings, she decided: he was either cautioning her against straying into insubordination, or he was warning her to be careful of the man before her.

She chose the latter, and looked at the hard-faced general with the right amount of diffidence that neatly masked her own hostility.

'Have you discovered anything about PS0, Colonel?'

It was a bolt from the blue; a question designed to achieve maximum surprise, in order to wrong-foot the person being interrogated. But having been forewarned, she was ready.

'What is PS0?' she asked.

The visitor glanced at the general. 'She does not know?'

'Obviously not,' the general replied, still giving nothing away.

'But I thought . . .'

'Wrongly, it would seem.'

11

The hard-faced man looked displeased, and made no effort to hide it.

'What is PS0?' Carey Bloomfield repeated, looking from one to the other.

The general looked at the hard-faced man, who looked back at him. Then the hard-faced general looked at Carey Bloomfield with some uncertainty, as if deciding whether to tell her.

'A weapon,' he finally said. 'A very special weapon. And we want it.'

'I'm sorry, General. I don't understand any of this.'

The general continued to stare at Carey Bloomfield. 'Your original mission was to shadow Müller, Colonel. That hasn't been changed. Müller may be the only link we have to that weapon . . . a very tenuous one; but we believe it to be there.'

The general chose not to explain about the 'we'.

'I'm still not with you, General,' she said, maintaining complete ignorance. 'What has Müller to do with this PS0?'

The hard-faced general turned to his fellow general officer. 'Why has she not been briefed about this, Dering?'

'To you,' Dering began, 'it's General or General Dering.'

A fierce look appeared upon the unknown general's face which twitched in response, as if he had actually been slapped. He glanced at Carey Bloomfield, clearly offended that he had been taken down in front of a subordinate.

'I'll remember this,' he said to Dering, features tight as if stretched by a plastic surgeon.

'So will I,' Dering said with pointed calm. 'Will you please continue, General?'

The still-faced general gave Dering a final glare, before turning back to Carey Bloomfield.

'You're going back to Europe, Colonel, and anywhere else necessary. You stick with Müller. You find that link to PS0.'

'But, sir . . . !'

'You suddenly hard of hearing, Colonel? You just got your orders.' He looked at Dering. 'Your responsibility, Dering. Air Force,' he added with a barely concealed sneer.

Before either could respond, he marched out.

Dering stared after his visitor, an unfathomable look in his eyes.

'He was an early bird,' Carey Bloomfield said. 'Want to tell me what just happened, sir?'

'Not sure I know myself,' Dering replied, still staring at the space where the hard-faced general had been.

'Since when do you take orders from generals without names?'

'We both take orders from people without names, Colonel,' Dering said. 'Even one-star assholes.' But it was as if he had addressed that to someone else.

Carey Bloomfield looked at him, bemused. 'General?'

'How about lunch?'

'Excuse me?'

Instead of replying, Dering returned to his uncrowded desk and pulled out a small, blank card from a black rolodex.

'I can't believe you still use that thing, General,' she said. 'There's nothing on it. Well . . . almost nothing. People use notebook computers, notebook phones . . .'

'All of which can be hacked,' Dering said as he wrote upon the card. 'Besides, I don't put important stuff on there.' Finished, he came round to hand her the card.

She stared at it as she read. 'But . . .'

'Yes, Colonel. I know. Those are your orders.' His eyes told her to say nothing more.

'Yes, sir.'

'Dismissed, Colonel.'

'Sir.'

Back in her office, she read the card once more, then put it into the small shredder attached to her desk. The shredder hummed the card into a fine powder.

'A hundred and fifty-eight miles for lunch,' she murmured to herself, '*tomorrow*? That's Saturday. My weekend. What the hell, General?'

Dering's choice of a place to eat was a beach-front café-restaurant at Virginia Beach.

*   *   *

In Berlin, Müller's seal-grey Porsche Turbo growled its way beneath the raised armoured door and into the underground garage belonging to the glass-rich building that housed the special police unit on Friedrichstrasse. The sensor-operated lights had come on automatically, and the door was lowering itself even before Müller had parked in his allotted space.

He pulled up next to a gunmetal BMW coupe, long appropriated by Pappenheim from the Semper. Though in the strictest sense 'evidence', the Semper had never claimed ownership, and never would. The car had been used by one of their killers.

Among the many vehicles, Müller spotted Hedi Meyer's original, and immaculately kept, black Volkswagen Beetle. Though severely wounded in a recent shooting by one of the Semper's most accomplished assassins, and barely escaping with her life, the goth – as she was known by her colleagues – refused to stay away.

'She did eventually kill her would-be killer,' Pappenheim had said when the goth had first made her determination to remain on duty known. 'We should humour her . . . for now. That wound will force her to see reason.'

'Somehow, I think the wound has surrendered,' Müller had replied. 'No shrinking violet, our ethereal Miss Meyer.'

Müller entered the lift that would take him up to his office. He got out on the top floor, stepping into a corridor festooned with no-smoking signs.

'Pappi's bane,' he commented with dry humour as he walked along the corridor that led to both his, and Pappenheim's offices; which was where that particular corridor ended.

Müller paused by Pappenheim's door, knocked, and entered into what felt like a smokers' convention. But only one man was producing all the smoke.

'There you are,' Pappenheim greeted. 'And shut the door. Do you want to poison me?'

'I can barely breathe!' Müller protested.

Pappenheim blew four perfect smoke rings at the nicotine-painted ceiling. 'I can.'

Müller gave a tolerant shake of his head. It was a familiar routine between them. 'You're impossible, Pappi.'

'You wouldn't want me any other way. So? How's Greville?'

'Looking fit.'

'But?'

'He thinks it will come any time soon,' Müller replied. 'He insists on cremation.'

'All things considered . . . best thing.'

Müller nodded. 'Under the circumstances, most definitely. There must be nothing for those bastards to get their hands on, no matter how remotely.'

'I second that. Does your aunt know?'

'Not yet.'

Pappenheim blew a single smoke ring, and watched it float to the ceiling. 'Rough.'

'He promised to tell her.'

'It's still rough.'

'Yes.'

'Seen the goth's car?'

Müller nodded. 'I think we've lost that argument.'

'Short of nailing her feet to the floor, we have.'

'How is she really?'

'According to our resident doc, she has the constitution of an ox. According to Berger, Reimer, even Klemp and, of course, my good self, she's off her tree.' Pappenheim grinned through his smoke, then shook his head in wonder. 'How someone so frail-looking could take a heavy calibre bullet near the heart and . . .' He paused as words temporarily failed him. 'The doc recommends a decent convalescent period. No one would object to her going on sick leave. But not our goth. She wants to be near the action. Specifically, she wants to give her all to the apple of her eye . . .'

'Don't you start on that.'

'She would die for you,' Pappenheim said without mercy. Cigarette clamped between his teeth, he gave another grin. 'And was prepared to do so when she took on Sharon Wilson, under the Moseltal autobahn bridge.'

'She saved our lives ... yours, Miss Bloomfield's, Berger's ...'

'And yours,' Pappenheim reminded him. 'We certainly owe her.'

'So if she wants to come in to work ...'

'Sharon Wilson couldn't stop her. We've got no chance.' Pappenheim grinned for a third time, shamelessly.

'I think I'd better get out of here before I begin to smell like a smoke factory.'

'Sticks and stones,' Pappenheim said without repentance. 'Sticks and stones. And your Friday will not be spoilt,' he went on. 'The Great White is not in residence, so he won't be hunting for you.'

'Aah ... *Polizeidirektor* Kaltendorf ...' Müller began.

'Probationary. Let's not forget that ...'

'Still probationary,' Müller corrected. 'What would my life be without him?'

'A life without bunions?' Pappenheim suggested.

'I can see you're in top form. I'll leave you to it and enjoy the small mercy of Kaltendorf's absence, while I can.'

'Jens,' Pappenheim began in a voice that had become serious as Müller turned to go.

Müller paused, waiting.

'When are you going to tell me about what you really found out there in Australia? And I'm not talking about all the killer information you picked up on the Semper.'

'In time, Pappi,' Müller said as he went out. 'In time.'

Pappenheim stared at the closed door, then stubbed out his cigarette in the already full ashtray on his cluttered desk.

'Yes,' he said to the door. 'But *when* exactly?'

In Washington, the un-named general was talking to three people in an office that was not at the Pentagon. One of them was a powerful woman in commerce, allied to the military.

'Is she going?' the woman asked.

'She was given an order. Of course she's going.'

'But will she find what we need?'

16

'It's anyone's guess,' the general answered. 'We have no firm indications. But it's all we do have. He is, after all, the man's son. If there is any link, it must be with him.'

'If he isn't killed first.'

'He has survived many attempts.'

'So far.'

'They got Sharon Wilson,' the hard-faced general reminded them. 'And as we all knew, Wilson was no pushover. One of the very best.'

'And flawed,' the woman said. 'She had a weakness that was her undoing.'

'We all have our weaknesses. Some are better at controlling them than most.

'Müller is very good at minimizing any weaknesses, or vulnerable flanks he may have. He knows how to protect himself,' the general continued. 'Colonel Bloomfield is an excellent shooter. If she stays close as ordered, she'll be of use to him in a tight corner.'

'While seeking to betray him.'

'It's a tough life.'

'Will she do it when the time comes?' one of the men began. 'Doesn't this . . . colonel have a reputation for doing things her own way? I remember her going against orders when she initiated that rescue attempt to save her brother.'

'Yes. She did. It has not been forgotten.'

'And you trust her to follow orders on this?'

'I trust no one,' the general said.

'Does that include – ' the woman glanced at her companions – 'us?'

'I trust no one,' the general repeated.

A long, and pointed silence descended.

Then the woman spoke again. 'Can we assume that you will be sending someone to keep an eye on her?'

The general gave her a look that was scathing. 'Don't try to teach me my job.'

She pursed her lips in disapproval.

The general gave her another hard look; this time, it was

one of contempt. 'It's a pity,' he went on, 'that Müller is so unreasonable.'

She would not let go. 'You sound as if you admire him.'

'Not "admire". I respect his capabilities. Many do. There's a difference. There is always more satisfaction in defeating a worthy opponent.'

'You see him as an enemy?'

'From where I'm standing . . . yes. Of course, everyone has a price.'

'Everyone?' She still would not let go.

'Everyone,' the general repeated coldly. His eyes stabbed at each of them. 'That includes all of you. That includes me.'

'Müller does not need money,' the woman said.

'Money,' the general said to her, the contempt naked in his eyes, 'is not the only price.'

Müller's office was the antithesis of Pappenheim's. It was a spacious, smokeless zone. Some items of modern furniture had been added at Müller's own expense. A wide and high curving window gave it an expansive view of the city.

A favourite routine of his every time he first entered the office for the day – or after some time away during the day itself – was to stand at the window, and look down upon the city. The curve of the huge glass panel gave him a substantial view both to the left, and to the right, enabling him to see almost along the entire length of the Friedrichstrasse.

He looked to his left, following the street to the junction where it crossed Unter-den-Linden, which disappeared between the buildings on its way towards the Brandenburg Gate. Müller tracked further left, following the wide boulevard in his mind's eye until he could actually see the quadriga atop the Gate itself. His office was at a level that enabled him to do so. It was, he reminded himself, a great view of a great city.

And it was his job to protect it from those who would threaten it. To him, that meant the Semper . . . the prime, current threat.

His continuing battle against the shadowy organization –

the invisible skeleton that had attached itself to the nation's very backbone – grew more vicious with every small victory he managed to secure. The biting irony was that at first he had been blissfully unaware of its existence . . . until he had been dragged into the nightmare by a distant cousin he had never known about, and who had been a rogue element within the organization. That cousin, Dahlberg, had once been a full colonel of police in the former DDR, with an Intelligence brief. Nursing a long-held familial grudge, Dahlberg had exceeded this brief to attempt a vengeance strike on Müller – for something which in his enraged mind he had held Müller guilty: simply for being a von Röhnen. By allowing his personal animosity to cloud his judgement, he had, apparently unwittingly, alerted Müller to the existence of the Semper.

But given what he now knew, Müller believed the entire thing had been a setup and Dahlberg, already out of favour with his masters, had been marked down for sacrifice if he failed in his attempt. Müller and Carey Bloomfield had killed him.

That had been Müller's first inkling, that something inimical existed within the nation's shadow; but something, he had begun to discover, that also went beyond the nation itself. Members of the Semper belonged to many nations.

And his father had been one.

Müller stared down at the city and let out a quiet sigh.

Müller had no idea at the time that for many years, his father had carried extremely high rank within the organization. It was only much later that he had begun to realize the dangerous life that his parents had led; that his father had in fact been a double agent, infiltrating both the Intelligence community of the DDR, and the Semper itself. Then somehow, he had been betrayed. The Semper had found out, and had taken a terrible revenge. Müller had then lost his parents in a mysterious plane crash, when he had been at the ripe old age of twelve.

The trauma had marked him, without his realizing it. For many years, he had accepted the crash as a shocking accident . . . until a dying Russian on Rügen had told him it had in fact been no accident, but murder.

This appalling piece of information had driven him into pursuing the Semper even more implacably. It had eventually led to his being pointed to the Hargreaves as prime informants by Grogan – who was still playing his own game – who had hidden themselves at Woonnalla, deep in the Outback of Western Australia.

But the Hargreaves had themselves given him the biggest shock of his life . . . the Hargreaves had turned out to be his supposedly long-dead parents. It had been no happy reunion, and very short-lived. This time, it appeared that the Semper had finally succeeded in taking their long-delayed revenge. He had been there to see it happen; to witness in person the second plane crash. In the beautiful sunset of Cape Leveque, he had watched their true death as the flaming pieces of the exploding Cessna 337 had showered down into the darkening ocean. With them had gone, after long years, the parents he had never really known.

Müller took a deep breath as he vividly remembered.

He had subsequently discovered that the Hargreaves had long expected him to turn up one day and had prepared extensively for such an eventuality. In a high-tech, secret bunker beneath the main house at Woonnalla, they had left him a dangerous inheritance, appropriately nicknamed Pandora's Box. In it was a treasure trove of highly devastating information about the Semper, incriminating many people across the globe. The seeds of its eventual destruction were planted there.

'And all in my hands now,' Müller said in a quiet voice to himself. 'And all the more dangerous if they ever found out.'

He hoped Carey Bloomfield would keep her promise not to divulge any details of the Woonnalla bunker to her own people. He trusted her not to.

She had seen the aircraft explode, and had accompanied him into the bunker. She had seen the rows of files stored there, along with the computer disks, all containing information on the Semper, and scrupulously collected over many years.

'I hope I don't live to regret it,' he muttered.

He had been handed a poisoned chalice; for one of the incriminated people was a man Pappenheim looked upon as a friend.

'I've got to tell him,' Müller said, talking to the city beneath him. 'And there'll never be a good time.' He went to his desk, and picked up one of the two phones. 'Time to talk, Pappi.'

'You sound as if I'm going to need a cigarette.'

'Not in here, you don't,' Müller said, forcing some humour into his voice.

'Ah. That air of strained levity. Now I know I do need a cigarette. I'll be with you right after.'

'All right.'

In his office, Pappenheim put the phone down, stared at it for some moments, then lit up a cigarette. He blew several smoke rings at the ceiling, in rapid succession. It was a measure of his agitation.

Jens and I have been friends and colleagues for years, he thought staring at the ceiling. *We watch each other's backs. So why do I feel like a boy on my way to see the headmaster?*

Despite his agitation, he took his time smoking the cigarette. At last, there was nothing left to smoke. As he stubbed out the dying end, his hand shook slightly.

He stared at it, as if it belonged to someone else.

So bad he has waited for two whole weeks before deciding to tell me? Must be a nasty surprise waiting.

He eased himself off his chair, brushed the specks of ash off his crumpled suit, and with a sense of foreboding, went out.

I hate nasty surprises, he considered. He sniffed at the smoke-free air of the corridor. *Poison.*

Two

'The Graf of the city, surveying his domain,' Pappenheim said to the Armani-clad Müller as he entered.

Müller, hands in pockets, was still looking at the Berlin cityscape. He gave Pappenheim a quick over-the-shoulder glance. 'You might want to sit down, Pappi.'

'Really that bad,' Pappenheim remarked as he approached. He stopped next to Müller, and studied the spread of buildings. 'I think I'd better stand. If I faint, you can catch me . . . if you can handle the weight.' His grin, unusual for him, was hesitant.

Müller was silent for a moment as they both looked out upon the city.

'My parents are dead,' he said at last.

Pappenheim stared at him, unsure of how to respond. 'Er . . .' he began, 'that's . . .'

'Old news?' Müller nodded, more to himself. 'I thought so too . . . for all those years.'

'Er,' Pappenheim repeated, somewhat urgently this time, 'I'll think I'll have that seat, after all.'

Pappenheim, a large man, was almost as tall as Müller, but because of his bulk, appeared shorter than he really was. Like many of his size, he was deceptively quick on his feet; something that had caught many a criminal by surprise. Expecting to be chased by a puffing, out-of-breath walrus they had frequently, to their eternal chagrin, discovered too late that they were within the grasp of his solid hands.

Pappenheim's clothes – unlike Müller's elegantly casual threads – were a nightmare to those looking upon them.

Crumpled as if he had slept in them for years, and ash-bespeckled, his dishevelled appearance inevitably led to wrong conclusions about him; something he aided and abetted shamelessly.

The perceptive would spot the incongruous, immaculate tie, always tastefully chosen; the hands that were remarkably unstained, given he was a chain smoker; but his eyes were the centrepiece of the camouflage. Conversely, Müller would never wear a tie, unless perhaps being forced to under torture. Not even Kaltendorf, a stickler for correct dress, could make him. Kaltendorf had been reduced to making pointed stares where the tie should be.

Pappenheim did not wear a tie because it was Kaltendorf's wish. If anything, he would probably have removed the tie, just for the fun of driving Kaltendorf mad. Baby blue eyes gazed out upon the world with apparent innocence. They were the prime weapons in his armoury. They were his fangs when he put a mind to it. When the eyes were at their most innocent, he was at his most dangerous.

He went to one of the two Italian-designed black chairs in the room, turned it towards Müller then lowered himself gingerly, as if afraid it would collapse beneath his weight.

Müller kept looking at the city as he continued to speak. 'I watched them die, Pappi . . . and it was my fault. I towed the people who killed them to where they were.'

Pappenheim gaped. He suddenly felt fidgety enough to rummage inside a jacket pocket. He touched the comforting shape of the crumpled, opened pack of his Gauloises blondes; but knew better than to take it out.

'You're thinking,' Müller went on, 'Jens has finally taken leave of his senses.'

'I wouldn't have put it quite like that. Not so flowery.'

'I've no doubt.' Müller would normally have smiled as he said this; but not today. 'Then you must assume Miss Bloomfield has also lost her mind. She was there. She saw it all.'

Pappenheim could not sit still. He got to his feet. 'Enough

of the riddles. How could you witness the deaths of people who have been dead since you were a kid?'

'No mystery . . . if the original "deaths" were faked.'

'*What?*' Pappenheim again joined Müller at the window. 'Your parents *faked* their deaths? Are you . . . ?'

'Mad . . . ?'

'I was going to say crazy.'

No, Pappi. Not crazy. Neither is Miss Bloomfield. Neither are Inspector Wishart of the Western Australian police; nor some of his colleagues who were also there . . . nor the other people who were there to see it happen.'

Pappenheim said nothing for long moments, staring at Müller as if he still believed his friend and colleague had really lost it. Then the implications sank in.

'Christ,' he said at last in a stunned, low voice.

'As well you might. They had received forewarning of the plot to have them killed,' Müller went on. 'They behaved as if they had no knowledge of it. They allowed the plan to go through. They even boarded the plane and flew off. They aimed the plane for the mountain – perhaps on autopilot – and jumped. I'm not sure of it all . . . just piecing things together from what I found at Woonnalla.' He made a noise that could have been a short laugh. It did not sound like it. 'Who would have imagined my mother knew how to make a halo jump?'

'High altitude, low opening . . .' Pappenheim said, as if in a dream.

Müller nodded. 'My father, given what he was doing, would have been trained. He must have trained my mother. That must have been done when they went off on flights without me. They must have gone where she could be taught in secret, perhaps at a military base, anywhere within NATO. Plenty of choices.'

'But the bodies that were found?'

'In many small pieces, and burnt out of all recognition. DNA investigation was not yet the norm in those days. The bodies were assumed to be theirs . . .'

'So whose?'

24

'Two Stasi agents working for the Semper. They were the ones ordered to do the job of sabotaging the plane. My father allowed them to do it, then caught them . . .'

'You mean killed them.'

'Yes. The bodies that were found belonged to them. As for the flight recorders . . . as you know, the Semper planted the false ones that were eventually retrieved, complete with the supposed recording of my screaming mother as she deliberately crashed the plane.'

'But the sudden disappearance of those agents?'

'Was taken care of. My father – in his capacity as a supposed Stasi senior officer – had prepared a report with a fake signature, showing that the agents – a couple – had died on a mission in the West. The Stasi agents were freelancers. The Semper would not have cared about them. Money was paid, and as far as they were concerned, the job was done. The fact that they died on an official mission was a bonus for the Semper. Matter effectively closed. Mouths shut for good. Perfect solution . . . and my father knew that was how it would be seen.'

'Thorough man.'

'He had to be, given what he was really up to. He was up against an implacable enemy. His survival instincts had to be extremely sharp. The shock of my sudden appearance at Woonnalla – even though they seemed to have been expecting me to turn up one day – must have dulled them long enough to his . . . and . . . and my mother's, eventual cost.'

The stunned Pappenheim, unsure of how to react to what he'd just heard, eventually said, 'So . . . who were they? Who were the people they became?'

'If you were to ask me who my parents were, I'd have to answer I never knew. If you're asking about who they were when I last saw them . . .'

Müller stopped, and at last turned to look at Pappenheim.

Pappenheim was shaken to see the measure of the haunted look in Müller's eyes. Something deep down inside seemed to be screaming.

'I think you may have already guessed,' Müller said.

'You mentioned Wishart, and Western Australia. You can't mean the Hargreaves . . .'

'I do mean the Hargreaves. They had created their own little Eden out there, deep in the Outback. A very successful, large spread with eco produce – vegetables, fruit, flowers – seeming for all the world like grown-up, rich hippies. All the while, they had another life . . . still fighting the Semper.'

'Grogan pointed you to them . . .'

'Our Russian-American . . . or American-Russian when it suits him, has been our unexpected, mysterious benefactor from time to time. He knew all about the Hargreaves. Miss Bloomfield suggested that my . . . the Hargreaves may have engineered the pointing. I tend to agree. All that remarkable, detailed information we found, comes from a bunker hidden beneath the main house at Woonnalla. Years and years of data on the Semper.'

'The goth and I did wonder when you started sending some of that through, where you could have found all that stuff.'

'Well . . . I got the sources killed . . .'

'No you didn't, Jens,' Pappenheim said without mercy. 'What happened was *not* your fault. How could you possibly have known?'

'Pappi . . . I turned my back on them. I was so shocked and angry, I behaved like a spoilt child. I could only think of how they had betrayed me; how they had left a boy of twelve . . .'

'Stop the tape. I'm not going to let you do this to yourself. You're a police *Hauptkommissar*. You followed a lead. You had no idea what was waiting down there . . .'

'I led the killers to them!'

'Rewind the tape,' Pappenheim said. 'Did the Semper *know* these people were your parents?'

'No. I'm certain of it. They intended to kill off what they thought were potential witnesses . . .'

'Exactly. I'm not saying that the lives of witnesses are any less important; but for the sake of the argument . . . you could say you may have inadvertently led the killer, or killers, to a pair of witnesses. *Not* to your parents!'

'Inadvertently.' Müller spoke with unforgiving bitterness. 'Nice way of putting it. This spares me nothing, Pappi. You did not see my mother's face as I turned my back on her,' Müller continued in a voice that was a wrenched groan. 'My father followed me. He talked. He began to explain why they had done it . . . to continue the fight against the Semper, of course . . . but mainly, to protect me. I did not even turn to look at him. He gave up, and walked away. Then I heard the plane take off some time after. Then came the explosion and . . . and I watched it fall in flaming pieces . . .' Müller tapped at his temple briefly. 'You have no idea what's sitting in here, Pappi. And it keeps playing, over and over . . .'

'I won't even try to imagine. I cannot begin to understand. I can only offer what you already know . . . my support, my backup . . . any time. Without limit.'

'I know, Pappi. I know. And I thank you for it.' Müller paused, nodded to himself, coming to a decision. 'But now comes the hard part.'

Pappenheim stared at him. 'There's something worse than what you've just told me?'

'For you . . . yes.' Müller sounded reluctant to continue.

'Do I need to sit down again?'

'You may need a smoke.'

'In *here*?'

'Given the circumstances, I might even consider it.'

Pappenheim's expression said it all. 'God. It must be bad.'

'There's not a good way to tell you,' Müller began, then went on quickly before Pappenheim could say anything, 'and there never will be. It looks . . .' He paused, as if uncertain whether to continue. 'It looks more and more likely that the person who put the killers on our trail – Mainauer, the three on the Great Northern Highway, even Sharon Wilson – was your friend Waldron . . .'

'*What?*' It was virtually a shout of disbelief.

'I am very sorry, Pappi. But Waldron *is* Semper. His name

27

is on the list of members we sent from the bunker at Woonnalla. There's so much information, I assumed you would not have seen this particular item as yet. I had hoped,' Müller went on, 'that perhaps there had been some mistake; but the Hargreaves were so thorough.' Müller paused again. 'And given all that we now know about them, the . . . Hargreaves would not have made such a fundamental mistake. Waldron is a second-generation member. His father is one.'

Unable to counter this, Pappenheim was silent for more than a minute. His eyes stared into nothing.

He was remembering two students in London, each travelling with the girlfriend he would one day marry.

He remembered how he'd first met Waldron, then a young Australian doing the European tour in his VW camper van, which he had parked in a back street near the Festival Hall on the South Bank. He remembered stopping in his dilapidated Beetle to help fix the camper van's engine.

He remembered the friendship that had sprung from that chance encounter and how after an evening of serious drinking, both couples had gone for a walk along the Thames. He remembered how Waldron, much the worse for wear, had begun pretending to walk along a straight line, and had fallen into the river. He remembered jumping in without a second thought, to haul Waldron out.

The river had been fast-flowing and with both men fully clothed, they were soon being weighted down by the water. But Pappenheim had gained a desperate strength and with the women screaming for non-existent help from the few passersby, he had somehow managed to cheat the Thames of two bodies that night.

Pappenheim at last drew in a deep breath, and let it out slowly. 'To think I saved that bastard's life.'

This was said in such a conversational tone that Müller peered at Pappenheim, half-expecting to see a smile. Then he saw the look in the baby blue eyes.

'You know,' Pappenheim continued in the same conversational tone, 'I can't remember the last time I took a proper holiday. With all the time I've accumulated, this might be a good moment to take one. Travel far, stay for a while. I could throw him into the Swan . . . let it finish what the Thames started.'

'That would be clever,' Müller said. 'Then the WA police would arrest you for drowning one of their citizens . . . the Semper would know we found their man out . . . and would immediately shift into high gear to discover just how we did find out. At one stroke, we lose our advantage.'

'Do you always have to be so . . . logical? Don't you ever have a rush of blood?'

'You ought to know better than most, Pappi. I have my rushes. I . . . control them . . . sometimes.'

'I'd hate to be around when you do blow. On the other hand, it might be interesting to watch. You've got a pressure cooker in there, waiting to go off . . .'

'So?' Müller said, deliberately interrupting. 'Are you going to head out to Australia? I could order you not to. But I won't.'

Pappenheim fell silent once more. Then said, 'I want to feel my hands around the bastard's throat.'

'So do I. He pointed the killers to my . . . parents. I want him just as badly. But I want more than that. A lot more. You were just telling me off for not thinking straight. Now it's my turn. So?' Müller repeated. 'Are you going?'

'Of course not,' Pappenheim growled after another pause. 'What do you think? But when we get to see him again . . .'

'We will. That's a promise.'

'Then I want first shot.'

'Let's tear him to pieces together.'

'That is an offer I won't refuse. I'm enjoying the image.'

'Red in tooth and claw?'

'Oh, yes.'

'Then let's do it the smart way. Let's use him, and rip him into little pieces, bit by bit. The means of destroying a person comes in many guises.'

Pappenheim stared at him, as if seeing him anew. 'What do you do when you're really angry?'

'I'm angelic.'

'Of course. Why didn't I think of that?'

About an hour after Pappenheim had returned to his office to mull over what Müller had told him about Waldron, he was still sitting back in his chair, blowing smoke rings at the ceiling. Both his phones had rung on at least four occasions each.

He had chosen to ignore them.

Angelic, he thought, remembering what Müller had said. *But what kind of angel?*

An insistent tone again interrupted his musings. It was the internal phone. No extension light was showing; so that meant the switchboard for unsecured external calls, which was manned by civilian staff.

'Leave me alone!' he snapped, glaring at it, but making no move to pick it up.

The phone kept ringing. There was a persistence to it that was at once annoying, and commanding. Pick me up *now*, it seemed to be saying.

Pappenheim picked it up mid-ring. '*What!*' he barked.

There was a brief, affronted silence. 'Why are you biting my head off, *Herr Oberkommissar*?'

'Ah . . .' Pappenheim began.

'You don't know who I am, do you?' The affronted voice now carried a hint of peevishness.

Somewhat taken aback, Pappenheim said, 'Of course I do . . . er . . .'

'Krista,' came the frosty reply. 'I took over this shift from Mahrenius who is on maternity leave. I've been doing this for *six* months.' It was an accusation.

'Ah . . . yes . . .'

'I've called you *four* times.' This time the voice was in perfect imitation of the reproach of a scolding nanny.

God, Pappenheim thought, glancing imploringly at the ceiling. Where did they find this one?

'I was not in my office,' he lied.

'Someone's been trying to reach you.' She did not sound as if she believed him. 'He spoke English, but not with a British accent. Not American, either. Not Canadian . . . I have a Canadian friend . . .'

'Krista . . .' Pappenheim interrupted in his smoothest voice when what he really wanted to do was shout at her. 'Before you take me on a tour of the entire English-speaking world, why not just tell me who?'

'I'm coming to that!' Her voice was starting an ice age of its own. 'Here's his number.' She passed it on.

Pappenheim stared at it when he'd written it down.

'He didn't give me the country code,' Krista went on as the icicles continued to form. 'Strange. I expect you know where he's from.'

'He doesn't need to. This is a Berlin number.'

'Oh!'

'Now Krista, if it's not too much trouble, the name would be nice to have.'

'Oh! Yes. Waldon, it sounded like.'

Despite being caught completely off guard, Pappenheim did not bat an eye.

'Waldon,' Pappenheim corrected. 'And he's Australian.'

'Oh! But isn't it midnight over there?'

'Where he would normally be calling from, it's past that. But as this is a Berlin number, I think he has the same time as us.'

'No need to be sarcastic, *Herr Oberkommissar*!' She hung up.

Pappenheim put his own phone down slowly. 'Well, Nanny's just told you off, Pappi.'

But his mind was elsewhere as he stared once more at the number he had written down.

Speak of the devil, he thought. *Nice address.* What was Waldron doing in Berlin? he wondered. And just two weeks after the events. Was he on a fishing mission?

The number belonged to a luxury hotel on Unter-den-Linden. It was virtually at the Brandenburg Gate.

31

He smoked two cigarettes, taking his time about it. He did not call Müller to tell him about Waldron.

Pappenheim stubbed out the second cigarette with the deliberation of someone who had made up his mind about something.

He picked up the phone, pressed a button to bypass the switchboard, and dialled directly.

The phone at the other end rang just once, before being picked up. 'Waldron.'

'Blast from the past,' Pappenheim said. There was a bonhomie in his voice that completely masked his true feelings.

'*Pappi!*'

The shout was of such genuine pleasure, that Pappenheim briefly found himself doubting what Müller had told him. Then the policeman in him took over. He knew that Waldron would have to be an accomplished performer. It went with the territory. Besides, doubting Müller was a non-starter.

'Hello, you old drunk,' Pappenheim greeted in perfect English. 'Fallen into any rivers lately?'

Waldron's laugh echoed the pleasure with which he had responded to Pappenheim's first words.

'Keeping away from them, mate,' Waldron said. 'At least, those with crocs swimming around.' He gave another short laugh.

'Wise. Very wise. What brings you to Berlin?'

'Diplo business. But thought . . . why not take some time to see my old mate and saviour, Pappi?'

'Flattery will get you everywhere.'

They both laughed.

'Well?' Waldron said. 'Slaving at the office? Or can you escape for a drink or two, then dinner? On me, of course.'

'As you're paying, I can definitely escape.'

They laughed again.

'I'm not far from where you are.'

'I know.'

'How about an hour from now?'

'I'll be there.'

As they hung up, Pappenheim favoured the phone with a baleful look, thinking that though the Spree was not the Thames nor the Swan, and it didn't have crocodiles, each river has its own special qualities and would do just as well.

He lit up, and blew a stream of smoke at the ceiling.

Pull yourself together, he thought, as the swirls of smoke rose. *You're supposed to stop criminals, not be one.* He took another drag. *Even if, in this instance, it may be very hard.*

In Washington, at about the same time, the hard-faced general, a remote control in his right hand, was in a small room that was comprehensively fitted out with state-of-the-art surveillance equipment. There was just one other person with him. They were studying an image on a large, wall-mounted screen. It was a head shot of Müller.

'Müller,' the general said. '*Hauptkommissar*, special police unit, Berlin. Very good at his job. Unconventional. Study that face well, until you can see it in your dreams . . . or nightmares.' He touched a button on the remote with his thumb, and the image zoomed out to full length.

'A girlie with an earring and ponytail, in a fancy suit.' The general's companion was disdainful.

The general said nothing, but his face stiffened. He did not look at the speaker. Instead, he touched another button on the remote. An image of Pappenheim, eternal cigarette in hand, joined Müller's.

'A fat slob with a cigarette,' the other said, still disdainful. 'Those are the two jokers I'm up against?' He sounded as if he wanted to laugh.

The general still did not react.

'They are supposed to be routinely armed,' he went on, as if to an exceptionally dim class of students, 'but it is known that they sometimes choose not to carry their weapons. However, I would advise you not to bet your life on it. They both use non-standard issue automatics. They have a taste for the Beretta 92R . . .'

'Cosy.'

The general ignored the interruption. He placed another image next to Müller and Pappenheim.

'*Nice*,' his companion said. 'Now *that*, I can . . .'

'Bloomfield,' the general cut in, 'Lieutenant-Colonel, US Air Force. Your mission. She also uses the Beretta.'

'What is this? Some kind of club?'

The general still continued to ignore the interruptions. A fourth image came onscreen. 'Kaltendorf, *Polizeidirektor*, and Müller and Pappenheim's immediate boss. No love lost between them and Kaltendorf. You can ignore Kaltendorf. He was a good cop once, but lost his nerve when someone got him cold – scaring the shit out of him – then let him live. Never quite got over it. He's a networker, more interested in keeping his nose clean and climbing up the ladder with the help of influential friends, leaving Müller and Pappenheim to do the dirty work. However, if they fall, he'll complete the job by stamping their faces in the dirt. He too has a 92R, but probably hasn't used it since the day his bowels turned to jelly.

'If you are under the mistaken impression,' the general continued, 'that you can take Müller and Pappenheim without breaking sweat if the situation demands, think again. Those two will nail your ass so fast, you won't see it coming. When they need to be, they are killers. And do not underestimate Bloomfield. She's good too.'

'If you're trying to impress me, you're failing.'

The general continued to keep a tight rein on his true feelings. 'Cars,' he said. Various shots of the Porsche Turbo were onscreen. 'Müller's. Bought and paid for by himself, but it is fitted with a communications suite, a police siren, and hidden flashing lights. If you give him cause to chase you – and I expect you not to – he can call up the cavalry in a heartbeat if he wants to, and have you nailed. Don't give him a reason.'

Pappenheim's BMW was next.

'Pappenheim drives this,' the general said. 'Appropriated.

The real owners will never ask for it to be returned.' He did not elaborate. 'Consider it a police car. It's got a mobile flashing light. And this . . . belongs to Colonel Bloomfield.'

Carey Bloomfield's classic red BMW M3 was now on the screen.

'A relatively old car,' the general continued, 'but in perfect condition. She won't, of course, have it in Europe; but study it well. Your mission begins as soon as you leave this building. All three cars are fast. The Porsche is obviously the fastest . . . by a large margin. It accelerates like shit under your shoe on a wet day. You won't catch him, and he'll catch you. If you need to, you'll have to trap him. It's the only way.'

'Of which there are many ways,' the man said.

'The secondary members of your interest group,' the general went on, ignoring the comment.

Three new images had appeared.

'That frail-looking young woman is Meyer, known to her colleagues as the goth. You can see why. She's an electronics genius. Her rank, *Meisterin* – that's sergeant to you . . .'

'I understand German.' It was not quite a censure, but it was close.

Yet again, the general chose to ignore the comment.

'She may *look* frail,' he continued, as if the other had not spoken, 'but she's tough. Splashed the last person – a pro killer like you – who went up against them. Two shots. One in the chest, one in the head. The pro, a woman, was one of the best. She underestimated the goth. Meyer is supposed to be carrying a torch for Müller. You may find that useful.

'Next, we have Berger, *Kommissarin*. She looks tough, and is. Look at those eyes. Beautiful, but don't let that fool you. Look again. Her eyes have been described as those of a hawk. You can also see why. She'll shoot you as soon as look at you. She has a thing for Pappenheim. No accounting for taste.

'Our last person in the team is Reimer. Last, but certainly not least. He looks as if he's never sure what planet he's on. Again, don't be fooled. Reimer is at least as good a shooter

as Berger, who is better than the goth. He has worked under-
cover. You two have something in common: he's a master at
fading into the background. These six are backed up by a
highly motivated and professional bunch of cops at their unit.
Understand what you'll be dealing with.'

The general then decided the moment had come for a
lesson. He switched off the display and turned to his
companion, a small, thin man with dead eyes, and a voice
that sounded like a croak. The thinness was hereditary. The
croak, courtesy of a bullet that had damaged his larynx. Apart
from the dead eyes, he was not remarkable to look at and
could blend into almost seamless invisibility, wherever he
happened to be. He used his inherited camouflage to
murderous effect.

'You come highly recommended . . .' the general began.

'I'm worth it—'

'*Don't* . . . interrupt me again.' The general's eyes appeared
to have even less life than his companion's. 'Underestimating
a potential adversary is a fatal flaw. I've tolerated your
apparent reckless over-confidence as a matter of respect for
those who recommended you. Don't prove them wrong. And
don't prove *me* mistaken for accepting that recommendation.
You foul up, and I'll be spitting blood – your blood – because
I'll be looking to have your ass nailed to a plate. I promise
you won't like that. You really would not enjoy having me
on your tail. And don't worry, I won't make the mistake of
underestimating you. I never underestimate even a fool.'

The dead eyes of the thin man looked back at the general,
and accepted the challenge.

The general placed the remote next to a computer keyboard.
'Run through the details you've just seen, as often as you
want. You've got your instructions. Do not exceed them.
Don't try to access anything else in here. You won't be able
to and worse for you, I'll know you tried.'

'Don't keep threatening me.'

'I never threaten,' the general said, and went out.

* * *

Face expressionless, Pappenheim took his shoulder harness out of a drawer and put it on with exaggerated care. He drew out the big 92R, checked it, then returned it to the holster. From the same drawer he took out a silencer, and put that into his jacket pocket.

He locked the drawer, then got to his feet. He was not smoking. He had still not told Müller about Waldron. He left the room, paused to pull the door quietly shut, glancing to his right at Müller's office as he did so.

Müller's door was closed.

Pappenheim did not attempt to check whether Müller was in. Instead, he hurried on silent feet to the lifts and entered one that was waiting, thankful that it was empty.

With a sibilant hum, the lift rushed at high speed downwards. It stopped at the ground floor. Pappenheim got out, and walked along the corridor to where the sergeant on duty sat at a bank of monitors, behind a raised counter. A wall of armoured glass went from counter to ceiling. To the left of the counter was a security door of solid steel, operated from where the sergeant was sitting.

Having heard the lift stop, he turned round to look.

'Eyes front, *Hauptmeister* Lötten.'

Klaus Lötten grinned. 'Taking a walk, are we? And where are we going?'

'*We* should not be so nosey, Klaus.'

'It's my job. I'm a policeman, just like you.'

'Imagine. What are you doing?'

Lötten had turned back to his console, and was writing something down in a large diary-like book.

'Logging you out . . .'

'*Logging* me . . . what are you talking about? Since when?'

'Since a few days ago. I log everyone who leaves this way.'

'And whose bright idea was that?'

'The—'

'Don't tell me. *Direktor* Kaltendorf.'

'Yes, Chief.'

'And what bright reason did he have?'

'He did not tell me personally. It came down from *Kommissar* Gatto. He handles things like that, as you know.'

'I know. Bet he was pleased.'

'He didn't sound it.'

'What a surprise,' Pappenheim said. 'What do you do when people go out via the garage?'

Lötten pointed to the monitors. 'The cameras . . .'

Pappenheim glanced about him, pointedly observing the small protrusions in the ceiling that looked like tiny, dead light bulbs. 'I think you've got cameras here too. Oh, look. There's me on that monitor.'

The sergeant looked aggrieved. 'What can I do? I've been told . . .'

'Ah, orders. The bane of humanity. Let me out of Kaltendorf's madhouse. I need some air.'

Lötten, looking worriedly at Pappenheim, pressed the button to release the door. It sighed open.

'Yes, Klaus. I know. I'm denigrating a senior officer in the presence of a subordinate.'

'I'm not worried about that, Chief. I'm worried about you.'

'Thanks for the thought, Klaus,' Pappenheim said as he went out.

Lötten shook his head slowly as Pappenheim left the building.

'Was that the chief?' a voice said from behind.

Lötten jumped. 'Can't you people walk loudly?'

'Guilty conscience?' Berger grinned at him. 'So? Was that the chief I just saw?'

'How many big men in crumpled suits do we have?'

'Watch your tongue, or I'll nail it to the roof of your mouth.'

Lötten gave her a searching look. 'I wouldn't put it past you.'

'You know me too well. So? Where was he going?'

'I'll tell you what he told me . . .'

'Which is?'

'Don't be nosey. And pull all the rank you want. I can't tell you more.'

'Hey. This is me. Lene. I was a sergeant not so long ago. Why would I pull rank on you, Klaus?'

'Promotion sometimes affects people.'

'You've been mixing with the wrong ones.' Berger gave the main entrance, through which Pappenheim had just gone, a speculative look. 'Thanks, Klaus.'

'What for? I didn't give you any answers.'

'You did,' she said, and left him to it.

Lötten stared after her, then shook his head again. 'I'm just an ordinary sergeant,' he muttered to himself, turning back to his monitors.

Berger made her way up to Müller's office, and knocked.

'I'm in,' came his voice.

Berger poked her head through. 'Got a few minutes?' She stared at his desk. Files were spread out on it, and he was writing on a sheet of paper. 'You're *writing* reports?'

'Don't make it sound as if I never do.'

'You never do,' she said as she entered, 'if you can help it.'

He sighed. 'You're right. But I'm months behind. This is just to keep Kaltendorf off my back.'

'This building is full of reports. He doesn't need more from you. He'd never be able to read them all in a . . . oh . . . thousand years?'

'What will you bet he'll always look for mine?'

'I don't gamble.'

'Hah.' Müller closed the files with relief, glad to be interrupted. 'So . . . what's exciting you?'

'Do you know where the chief is going?'

Müller was surprised. 'I didn't even know he'd gone out.'

'Well, that's a nice little mystery.'

'Can you break the code for me? I'm certain you're trying to tell me something.'

She gave him a sideways look. 'You know, don't you, boss?'

'No, Lene. I don't know.' He looked at her, waiting.

'He left by the main door. When Klaus Lötten asked where he was going, he told him not to be so nosey.'

Müller was thoughtful. 'Walking. How did he seem?'

'No idea. I only saw his back as he went out.'

'Perhaps he just fancied a walk.'

'You don't believe that. I don't believe that.'

'Is that your way of saying you would like to follow him? If so, it won't make him a happy man.'

'I'm worried about him.'

'You're always worried about him, Lene,' Müller told her gently. 'Everyone in this place knows it . . . even Kaltendorf, who normally has no time for anything that is not in his interest.'

'Perhaps he needs the distraction.'

'You said that. Not me. Why are you more worried than normal?'

'We spoke on the phone earlier. He just didn't sound like . . . well . . . the normal Pappi.'

Müller tried to make a joke of it. 'What's normal for Pappi can sometimes be abnormal for some. Just ask Kaltendorf.'

She did not smile.

'Woman's intuition?' he said at last.

'Don't knock it.'

'I'm not. My mother used to say . . .' Müller stopped, remembering Woonnalla. 'So? Are you going to follow Pappi?'

'Are you giving me the OK?'

'No,' Müller said. 'But if you have a *personal* interest . . . none of my business.'

'I'll do it.'

'He could be going anywhere. Berlin may not be as big as London, Paris, or New York, but it's big enough.'

But Berger had gone.

'Lene, Lene,' Müller said, looking at the closed door; then he stared with disgust at the files on his desk. 'You're right. They can wait. Back into the cupboard.'

He was about to get to his feet, when one of the phones rang.

He picked it up, glad of the distraction. 'Müller . . .'

'Mr Müller . . .' a familiar, American-accented voice greeted. 'I knew your parents . . . the Hargreaves . . . And don't worry. I know this phone is secure long enough for the time we need. Your secret is still safe from those who would like to know.'

'*You!* You called my home two weeks ago and left the first part of that same message on my machine. Who are you? And how did you get this number?'

'Beware of shadows. Time's up.'

The caller hung up.

Müller put the phone down slowly. 'So what was that about? Blackmail?'

The phone rang again. Müller picked it up, but did not speak.

'In case you're wondering,' the same caller said, 'this is not a blackmail attempt.'

The phone went dead once more.

Again, Müller put it down slowly. He stared at it, half expecting it to ring a third time. But it did not.

'If not blackmail,' he said to himself. 'Then what?'

Three

Pappenheim had turned left as he stepped outside and had begun walking up Friedrichstrasse, in the direction of Unter-den-Linden.

He did not hurry. He was as eager to get to the hotel where Waldron was staying, as he was reluctant. So he ambled along, delaying the moment when he would arrive there. It should take him about twenty minutes, he reasoned, at his current pace. Plenty of time to get his thoughts in order.

He did not smoke; which was a remarkable thing in itself.

Klemp and Reimer were in the sergeants' office. Reimer was busy writing something down, while Klemp was deeply engrossed in his usual reading fare.

The centrefold of his favourite fitness magazine displayed a strong-looking, well-built sports woman in a bikini. He turned the magazine this way and that, admiring the view.

'Hold it closer, Klemp,' came Berger's voice from the door. 'That way your eyes won't have so far to reach. Ease the strain before they fall out.'

Klemp shut the magazine with a guilty snap.

Before he could say anything, she said to Reimer, 'The chief say where he was going?' She entered the room, but seemed poised to leave again.

Reimer looked up. 'He's going somewhere?'

'Never mind.' She went out.

Reimer stared after her. 'What was that all about?' he asked no one in particular.

'I'll be glad when she gets her own bloody office,' Klemp remarked sourly. Then he snapped his magazine open with a smirk. 'What she needs is . . .'

'Shut it, Klemp!' Reimer said in a harsh voice.

'Hey! Don't talk to me like that. I outrank you!'

'Let's put it this way, Klemp,' Reimer said, spectacularly unintimidated. 'The chief walks by one day and hears one of your comments about Lene, your rank won't be worth shit. You'll find yourself doing foot patrols in Hamburg. St Pauli. He can arrange that faster than you can read through that rag of yours.'

Klemp grinned. 'He threatened you with that once, didn't he? St Pauli,' he said. 'The Reeperbahn . . . that wouldn't be so bad.' A dreamy look appeared on his face.

Reimer stared at him with pity. 'You're sick.'

'So what's new?'

Klemp returned like a deprived child to his magazine. He had barely begun to resume his study of the centrefold, when Berger returned.

Klemp again shut the magazine, this time with slow deliberation. Reimer chose not to look up.

Berger went to her desk, and picked up her phone. She pressed a button. 'Krista,' she began, 'have you spoken to *Oberkommissar* Pappenheim today?'

'Yes,' came the frosty reply. 'He was rude.'

'Was he? Why?'

'How should I know!'

Berger waited.

'I called him to give him a message, and he was rude to me.'

Knowing there was rudeness, then Krista's version of rudeness, Berger continued to wait.

'Someone from Australia rang him,' Krista continued with an I-know-something-you-don't air of triumph.

'That sounds interesting . . .'

'I gave him the Australian number to call, but he said it was a Berlin number.'

'Imagine that. Can I have it, please? Perhaps he's gone there. I've got to get a message to him.'

Krista passed on the number.

'I know that number,' Berger said to herself as she wrote it down.

'What?'

'Oh . . . nothing. Just talking to myself. Thanks, Krista.'

'Strange people,' Krista said as they hung up.

'You can talk,' Berger said.

She went out again.

Reimer looked at Klemp, who was looking at the departing Berger.

'Don't even think it,' Reimer said.

'Fuck you!' Klemp snarled, and went back to his magazine.

Reimer shook his head in pity.

On the left side of Unter-den-Linden, Pappenheim walked even more slowly as he approached the big, historic hotel.

He stopped, watching as a gleaming limousine pulled up at the entrance. A single passenger – a woman casually dressed in a manner that spelled wealth by someone with little need to impress – began to climb out. One of three hotel doormen in red coats swiftly arrived at the car without appearing to hurry, and held open the door. The other two hovered by, looking out for arriving guests.

'He was a little late,' Pappenheim muttered to himself as he observed the scene. 'Do I really want to go in there?'

The woman swept past the doorman with a nod that was at once courteous, and dismissive.

What it is to have money, Pappenheim thought drily.

He waited until the limo had whispered away, and the doorman was back at his post with his colleagues.

When he arrived, all three gave him the swift scrutiny of the accomplished professional, assessing his probable bank balance in fleeting seconds. Nothing of this was betrayed by their collective expressions as the one who had opened the car door turned to face Pappenheim.

'Yes, sir?' Politeness itself.

'My name is . . .'

'*Pappi!*' came an uninhibited shout. Waldron was almost bounding through. He grabbed Pappenheim's hand. 'I was waiting. Saw you arrive.' He looked at the doormen. 'No worries, mates,' he said in English. 'This guy's a most important person.'

The doorman with Pappenheim recovered with a swiftness born of years of practice. 'Of course, Mr Waldron,' he said in perfect English.

Waldron grinned at Pappenheim. 'Amazing, he is. He speaks four languages, fluently.'

'Five, sir,' the doorman corrected with a smile, 'if you count German.'

His colleagues allowed themselves the most polite of smiles.

'There you go,' Waldron said to Pappenheim. 'What did I tell you? My God, Pappi! After all these years! Come on, mate. I've got stuff coming up to the suite for us to kill while we catch up.'

Putting on a cheerful face, Pappenheim allowed himself to be ushered inside. The doorman even held the door open for him.

Berger drove up just in time to see Pappenheim entering the hotel. She parked the unmarked car on the opposite side of the wide thoroughfare at the entrance of a small crescent. She was certain that Pappenheim had not spotted her.

A patrol car was parked just a little way into the crescent. One of the two policemen inside the vehicle got out, and began walking towards Berger. His partner got out as well, but stayed with the car, hand on pistol.

'You can't park here . . .' the approaching officer began, then stopped as Berger got out. 'Oh,' he said. 'It's you.'

Surprised, she said, 'You *know* me?'

'You don't remember,' he said, looking disappointed.

'Er . . .'

'Last month. We spotted someone you were looking for.'

'Ah!' Berger said, remembering. 'Yes. Yes. That was good work. My chief was impressed.'

He beamed. 'Nice to be remembered by the stars.'

'I wouldn't go that far.'

'So?' It was eagerly said. 'Another chase?'

'Boring stuff. Just watching.'

'The hotel?'

'Now you know I can't answer that.'

'Of course. Of course. Well . . . if you need us.'

'As you're on the spot, so to speak, I'll definitely alert you if I need to.'

He beamed again. 'Anytime.'

He kept the beam as he hurried back to his colleague who in the meantime had removed his hand from his sidearm, when he had also recognized Berger.

It would happen, Berger thought as she got back in.

She looked towards the hotel. What, she wondered, was Pappenheim doing in there?

Pappenheim was admiring Waldron's suite.

'Bit different from a camper van,' he remarked with dry understatement.

'That it is,' Waldron said, smiling. He opened a bottle of chilled beer, and handed it to Pappenheim. 'Here, mate. Have nectar from Oz. They can get you anything here. I said I wanted Oz beer, I got Oz beer.'

'Handy being a diplomat.'

'It has its uses.' Waldron uncapped a beer for himself, clicked it against Pappenheim's. 'Cheers, mate. Really good to see you.' He gave Pappenheim an amused scrutiny after they'd had a swallow. 'You look just the same.'

'I doubt that. Older, and – ' Pappenheim patted his stomach – 'some extra girth.'

'Not that you'd notice.'

'Are you saying I was fat when we first met?'

Waldron grinned. 'Let's say you were . . . solid. Bloody good thing, too, or I wouldn't be here today.'

Pappenheim clinked bottles. 'I'll drink to that.'

'Amen,' Waldron said.

Outside, Berger was getting impatient. She decided to have a closer look, and got out of the car.

One of the patrolmen came up. 'Action?'

'Let's wait and see,' she said mysteriously.

'If you need us . . .'

'I'll call.'

'OK.'

She nodded at both of them, then crossed the wide avenue to the hotel. One of the three doormen approached as she reached it.

'May I be of service, madam?' he said in German.

She took out her ID. 'Berger, *Kommissarin*. Can you keep a confidence?'

'Of course, madam,' he responded, as if the question did not need to be asked. His colleagues kept a respectful distance.

'One of my colleagues, *Oberkommissar* Pappenheim, is visiting someone . . .'

'Ah yes. I remember. He is meeting one of our respected guests. They are friends . . .'

'That's the one,' Berger interrupted quickly. 'I need to speak with him.'

'No problem. My colleague here will take you to . . .'

Berger gave him her best smile, which could be devastating when she felt the need. 'No. I'll do that myself, thank you. Discretion.'

'Of course.'

'May I wait somewhere?'

'The lobby . . . or perhaps the summer terrace? You can have a coffee while you wait.'

Berger glanced at the hotel's open-air café/restaurant and decided to choose inside.

'The lobby, I think.'

'Very good, madam.' He held the door open for her.

* * *

47

There was a knock on the door to Waldron's suite.

'Ah!' Waldron said. 'Not only do they have Aussie beer, they've got some genuine Aussie crayfish. North Queensland. Up by Cape York. Hope you like shellfish.'

'Like it, but can't afford it like Jens.'

'Now I know you're pulling my leg,' Waldron said as he made for the door.

'Perhaps . . .'

The door opened to a white-jacketed member of the hotel staff pushing a laden trolley. Waldron directed him to a table seemingly big enough for a small banquet. He laid the table with expert speed and when everything was set to his liking, lifted the silver covers of the dishes with a flourish, and placed them on the trolley.

'Absolutely fantastic!' Waldron acclaimed in admiration.

The young man gave a wide smile. 'Thank you, sir!'

'I'm the one who should be thanking you,' Waldron said. 'My compliments to the chef.'

'Thank you, sir,' the hotel staffer repeated. The smile flashed back on as he went out, pushing his trolley.

Waldron shut the door. 'You look as if you're in a store with all the toys you've ever wanted.'

Pappenheim was staring at the table, dumbfounded. 'You call these monsters *crayfish*? They're bigger than any lobster I've ever seen. They're huge.'

'Cape York beauts, mate. They don't get bigger than these.' Waldron went up to the table. 'Fit for a king. Take a seat, Pappi. Let's tuck in.' He took one of two bottles of wine out of the chiller, and studied it with a critical eye. 'Yep. This should go down well, I reckon.'

As they ate, they talked about old times and reminisced about their time in London all those years ago, laughing as they remembered their antics, particularly their drunken swim in the Thames.

'Tell you, mate,' Waldron said, waving a giant crayfish leg at Pappenheim. 'I've said this to myself for years . . . without you that night, I was a goner. I shudder to think of it. I can never pay you back. Never.' He waved the leg at the room. 'I'd never be around to stay in a place like this. All due to you, Pappi.'

Pappenheim's baby blue eyes looked at Waldron, betraying nothing of the way he truly felt. 'You give me too much credit. I was drunk. I had no idea what I was doing.'

Waldron began to laugh. 'You certainly were drunk!' Pappenheim joined in as Waldron refilled their glasses, then raised his. 'A toast to drunkenness.'

Pappenheim did likewise. 'To drunkenness . . .'

'Long may it reign!'

They drank, and continued to attack the crayfish.

After having eaten as much as he could, Pappenheim said, 'I think I need . . .'

'The dunny?' Waldron waved a vague hand. 'Over there. It's big enough to fetch a great price as an apartment in London. Don't get lost.' He giggled.

Pappenheim, keeping to the game, smiled as he got to his feet. 'Won't be long.'

'No worries, mate. Take the grand tour.' Waldron was still massacring the crayfish.

Pappenheim went into the bathroom, shut the door, and looked about him. Despite Waldron's joke, it was not a small bathroom.

'I see what you mean about a London flat,' he shouted through the door. 'If you swung a cat in here, it would suffer agoraphobia.'

Waldron's laugh came back at him. 'Told you!'

Pappenheim had no need of the bathroom and despite the show for Waldron, was coldly sober. He had kept his jacket on throughout and now, he drew his pistol from its holster, reached into a side pocket and took out the silencer he had brought with him. Very deliberately, he attached it to the gun.

'Show time,' he said quietly through tightened lips.

He flushed the toilet then ran the tap long enough for effect, before opening the door.

Waldron had finished with the crayfish, and was in the act

of raising his glass. He paused. 'Funny thing, Pappi,' he said without looking round. 'You haven't smoked. Given up the weed at last?' He took a drink.

'And deprive myself of one of my pleasures?'

'Then why . . .' Waldron paused once more, and slowly put his glass down. 'Something in your voice. What's wro . . . ?' He turned to look, and saw the silenced gun. His eyes widened to their limit. '*Jeezus, Pappi!* That's not funny!'

'It isn't meant to be.'

'What the hell's going on?'

'That's what I'd like you to tell me, *mate*.' Pappenheim used an exaggerated Australian accent on the word.

'Jesus!' Waldron repeated. 'What the hell are you talking about?' He stared at Pappenheim, clearly believing his friend of many years had suddenly gone mad.

'As I've said, why don't *you* tell me? Why have they sent you?'

'*They?* Who the hell's "they"?'

Pappenheim's baby blues had a coldness in them that even those who knew the chill that could sometimes reside there, would have been startled to see.

'What I would like to do, *mate*,' he said, 'is give your head a close acquaintance with every wall in this suite and afterwards, shoot you. But your brain would not be in a state fit to be used, and your body would not be functioning either. Unfortunately, I need both brain and body in working order. For now.'

'Is this one of your crazy jokes? If so, pack it in, mate. Sit down and let's finish . . .'

'I never point a gun at people as a joke.'

Waldron now stared at Pappenheim in a mixture of confusion, and growing unease. 'Jesus, Pappi.'

'And you can stop calling me that. It's reserved for people I like.'

'For God's sake . . . you saved my life . . .'

'And I'm regretting it by the second. Some people, worth a lot more than you, would still be alive if I had let you drown that night. Why did the Semper send you?' Pappenheim fired off the question without warning. 'To find out what we know?'

'You're not making any sense! What the fuck's the Semper?'

Pappenheim's smile was frightening. 'Feigning ignorance. That's good. But it's not going to help you, Waldron.'

'It's *Waldron* now? What . . .'

'Shut the fuck up and *listen!*' Pappenheim cut in with unexpected savagery. 'I sent Jens Müller and Colonel Bloomfield to you in Australia, because I *trusted* you. But important witnesses they were going to interview ended up dead. A sniper magically trails them right to the home of the witnesses. An unsuspecting Oz policeman ends up being shot dead at point-blank range. Three men ambush Jens and Miss Bloomfield on the Great Northern Highway. By rights, they should have died there. Only their own skills saved them. No matter how often I run this through, I come up with the same thing: you. You are the only person who could have given Jens and Miss Bloomfield away, and whose information caused the deaths of the Hargreaves, blown up in their own plane.'

Waldron was staring open-mouthed. 'Jesus!' he said at last. 'You *are* crazy. If not for that gun, I'd think I'm in a nightmare . . .'

'You are in a nightmare. But you're not dreaming.'

Pappenheim suddenly began to remove the silencer, while Waldron continued to stare at the gun, mesmerized. Pappenheim put both gun and silencer away.

'Do you know,' Pappenheim began, not looking at Waldron. 'When we had that call after Jens first arrived in Perth, I remember putting the phone down and thinking – I hope Pete isn't dirty. I thought that would shatter what few remaining illusions I have about people. Congratulations. You've just shattered a few more of my fading supply. So tell you what . . . we'll just let it be known to the Semper that you talked to us. That won't be hard to do. Let's see how they respond.' He began to leave. 'Thanks for the meal. Nice crayfish. Really good. But right now, I need a smoke. Gasping.'

51

He was at the door when Waldron said, 'Wait!'

But Pappenheim opened the door. 'Don't leave the planet just yet, will you? You need to talk to me.'

He went out, and closed the door on Waldron.

'Sweat, you bastard,' Pappenheim muttered as he walked along the richly carpeted corridor.

A minute or so later he was heading down the horseshoe marble staircase to the lobby, when he saw a guilty-looking Berger rising to her feet.

'What are you doing here, Berger?' he asked in an urgent low voice when he reached her.

Her look was now one of uncertainty. 'I . . . was worried.'

He kept walking. 'About what?'

She trailed hastily behind. 'You!' she hissed.

He said nothing to that, and continued, without pause, towards the entrance.

A blonde with a wide smile that said the world should recognize her swept through, eyes seeing no one.

'*Scheisse!*' Berger observed under her breath. It was definitely not complimentary. 'Look at that.'

Pappenheim went past the blonde without looking. The eyes that saw nothing somehow managed to detect the apparent slight. She gave Pappenheim a cutting look as she swept on.

Berger observed Pappenheim's behaviour with something akin to a sense of pride. She gave the doorman one of her best smiles as he held the door open for her.

Pappenheim finally decided to speak when they were out of earshot. 'Did you walk, or come by car?'

'Car. It's across the road.' She pointed.

'Ah. And who's the admiration society staring your way?'

'The two colleagues who spotted that "stolen" BMW—'

'That Sharon Wilson was driving some weeks ago?'

'That's them. They're hoping we've got something more to pass their way. They seem to think we're some special unit.'

'Imagine that. Well, they're out of luck today.'

The patrolmen were grinning expectantly.

'*Herr Oberkommissar*,' one began in greeting.

Pappenheim nodded at them. 'My colleague tells me you are the two from the last time.'

They looked eager. 'Yes, sir,' the one who had spoken replied.

Pappenheim seemed to pause for thought. 'Tell you what. Keep an eye on the hotel entrance. A tall blonde you might like might come from there. Take note of anyone she may be with.' Pappenheim handed over a card. 'Call this number with a description of her escort.'

'Yes, sir!'

'How long can you stay?'

'We're on routine patrol, so it's flexible.'

'If you're called to an incident, call the number. I'll fix it so you can stay here on watch.'

The patrolmen liked that. 'Yes, *sir*!' the speaker enthused.

When Pappenheim and Berger were on their way back, Berger said, 'I thought you said . . .'

'I changed my mind.'

'I thought only women were supposed to do that.'

'You've been reading the wrong books.'

A silence fell in the car, then Berger continued, 'So you didn't shoot him.'

'Shoot whom?'

'Come on, Chief. This is Lene you're talking to.'

'Why would I want to shoot him?'

'You tell me.'

Pappenheim said nothing for some minutes.

'It was close,' he admitted eventually.

He added nothing further.

Waldron was surveying the remains of the crayfish when three sharp knocks in rapid succession sounded like a drum roll on the door.

He knew who it was. He rose to his feet, and went to admit his visitor.

The blonde that Pappenheim and Berger had seen, stood there. The hello smile was gone. Very dark eyes looked at Waldron.

'You just missed . . .' Waldron began.

'I just saw him,' she corrected, entering. 'I only came up because I saw him leave. Any luck?' she added, surveying the debris of the meal critically.

She went over to the table, spotted untouched crayfish legs, ripped one off, then bit into it. Her teeth clamped upon it with the sound of the snap of a predator cracking bone. She crunched into the leg, chewed on it, then spat the shards of shell on to an empty plate. She continued eating.

Waldron shut the door, and looked at her with open curiosity. 'How do you do that? Your mouth must be full of bits of that shell.'

She shook her head. 'Nope. No shell. Just the flesh. I've got an acrobatic tongue . . . as you know.' Finished with the leg, she grabbed another. The crunching sound came again.

Waldron gave an expressive shudder. 'Jesus.'

She seemed to crunch and grin at the same time, spitting out the shell residue then continuing to eat as before.

She swallowed the crayfish meat. 'Good, that.' She was English, the accent of an educated southern counties woman. 'So? Any luck?'

Fully recovered for the moment from Pappenheim's bombshell, Waldron lied smoothly. 'Early days. This meal was a softener.'

The dark eyes were pools of obsidian as they looked at him. Waldron got the uneasy feeling that he was being studied by an implacable and ferocious reptile.

'Was it worth it? Will he say anything of use to us?'

'He's an old mate. He . . .'

'Saved your life. We know all that . . . which is why you were so well placed to . . .' She smiled. 'Betray his trust.'

'Now steady on . . .'

The implacable eyes pinned him. 'It's true, isn't it?'

'I have one loyalty,' Waldron said with the right amount of outrage.

'And you've already proved it in a way that leaves no doubt. After all, it's all in the family, isn't it? Son of the

54

father . . . generations of membership.' She ripped off a third leg of Pappenheim's crayfish.

Snap. Crunch-crunch.

'Do you have to eat it like that?' Waldron asked.

The beautiful mouth smiled, the reptile eyes did not. 'As nature intended. Is there another way?' She crunched some more, then went into the familiar spitting routine. She wiped at her mouth with the back of a hand. 'Mmmm. That was good. Can we start betraying your wife now? I can finish off the rest of the legs later.' She looked at a glass, still containing wine. 'Yours? Or his?'

'Mine.'

She picked up the glass, and emptied it in a single swallow. She put the empty glass down, and the dark eyes seemed to grow huge. 'I'm hungry. You know what that means.' She glanced at the bedroom, then the bathroom. 'Bathroom first.' She then gave the destroyed crayfish another glance. 'This really worked up my appetite.'

The reptile eyes brooked no resistance as she explored her lips with her tongue.

Waldron was not about to offer any. He never had; from the first time they had met at a small Semper gathering in the States, two years before. His father had made the introduction.

An hour later Pappenheim, cheerfully polluting his lungs, picked up his phone at the first ring.

'Pappenheim.'

'Er, sir, *Hauptmeister* Walde, Brandenburg Gate. You wanted to know . . .'

Pappenheim killed the cigarette as he straightened in his chair. 'You've seen her?'

'Just came out. She is very . . .'

'She is something,' Pappenheim interrupted, hearing the excitement in the patrolman's voice. 'Anyone with her?'

'Yes, sir.'

He gave Pappenheim a detailed description of Waldron.

'Excellent,' Pappenheim commended, giving nothing away. 'Good work. Thank you.'

'A pleasure, sir. Any time you need us . . .'

'I'll know who to call. Thanks again.'

As they ended their conversation, Pappenheim leaned back in his chair, and stared at the smoke-stained ceiling.

Even to the bitter end. I was hoping against hope . . .

Pappenheim lit a fresh cigarette. *But hope is the last to die.*

He blew several smoke rings at the ceiling. *If I could have seen into the future, I would have let you drown that night*, he thought angrily.

He smoked the cigarette down until it was almost burning his fingers. He finally took it out of his mouth, looked at it with regret, then stubbed it out.

He picked up one of his phones. 'Miss Meyer,' he said as the goth answered. 'Can we meet in the Rogues Gallery? I won't keep you long. Say . . . ten minutes?'

'I'll be there,' she said.

They arrived at the armoured door with its keypad entry, at the same time.

The room it protected was atmosphere-controlled, and housed all of the unit's sensitive information – particularly on the Semper. Only Müller, Pappenheim, and Kaltendorf had unaccompanied, authorized access. Though Kaltendorf could enter the vast room, he did not have access to the Semper information that Müller had found at Woonnalla, and plenty more besides. As far as Müller was concerned, the jury was still out on Kaltendorf.

Pappenheim gave her a swift glance as he punched in the code on the keypad. The goth was dressed in ankle-length, diaphanous white, with sleek red trainers on her feet, and matching blood red fingernails. Her eye shadow was a pale blue, and her changeling eyes surveyed Pappenheim critically.

'Don't tell me,' he said. 'Your white period.'

'Wrong,' she told him. 'This is my red period. Fiery.'

'Er,' he said as the door hissed open to save him. 'Go in, shall we? How are you feeling?' he continued as he followed her. 'Not so long ago, I pushed you here in a wheelchair. Now you're walking as if the wheelchair never happened.'

'That was then,' she remarked as she went straight to the advanced, powerful computer at its console at the far side of the room. 'I'm a strong woman.'

The huge plasma monitor came alive as the machine got into its stride.

'Ready,' the goth said. 'What are we looking for?'

'It's not a "what".'

'I've got everything the boss found in Australia filed. Just give me a name.'

'Waldron,' Pappenheim said without emotion, hoping for information on the father of the man who had betrayed him.

The red-nailed fingers did their fleet work on the keyboard. 'Just look at that!' she exclaimed softly as the information appeared.

There was plenty of it.

Pappenheim stared at the screen, face still. ' "Sir Ralph Waldron",' he began to read, ' "born Surrey, England. Moved to Australia aged six, with parents. Sent back to England aged twelve for public school education . . ." ' Pappenheim paused. 'Public school in England means . . .' he started to explain.

'Private, elite school. I know.'

'You *know*?'

She glanced back at him. 'The boss went to one, before going on to Oxford and, of course, university here in Germany.'

'How do you know this?' Pappenheim was intrigued.

'Easy to find out, if one is interested. It's not a secret.'

'Of course.'

'Shall we continue?'

'Er . . . yes. Yes.' He continued to read but this time, silently. 'Knighted,' he said aloud after a while, 'for services to industry. Wonder whose political purse he contributed to?' he added with dry scepticism, before continuing to read.

'And now,' he said almost to himself, 'we come to the next generation. Like father, like son.'

He lapsed into another silence.

Fifteen minutes later, he said to Hedi Meyer, 'I've seen all I want to. Thank you, Hedi. You can close that file.'

She gave him a sympathetic look over a shoulder, noting the grim expression he wore. 'Sorry, sir.'

'Not as sorry as that bastard's going to be.'

The harshness of his tone was unlike anything she'd previously heard from him; and there was a cold implacability that did not promise anything good for Peter Waldron.

Pappenheim glanced at two items on either side of the keyboard that looked exactly like the sidestick and throttle of an F-16. They were a fixture now, and belonged to the goth who had a penchant for one of the most realistic jet fighter simulations around. Both Müller and Pappenheim indulged her, as a sort of payment for the electronic miracles she performed.

'If Hermann Spyros is not screaming for your services, have a flight. Kill some bogeys for me. Imagine Waldron is flying all of them.'

Spyros, *Kommissar*, of German-Greek descent and fondly dubbed by Pappenheim as 'our resident Greek', was the head of the unit's communications and electronics department. Good as Spyros was, he readily admitted that the goth left him standing.

Pappenheim went out, leaving her staring at the closing door.

'I would not like to be in your shoes, Mr Waldron,' she said as she turned back to the computer and launched her flying game.

Waldron was strolling in the vast grounds of the centuries-old baronial mansion just outside Berlin, where, the previous August, Müller and Pappenheim had encountered the retired general of the Bundeswehr, Armin Sternbach, for the first time. The mansion was owned by the general, which had led Pappenheim to voice his thoughts to Müller, on the question of where all the money had come from to pay for it, and for the living-in staff. The general's staff, despite their civilian attire, looked more like a small specialized unit that would be at home in an army. Indeed, many were ex-soldiers.

The original owners of the faithfully renovated building had chosen the location with an eye on defence. It nestled within a horseshoe of wooded high ground, but sufficiently far from it to allow a clear field of fire in that direction. An attack from that quarter would expose the attackers once they had left the screen of trees. The front of the building looked upon a wide vista of scrupulously attended gardens, dissected by a long, wide gravelly drive. The entire grounds were unobtrusively patrolled by Sternbach's hard-faced 'staff'.

Sternbach was high-ranking Semper.

'We are very pleased with you, Peter,' he said in perfect English to Waldron as they strolled along. 'It was excellent work.'

'Thank you,' Waldron said.

'No need to thank me. The praise is well-deserved. Your father and I go back a long way, Peter, and I look upon you almost as a son. I have watched you grow within our organization. I am impressed . . . as are many others.'

Waldron looked pleased. 'I try to do my best.'

'And you've done it well.' Sternbach gave Waldron's shoulder a fatherly pat. 'Thanks to you, we have deprived Müller of his valuable witnesses, before he could have learned anything from them. But as you know, we are not yet finished with that aspect of things. Who were the Hargreaves? We had no idea they existed. It was a secret well kept. But by whom? And who led Müller to them?'

'As I said in my original report,' Waldron said, 'Müller has managed to put a blanket on all information. Nothing about the Hargreaves is getting out – no stories, no photographs. There is an embargo on everything out there. Journalists are not even allowed to visit the Hargreaves' place at Woonnalla Station. There's a cordon sanitaire for miles around the area. The Aborigine brothers currently running the station have replaced the bombed plane and are flying patrols in co-operation with the local police. Anyone trying to get through will be stopped by the coppers, and Müller will know almost instantly after that. This state of affairs will continue, I suspect, until Müller decides to end it. So if we try to send anyone in for the foreseeable future, they'll definitely be caught.'

'Not what we want,' Sternbach admitted. 'Invisibility, as much as possible, has always been our watchword. There are times when necessarily obtrusive steps need to be taken and even then, we keep the matter as low-key as possible. It is not always so, naturally. Since Müller began poking his nose into our affairs, the obtrusiveness appears to have spiralled. He forces us to act in ways we would prefer not to.' Sternbach's voice grew hard with outrage. 'He even came to my home! He and that rough . . . forgive me. Pappenheim is your . . .'

'Friend. Yes.'

'Which is why you have been so uniquely placed, and why we need you to help us find out the truth about the Hargreaves. Much is at stake, Peter.'

'I know.' But Waldron was thinking of something quite different from the general.

'On another matter,' Sternbach was saying, 'but not so far removed. I have observed your relationship with Rachel over the last year or so. Some advice from a hopefully wiser head, Peter. You should be more careful. She is a highly attractive young woman, and I can understand your . . . interest. However, she is also one of our most accomplished killers. We have found over the years that our female assassins have been quite remarkably successful. Our organization will not look kindly upon any influence that might dim those successes.

'In the case of Rachel, she is like those who have gone before her, only better.

'*Anyone* with whom she may become involved will *always* take second place to the job. Mary-Ann was like that . . .' Sternbach paused. 'Mary-Ann,' he repeated softly. 'She was . . .' He stopped again, then continued. 'Then there was Sharon Wilson. Implacable. Brilliant. Ruthless. But she had a weakness we did not discover until too late. This weakness betrayed her in the end. Her sexual appetite finally got the better of her. Müller's people killed both Mary-Ann, and Sharon Wilson.'

Waldron said nothing.

'We choose our candidates well,' Sternbach continued. 'They are usually loners, for various reasons. No family, no attachments through estrangement, down and outs. Sharon Wilson had left home at fourteen. Rachel comes from a good family, but took to drugs and was thrown out. She was well on her way down when we found her, cured her of drugs permanently, gave her purpose. Today, doors open for her. She can be anything she chooses to be to the outside world. She has money, and she mixes easily with so-called high society. She has modelled for fashion houses, and is actually a very good singer. She has – in her own words – "jammed" with bands. All perfect cover for what she really does.

'The reason women assassins are so successful,' Sternbach continued, 'is because even today, their intended victims are always taken unawares. A man walking down an empty alleyway discovers he is being followed by another man. He is instantly on the alert. It is an instinct that goes back to the very dawn of man. Yet that same man, with all those survival instincts intact, seeing a woman following him will almost certainly be first wondering how good she might look and may even slow down for her to get close enough, so that he can check. This has actually happened to Rachel. The man in question never knew what hit him.

'Even a female target – unless she is in the, er . . . trade herself, is also usually guard-down to a female assassin. Again, if a man is following her, she instinctively thinks of a possible attack. With a woman follower, it is again different. Equally interesting is the fact that in each case, we lost Sharon Wilson and Mary-Ann to women. Colonel Bloomfield got Mary-Ann, and Müller's female colleague – someone who outwardly seems fragile – actually shot Sharon Wilson. Wilson had already shot this woman some time before and though hitting her, had not fired a killing round. The young woman in question eventually took her revenge. Wilson –

who should have known better – made a classic mistake. She underestimated her opponent.'

'What is this leading to, General?' Waldron asked.

Sternbach halted. Waldron stopped to turn to face him.

'Always remember, Peter. If for any reason Rachel were given the order to kill you, she would.'

Waldron looked at the general for long moments, in silence. 'And is that likely to happen?' he eventually asked.

Sternbach continued walking. 'No, no! I used that example to illustrate a point. She would kill *me*, just as easily. She is colder than either Mary-Ann, or Sharon Wilson could ever have been. Be warned. Her original name is not Rachel, of course. After we cleaned her up, she chose the name herself – Rachel Worth. I asked her why Rachel and why Worth. She only answered about Worth. She was now worth something, she said. Now let me show you my koi. Beautiful, expensive creatures.'

They walked on to a large and deep pond in which an astonishing number of ornamental carp went about their leisurely, pampered business. Some were very big, at least six comfortably passing ninety-five centimetres in length.

Waldron stared at them. 'These are huge! I've never seen carp this big.'

'They are special,' Sternbach admitted, pleased by the reaction. 'Frighteningly expensive. Look at them. Fat, complacent, lazily swimming their way through life, their every need catered for.' The general began to point to the larger ones. 'My specials: that gloriously golden beauty; or this stunning black and white jewel; or the red crest with its pure white body. All beautiful. But they are not my true favourites. That is reserved for this magnificent specimen.' The general pointed to the largest of the koi. This looked as if it were made of metal. Its skin was a mixture of gold streaks, steel blue, black patches, and a silver mantle-like pattern directly behind the head. 'Truly magnificent, and unique. Not another like it. Anywhere. This one alone would buy Müller's car.

'See these koi as the outside world. Now imagine a great

predator among them; a ferocious pike introduced in there. How long would they last? But in with the hunting pike is another, smaller, yet equally ferocious pike. It knows it cannot win in a straight competition against the bigger pike. However, it is not after the koi. *It is after the pike.* Its method is to attack its bigger adversary, taking bites here and there, and vanishing into the reeds. The big pike has two options: continue attacking the koi and risk continuing attrition until weakened . . . or, it turns from the koi for the time being to first save itself, and concentrates all its fury upon the smaller attacker.

'But there is a problem with that strategy. It allows the koi to recover. Valuable time is spent on eliminating the smaller pike. Unless it can defeat the smaller pike completely, it risks being weakened, defeated, and ends up losing the koi as well as its life. The solution? More big pike . . .'

'The Semper are the big pike,' Waldron said, 'and Müller the smaller.'

'Remarkable. You've not met Reindorf, have you?'

Taken off guard by the switch in subject, Waldron replied, 'No. Who . . . ?'

'Like me, Reindorf is ex-military. Colonel. We briefly served in the same unit. Reindorf is an absolutely sound man. The classic adjutant who knows where everything and everyone happens to be at a given time . . . and when to administer punishment of a permanent kind. His strength is that he does not look it. He runs this place, and commands the personnel. He does not live here as most of the others do, but has a home a few kilometres away. Last August, we were standing here, admiring the koi. I posed the same analogy. He came to the same conclusion as you have; but I had the feeling he did not quite agree with my conclusions.'

Waldron looked at Sternbach, and waited.

'I suggested that Müller would be swamped by the many bigger pike. Reindorf did not say out loud that he disagreed with my conclusion. It was all in his stance. Later, I thought about that. I decided that perhaps there was coinage in his apparent caution; that perhaps he was right to believe that

Müller had weaponry that would be as effective – if not more so – than several big pike. That was why you were instructed to act . . . and you were most successful.

'But now, we need to know what lay behind the Hargreaves, and how they came to have whatever knowledge Müller thought would be of sufficient use to him, to make him travel all the way to Australia in the first place . . . and more than once.' The general paused, his face tightening. 'We are not immune to infiltration. Müller stormed in here and I could do nothing. He carried the double signet rings of high rank within the Order. His father's. The Order dictates that sanctuary must be given to anyone legitimately carrying the insignia of rank. A father may pass this on to a son. It is the only level of rank where this is allowed. That man's father once held one of the highest ranks – higher than your own father's, or mine. He used his position to seek to destroy us. We responded in the only way possible. Müller was twelve at the time. He has a blood feud with us. He will not stop, unless he is stopped . . . like his parents. Until this is achieved, the fight will continue. Müller is actually a high member of the Semper . . . if only in name. He could, if he wished, demand to attend a meeting of the Council.'

'Would this be granted?'

'No. But he is free to demand it . . . as long as he holds the signets, which I am certain he has placed somewhere currently inaccessible.'

'Do you want me to try and find out?'

Sternbach shook his head. 'It will be difficult enough trying to learn about the Hargreaves without arousing suspicion. If the whereabouts of the insignia fall into your lap, then of course seize the opportunity. But do not waste any effort in overtly, or covertly, trying to find out.'

Waldron nodded. 'OK.'

Distant movement made them both look in its direction.

'And here she comes,' the general said. 'I was about to remark she is dressed to kill, but I believe she has other activities in mind. Remember my warning, Peter. She shares something with Wilson, and Mary-Ann . . . a DNA map that a female spider would recognize.'

Sternbach walked on, leaving Waldron to wait as Rachel approached.

'So?' she began, glancing in the direction Sternbach had taken. 'Was he talking about me?'

'What gives you that idea?' Waldron countered.

'I can tell,' she said, dark reptilian eyes probing.

'Only in passing,' Waldron admitted as lightly as he could.

'What's "in passing" exactly?' The eyes gave him a slanting look.

'He said you can sing,' Waldron sidestepped neatly.

She brightened in a sudden metamorphosis from searching predator, to the pleased receiver of an accolade. 'Did he, really?'

'He did. And can you?'

'Some people I've jammed with say I've got a good rock voice.'

'Perhaps you should record a few songs.'

'One day, I might.' She glanced to where the distant Sternbach was talking to someone who had just driven up in a steel grey Mercedes. 'Colonel Reindorf,' she explained.

'The general talked about him,' Waldron said, looking at the two men as Reindorf got out of his car.

'His right-hand man. Sometimes, I feel sorry for him.'

'Who? Reindorf? Or . . .'

'The general. He's never got over what happened to Mary-Ann. She was . . .' Rachel chose not to explain. 'I promised him I'd get the person who did it . . . and I will.' The mood changed again. 'Come on. Back to your hotel. I'm hungry. Let's have another session of betraying your wife. You're so good at it. I really like that.'

Her tongue darted out at him, then licked at her lips.

Four

Pappenheim picked up the phone at the first ring.

It was the keen patrolman. 'They've just got back, sir.'

'They as in the man and the woman?'

'Yes, sir. Same woman.' The patrolman sounded pleased he had been on station to spot Waldron and Rachel Worth's return. 'Should I wait to see what happens next?'

'No need. I have a feeling it will be a long wait.'

'I think I know what you mean, sir.' The policeman sounded as if he shared a secret with Pappenheim.

'No penalties for thinking.'

'No, *sir*!' the patrolman said, warming to whatever theme he thought was Pappenheim's.

Pappenheim turned his eyes briefly heavenwards. 'I think that will be it for today. And thank you again for your help. Much appreciated.'

'Thank *you* for giving us the opportunity, sir. Anytime you need us . . .'

'I know how to find you.'

'Thank you, sir.'

Pappenheim could almost see the other's grin of pleasure as the call ended. After a moment, he picked up the phone again and dialled.

'So many things I didn't know about you, Pete,' he said to the phone. 'How long have you been cheating on your wife?'

The phone began to ring in Waldron's suite.

Rachel was in the bedroom, stepping out of her knickers. She glanced at the extension on the bedside table, letting the

66

transparent underwear drop to the floor, still tethered to her left ankle. She was close enough to pick up the phone.

'Waldron suite?' she answered in a soft, warm voice.

'Er . . . can I speak to Pete Waldron, please?'

'You were surprised, weren't you?' she said, smiling. 'You called him Pete. Are you a friend?'

'A very old friend.'

She paused. 'Don't tell me . . . you're *Pappi*!'

At the other end, Pappenheim contained his astonishment with aplomb. 'You *know* about me?'

'Of course! Pete talks about you a lot. You're his big hero!'

'I am flattered. I never imagined . . .'

'Don't hide your light. He's told me about your saving him from the Thames.'

Pappenheim gave what sounded like an awkward little laugh. 'That old thing. That was years ago. Not sure I could do it again.'

'From what he's said about you, I'm sure you could.'

'You sound English. Known Pete long?'

'I am, and we met . . . oh . . . a couple of years ago on one of his diplomatic rounds. We're very good friends.'

'I see. Well, very pleased to talk with you . . .'

'Rachel.'

'Very pleased to talk with you Rachel.'

'And here's Pete.'

'Thank you.'

Waldron had come out of the bathroom, and was staring at her in horror. 'Are you crazy?' he mouthed at her.

She handed him the phone with a sweet, unrepentant smile.

'Sorry about that,' he said to Pappenheim in a normal voice when he had taken the phone from her. 'Was pointing Percy.' He gave an easy laugh, as if all were perfectly OK. 'See you've met Rachel.'

'She sounds very nice.'

'She is. Good friend.'

'We're both grown men, Pete. You don't have to explain anything . . .'

This threw Waldron slightly off balance. 'All above board, mate.'

'Of course.'

'Anyway, what can I do for you?'

'How about a coffee ... say in one hour? I'll pick the place.'

'Aah, not so sure I can make it, Pappi.'

'How about a coffee in one hour?' Pappenheim repeated firmly.

Waldron got the message. 'But I suppose I could just about manage it.'

'Good. I'll meet you outside the hotel. And don't bring Rachel.'

'You've got it, mate.' Waldron smiled at Rachel, giving no indication that his last words had been directed at a dead line.

'So?' she began. 'When are you going to meet him?'

'In about an hour.'

She had stepped fully out of her knickers which she now twirled round an upheld index finger.

'First instalment first.' She smiled.

The reptile eyes did not.

Pappenheim was waiting a little way from the hotel entrance, on Unter-den-Linden.

Pappenheim watched Waldron appear, speak briefly with one of the doormen, before turning his head, searching. Waldron saw him and came quickly over.

'No car?' he said as he came up.

'We're walking. It's not far – a hundred and fifty metres or so. Let's cross to the sunny side. The café's there.' Pappenheim gave Waldron a critical glance. 'Can you walk?'

A flush briefly darkened Waldron's cheeks as they crossed the wide boulevard, and began walking in the direction of Friedrichstrasse.

'Pappi ...'

'Save it. If you want to betray your wife as well, that's your business.'

'It's not what you think.'

'What I think about that does not matter.'

Waldron kept trying to explain. 'She's . . . she's one of them,' he said in desperation.

'*You're* one of them,' Pappenheim said coldly without looking at him.

'She's . . . she's one of their killers.'

Pappenheim stopped, and turned his baby blues on Waldron. 'Now *that* is interesting. Are you telling me the truth?'

'Yes.'

'You must enjoy living dangerously.'

'I've already been told she would turn on *me* . . . if ordered to.'

'And you still sleep with her? She must be something. Who gave you the smart warning?'

Waldron hesitated.

'This is no time to be coy,' Pappenheim said without mercy, and waited.

'Someone I saw earlier today. A man called Sternbach . . .'

Pappenheim gave Waldron a cold smile. 'Retired general. Small world.'

'He said he'd met you, and Müller.'

'I hope he said nice things about us. It was fun.' Pappenheim continued walking. 'You see? In less than a day, you've put some important pieces together for me. Definitely worth a coffee.'

'He asked me about the Hargreaves,' Waldron said, first trailing, then catching up.

'Did he now? What did he want to know?'

'Who they were. How much did you find out? What pointed you to them . . . or who?'

Pappenheim said nothing for several moments as they walked on.

'Poor Pete,' he said after a while. 'The Semper on one side, me on the other, and a killer in your bed.' The words were not spoken with sympathy. 'Life is hard. She must be worth it.'

'Worth,' Waldron said, wanting to say something. Anything.
'What?'

'Worth. She calls herself Rachel Worth.'

Pappenheim glanced at him. 'Is that a joke?'

Waldron shook his head. 'The truth. Not her real name. I don't know what it is. Sternbach simply said she calls herself Rachel Worth.'

'Why?'

Waldron explained.

'Very humanitarian, your organization,' Pappenheim remarked acidly. 'And here we are. I like this place. Hemingway once had coffee here.'

'Now that's a leg pull,' Waldron said.

'I'm not in a joking mood,' Pappenheim said, killing the smile that had begun to appear on Waldron's face.

They entered the long room that was the café. Its walls were adorned with large black and white photographs of Marilyn Monroe in a white dress.

Waldron stared at them. 'These look like the real things.'

'They are.'

'And that dress looks just like the one she wore in the movie she did with Tom Ewell . . .'

But Pappenheim was already moving to a table in an alcove-like space near the door. It was hidden from people entering, and gave a degree of privacy. There were no occupied tables nearby.

Pappenheim sat down as Waldron joined him.

A young woman came up as Waldron took his seat. She beamed at Pappenheim. 'The usual?'

'Yes, please.'

She looked at Waldron.

'I'll have what he's having,' he told her in perfect German.

She smiled at them both and went off to fill the order.

Pappenheim gave Waldron a sideways glance. 'Your German is a lot better than I remember,' he said, reverting to English. 'You've even got a touch of Bonn in there.'

'Not surprising. I did spend some uni time there, when it

was still the capital, and when my father was an active diplo. Must be how I picked it up.'

'Is that where they recruited you? Or was it like father, like son?'

'Sternbach told me Müller carries high rank in the Semper,' Waldron countered.

It was a mistake.

Pappenheim's eyes became frosty. 'I am forcing myself to remain civil. Don't you *ever* again attempt to equate yourself with Jens Müller!' he said in a biting putdown, his voice a sharp hiss. 'You are not remotely comparable. If I were to contemplate too long upon the reasons that have brought us here to this café, you'd be a dead man, and they'd be hauling me off to jail. So don't try me.' He looked up, smiling, as the young woman brought two tall cups of coffee. 'Ah,' he said to her. 'Perfect as usual.'

She gave him another beam and left them to it.

'You'll really like this,' he said to Waldron, as if the hostility in his voice had never been. 'Now tell me about Rachel Worth.'

Waldron, subdued, stared at his coffee, before sugaring it, and taking a sip. 'Hey,' he said in pleasant surprise. 'This *is* good. Rachel Worth,' he continued. 'According to Sternbach, she's very, very good. Better than the other two you had to deal with – Wilson, and Mary-Ann – for whom it seems he had a soft spot. Don't know what's behind it, but he's asked Rachel to avenge her. He knows who killed Mary-Ann. I expect Rachel will be hunting her.'

Pappenheim's face remained still, giving nothing away. 'And the Hargreaves?'

'As I've said . . . they'd like to know how you got to them, and what you got out of them.'

'You were too successful,' Pappenheim said in a hard voice. 'You got them before we could find out anything. So from your point of view, an own goal. You can tell that to Sternbach. Anything else from your little meet with him?'

'I heard him on the phone to someone . . . Whether he

had called or the person had called him, I've no idea. I heard the conversation in passing. They are worked up about something I heard him call the "weapon". I've no idea what he was talking about.'

Pappenheim said nothing.

Waldron looked at him warily. 'I . . . could ask my father. Perhaps he knows.'

'And where is he?'

'At this moment, in Oz.'

'And how would you get that information securely to me, assuming he knows anything?'

'You've got scramblers, we've got scramblers. I'm certain a way could be found without alerting the wrong people.'

Pappenheim stared at him. 'The question is . . . can I trust you? Especially after what has happened?'

'Wrong question. It should be can *I* trust *you* to carry out your threat if I tried anything. The answer is . . . yes. I have no doubt whatsoever that you would dump me right in the shit.'

Pappenheim's eyes were merciless. 'I am not the one who put you there, Peter. You did it all by yourself.' He got to his feet.

Waldron looked surprised. 'You're *leaving*?'

'You've given me some interesting information . . . on the surface. I'm going to check it out. You *will* be *very* deep in the shit if you've been playing with me. I'll be in touch. And Peter, I hate repeating myself. You do *not* have the right to call me Pappi anymore. Give that young lady a good tip. I have my reputation to think about.'

With a wave at the one who had served them, Pappenheim went out before Waldron could marshal his thoughts.

Pappenheim thought he'd caught a peripheral sighting of Rachel Worth as he left the café. He did not turn to check, but kept on walking, crossing the road, and turning a corner. When he felt it was safe to do so, he stopped, and made his way slowly back until he could see the café, but was himself out of observation from there.

He remained in his position for about three minutes and was about to convince himself that he had been mistaken, when he saw her enter the café.

'So even you don't trust lover boy,' Pappenheim murmured. 'Shit is not the word for it, Peter.'

He eased back, then turned and continued on to Friedrichstrasse.

Waldron gave an involuntary start as Rachel Worth appeared at his table.

'You *followed* me?' he said in a low voice.

'I fancied a walk.' She took the seat Pappenheim had just vacated, placing a hand between her legs as she did so. 'And she needs some air, after the workout you've just given her.' She smiled. 'Ready for the second instalment?'

'Are you crazy?' Waldron said in a sharp whisper. 'What if Pappenheim had seen you? He just walked out of here.'

'I know. I saw him leave. He didn't see me.'

'Are you sure?'

'Of course I'm sure,' she said, affronted. 'He was going away from me, looking away from me. I stopped until he was long gone. Don't try to teach me my job, love. OK?' She smiled again, her reptilian eyes cold. Then she looked past him. 'And why is that woman staring at me?'

Waldron glanced round. 'You're in the seat Pappenheim used. This is his favourite café. She knows him.'

'Does she like him, and he . . . her?' She sounded thoughtful. She gave the waitress a quick smile.

'Whatever you're planning,' Waldron cautioned, 'don't.'

'If he likes her . . .'

'You won't hurt him, but you will enrage him if you do anything to her. Pappenheim is not in love with anyone except his wife . . . and she's dead.'

'How gruesome.' Rachel Worth gave an exaggerated sigh. 'Shame.' She gave the waitress another quick smile. 'Your lucky day,' she said, almost inaudibly, through the smile.

She looked away from the waitress to scan the Monroe photographs.

'She looks like me, don't you think?' she went on to Waldron in a casual aside. 'Except I'm not that big, thank God!' It was said with a subtle vitriol. Then she turned her attention to Pappenheim's unfinished coffee, and picked it up. 'I'm always having his leftovers . . .'

'I can order a fresh . . .'

'Umm,' she said, drinking. She put the cup down. 'This is fine. So? Learn anything?'

'Well, they got nothing out of the Hargreaves. Our people did their job too well and got to the Hargreaves first.'

'You believe him?'

'You should have been here,' Waldron said, glad she hadn't been. 'He was livid. Frustrated.'

'Thwarting Müller and Pappenheim is always good.'

'Yes . . . but it would have been better to have found out who led them to the Hargreaves, and what the Hargreaves knew. Now everything will be locked down. I can't talk further about the Hargreaves without causing suspicion.'

'I'm sure you'll find a way.' It almost sounded like a threat. 'Come on, lover. Pay up and let's go for the second round.'

Pappenheim entered Müller's office after a brief knock.

'I've had an interesting few hours,' he began as he strolled in, and told Müller about his encounters with Waldron.

'I'm glad you did not shoot him in cold blood,' Müller commented.

'Oh, my blood was very hot. Believe you me.'

'You wouldn't look good behind bars.'

'Oh, I dunno. I could run a nice little network from there.'

Müller stared at him with a ghost of a smile. 'You probably would. So now we've got your erstwhile friend betraying his wife with a Semper killer. Nice.' A hard look came to Müller's face. 'And to think I got drunk with that man on his terrace overlooking Swan River. That oh-so-genial host is one of those responsible for the murder of—' He stopped suddenly, switching subjects. 'The "weapon" he heard Sternbach talking about must be the DNA weapon.'

'Can't be anything else. The good part is that they have no idea where to look.'

'Long may it remain so. I'm going home,' Müller went on. 'I was waiting for you to get back. I'm going to have a long soak in a hot bath, play the Hammond, then to bed. You?'

'I'll stay for a while. If the goth will put up with it, I want her to check out Rachel Worth. See if there's anything on her in the Woonnalla stuff.'

'Good idea.'

'If the goth complains, I'll tell her you asked.' Pappenheim grinned.

'Thanks, Pappi. You're so kind.'

'That's what the higher rank's for. I can always put the blame on you. And as we both know she'd die for you . . .'

'Out.'

Pappenheim grinned again. 'To hear is to obey. Need a cigarette, anyway.'

'And don't call me unless the world's coming to an end.'

'Too late by then,' Pappenheim said, making his retreat.

'He really asked?' the goth was saying in Pappenheim's ear.

'He really did,' Pappenheim lied without shame as he blew repeated smoke rings at the nicotine-painted ceiling of his office.

'I'll be there,' she said.

'Thanks, Hedi,' Pappenheim, at his most innocent, said. 'I promise not to keep you too long once we've found what we're looking for.'

'No problem,' she said, and hung up.

Pappenheim replaced his own phone slowly. He smiled, and blew a few more smoke rings.

He finished the cigarette, then set off for the Rogues Gallery.

Hedi Meyer was already waiting by the door. 'I might as well have a little studio apartment in there.'

Pappenheim gave her a look as he tapped in the entry code. 'Are we being funny?'

'Who? Me?' She went in ahead of him as the door started to open. By the time Pappenheim was inside and the door had shut again, she had powered up the computer. 'What are we looking for?'

'A name,' he answered as he approached to stand to one side. 'Worth, Rachel.'

She typed in the name. There was barely a wait. A host of files came onscreen.

'Look at that!' she exclaimed softly. 'Which one should I open?'

'Take your pick. See what turns up.'

'This one looks interesting. "Kill History". Shall I try it?'

'Seems like a good place to start.'

She opened the file.

'Oh!' she said. 'Oh, oh, oh, oh, my God! Look at the people this woman has killed. More than Sharon Wilson!'

'It looks as if my former friend did not lie,' Pappenheim said, expression grim.

'Sir, she *married* two men, just to get close enough to kill them . . .'

'That's dedication for you. There's someone she seems dedicated to who perhaps should be watching his back.'

'Is he in the files?'

'Oh, yes.' Then an item caught Pappenheim's eye. 'Stop scrolling. There.' He pointed at the screen. 'Highlight this. Well, well, well,' he added when she had done so. 'Just hold it there. Jens should see this.'

He went to the phone and called Müller's office.

'I was just leaving,' Müller said. 'Has the world ended?'

'No one's told me. But you should definitely see this.'

'It had better be good.'

'Oh, it is.'

Müller was there almost immediately. When he entered, the goth swivelled her chair to give him a welcoming smile before turning back to the computer.

Noting this, Pappenheim glanced heavenwards and shook his head slowly.

Müller gave him a semi-stern look.

'Feast your eyes,' Pappenheim said.

Müller began to read the passage the goth had highlighted.

She was trained to handle extremely powerful but tiny charges and how to plant them unobtrusively. She is very good at it, and is responsible for blowing up at least six small aircraft in midair, one of which belonged to one of her convenience husbands.

Müller stopped reading and stared at the screen. 'What?'

'Thought that might excite you,' Pappenheim said.

Müller straightened from the screen to face Pappenheim. 'Are you saying *she* might have been the one . . . ?'

'I'm not saying anything. But she has the CV.'

'She was not in Australia.'

'We don't know that . . . but I know a man who might. If she really is as good as this says . . . and knowing the source, we have every reason to believe it . . . she could have been down there at any time, planted the stuff with a timed period from hours to days, to weeks . . . once the Semper got to know of the . . . Hargreaves. We – *I* – conveniently gave them the scent via my old pal Waldron. The rest was easy. All they had to do was find out where the Woonnalla plane made its stops, check filed flight plans . . .'

'Not so hard to do, given their organization.'

'Exactly.'

'Bastards,' Müller said tightly.

'I've got a tame one of those dangling on a string,' Pappenheim said. 'He can give us the information we need about how they did it.'

'As long as he has Rachel Worth in tow, best not to contact him again today. That would alert her, and hasten his demise.'

'I should bleed.'

'Nor me, God knows. But we need him to continue dangling.'

'Then I have an idea, I know a couple of eager patrol colleagues who could keep watch . . .'

'You're press-ganging patrol colleagues now?'

'I think they're hoping to transfer to us.'

'And of course you're letting them believe they've got the slightest chance.'

'Calumny!'

'Contact them.'

Pappenheim gave the sort of grin that went with a cigarette clamped between his teeth.

'Done.'

Wilmersdorf, Berlin. 2200 local

Müller had soaked his fill in the hot bath and feeling rejuvenated, had gone into the Hammond room of his apartment with its two Hammonds – a B3 and an XB3 – for some serious playing. He had decided to play the enhanced version of Mancini's Pink Panther theme. Using a mixture of the preset voice keys and his own drawbar selections, he emulated every section of the orchestra, while using the pedals to give him the bass line. He also played every solo, and played the drums in his head. He was deep into the organ solo, when the phone began to ring.

'I'm busy, Pappi!' he shouted at the phone. 'And the world hasn't ended yet!' He kept on playing.

The phone stopped.

'Thank *you!*' he shouted at it.

But his respite was short-lived. He had finished the organ riff with a flourish, moved on to the sax, and was about to cap that with a repeat of the famous intro, when the phone rang again.

'No, no, *no!*' he shouted, and continued to play.

The phone stopped again.

He kept playing until the end, closing the piece with the well-known descending slide.

As if on cue, the phone started again.

'All right, if you must.'

The mobile unit was on the Hammond. He picked it up. 'The world hasn't ended yet, Pappi.'

'What have you been eating, Müller?' the familiar voice of Carey Bloomfield asked.

'Ah!' Müller said, taken completely by surprise.

'I've been calling you. Were you in?'

'Aah . . . yes.'

'You don't like picking up your phone? And what has Pappi done?'

'Ah. Well. I was . . . er . . . playing. And Pappi's not guilty of anything.'

'Hah! Even Pappi would not believe that. So you're in the Hammond room? You still haven't played for me, Müller.'

'You're never here when I do play.'

'We can change that. Could you use some company?'

The way she'd said that made him pause. 'When?'

'Sometime next week.'

'I'll pick you up at the air—'

'I'll make my own way.'

That too made him pause. 'All right.'

'Gotta go.'

'All right,' he repeated.

The call ended.

Müller put the unit back down on the Hammond. 'Someone's pushing over there,' he said to the organ. 'But who? And why?'

He began to play Booker T. Jones' 'Time is Tight'.

Washington DC, 1601 hours

Carey Bloomfield looked at her phone and thought of the still-unnamed general's unwelcome visit.

'Did you listen-in, General?' she asked of the phone. 'I'm going over there. Happy now?'

'Talking to yourself is a sign of screws going loose.'

'Oh!' she said, looking up, taken unawares.

Dering was looking down at her with a tiny smile, but his eyes held a warning which she immediately understood. Dering seemed on his way out.

'I was not talking to myself,' she said. 'I was talking to the phone.'

'So it would seem. But rank protocol is rank protocol, Colonel, even in absentia. Even to dead phones. Let's not forget.'

'No, sir.'

'I have a meeting. Day's nearly gone, so I'll not be back before you leave. Have a nice weekend, Colonel.'

'You too, sir.'

Berlin. 2330 hours

Pappenheim was having a late night of it, having long since sent the goth home. He picked up his phone at the first ring.

'Pappenheim.'

It was one of the eager patrolmen, still doing their hopeful audition for a transfer. 'She's just left, sir.'

'And the man?'

'So far, no sign of him.'

'All right. Thank you, and good work.'

'Anytime, sir.'

'Well, you can stand down for tonight. Go home to your wives, families, or girlfriends. I'll sort out any problems with your commander.'

There was a slight pause. 'Well, actually, sir . . . we're on our own time. Not in a patrol car, and out of uniform.'

'You're very keen. I'm impressed. Thank you again. Now you really can take off. I'll be in touch.'

Misunderstanding completely, the patrolman was full of eagerness. 'Whenever you're ready, sir.'

If I'm not very careful, Pappenheim thought as he put down the phone, *they'll get the better of me and actually manage a transfer to this unit.* He picked up the phone again and called Waldron.

'Lunch tomorrow,' he said as soon as a tired-sounding Waldron had answered.

'Can't,' Waldron said. 'I've got a small diplo lunch to attend.'

'You can be late. Our lunch is no bigger than a coffee break.'

'Rachel's going to be there,' Waldron countered. 'She's supposed to be accompanying me.'

'She can still accompany you. Is she staying at the hotel?'

'No. She has an apartment.'

'Perfect. Give yourself some time before you pick her up and meet me.'

Pappenheim could almost hear the sigh.

'OK,' Waldron said. 'My lunch is at . . . one. Meet you at . . . eleven? Gives me time to get back and change into diplo togs.'

'That will do.'

'Where?'

'I'll pick you up.'

'Shouldn't we be more careful? People could be watching . . .'

'You let me worry about that. I'll pick you up.'

Pappenheim hung up before Waldron could say anything more. 'Hope you have a sleepless night, you bastard.'

He got out a Gauloise and smoked it furiously.

Berlin, Saturday. 1100 local

Pappenheim was waiting across the street from the hotel, when he saw Waldron emerge.

Waldron looked about him, saw Pappenheim, and began walking over.

When he got there, Pappenheim was coldly matter-of-fact. 'This way.'

They walked through an alley that went past the Brandenburg Gate to the right. A big café/restaurant was tucked into a corner, but they did not enter.

81

'That looks like a nice place,' Waldron commented. He sounded hopeful. 'Right across from the hotel too. Convenient.'

'We're not going in,' Pappenheim said, voice abrupt. 'This is one of Jen's favourite places. I won't take you there.'

They walked on in silence until they came to the street that led to the Reichstag. They crossed on to the pedestrian square behind the building, and walked down to where the Spree curved past.

They stopped by a railing with black crosses on white panels, marking the deaths of those who had attempted to flee West in the days of the DDR.

'Lunch,' Pappenheim said, leaning against the railing, some distance from the crosses. He looked about him. No one remotely within earshot.

'We're not eating?' Waldron asked.

'We're not eating. Don't want to spoil your appetite at your function, do you?'

Waldron, sensing the palpable hostility, tightened his lips and said nothing.

'I did some checking,' Pappenheim began. 'Some people I know gave me some information about Rachel Worth.' He told the lie easily, and believably. 'Quite a person, your Rachel.'

'What did you find out?'

'That you told me the truth, for a start – which is lucky for you. But I discovered something you did not tell me . . . that she is an expert with micro explosives.'

Pappenheim gave Waldron an unwavering stare, to gauge the reaction to this piece of news.

Waldron paled. 'You . . . you know people who *know* this?'

'What do you think we're doing?' Pappenheim said harshly. '*Sleeping?* What you need to concern yourself about is with the fact that we know more than you imagine. That's it. So if ever you get it into your head to lead me a dance, you'll be the one dancing, and you won't like it. So here's a question, and I want a straight answer. Did Rachel Worth bomb the Hargreaves plane?'

'I don't know. I honestly don't.'

'Was she ever in Australia at a time that would make that possible?'

'I never see her in Western Australia.'

Pappenheim's mouth turned down. 'Naturally not. She might run into your wife. Tell you what. Find out what your killer doxy was up to around that time. See if she can be placed in the area, and what she did when she was there. You're seeing her today. Who better to tell you?'

Waldron looked alarmed. 'Christ. How do I do that without . . . ?'

Pappenheim smiled coldly. 'I'm certain you'll find a way. You can also find your way back to your hotel, can't you?'

Pappenheim eased himself off the railing, and walked away from Waldron without a backwards glance.

Annandale, Saturday. 0800 local

Carey Bloomfield set off in her classic red BMW M3. The car, beautifully preserved, had belonged to her father. He'd passed it on to her when he had decided that his M3 days were over. She loved the car. It was fast and loud but today she decided that the journey to Virginia Beach to meet up with Dering would be done at an easy pace. She also intended to take a roundabout route, to flush any possible tail the hard-faced general might have decided to employ. It would add a good sixty miles to her journey, but it had to be done.

She flushed the tail almost as soon as she had joined the interstate 495 on her way to take the 95 south. It was a dark blue SUV that was driving a little too correctly, keeping a precise distance.

She cancelled the idea of the 95 and decided to tow whoever was following on a little tour. As soon as she could, she left the highway, in no particular hurry, heading back towards Annandale. The SUV followed, still keeping distance.

Now she was certain. She kept an eye out for other trailers, in case the over-confident SUV was a decoy. She saw nothing to excite her interest.

She did not return to Annandale but instead, headed west-wards, towards Centreville. The SUV kept station. She still made no effort to lose the tail. She wanted them to believe she was quite unaware.

Before reaching Centreville, she turned southwards towards Manassas.

'Might as well ditch you in Manassas,' she said to the trailing vehicle.

It was not difficult. They had probably by then been lulled into complacency, she reasoned. She took the first right just before reaching Manassas, then just about every turning she came to after that. She drove without seeming to hurry, but with increasing speed. Caught out, the SUV began to increase its own speed; but after a few turns, it lost the chase.

Carey Bloomfield did not enter Manassas. Instead, she headed for the 211 from which she took the 17 heading east and south to join the 95 through to Richmond. After Richmond, she took the 460 to Suffolk where she joined the 58 to Virginia Beach.

She never saw the SUV again, nor any other tail. It had cost her more miles than she had originally intended; but she was satisfied she had not been followed.

She parked the car where Dering had suggested, and made her way to the beach-front café.

The section of beach area where she waited near the restaurant was not crowded. Closer to the water some metres away were a few coloured beach umbrellas, with people lying near them. It was a bright day, with a clear blue sky. As she waited outside, something twinkled high above the ocean. Jet noise percolated down.

'Hornet jock from Oceana showing off,' Dering said from behind her. 'I'll miss the old Tomcat, though. Great bird.'

She turned round, not startled by his sudden arrival. 'The Navy let you into one of theirs?'

'The Navy/Air Force rivalry is grossly exaggerated.' He smiled. 'Well, sometimes. Glad you could make it. Any problems?'

'I had to shake off an SUV.'

'And?'

'Successfully. They should still be looking for me up by Manassas.'

'Couldn't have happened to nicer people.'

'What's this all about, General . . . ?'

'First rule while we're down here. I'm Jack, and you're Carey.'

'OK.'

'And before you ask again, let's go eat. Then we'll have a walk, and a talk.'

'In that case, I think I'll overdose on shrimp and crab.'

Huge panes of glass looked out upon the beach. They took a table near one that afforded them a wide view, and that was well away from other diners.

'Good time to be here,' Dering said. 'Gets busy later . . . but we'll be done in here by then.'

Carey Bloomfield took the card menu out of its holder as they sat down.

'Yep,' she said after a quick perusal. 'Got it. I'll start with the Malibu coconut shrimp, followed by the seafood platter. It's my jumbo shrimp day.'

'To make life easy, I'll have the same.'

A friendly waitress in a blue T-shirt and pale, rolled up shorts came to their table to take their order.

'Hi, Jack,' she greeted.

'Mary. We'll have the Malibu, and the seafood platter . . . twice.'

'That's an easy one.' She went away smiling.

'You a regular here?' Carey Bloomfield asked.

'Not really. But I've come here a few times with some navy guys.'

Dering, in short-sleeved shirt and pale trousers, did not look like a general. His hair was short, but not overtly military in cut.

'I'm going to have a hard time eating without wanting to know why we're down here.'

85

'Enjoy the shrimp and the crab,' Dering said. 'Plenty of time to talk later.'

Dering seemed to be waiting for something. Or someone.

'Woo!' Carey Bloomfield said as they left the restaurant. 'I don't want to see another jumbo shrimp, or more battered crab meat, for a hundred years . . .'

'Did you not enjoy it?'

'Jack, I wolfed it all down. What do you think?'

Dering smiled. 'A hundred years seems drastic.'

'Tomorrow would be long enough.' She grinned at him.

'Then let's walk it off. We'll head this way.'

This way took them along a stretch of beach that was almost empty of people, becoming even more so in the distance.

'I'll talk,' he began, 'you listen. Confirm nothing. I won't ask questions. You don't ask questions. Just listen. Deal?'

'Deal,' she agreed, despite a raging curiosity.

'During the second world war,' Dering continued as they strolled, then he paused, glancing up at the sky. 'Just think of it. Up there, are satellites that can zero in on a target to the resolution of a close-up photo. A face can be clearly identified. We've both seen high-res shots of unknowing bikini beach babes from all over the world.'

Carey Bloomfield smiled neutrally, but said nothing to that.

'All that high-tech,' Dering went on, 'and people still die of starvation. We spy on each other instead.'

'I think I'm getting your drift. Do I ask a question?'

'No.'

'OK.'

'If you're wondering whether I've turned into some kind of philanthropist all of a sudden . . . I've always been disturbed by this wasteful imbalance. But I chose to be a warrior. I chose a different fight.' Dering gave the sky another glance. 'The people we don't want to know we're here won't be scanning this area. They have access to surveillance sets, but there's not one currently available to them for here, at this time. I made certain.'

Dering gave no explanation, and she did not ask for one.

'There were some people during the war who knew the Nazi regime would be devastated . . . from the very beginning; particularly among some of the Nazis themselves. They were already planning for this eventuality. A small group began research for a DNA weapon, but without success. As the war progressed, the organization they planned – let's call it an Order – also evolved. They found like-minded people from other nations, even during the war. By the time the war had ended as expected this Order, the Semper, was well advanced in the plans it had laid. The subtle infiltration of post-war Germany began, as did its initial probes beyond Germany. The East/West divide helped it enormously. Many of its leading lights were in the military and police forces of both.

'The infiltration of the Order itself was also begun, and one of the best double agents of more recent times was Müller's father. He rose to very high rank within the Semper, and was a colonel of police in the DDR. His wife, Müller's mother, played her part as well. Then the Semper began to suspect von Röhnen. The decision was made to terminate them and it ostensibly happened, when Müller was a boy of twelve.' Dering paused to look at Carey. 'Of course, you know all this.'

He walked on, without waiting for an attempted response. 'But there are some things that you do not. Work on the DNA weapon progressed fitfully. A highly secret lab was set up in a Middle Eastern country, far from prying eyes. The nation itself had little to do with what went on. The pay-off came in many forms – money, arms, you name it. Then one day, bingo. The prototype was developed.

'The Brits were the first on the scent. They inserted a special unit to steal it, and destroy the lab. They succeeded in their mission; but the man who led them vanished, believed dead. The weapon prototype never made it. Big mystery for decades.

'Gulf War One. A combined special unit of Brits and Americans set out to find the site of the lab. Someone had sent a rumour down the line that just maybe, the prototype was lying somewhere out there. The lab was not in Iraq, and under the cover of the war, the unit went into the nation in question. Somewhere along the way, the Brit and American elements split up. Given what happened next, it was lucky for the Brits. The American contingent was led by a young lieutenant who was either too gung-ho, too green, or both. His second-in-command was a hardened sergeant called Jan Brannic. Brannic was a third-generation American whose family originally came from Serbia. His mother was of Swedish descent. Her family were in the States since the nineteenth century.' Dering gave a sudden chuckle. 'Hell, my own family on my father's side come from Germany.

'According to Brannic, they ran into an ambush. He was wounded, the lieutenant killed. As were the rest of the men. Brannic staggered back, carrying the lieutenant who was still alive at the time, hiding from pursuit, and continuing when he could. He made it back, still carrying the lieutenant, who was by that time dead. Brannic was decorated, and given a field commission. You met him yesterday.'

'*What?*'

'Our asshole general. Yes. Brannic is playing a double game. He is ostensibly hunting the DNA weapon for us, but in fact he wants it for the Semper.'

'Jesus! Brannic is Semper? Sorry. I'm asking questions.'

Dering seemed prepared to let that go. 'He always was. At which point in time they got to him is still a mystery. What is definitely known is that he – more correctly the Semper – arranged that ambush. But the timing was all wrong. It was supposed to happen after the weapon had been found, assuming it still was there to be found. The whole thing turned out to have been a wild goose chase. The rumour spreaders got what they wanted: the unmasking of a Semper member and the Semper intentions – but it cost lives that might otherwise not have been lost. He was left alone, but monitored by those who are fighting the Semper. It is also known that Müller's parents escaped the attempt to murder them; known, I should clarify, only by those who were on their side; *not* by their enemies.'

Carey Bloomfield felt a sense of shock. She wanted to ask several questions, but forced herself to obey Dering's pre-conditions.

'They hid themselves in Australia, where they continued to compile information. They were still active but now, only a very trusted *very* few knew it. These few continued to feed them information that enabled them to carry out their own missions. Some of us – yes,' Dering said, knowing the reaction that would come from her, 'I am one. Some of us visited them on rare occasions with valuable information. Grogan, as you no doubt have guessed, is also one.'

'I'm not so sure about Grogan.'

'Grogan's cover is his . . . protection. Tell Müller not to try to find out too much. This might expose Grogan. As for me, the hounds are drawing nearer . . .'

Carey Bloomfield could not stop herself. 'General . . . Jack, what are you *saying*?'

He gave her a look with sadness in his eyes. They were already saying goodbye.

'I am Semper. Correction . . . I am an infiltrator, and I'm afraid my time is up. Brannic has been hunting me for – ' he paused, not saying for how long – 'and I believe he may have at last found something to tag to me. I've been watching your back, Carey, keeping Brannic's people off you. He suspects that Müller may know more about the DNA weapon than appears. He does *not* know for sure. He only suspects, because of who Müller's parents were. Neither he nor the Semper know they were the Hargreaves. So that secret is safe. I don't even want to see by your expression whether what I have said is correct or not. Got it?'

She nodded, trying to prevent herself from shaking as a result of Dering's revelations.

'Let's walk. Brannic wants you to betray Müller,' Dering

went on, 'but I know you will not do so. He will try to pressure you, using his rank. I believe I've taught you well enough. Use everything you've got to counter him. And warn Müller . . .'

'Jack . . .'

'If,' Dering interrupted, 'I am not back in my office, Monday . . . you'll know. And you'll be on your own. More or less. Grogan will still be there, of course. But his help can only be in the way he's been giving it. There are more of us, but even I don't know them all. I'm . . . I'm sorry to dump this on you.'

Dering stopped, and turned to face her. 'Don't go back the way you came. Take the Bay Bridge route. See you Monday. If not, it's been a privilege to serve with you, Colonel.'

Dering turned and walked away.

'Sir . . .' she started to say.

But he did not turn, or look back. She stood there, until she could no longer see him.

Five

A marvel of engineering, the bridge swooped and curved its way across the Atlantic mouth of the bay for 17.6 miles, its twin spans carrying their own individual one-way traffic. Carey Bloomfield knew that the actual, tolled shore-to-shore journey was about twenty miles. She liked driving on the bridge, sweeping over the waters below; but she hated the narrow tunnels, ninety feet beneath the seabed. She was always relieved to exit the tunnels.

Good places for ambushes, she thought as she watched the bridge curve into the distance, seemingly forever.

But she knew that Dering had given her smart advice. If by any chance the people in the SUV had somehow managed to head for Virginia Beach, they would not expect her to return this way . . . unless they had people waiting at the other end, just in case.

She decided not to think about that. If they were waiting, she would handle the situation. They did not know she had met with Dering. They would question her, no doubt; but she had answers ready for anything they might try to pull.

She sniffed at herself to check if there were any hint of the smell of seafood about her. There wasn't. At least, not that she could tell. She had an answer for that too, just in case.

Dering, she knew, was running interference, taking a bold but risky route back. It was almost as if he wanted them to find him, now that he had told her the secrets he had been sitting on for so long.

'My God,' she whispered. 'Dering! All these years I've known him.' She shook her head slowly in wonder. 'You've got to make it,' she added softly, feeling a moistness in her eyes.

Who would she be able to trust if Brannic got Dering?

'I'm alone,' she said to herself. The realization shook her. 'No,' she went on. 'Not alone. I've got Müller and Pappi.' She gave a soft chuckle that was without humour. 'The man I was sent to spy on is my best protection.'

She glanced to her right, at the open ocean. A warship, a big cruiser, was heading in, towards one of the channels above a tunnel.

'Müller,' she said, 'have I got some news for you.'

Dering was on the 460, heading for the 95, for the journey back. He made no effort to alter his planned route. It was a straight run back.

He had an untroubled run . . . until he was just a few miles from the massive construction site of the Springfield interchange roadworks. Suddenly, he had company. Four blue SUVs came up fast. Two went ahead and slowed down. Two stayed close behind. Boxing him in, they guided him off the highway. None of the vehicles touched his car.

The strange convoy went on for some several miles, then turned on to a deserted road that was more of a wide track. They continued for at least twenty minutes, when the road came to an end in a wide, unpaved circle. The SUVS, like hunting dogs, fanned out, blocking all escape.

Dering remained in his car and waited, face still. He kept the engine running.

No one moved out of the SUVs for several minutes.

Dering still remained where he was.

At last, a door in one of the vehicles opened, and a suited Brannic got out. He began walking towards Dering's car.

Dering made no move to get out.

Brannic came right up to the car, stared at Dering for some moments, then rapped on the driver's window.

Dering lowered it, and looked up at his adversary. 'You're a highwayman now, Brannic?'

'Very funny. Cut the engine and get out!'

'And if I don't?'

'You'll be hit by a platoon-sized broadside of automatic fire.'

'Well, that's clear enough. After what happened to Lieutenant Driscoll back in the Gulf War, I suppose shooting your own comes naturally. Have you ever felt shame for accepting a decoration, and a commission, falsely?'

Brannic's hard face went bright red. He drew an automatic from a shoulder holster. 'Get out of the fucking car! Now!'

Dering remained absolutely calm. 'Or what? You'll shoot me?'

'Get out!' Brannic screamed.

'Temper, temper. But as you asked so nicely . . .' Dering turned off the engine and climbed out.

Brannic took two long, rapid steps back.

'Don't be afraid, Brannic,' Dering said. 'I'm not going to jump at you in front of all your friends, hiding in their SUVs. Don't they want me to see who they are?' He leaned against his car.

Brannic's face tightened, finger seeming about to squeeze the trigger. But he stopped short of doing so.

'Where's Colonel Bloomfield?' he demanded.

'Why would I know what the colonel does on her weekend? Unless she's on a mission, her whereabouts in her free time are of no interest to me.'

'Do you take me for a fool?'

'Only you can judge that.'

'She was seen driving away . . .'

'And you expect me to know where she was headed? Perhaps Florida. Her parents have moved there. Perhaps she wanted . . .'

'To drive to Florida for a weekend?'

'Ever heard of airports? And please don't ask me again whether you're a fool. You might get an answer you won't like.'

'Ever heard of loyalty?' Brannic countered in a snarl.

'That depends. Loyalty to country, family, buddies, friends . . . to your Service. Where are your loyalties, General? You wear the uniform of a general in the US Army . . . where do *your* loyalties lie?'

Brannic gave a hard smile, gun still pointing. 'The world, Dering, is global. Isn't that what you . . . "intellectuals" say? What we do is supranational . . .'

'Ah yes, tomorrow the world . . .'

Brannic did not seem to mind the comment. 'Our reach is very wide, as you know. You also know the penalty for betrayal.'

'Our ideas on what constitutes betrayal differ . . .'

'We want answers from you, Dering,' Brannic said, bypassing the comment. 'Who you passed your information to would be a good place to start . . . then we move on to what you told Colonel Bloomfield.'

Dering glanced at the SUVs. No one else had made a move to get out. 'You're hard of hearing, Brannic. I have not seen the colonel. Therefore, I could not have said anything to her, had I wished to.'

'And you expect me to believe that.'

'Believe what you want.'

Brannic gave another of his hard smiles. 'Nice try tying up the access to the satellite we would have used. But we found other access in time to find you. As a general, General, you'll know all about protecting your flanks . . .'

'And I'm certain *you* do . . . *Sergeant.*'

It was meant to wound . . . and it did.

Brannic's face went red again, this time with rage. 'I spent years as a sergeant, wiping the asses of incompetent officers. I *deserve* my commission *and* my rank! All right, Dering!' He raised the gun and came forward. 'Into my vehicle! We need information, and you'll give it . . . one way or another. Move!'

It was what Dering had wanted. In his rage, Brannic had forgotten his caution. When he was close enough, Dering moved swiftly. He opened his door with a savage swing. The edge of the door hit Brannic on the kneecaps.

Brannic roared in pain and staggered back.

It was enough. Dering leapt into his car, started the engine, and began to move even as the door swung shut.

Suddenly, a barrage of automatic fire erupted from all the SUVs. Bullets raked Dering's car, which stopped moving almost immediately.

A silence fell.

There was no movement from inside the car. Brannic straightened painfully, glared first at the car, then at the SUVs.

'Goddammit!' he roared in frustration. 'You *idiots*! You did exactly what he wanted! He's dead!' He looked back at Dering's car. 'Shit. Shit! Damn you, Dering!' He turned again to the SUVs. 'Come clean up your mess!' he yelled at them. 'Now we've got a damned general to make disappear!'

Men piled out of the vehicles.

Carey Bloomfield made it home without incident. No one followed her. At least, no one she could spot. But she felt certain that her journey back had been clean. And there was no reception committee waiting when she arrived.

She parked the BMW in front of her home. This was deliberate for on the way back, she had come to a decision.

She began to pack and afterwards had a shower. She then got dressed, and called a taxi.

'If you make it back, General,' she said as she put down the phone after the call to the cab company, 'and you see I'm not there on Monday, you'll understand. If you don't make it . . . you'll understand.'

When the taxi arrived she took it to the airport, leaving the BMW where it was.

Half an hour after she'd gone, an SUV cruised past. There were two men in it.

'Car's there,' the one in the passenger seat said into his solid-looking radio-phone. 'Lights out in the place.'

'Park somewhere and watch,' the voice at the other end commanded.

'Yes, sir.' The man turned to the driver as the conversation ended. 'You knew the general before, didn't you?'

They were not from the same group who had killed Dering.

The driver, older than his partner by several years, nodded. 'Knew him when he was still a sergeant. Best damned sergeant I ever knew. Last time I saw him before he got in touch, was years ago. He was going on a mission . . . special patrol. I was supposed to be on it, but got sick with some goddamned Mid-East bug. The patrol and the LT in command got wiped. Brannic was wounded, but he walked all the way back, carrying the LT on his back, thinking the guy was still alive. Brannic got a medal and a commission. I was sent back home. Hospital case. Left the man's army not long after. Years later, I get this call from Colonel Brannic. Would I like to join a special security unit he commanded, as a civilian. I was bored, marriage so far on the rocks, the rocks were pissed off with our presence. It was no contest. I took the job. Been with him ever since.'

'How long?'

'Three years now.'

'When did he make general?'

'Two years ago.'

'That was fast. Sergeant to general . . .'

'He's a good soldier. One of the best.'

The younger man fell silent. 'What do we do,' he began after a while, 'if a concerned citizen comes to question what we're doing here?'

The driver looked at him. 'Are you serious? We're national security. *We* question the "concerned" citizen. If he does not get the message, *we* give him a very bad day.'

Sunset and The Major

Müller was getting ready to drive down to the Schlosshotel, when the doorbell gave its two-tone ring. Surprised, he wondered who it could be.

'Pappi would have called,' he said to himself.

Unless it was so important, Pappenheim had decided to attend in person.

Frowning slightly, Müller went to the door monitor, and got a bigger surprise. There, looking ghostly on the screen, was Carey Bloomfield, a travel bag in hand, looking for all the world like a waif without a home. She was staring up at the camera she could not see. As Müller's car was in the garage, she had no way of telling whether he was home.

He panned the camera to check whether anyone was perhaps hiding behind, or trailing her. There was no one.

'She said next week,' Müller said in a voice that was almost a whisper. Something must have gone seriously wrong.

Pappenheim liked to call Müller's penthouse apartment the luxury fort. Carey Bloomfield called it a palace. Müller termed it his 'little flat'. There were just three apartments in the three-storey building, each occupying an entire floor. Once the family home, Müller had inherited the building. It was a very secure building, with its own underground garage. Each apartment had a separate access. Access to Müller's was via a heavy steel door so thick, Pappenheim had once joked it could take several 20 mm hits without damage.

Instead of pressing the remote button to open the door, Müller went out of the main door to the apartment, and virtually ran down the wide, six flight internal staircase. A second door led off the ground floor landing, behind which another flight of stairs went down to the garage, and cellars.

'Hi, Müller,' she said, entering as he opened the massive door. 'Wasn't sure you'd be in.' She dropped the bag.

He let the door swing back to click shut.

Müller looked at her, an uncertainty in his eyes. 'Are you all right? I expected you later in the week.'

'No, Müller. I'm not all right. I'm jet-lagged, and I'm feeling exposed. And I'm scared . . . kind of. So if that strange look in your eye is what I think it is, tell that mixed-up correct German, English-influenced mind of yours not to wait for written permission, plus twenty copies, and just give me a hug, will you?' Her words ended in a small plea.

Very gently, he put his arms about her and she relaxed against him with a small sigh of relief. She trembled slightly as he held her, and her arms tightened about him. They stayed like that, not speaking, for a full minute.

'I needed that,' she said as they let go of each other; he uncertainly, she reluctantly.

'Come,' he said. 'I'll make you some coffee, then you can tell me all about it.' He picked up her bag.

She shook her head. 'No coffee. What I'd like to do is sleep.'

'All right,' he said, wondering. It was not like her to look so vulnerable. The Carey Bloomfield he thought he knew was no shrinking violet.

As they made their way up the stairs, she said, 'Müller, I think they may have killed my boss yesterday.'

He paused. 'What? And who's "they"?'

'The Semper. I hope not . . . but my gut tells me they did. I'll tell you all after I've slept.'

He nodded, giving her a sideways look full of questions, and they continued up the stairs.

When they had entered the apartment, she glanced at his clothes and said, 'Were you about to go out?'

'To Aunt Isolde's.'

'The major still OK?'

'He's in good health, but he seems to think his nemesis has finally caught up with him.'

'Then what I've got to say will hit the radar . . . hard. But I need that sleep first. I don't . . . want one of the guest palaces . . . er . . . bedrooms. Can I use yours? Müller . . . would you mind if I slept in your bed? Don't panic. This is not . . . not a . . . look . . . I'd just feel . . . safer. Would you mind? Humour me. Blame it on jet lag.'

She spoke rapidly, as if afraid he would refuse if she spoke any slower. Again, there was that plea in her eyes.

Wondering what could have spooked her so much, he nodded. 'Help yourself. You know where it is. It's got a wide view of the city. If that is too much window for you, pull the roman blinds. You can't be overlooked up here. We can go down to Aunt Isolde's when you've slept.'

'Thanks, Müller.'

'The sheets . . .'

'Don't need changing.' She picked up her bag, and went off to his bedroom.

He stared after her as she closed the door, at a loss to understand what was behind it all.

A little later, he went to the door and knocked softly.

'It's not locked,' came from inside.

He opened it, and poked his head round. She was already in bed, head peeping out from beneath the sheet. She had drawn the blinds across the wide, almost panoramic window.

'I'm going out for a while,' he said to her. 'Don't open up to anyone. I am not expecting visitors.'

The head nodded. 'OK.'

'I won't be long.'

She nodded again, and he closed the door.

Frowning slightly, he went into the Hammond room and called Pappenheim's office on spec.

'I thought this was a day of rest,' Pappenheim said immediately.

'I could say the same to you.'

'Ah, well . . . I've got a few things to attend to,' Pappenheim countered. 'That's my excuse. What's yours?'

Müller heard Pappenheim's loud drag of his cigarette.

'My office, in one or two of your *blondes*.'

'Thought it might be something like that. I'll curb my curiosity till then.'

'You'll have to.'

'Ah . . . you're such a hard man,' Pappenheim said.

They hung up together.

99

Müller left the Hammond room to have another look-in on Carey Bloomfield. She was fast asleep. The head was still poking out of the sheet which was rolled about her, but this time, a shapely leg was poking out as well.

He closed the door quietly, a tiny smile upon his face.

Pappenheim had just finished his second cigarette, when Müller arrived at his door. Müller gave a soft knock, and walked in.

Pappenheim joined him less than thirty seconds later.

'I'm keen, as you can see,' Pappenheim said in greeting.

Müller was standing in his favourite spot by the window, looking down upon the city. 'You'll be even keener when I tell you about my Sunday surprise.'

'Try me.'

'Carey Bloomfield is here.'

Pappenheim stared at him. 'OK. When?'

'Less than an hour ago.'

'Where?'

'Right at this moment, she's sleeping . . . in my bed.'

'Ah.'

Müller turned from the window. 'What do you mean "ah"?'

'Just ah. I'm waiting for the rest.'

Müller turned back to the window. Pappenheim joined him, and they both looked down at the city.

'We seem to be having a kind of gathering. First Waldron and his killer doxy are in town . . .'

'Doxy?'

'Doxy. Now we've got Carey on your doorstep . . .'

'I got a call from her on Friday night,' Müller said. 'Would I like some company? That was strange enough, so I assumed a message of some kind. I said yes, and she said she would see me next week. I was getting ready to go down to my aunt's this afternoon, when the doorbell rings. There she was on the monitor, looking for all the world like a refugee. And here's the astonishing thing, Pappi . . . she is frightened.'

Pappenheim stared at him. 'Our favourite colonel frightened?

This is the woman who went to the Middle East against orders, to rescue her brother, who took down Dahlberg with you, who took on Mary-Ann . . . and won, who shot von Mappus at long range, sniper on sniper; who surprised and shot Mainauer, one of *the* best snipers around at the time. This woman is not easily frightened. Only snakes can terrify her.'

'Exactly.'

'Which means either she's really frightened . . .'

'Or she's playing a game.'

'But?' Pappenheim asked.

'Remember when she first came into our lives?'

'Your life,' Pappenheim corrected.

Müller let it pass. 'I did not trust her then. *You* did not trust her. Later, you ended up trusting her even more than I did.'

Pappenheim cleared his throat. 'What can I say? I've got a soft centre. She's like one of the team now . . . almost. We've trusted her with plenty.'

'Exactly,' Müller repeated. 'I don't think she would have said she was scared, unless she meant it. She also said she believed the Semper killed her boss yesterday.'

'Keeps getting better . . .'

'It's just the beginning. She has promised full revelations when she's had her sleep.'

'She came to you and just went to sleep?'

'Didn't even pause for coffee.'

'Whatever it is,' Pappenheim said after a while, 'it must be a doozy as she would say . . .'

'She never says that . . . or does she?' Müller added absently.

Pappenheim gave a tiny shrug. 'Details. Whatever it is, it was enough to send her running across an ocean to you . . . and fall asleep in your bed.'

'Enjoying that part, are you?'

'Oh, yes.'

'I don't think we're going to like what she has to tell us.'

'So what's new?'

'She asked about Greville,' Müller went on. 'One of her first questions. When I told her he thought nemesis was about to get him, she suggested that what she had to say would "hit the radar hard", as she put it.'

'The DNA weapon.'

'The DNA weapon,' Müller agreed. 'If someone really is after her, she's safe enough at my place. I warned her to open up to no one.'

'I can't wait for her to wake up,' Pappenheim said. 'I think I need a smoke.'

'And I'd better get back.'

'Should I alert the goth?'

'Let's not ruin *her* Sunday . . . unless we have to,' Müller said. 'Let's first see what our colonel has to say.'

Carey Bloomfield was still asleep when Müller returned to his apartment; but a bare forty-five minutes later, she appeared in the kitchen, fully dressed.

'Do I smell coffee in this stainless steel temple?'

'No,' Müller said, 'but you soon will. I'm surprised you're already awake. You look . . .'

'Terrible. I know.'

'You can never look terrible . . .'

'So gallant.'

'And I was going to say you look amazingly refreshed.'

'Don't let this exterior fool you. I'll soon look like a hag if I don't get my caffeine hit.' She smiled at him as she took a seat at the breakfast bar.

Müller was already at the machine. 'Gurgling of the finest Guatemalan is about to be heard. How do you want it?'

'Right now . . . sugar, black, in a big cup.'

'The lady commands, the lady gets.'

There was silence as she watched him work, enjoying the aroma of the coffee. When the coffee was done, he handed her the steaming cup.

She took an exploratory sip. 'Mmm. Oh, yes. You'll make someone a good wife one day, Müller.'

'So you keep telling me.'

'You shouldn't know how to cook so damn good. Your

fault.' She drank some more. 'Guess I'd better explain what's going on.'

'In your own time.'

'None like the present. On Friday, a general I'd never seen before stomps into our patch of the Pentagon—'

'Stomps?'

'A marching stomp. A rude bastard, too. He opens up with something not very nice about you.'

'*Me?*'

'This *is* all about you, Müller, as you'll soon see. The rude general's name is Brannic – a name that should be on the Woonnalla files.'

'Semper?'

'Seems this Brannic is in overall command of my mission – news to me, news to my immediate boss, Dering, also a general.'

'And your mission is?'

'My mission *was*,' Carey Bloomfield corrected, 'to shadow you. But you know that. My *real* mission was . . .' She stared into the coffee, then looked at him. 'My real mission was to try and find out about the DNA weapon.' She stopped, waiting for his reaction.

'You said "was",' he told her quietly after a while.

'I *mean* was. I'm not going to betray you, Müller. If I were, I'd have told him about Woonnalla. I did not. Not even Dering knows . . . But Dering had a surprise of his own. Boy . . . was it a surprise.'

'Go on.'

'Brannic made a big deal about needing the information for the country; but until Dering dropped his own bombshell, I had no idea that Brannic was Semper, and was really hunting out the info for them. Dering and Brannic don't like each other . . . and that's an understatement. Next to them, freshwater and saltwater crocs are bosom pals. After Brannic had stomped off, Dering did something strange – he invited me to lunch on Saturday, one hundred and fifty miles from Washington. Virginia Beach.'

Müller said nothing, and waited.

'I set off in the morning, and got followed by an SUV. I took it on a tour and ditched it, then went on to meet with Dering. Turns out Dering is Semper too.' She paused, studying Müller's expression.

Müller still said nothing.

'But . . .' she continued, 'and get this, Müller . . . he's like your . . . dad. He's an infiltrator just like him . . . as . . . as he was . . . and, he *knew* him! In fact, he knew all about Woonnalla, and used to go there!'

This at last got a reaction from Müller. 'What?'

'The truth. Dering did all the talking . . . well, pretty much most of it. He told me he would speak and I would listen, but neither confirm nor deny. He did it that way to show he was not trying to trick me into revealing anything. Müller, I'm certain he was the "other" your father wrote about. He knew all about the Hargreaves. He was one of those who passed them information.'

She told the astonished Müller all that had occurred, and everything that Dering had revealed to her. By the time she had finished, the rest of her coffee had grown cold.

He stared at the cup. 'Another?'

She shook her head. 'Well, Müller? Did that hit the radar?'

'It's swamped it. Are you so certain that they've got him?'

'After what he said, I don't think he's going to be in Monday. Funny, isn't it? You think you know people . . . Remember how Toby Adams – who'd been my backup for years – was Semper, and I never suspected. Then Mary-Ann killed him, and the bastards tried to frame me for it. But who would have thought Dering was doing something so dangerous? Exactly like your father? He always came across so . . . easy-going . . . When they're done with him, they'll be heading my way. Brannic's an asshole, but he's not a dumb asshole. He'll soon work out that I'm not doing his mission. I'm out on a long limb over a precipice, Müller . . . and it can break at any time. I travelled as an ordinary citizen. No diplomatic immunity. No backup. And I travelled on a passport that does not say

I'm Carey Bloomfield. He can haul me in for going AWOL, then I disappear.'

'That is not going to happen.'

She gave him a tired smile. 'You going to protect me, Müller?'

'Yes. And Pappi, and even Berger. All of us.'

'You know how to make a person feel at home. Brannic's not going to love you for this.'

'As he already does not love me, I don't think I shall worry unduly about that.'

'So what now?'

'We go to the Rogues Gallery to check on Brannic. Pappi's in the building . . .'

'Does he ever go home?'

'He's been known to, believe it or not. After that, we go to the current source of the DNA weapon.'

'Greville.'

'Greville. You'll be safe down there . . . but if you prefer, you can stay here, or at the unit. We've got protective apartments there.'

'No way! Where you go, mister, I go. I'm not some weak flower, Müller.'

'Never imagined it.'

'I just needed to find my feet.'

'As I thought.'

'Make me another coffee, Müller, then let's hit the road.'

'Coming up. I've got some news for you too,' Müller went on as he began preparing a fresh cup. 'Pappi's erstwhile friend, Waldron, is in town.'

'You *told* Pappi about Waldron?'

'No choice. I could not keep that from him.'

'Guess not.'

As the machine began to gurgle again, Müller realized it must have been Dering who had made the mysterious calls, warning him, letting him know that he was one of the Hargreaves' informants. Dering must also have known even then, that the hounds were getting closer.

'Waldron called him,' Müller continued, 'inviting him to meet. Old times.'

'Bet Pappi enjoyed that.'

'As a matter of fact, I believe he *is* enjoying it, though not in the way Waldron originally expected. It would appear that the Semper sent Waldron in to get information about the Hargreaves out of Pappi. Pappi let Waldron know that he *knew* Waldron was Semper. Now the situation is reversed. Waldron is . . . call it "working" for us.'

She gave a little laugh. 'Pappi's blackmailing him?'

'Perfect way to describe it.'

She laughed again. 'Neat.'

'I thought it was. Point of interest for you. Waldron's having an affair with someone called Rachel Worth.'

'The guy's even cheating on his wife? He deserves everything he gets. The bastard.'

'He might get more than he bargained for. Rachel Worth is a Semper killer. She will kill whoever she's ordered to, including Semper members.'

'Nice.'

'Coffee's up.'

They made their way down to the secure garage, where each apartment had been allocated three wide parking bays. Müller had called Pappenheim to say they were on their way.

'When I was last here,' Carey Bloomfield said as they walked towards the nearest trio of bays where Müller's two vehicles were parked, 'there were mainly bimmers in here . . . apart from your cars, of course. Now I see Audis, and the place is still clean enough to eat off. You should see where I park.'

'Speaking of bimmers, how is your M3?'

'Sweet as ever, and parked outside my place as a decoy for Brannic's foot soldiers. If they damage it, I'll kill them.'

They stopped by Müller's gleaming seal grey 911 Turbo. Next to it was a Cayenne S.

'Müller . . .'

'Yes.'

'You going to put a third Porsche in the next bay one day?'

'Is that a trick question?' he asked, pressing the remote to unlock the car.

'Just curious.'

'Get in,' he said.

'Masterful.' She got into the passenger seat. 'You could let me drive,' she suggested.

'You're jet-lagged. Remember?'

'Not that jet-lagged. I've had a sleep.' The engine barked into life. 'God. I love that sound.'

'Then enjoy it,' he said, driving towards the slight incline of the exit.

The rollover door began to raise itself.

'If you're here on your own,' Müller said as they waited, 'and anyone tries to enter this way, it won't happen. This door will only open to a coded command. Each car in here has its own. The door will only raise when it recognizes one of the codes.'

'What if that person follows a car in on foot?'

'He can't do that without being seen. He can of course try to force his way in with a weapon; but that won't work in his favour. He'll have to use a hostage, which rules out the entire concept of a clandestine entry.'

The door was fully open and Müller drove out.

'If the person happens to be Semper,' he continued, 'then they're after you, or me. Taking a hostage would be seriously counter-productive.'

'Is this supposed to make me feel better?'

'Doesn't it?'

'Nope. As I did not travel with a gun, can you lend me one?'

'Yes.'

'Boy . . . is that a relief.'

Müller smiled to himself as they drive towards Friedrichstrasse.

* * *

In an eavesdropping sub-centre with wall-to-ceiling monitors and a large digital map of the world that could be zeroed-in on any location on the planet, an operator, with one hand to a headphone, was trying to clean up a recording he had made of Müller's latest conversation to Pappenheim. The map showed that other conversations were also being monitored.

After some minutes of futile attempts, he gave up, leaned back in his chair to look up at the man standing next to him.

'Nothing worth shit. All he said was "On my way": then static.'

'That's it?'

'That's it.'

'Just those three words in the clear.'

'As a bell. If he said anything else, it's scrambled. Completely. As usual, they expect to be eavesdropped.'

'Anything on those other calls?'

'Nothing.'

'And from Colonel Bloomfield?'

'Nothing.'

'Damn it!'

Pappenheim was already in the Rogues Gallery when Müller and Carey Bloomfield got there.

Pappenheim grinned a welcome at her.

She gave him a quick hug. 'I come seeking asylum, Pappi.'

'Granted immediately.' He studied her closely. 'Bad?'

'You said it. I'll let Müller update you.' She looked at the computer. 'No goth?'

Pappenheim glanced at Müller. 'Depends on what we need.'

'Just a name. I guess I can hack it if the goth won't strangle me for touching her machine.'

'Can you do it?' Müller asked.

'I've got my own at home, and at the Pentagon. I worked that monster machine at Woonnalla. How difficult can it be? I just hit the power button . . . right?'

She did so. The machine powered up. The screen remained black; then a single small window, white-bordered on the

black, appeared. A single word appeared in the window.
PASSWORD.

'Er . . . guys?' Carey Bloomfield said.

They looked, then looked at each other.

'Ah,' Pappenheim said.

'Knowing the goth,' Carey Bloomfield began, 'she'll have
this locked up tight which, if you think about it, is smart. If
anyone you don't want to ever managed to get in here, this
will be dead to them. I'm not even going to try to play with
it. I could end up burning your system out. Do you want to
risk that?'

'No,' Müller said.

'Looks like the goth, after all,' Pappenheim said.

'Come on, guys,' she urged. 'Doesn't one of you have the
password?'

'Ah!' Pappenheim said. 'I may have. She gave me one.'

He went to a cabinet, and tapped in a code on its keypad.
It popped slightly open. He pulled it out, and searched among
some discs.

Then he took out a jewel case with a slip of paper in it.
'That's the one . . . I think.'

'You hope,' Carey Bloomfield said as he passed it to her.
'Jesus,' she went on, staring at it. 'This is not a password.
It's a novel. No hacker would ever get this.'

'She's a hacker,' Müller said. 'Who better to stop one?'

'Well, wish me luck.'

'Wish *me* luck,' Pappenheim said. 'She could have changed
it without my knowing.'

'Oh, great. Well, here goes. I'm going to do this very carefully.'

Carey Bloomfield made each key press with great care.
The first one brought up a green asterisk. At last, all digits
and letters were entered. The window was now filled with
green asterisks. They all waited to see what would happen
next.

For long, agonizing seconds, nothing at all happened. Then
the screen went ominously black.

'Oh, no!' she cried. 'I've just killed your system . . .'

But then the computer powered up normally. They all heaved sighs of relief. In fleeting seconds, the desktop icons came on; but there was no sign of anything related to the Semper, or Woonnalla.

'I'll have to navigate my way through this,' she said. 'Hope the goth hasn't laid any traps.'

'She wouldn't have,' Pappenheim said. 'She practically told me she had made it so simple, even I could find my way through.'

'Really encouraging, Pappi. Müller, why don't you bring Pappi up to date while I try to find my way around here? I feel nervous with you guys hanging around.'

'Are you suggesting we leave?' Müller asked.

'Just give me a few minutes.'

'Can we trust you?'

'Bit late for that question,' she retorted, not looking round.

Müller glanced at Pappenheim with a tiny smile as she said that.

'And don't you forget I'm in here . . .' she said.

'We won't.'

They left her to it.

It took her some minutes of anxious trial and error but in the end, she found a folder entitled Woonnalla – 1.

'Might as well start with this,' she murmured to herself. 'Brannic is right up the alphabet, so he should be in this one.'

She opened the folder. Gold came onscreen. There were many files tagged 'Brannic'. She started reading.

As if on cue, Müller and Pappenheim returned.

'Any luck?' Müller asked.

'Take a look,' she replied, pointing to the large screen with a flourish. 'I had a quick read. Apart from being with the Semper, it seems Brannic is also tied in with militia groups. Some of his men are of the "ethnic hero" kind. I think we know what that means.'

'We do indeed.'

As they came forward to read the information, Pappenheim gave her a quick glance. 'Brannic will crucify you if he ever gets the chance.'

'Let's hope he never does.' She pointed to the screen. 'Dering knew what he was talking about.'

'He certainly did,' Müller agreed quietly as he read. 'And in all those years since that mission during the Gulf War, Brannic has never stopped looking for the DNA weapon.'

'Sooner, or later,' Pappenheim said, 'he will be heading our way.'

'He was always headed this way,' Müller said. 'Even all those years ago. We must be ready for him. Pappi, we're going to have to disturb the goth's Sunday. If she's not home, try her mobile. We need to have a special file on Brannic – printed and bound – for me to look at closely. I only wanted information that covers his method of operation. Every little quirk – if it's mentioned in the Woonnalla files, I want in that file. I leave you to judge what will be of most use if we have no choice but to go up against him.'

Pappenheim nodded. 'Where will you two be?'

'Where the DNA weapon happens to be . . . at my aunt's. Time to warn Greville.'

Again, Pappenheim nodded. 'I take it you won't be back tonight.'

'No. Perhaps tomorrow afternoon.'

'And if Kaltendorf asks . . . if he comes in?'

'I'm following a lead,' Müller said.

'One of those. That should keep him happy.'

Müller turned to Carey Bloomfield, who was looking at him.

'Shut down?' she asked.

'Shut down.'

Six

B ack in his office Pappenheim lit up, picked up the phone, and called Hedi Meyer.

She answered immediately. 'Meyer.'

'Miss Meyer,' Pappenheim said. 'Doing anything special?'

'Reading. Dostoevsky.'

'Sorry to spoil your literary Sunday . . .'

'He needs me?' she asked eagerly.

Pappenheim glanced briefly at the ceiling and shook his head slowly. 'He needs you.'

'I won't be long.'

'So much for Dostoevsky,' Pappenheim murmured after he had hung up. 'No contest. You're not going to be pleased when you know who's here.'

He took his time finishing the cigarette, then immediately lit another.

Autobahn A9, heading south. 1630 hours

It was one of those bright, late afternoons where hints of the coming autumn could be seen, but also where summer was stubbornly refusing to give in. The colours of that fight were glorious. Greenery was still very green. The September sky held a light to gladden the heart of a dedicated landscape artist. The speeding asphalt beneath the wheels of the car seemed darker than usual, a sharply delineated ribbon that etched itself into the distance.

The Porsche was holding a steady 200 kph in the fast lane. Traffic parted before it with smooth alacrity.

112

Except for a white van whose driver seemed to have fallen asleep.

Müller did not slow down as the van appeared to be reeling itself in at a high rate.

'Müller . . . !' Carey Bloomfield began.

Müller glanced in his mirrors. No one following. Not a sandwich.

'Müller,' she said again. 'We're going to hit that guy!'

'Think so?' Müller again checked his mirrors. No tail.

The van was getting bigger by the nanosecond.

'Give him the police lights you've got on this thing, Müller!'

'No. I've got a better idea.'

At the very last moment, the van driver seemed to come to his senses. He swerved dangerously out of the way.

The Porsche swept past.

'He needs a lesson,' Müller said. 'Here's his plate number. You know how to work the comm system. Key it in and send it to Pappi to check. If it's an ordinary white van tell him to find a way to get him charged for dangerous driving. If it's not an ordinary van, Pappi will know what to do.'

'You can't believe they've already zeroed in on us,' she said as she worked at the car's communications and navigation console. It contained capabilities not supplied as standard equipment.

'I'd be surprised,' he admitted. 'But you never know. He could just be one of those frustrating drivers on these autobahns who never let you pass, especially if you're driving a car like this. Or he could also be someone we don't want to know where we're going. Let's see what Pappi says.'

Müller pointed to the glove compartment. 'In there, when you're finished.'

She sent the message. 'Done.'

She opened the glove compartment, and saw a shoulder holster of strong, black webbing. In it was a big automatic she recognized as a Beretta 92R, her favourite weapon. It was a preference she shared with both Müller and Pappenheim.

'Nice,' she said, taking gun and holster out. She drew the weapon and checked it with smooth expertise.

'Spare magazines too,' he told her.

'How many of these things do you have now, Müller?' she asked as she balanced it for feel.

'I normally have three. This is newly acquired. Yours for whenever you come over without one.'

'I'm touched. Guys give jewellery, flowers . . . I get a gun.' She smiled. 'Just kidding, Müller. Thanks. I feel a little less exposed.'

'Thought you might.'

The communications unit pinged.

She looked down. 'That was quick. The goth must be there.' Then she gave a sudden giggle.

'What's funny?'

'Well . . . seems like we came up against an ordinary driver. To quote Pappi: "I just ruined his Sunday."'

'Serves the idiot right. Unfortunately, I doubt he will have learned his lesson. An accident waiting to happen.'

The unit pinged again.

Carey Bloomfield stared at the screen. 'Yep. The goth's in. I just felt the chill.'

'What does it say?'

'"Have fun": I don't think that's from Pappi, do you?'

Müller gave a smile. 'No.'

In the eavesdropping sub-centre, the operator shook his head in frustration.

The man who had previously been standing next to him hurried across from another terminal. 'What?'

'Just got a burst of transmission. Not voice.'

'And? From where to where?'

The other shook his head. 'Blocked.'

'Shit!' It was an angry outburst. 'We've got to burn through this. Find a way!'

Sunset and The Major

In the SUV, the man in the passenger seat rubbed his tired eyes as he stared at the red BMW.

'She's having a long lie-in.'

'Eh?' the driver said, looking slowly round. His eyes were slightly bleary. 'Some people like long Sundays in bed . . .'

'Which is where I'd like to be right now,' the younger one said through a yawn. 'A whole night in here . . .'

'Listen, soldier. You were picked because the general thought you could hack it. Not going to make the general a liar, are you?'

The other straightened in his seat and looked horrified. 'No, sir!'

'Much better. Now keep your eye out while I take forty. And besides, we've got bunks in back.' The driver reclined his seat, lay back and closed his eyes.

His partner looked at him uncertainly. 'Uh . . . yeah. Sure.'

'I've got a feeling about this,' the younger one said after a while.

Irritated, the driver opened one eye. 'If you're trying to get me pissed, you're on the right track. Got a feeling, have you? What feeling?'

Despite his uncertainty, the younger man stood his ground. 'We've been watching since yesterday.'

'As I was here as well,' the driver began with heavy sarcasm, 'tell me what revelations I've missed.' Both eyes, baleful, were now open; but he kept his seat reclined.

'I . . . I don't think she's in.'

'He doesn't think she's in. We've been here all goddamned night. Has that car moved?'

'No.'

'No! You were supposed to be watching when I wasn't. Have you seen her leave?'

'Er . . . no.'

'Er . . . no! Exactly! Now let me have my forty—'

'But that's just it . . .'

'Jeezus!' Furious, the driver brought his seat upright. 'What the hell are you flapping your mouth about, Harmon?'

'Perhaps . . . perhaps she never came home.'

'Perhaps . . .' The driver sighed heavily. 'How the hell did that car get here? It walked?'

But Harmon pursued his line of thought. 'What . . . what I mean is that she came home, but went out again . . . leaving . . . leaving the car . . . so we could watch it . . .' He stopped, worried by the look in the driver's eye.

The driver looked away to the car, frowned, then looked at Harmon again. 'You could be right.'

Harmon looked as if he did not quite think this was a better situation.

'But you have a problem,' the driver said.

'I . . . have a problem?'

'Say you're right. It means she's got several hours' start. We should let the general know. If you're wrong and one of us goes to check, that lets her know we're here. Not a good idea. Right now, she can't see us if she looks out of any of her windows. If she comes out to the car, we can pull out of sight, then follow her. As it's your idea she could be already gone, how do you want to play it?'

Harmon could see all the pitfalls mirrored in the driver's stare.

'Er . . . perhaps we should give it a bit longer.'

'Perhaps we should give it a bit longer,' the driver repeated, eyes lacking all humour. He reclined his seat once more. '*Don't* wake me unless you spot her.'

'Er, yeah. Sure . . . sure.'

Less than half an hour later, the driver brought his seat upright. 'Damn it, Harmon, you've planted that idea in my head. I'd better check with the general.'

He made the call. Brannic answered immediately.

'Sir,' the driver began, 'we may have a problem.'

'What is it, Jake?'

Brannic always addressed Jake Dixon by his first name, a habit going back to when they were NCOs.

'Harmon has the crazy idea that the colonel may not be home at all.'

There was a long silence.

'Sir?'

'What is this crazy idea?' Brannic eventually asked.

Dixon told him.

Again, the silence. Then, 'He could have a point.'

'That's why I thought I would run it by you, sir.'

'Smart to do, Jake. If she did manage to skip off before you got there, you've saved us from losing more time.' Brannic paused again. 'That's one smart bitch.'

'Yes, sir. What are your orders?'

'You're good with locks and alarms. Go find out . . . but make it quiet. And don't excite the neighbourhood.'

'Understood. And if she *is* there?'

'Make sure she does not see you.'

It was a warning, as well as advice.

'Yes, sir.'

'Jake?'

'Sir?'

'The more I think about it, the more I believe Harmon's called it correctly. You won't find her in there. But go check.'

'Yes, sir. All right, Harmon,' Dixon said as the call ended. 'The general's bought your idea. I'm going in for a quick recce. Watch out for nosey citizens.'

'You got it.'

It did not take long. Harmon saw Dixon returning, expression giving it all away.

'Goddamn it!' Dixon swore as he got back into the SUV. 'We've been watching a goddamned empty place. I feel like kicking that BMW to hell and beyond.'

He made another call to Brannic. 'Sir, Harmon was right. She's been long gone.'

The familiar silence came.

117

'All right, Jake. I'll take it from here. You come on back.'

'Sorry, sir.'

'Not your fault. I should have anticipated it. She got on my flank. She's won a small skirmish. That's all.'

A click ended the conversation.

In the Rogues Gallery, the goth, wearing a flaming red dress, was working on the Brannic file. Pappenheim had gone out for a much-needed smoke.

Face still, changeling eyes ablaze, she stared at the screen as if not seeing it.

'Yes,' she muttered. 'Have . . . *fun.*' She stabbed at a key.

Then she paused, staring at a passage that had come onscreen. The passage was sub-paragraphed Modus Operandi.

One of Brannic's favourite ploys is hostage taking for use as a bargaining chip. The mistake anyone dealing with this situation is likely to make, is to believe any promise he makes. None of Brannic's hostages have ever made it back alive, even when his demands have been met. He once kidnapped the son of a foreign government official whose services he needed. The act was naturally clandestine, as were the negotiations, which appeared to go well. After Brannic had got what he wanted, he told the official where to find his boy, who was six years old. The boy was found dead. Below is a list of known Brannic kidnappings, internationally. The mortality rate is one hundred per cent.

The goth stopped reading aloud. 'My God,' she whispered. She looked down the list of Brannic's victims. 'My God,' she repeated.

For a brief moment, she considered permanently deleting the entire sub-paragraph, to remove the warning. In her mind, she saw Carey Bloomfield being taken.

'You can't do that, Hedi Meyer,' she said to herself. 'You would never forgive yourself . . . and *he* would never forgive you, if he ever found out, no matter how long afterwards. I don't betray,' she added, incorporating the passage into the file she had created.

But she still hammered at the keys.

In his office, Pappenheim was having his troubled smoke. I can't talk to her, he thought. Not about this. She won't listen. Besides, I'm not that crazy.

The phone rang.

He picked it up. 'Pappenheim.'

'Mr Pappenheim . . .' an American voice began.

'Who is this? And how did you get this number?' Pappenheim began to reach for the button on the phone which would automatically set tracing in motion.

'And don't try to trace this. I won't be on long enough for you to breach my defences . . .'

'Defences. Are you a military man on Sundays?'

'Very funny. Where's my colonel?'

'You've got me there. I don't know who you are. How should I know if you've got a colonel?'

'Very funny,' Brannic repeated.

'You've said that already. Going to tell me who you are?'

'Don't make the mistake of underestimating me, Pappenheim.'

'Don't *you* make the same mistake . . . whoever you are.' Pappenheim's voice was cold.

A brief silence followed. 'I think we understand each other.'

'You might,' Pappenheim said. 'I don't.' He hung up, staring at the phone, wondering if he would call back.

There was no second call.

He was about to pick up the second phone to call Müller, when he drew his hand back.

'If this was who I think, they'll be waiting.' He lit a cigarette. 'Let them wait.'

In the eavesdropping sub-centre, the operator waited for the call he believed would be made.

119

After ten minutes, he shook his head at his colleague.

Half an hour later, he shook his head again. It was the same another thirty minutes later.

'It's not going to happen,' he said.

Pappenheim was on his second blonde, when the phone rang again; but it was not Brannic.

'File's finished, sir,' the goth said. 'And ready to print. Would you like to have a look before?'

'Yes. Be with you in a moment.'

'It's OK to finish your cigarette.'

'Thank you for the permission, *Meisterin* Meyer.'

'That's OK.'

Pappenheim sighed as they hung up. 'Respect for age. Where's it gone?' He finished the cigarette, then stood up. 'Now let's see what the general who likes to make anonymous calls is really all about.'

When he got there, Pappenheim scanned the file as the goth scrolled through. She paused at the hostage section, and highlighted it. Pappenheim read it through silently. He read the entire file without comment.

'Charming, murderous bastard, isn't he?' he finally said. 'You've done a great job. Thanks, Hedi. OK. Print and bind it. When you've done that, I want you to send a memo to all departments so that everyone on duty today sees it, and all those coming in tomorrow. Everyone is to be especially alert for kidnap attempts on members of this unit. Phrase it as you wish.'

The changeling eyes stared at him. 'You're serious, sir?'

'Do I look as if I'm joking, Hedi?' He spoke very quietly.

'Does that include me?'

'That especially includes you. The Semper still owe you one for Sharon Wilson. You've seen in that file, the kind of person we're going to have to deal with. I just received a call from the man himself.'

'Brannic? When?'

'Just before you called. Seems he's lost a colonel, and believes we may have her.'

'But how did he . . . ?'

'He assumes she's here. That's all that matters. Which reminds me: the second thing. Send a message to Jens' car. Tell him Brannic called, looking for a colonel. Send that in the usual burst.'

'When?'

'Time it for about an hour from now. He should be arriving about then.'

She nodded, and began to print the file on Brannic.

'Oh, Hedi . . .'

She looked back at him, waiting.

'As we both know our friends will be monitoring us again . . . or trying to, can you send them another of your little surprises?'

Her answering smile said it all. 'I've got just the surprise for them.'

'Surprise away,' Pappenheim said as he left.

An hour later, Pappenheim was still in his office, but he'd sent the goth home. Right on time, the message sent itself to Müller's car.

In the sub-centre, the operator remarked with some excitement, 'I've got something!'

'At last!' his senior colleague said, coming over to look. 'What have you got?'

'A transmission. I've done some cleaning up and . . . what the *fuck*?'

'What? What?'

'Something's tagging on to . . . oh, shit!'

One by one, the monitors began to die. Then whatever it was spread to the global map, which soon died. It was all over in seconds. The entire monitoring systems were good only for scrap.

The operator's eyes stared, his mouth agape as he surveyed the wreckage.

'What the fuck's just happened here?' his colleague shouted at him.

121

'They, they piggy-backed a virus to us. It's like the home-on-jam thing combat pilots do. Some of their planes have systems that will home on to other systems that paint them, and they send a missile along that. Whatever's been painting them – another plane, or a ground station – gets flamed. We've just had the same kind of thing done to us.'

'Are you telling me that they've got someone out there who can beat you, lock on to our scans, and send this shit back?'

'I'm not telling you anything. Look around. See for yourself.'

'Shit! Shit, shit. shit!' The senior eavesdropper looked around. 'What the hell do we do now if every time we start a surveillance, we collect a nasty infection?'

'Whoever's doing this is *very* good. Take it from me. It takes a hacker to know one. They must have someone who's definitely better than me. And I don't mind saying it.' He sounded respectful.

The other noted it. 'Cool your respect and come up with something to take that bastard out!'

'Well, he's got to be a special,' the other said. 'A true master. They don't come often. If you were really serious about taking him out . . .'

'What does that mean . . . exactly?'

'Exactly? Take him out.'

'You mean . . . kill him.'

The operator gave a shrug of indifference. 'Sounds permanent to me.'

'And how do we do that?' came the sarcastic retort. 'We tell the people who set this centre up that we have the bright idea of killing a police hacker? What do we suggest? That they go to that police unit and say please, can we see your hacker? We want to kill him.'

'It's not as crazy as it sounds. They can send me with the people who would do the job, to keep watch . . . see who comes in and out.'

'You can spot a hacker just by watching people go in and out of a building? Give me a break.'

'Laugh if you want. I'm a hacker. I know my kind. Suggest

it to them. All they can do is shoot us if they don't like the idea, but remind them of how often they're going to keep losing expensive equipment like this.'

In his office, Pappenheim gazed up through the smoke at his stained ceiling, and was smitten by a thought.

He picked up a phone. 'What are you doing here?' he asked when the call was answered. 'Doesn't anyone have homes? It's Sunday . . .'

'Why did you call this number if you did not hope I'd be here? And look who's talking.'

'What's this? Q and A?'

'Are we going to talk in questions all day?' Berger said. 'Well, it's nearly evening and if you really want to know why I'm here, I'm on duty. I decided to come in early. Reimer will be in soon. What's your excuse?'

'I don't need one.'

'Now we've got that out of the way, what do you want?'

'Lene, have I done something? Are you mad at me?'

'Why should I be mad at you? Feeling guilty?'

'Me? Innocence itself . . .'

'If it helps. The call. Why . . . sir?'

'That one bit,' Pappenheim said. 'It's about the goth,' he added.

'She's here too?'

'She was. Something important she had to do. She's gone home now.'

'I know there's an "and" coming . . .'

'Could you and Reimer keep an eye on her? You know how she's in a world of her own.'

Berger's attitude changed instantly. 'Is this to do with the memo you sent to all departments?'

'Yes.'

'Why her specifically?'

'It's a feeling.'

Berger fell silent, then, 'All right, Chief. I'll see to it. We'll babysit.'

'Don't let her know. I don't think I could survive the reaction.'

There was the hint of a smile in Berger's voice as she said, 'Don't worry. She's our goth. We'll look after her.'

'Thanks, Lene.'

'Care to tell me why the panic?'

'It's not panic . . . and no.'

Berger hung up on him.

What *is* the matter with them today, he wondered, staring at the phone, Gauloise gripped between his teeth.

In Washington, Brannic was again with the three people he had met earlier to discuss Carey Bloomfield's mission.

'You said it was urgent,' the powerful businesswoman with military ties began. 'I hate interrupted Sundays.' They were in her large study in her large home. 'I've got guests . . .'

'I've seen your guests,' Brannic interrupted bluntly. 'I considered this urgent enough to interrupt your Sunday and call this meeting. Your guests will think I am just another guest. I arrived in a limo, just as they did . . . and just as you two gentlemen did,' he added to the men with her. 'Happy now?' He looked at all three without expression. 'She's gone.'

'Who's gone?' one of the men asked.

'Who do you think?' Brannic's question held a tinge of irritation.

'But did you not tell us the colonel was under orders?' the woman asked.

'She is,' Brannic said coldly.

'We all know of Colonel Bloomfield's propensity for . . . let us call it . . . autonomous action. Do you know where she has gone?'

'Where she was supposed to. Germany.'

'Are you certain of this?'

'It's where she would go. The corns I do not have tell me so.'

This bizarre remark was one Brannic had used since his

days as a sergeant. His non-existent corns had never been proved wrong.

The woman raised an eyebrow. 'How did she get past you, General?'

'She's a good agent. She travelled under an assumed name. Obviously.'

'Do you know which one?'

'I've already checked all her known aliases. She did not use any of them.'

'She's smart.' The woman appeared to say this with approval. 'So you don't know for certain . . .'

'She's there. Count on it.'

'I trust you will do as you promised, and have someone keep an eye on her.'

'I've got people on it.'

'You seem to have everything in hand, General. Why then have you called us?'

Brannic's normally hard expression seemed to get harder. 'I believe she will betray the mission.'

The woman's eyes grew cold. 'That would not be good, and certainly not in our interests.'

'Tell me something I don't know. I called this meeting to give you a heads up, so that you can pass it on. If Bloomfield does betray the mission, as I believe, the repercussions could rattle right through the Order. I am convinced that Müller knows much more than we believe, and I intend to find out. That's it. I'm out of here. Enjoy your Sunday.' At the door, he paused. 'You probably haven't heard. Dering is dead.'

This stunned them.

'Dering?' the second man exclaimed. 'He is . . . he was one of us!'

'Not any longer, he isn't. And he never was. You know what that means.' Brannic went out.

The woman stared at the door that Brannic had closed just short of a slam.

'Our general seems to be getting a little too big for his boots,' she said with a thoughtful frown.

'Do you believe *he* killed Dering?'

'Not without sanction, I would hope. But one can never be sure with our pet bull terrier. But if Dering *was* an infiltrator, we might have suffered substantial damage without knowing it.'

'We need Brannic, but . . .'

'Perhaps Müller will kill him,' the man who had not yet spoken said. It was more than an expressed hope.

They looked at each other. 'As long as he finds the DNA weapon first,' the woman said. 'Our general is a little too . . . high profile for comfort. We prefer less of that. The world outside has little idea of who we are, and how much we influence it; and it must remain so. If Müller fails to kill him . . .'

'We've got Rachel.'

'Exactly.'

At the Schlosshotel Derrenberg, Pappenheim's message had arrived just as Müller was driving through the gate to the owner's wing of the hotel. Aunt Isolde and Greville – in his customary white suit but with open-necked shirt – were waiting with welcoming smiles.

'I think those grins are for you,' Müller observed.

'I'm well-liked,' Carey Bloomfield quipped. 'Uh oh,' she went on. 'Not so well-liked.' She was looking down at the communications screen.

'What?'

'Brannic's on my tail. See for yourself.'

Müller read the message. 'Not good. Better smile for the welcoming party. We'll talk about this later.' He turned off the engine and began to get out.

As she too got out, Aunt Isolde and Greville approached. Aunt Isolde gave her a warm hug. 'Hello, my dear.'

'Aunt Isolde. I keep turning up like a bad penny.'

'Nonsense.' Aunt Isolde released the hug, but still held Carey Bloomfield's shoulders in a gentle grip. 'This is your home, your bolt-hole, your refuge . . . whatever you want to call it. Your room will always be waiting. Don't you ever forget it.'

'Thank you. I won't.'

Aunt Isolde went over to Müller, and Greville stepped forward with the tiniest of secretive smiles.

'Hullo, young gel,' he said, giving her two quick pecks on the cheeks. His eyes probed at her. 'Some tightness about the eyes,' he continued in a low voice. 'Something in the car changed your expression.'

'Do you ever miss anything, Greville?'

'Some blind spots down the years . . . yes.'

Unobtrusively, he began to lead her away from Müller and Aunt Isolde. But Müller noticed and glanced in their direction.

'Not stealing her, old boy,' Greville called cheerily. 'Do you mind?'

Müller's eyes were guarded. 'Of course not.' He turned back to his aunt.

'There,' Greville said to Carey Bloomfield. 'All in order. But of course, his eyes too hold some secrets. Care to tell me?'

'Greville . . .'

'Ah. Understood.'

Greville abruptly left her to go over to Müller, while she stared at him in mild consternation.

'If I may interrupt,' he said to Müller and Aunt Isolde. 'Would you mind, old boy,' he said to Müller, 'if I took the lovely young gel for a walk in the main garden?'

Müller saw a message in Greville's eyes. 'Be my guest.'

'Jolly good.'

Greville gave him a smile and went back to Carey Bloomfield.

'He's really taken to her,' Aunt Isolde said to Müller. 'Treats her like a favourite daughter. What about you, Jens? She's perfect for you.'

'Stop matchmaking,' he said to her. 'You do that every time we come here.'

'Can't blame me for trying. You need a good woman in your life.'

'Thank you, Aunt Isolde. I've got the message.'

She glanced to where Carey Bloomfield and Greville were walking through to the main hotel gardens.

'Then stop dodging it. I'm not going to last forever, and as for Greville . . .' She stopped, not wanting to think of Greville's nemesis.

Müller smiled fondly at her. 'Stop worrying.'

Carey Bloomfield and Greville were strolling towards the bank of the stream.

'This spot holds many memories . . . one in particular is not very . . .'

'Pleasant, I know. This is where you and Jens got Dahlberg while the bastard held Isolde hostage,' Greville said.

'Yes. It was raining cats and dogs at the time, and the stream was swollen. I was in it, dragging myself against the flow to get one of his men.' She gave a slight shudder as she remembered. 'I don't want us to bring that kind of stuff down here again.'

'And do you think that is likely to happen?'

She paused, then decided to tell him. 'Greville . . . a man walked into my life . . .'

'Oh,' he said, misunderstanding. 'I thought you and Jens . . .' He made awkward motions with his hands as his words faded.

She smiled tolerantly at him. 'No, Greville. Not that kind of man. There's no one like that.'

Greville cocked his head to one side. 'No one? Ah,' he went on. 'That tiny blush says it all.'

'Stop it, Greville.'

He raised his hands in mock surrender. 'I shall probe no further. Tell me about the man who is not that kind of man.'

'A general called Brannic—'

'Brannic?' Greville interrupted. The name was said in shock.

She stared at him. 'You *know* Brannic?'

'I know of him, and what I do know is not pleasant. And

that is putting it mildly. At the time of the Gulf War – if we are talking of the same bod – he was a sergeant in a special unit which undertook a secret mission under the cover of the conflict. It was a cross-border operation. They were after the DNA weapon, which those who had sent them believed could be found out there. The unit ran into a set-up ambush. All killed except Brannic, who was wounded to give him cover when he made it back. Unfortunately the timing was all wrong. The ambush was supposed to happen *after* they had found what they were looking for. Brannic was the only one intended to survive, with the weapon safely found. Of course, no weapon to be found . . . but they were not aware of this. Another trap had been set . . . to fool the Semper into showing its hand.'

'Jesus, Greville,' she said, astonished. 'How do you know all this?'

'Grapevine. I talked to one of those who had mounted the ambush . . . a former agent, freelancing. He was neither Brit, nor American. He was the only one to survive. Temporarily. They eventually got him. Marseille, I think. Supposed bar fight. You see, the ambushers were themselves just hired hands, intended for elimination afterwards.'

'Nice people. You took a chance, Greville. He could have blabbed to someone about you . . .'

'He might have . . . if he'd known I was Greville.'

'And I should have known you did not survive this long by being careless.'

'Carelessness is one's implacable enemy in our line of business. Tell me about Brannic the general,' Greville added.

'He killed my boss. I'm certain of it. Now he's after me.'

'Aah. How did this come about?'

'This will pin your ears back.' She told him about Dering, and all that Dering had said.

'Aah,' Greville said again, after she had finished. 'Now I understand why you are so worried about revisiting that kind of trouble upon this place, and upon Isolde.'

'As I've said . . . he has no idea that you exist; only that Müller knows more than they think, and through me . . .'

129

'He hopes to get to Jens.'

'That has to be his plan.'

'I agree, dear gel. Totally. And we must ensure he fails, equally totally.'

'He will not be easy to take,' she said. 'Or stop, if he ever gets to find out who you are . . . or *what* you are.'

'I know it. But don't let my age fool you. I am as good as I ever was . . . perhaps even better and certainly fitter. Strange thing, my nemesis. It gives me excellent health, perhaps even augments it, while inexorably killing me. I have always considered the possibility that if that single element were removed from it, we would have a magic cure for all diseases on our hands – perfect health and on the evidence, a subtle anti-aging cure. I have no lines on my face. At my age, I should. And my eyes see better than they ever did. False dawn before the eternal darkness . . . Or should that be twilight? Never sure about that one.'

'Are you telling me the DNA weapon can be altered to be completely benevolent?'

'Who knows? But if so, imagine the scramble.'

'You're having second thoughts?'

'Absolutely not. If anything, I am more determined than ever that this should not be put into the hands of anyone. The years in the field and in the cold have taught me too much about my fellow man. I still have no wish to turn this loose upon the world. True, in its benevolent form it might save millions of lives, give perfect health, prevent aging . . . But both you and I know it would be abused. Commerce would want to make enormous sums out of it; and the military of any nation would want to use it as a weapon. Who knows what else it is capable of, once its key is unlocked? I am not a man who normally believes in such things, but for years now, I have thought that perhaps I was sent to do exactly what I am doing. Another person might not have done so, and we would now be facing the real horror of a biological weapon, one which would be capable of specific dedication. Life and death together. My fellow man would

130

choose to unleash death, as this frantic, decades-long search already proves.' Greville paused. 'It dies with me.'

'I can't disagree,' she said.

'I must say,' Greville began after another pause, 'that I am pleased you chose not to betray Jens. Rather reminds me of my own refusal to deliver the DNA weapon. Puts one out in the cold . . . but no choice.'

'I could not do that to him, Greville.'

'You have no idea how this pleases me.'

Something in the way he said that made her look at him closely. His eyes were fastened upon her.

After a while, she remarked softly, 'Would you have killed me if I had, Greville?'

He looked away. 'Perhaps we should not go there, eh, dear gel?'

She felt a tiny, involuntary shiver.

But he had turned to face her once more, and was smiling slightly. The almost unworldly chill she had seen in his eyes was gone.

'Brave man, your Dering,' he said. 'Absolute salt. Never knew him, or heard of him. As it should be, given what he was up to. But absolute salt to do what he did. Took courage, that. If that unmitigated bastard Brannic did get him, I am truly sorry. Make him pay.'

'Count on it.'

Greville gave her shoulder a light pat. 'That's the spirit. Now let's get back to Jens and Isolde, before they send out a search party, eh?'

He gave a soft laugh.

As they made their way back, Carey Bloomfield thought again about how the charming, very likeable man walking next to her would kill her without compunction should she attempt to carry out the orders Brannic had given her.

In the bedroom of his hotel suite in Berlin, Waldron looked at the naked body of Rachel Worth lying next to him. She appeared to be asleep. Then one of her eyes opened. It was, he thought with an uncomfortable frisson, like watching the eye of something fearsome come alive.

'Thought you were asleep,' he said.

'I was. I sensed you watching me. Like what you see?' She had still opened just the single eye.

'I think I proved it a while ago. It sent you to sleep afterwards.'

'Mmm!' She stretched, a lethal predator after a satisfying meal. Both eyes were open now, doubling the unsettling effect that had so disturbed Waldron. 'I've got to be going soon, lover.' She stretched again. 'Things to do. Last time I felt this good was that time I blew up those people you so nicely pointed us to, in their little dinky plane.'

And there it was. He had not yet been able to find a way of asking her about it without arousing suspicion. Yet now, presumably because she currently felt so satisfied, she had told him without prompting. It had literally fallen into his lap.

They had made energetic love during the night, and most of the day; and apart from calls of nature, had remained in bed. Waldron himself had only made one extra excursion to open the main door for the large ordered breakfast to be brought into the suite.

'Imagine,' she said, eyes gazing at him with an implacable indifference, 'if your good pal Pappenheim knew it.'

'He'd want to shoot me,' Waldron said, truthfully enough.

'Bet he would, lover,' she said, giving him a quick kiss.

The smell of her intoxicated him, and he reached for the body for which he continued to betray his wife.

She pulled away with a wide smile. 'Sorry, sweetie. Much as I love your . . . exercises and would enjoy finishing the Sunday with you, I've really got to go, and I can't be late.'

She seemed to be in a controlled fever of anticipation.

'So what's exciting you, if not me?'

She bared her teeth at him. 'Action.'

She did not elaborate as she easily evaded him to get out of bed, and headed for the bathroom.

She had one of the quickest showers he could remember

her taking and was dressed and ready to leave, while he was still in bed. All in white, in a close-fitting linen top that left her arms bare, complemented by what looked like skin-tight cycling shorts, she was a vision that continued to enthral him. The muscles of her tanned bare legs moved sinuously beneath the skin as she walked. Flat-soled white shoes were on her feet.

She fluttered a hand at him as she passed. 'See you soon, lover.'

She went out, leaving a bemused Waldron to wonder what was behind her suppressed excitement.

He waited for long minutes, until he was certain she was not returning. He need not have bothered. As soon as she had come out of the hotel, a big car with darkened windows had pulled up to whisk her away.

Pappenheim picked up the phone at the third ring.

'Pappenheim.'

'It's me.'

'And how's your Sunday?' Pappenheim asked brightly.

'Great. What are you doing at work?'

'You know how it is. Criminals don't respect holidays and weekends.'

Knowing that the eavesdropping centre was down, Pappenheim was not unduly worried about the security of the call. Even so, he hoped Waldron would be cautious.

With his own life at stake, Waldron was caution itself. 'Pity,' he said. 'I was hoping we could meet as arranged.'

Well aware there had been no such arrangement, Pappenheim said, 'Sorry. Something came up.'

'Solitary Sunday for me, then. It happened as you said, after all. Exciting times coming, eh?'

'I'm afraid so,' Pappenheim said. He understood what Waldron meant, but played the game in case there was a remote chance of being overheard.

'Perhaps another time then, mate.'

'Yes.'

As they ended the conversation, Pappenheim blew several smoke rings horizontally across the room.

'So the bitch did it,' he said to them.

Müller was in the spacious kitchen-cum-breakfast room with Aunt Isolde, who had again worked her magic and prepared an impromptu feast for her unexpected visitors.

Müller was studying the big table with anticipation when his phone rang.

'Yes, Pappi.'

Aunt Isolde discreetly went out.

'In case you're wondering about security,' Pappenheim began, 'have no fear. The goth detected another snoop centre and turned it into an ex-snoop centre. It's a matter of how long it takes them to switch to another, or replace it. The goth is certain her present was lethal, so it's a terminally dead centre now. She has a permanent, passive scan routine on guard.'

'Where is she now?'

'Gone back. She's not supposed to be on duty, as you know. For some reason, she's not a particularly happy bunny today.'

'Why? What's wrong?'

Pappenheim's silence was pointed.

'Oh,' Müller said.

'Yep. She knows we've got a visitor. Oh, and I've got Berger and Reimer to do some babysitting.'

'Dare I ask why?'

'The reason I called.'

'Which you're going to tell me when you're ready . . .'

'Such humour the man has. A quick look at the file brought up something interesting about the general's habits . . . he likes taking hostages, and has a hundred per cent mortality rate.'

It was Müller's turn to fall silent. 'We could be vulnerable to that,' he said after a while.

'You've got four prime targets with you . . .'

'Four?'

'Count yourself, and I've got one, which Berger and Reimer can handle . . .'

'The four of us can handle ourselves quite nicely, thank you. And what about yourself?'

'He's not after me. The goth would be a flanking attack. He likes using military terminology. What else? Where you are gives him all targets nicely together . . .'

'We've had two colleagues of the Ready Group on permanent rotation down here for some time, so we're not short-handed.'

'He's not on this side of the ocean yet,' Pappenheim said, 'but that won't last long. Be prepared.'

'Thanks for the warning. Good work by the goth.'

'She's priceless. I thought it best to warn you right away. I'll expect you when I see you. Better cut this short . . . before our keyhole friends attempt another go.'

'All right, Pappi. Thanks again.'

'Some more news.'

Müller waited.

'Rachel Worth bombed the plane.'

Müller felt a sudden tightness across his chest.

He was silent for so long, Pappenheim's voice came at him with some anxiety. 'Jens? You OK?'

'I'm fine, Pappi. I'm fine. Thanks for that news. It helps.'

'How?'

'To focus me.'

'Well, here's something else to focus upon. I was also told that exciting times were coming. I'm certain it's to do with her.'

'Brannic teaming up.'

'Could be. Just be careful.'

'I will.'

Aunt Isolde returned as the call ended. 'Trouble?'

'Policeman's lot.'

She gave him a sideways look. 'Jens, I know there's something you're not telling me . . . well, there's plenty you don't tell me. But I can understand that. It's just that . . .

Timmy thinks you found something in Australia that shook you.'

Müller's face was still. 'Aunt Isolde, now's not the time . . .'

She came to him and put a fond hand on his shoulder. 'All right, dear. When you're ready.'

He put his own hand to hers. 'Thanks. I'll tell you. Promise.'

'Good enough for me. Now where are those two? The food's waiting . . . ah,' she said as Carey Bloomfield and Greville entered. 'Where have you been? We were almost about to send out a search party.'

Greville turned to Carey Bloomfield with one of his impish smiles. 'There. Did I not tell you?'

'He did,' she said to Aunt Isolde and Müller. 'The very words.'

'Clairvoyant, me,' Greville said.

Berger's hawk eyes stared at Reimer as he came in, looking harassed.

'Reimer,' she began, 'I don't know which is worse . . . the haunted look on your face when you were with your skinny-ninny diet-freak girlfriend, or the haunted look now you're not with her anymore. Can't live with her, can't live without her?'

'Leave me alone, *Kommissarin* Berger,' Reimer complained, stressing the rank.

'Hey! Don't play the Klemp game with me. Since when does my rank matter with you? I've only had it for . . .'

'Since now. Leave Nina out of it!'

'Oh, Johann, *Johann*. Don't tell me you're seeing her again. That woman tears you to pieces.'

'She only wanted to talk things over . . .'

'Talk things over? I thought she'd left for good.'

'She said she made a mistake.'

'OK . . . She came to talk. Then what?'

Reimer cleared his throat. 'We . . . we . . .'

Berger needed no further explanation. 'My God,' she said, shaking her head in resignation. 'You men. Such fools. Good thing Klemp isn't here today. I can just imagine what he'd say to this. He'd have had a field day sniggering and making his usual, I'm-such-a-macho remarks. Well, Reimer, something to take your mind off your woes. The chief wants us to babysit the goth.'

'What? I don't need this!'

'You need,' Berger began in a hard voice, 'what the chief says you need.'

'Hedi Meyer doesn't know which end of the day it is. Why do I have to.'

'Reimer! Shut it! If the chief says we babysit, we babysit. If we ever, God forbid, have to take any action to protect her, you'd better be sure you can think and shoot straight enough, or I'll blow your brains out myself!'

'You bloody well would too,' Reimer sulked.

'As long as you know. Now forget about your girlfriend and behave like a cop who belongs here!'

Seven

Having eaten, Müller was making his way up the sweeping central staircase to his room; but he was not going to bed. Carey Bloomfield had remained with Aunt Isolde and Greville in the kitchen. Overlooking the staircase was a portrait of a beautiful young woman.

He was halfway up, when Greville's soft call came from the bottom. 'I say, old boy, may I have a word?'

Müller paused, to look back. 'Of course.' He waited for Greville to join him.

They continued together, and paused on the landing at the top of the staircase.

They studied the portrait.

'She was indeed beautiful,' Greville said.

'Yes,' Müller agreed, his voice softened by years of memories. 'She was.'

The wide landing formed a rectangular border for the staircase. Doors led off it into various rooms. Müller turned from the portrait and moved to go to his room.

When they were inside, Greville said, 'Hope you don't mind, old boy. I had a wee chat with the lovely colonel.'

'About?'

'Everything, more or less.'

'She told you about Brannic and her boss?'

'Yes. And I told her about Brannic.'

'You?'

138

'I know the unpleasant cove's reputation. Not someone you would give your hand to. He'd most likely cut it off.'

'We have detailed information on him and his methods,' Müller said.

'From what I've gathered from Carey, what you have tallies with what I do know. You've got a nasty on your hands.'

'I don't want him to come this way. We'll be leaving, perhaps tonight, to be safe . . .'

'As he'll clearly come after her, might be safer to leave her here. She and I, plus your two rather heavily armed colleagues can handle—'

Müller shook his head. 'And I don't want him near you . . . or my aunt. I can't take that chance. She comes back with me . . .'

'Keeping him focussed on where you are.'

'Yes.'

Greville nodded. 'I fully understand.' Greville paused. 'It seems to me that Dering was engaged in similar activities as your father. Are you ready to tell me what happened in Australia?'

Greville's eyes seemed to be telling Müller they knew more than he thought they did.

'Do you *know* something, Greville?'

'I have strong suspicions which, based upon my own experiences, lead me to certain conclusions. Of course, could be wrong, I hope I am . . . because if I am not, then I'm afraid I understand the look you just gave that portrait.'

Müller said nothing.

'You found them, did you not, Jens?' came Greville's soft voice. 'After all those lonely years, you found them . . . alive. They did as I did. They hid themselves in their supposed deaths. Your investigations eventually led you where you were always destined to go. So sorry, old boy.'

Müller still said nothing.

Then in a hoarse voice, he said, 'I watched them die, Greville. This time, it was the real thing. And I . . . never . . . made my peace with them. They tried and . . . in my anger . . . I rejected them. God forgive me.'

139

'It is not God, old son, who needs to forgive . . . but you. You need to forgive yourself.'

'You must never tell my aunt. Promise me that. I will do that myself. It has to come from me.'

'My word as an ex-officer, what's left of a gentleman, and the man who loves Isolde more than life itself.'

Müller cleared his throat. 'Thank you, Greville.'

'Thank you for telling me, dear boy. I really am so very, very sorry. You've no idea just how much. So many casualties in this long, damned secret war.' Greville gripped Müller's shoulder briefly. 'Now I had better leave you to it. You and the colonel have plenty to discuss. Look after that gel, Jens.'

'I will.'

Autobahn A9, returning to Berlin. 2330 local

The Porsche hurtled through the night in the fast lane, holding 255 kph, its bi-xenon lights turning the darkness into virtual day.

Carey Bloomfield watched as the mesmerizing flow of the road ribboned its way towards them. She had made no comment about Müller's decision to head back to Berlin.

'Why do we have to go back tonight?' she now asked.

'I'm a policeman, remember? This is not my long weekend.'

'You know what I mean, Müller.'

He said nothing.

'I know what you're trying to do,' she continued. 'Brannic has no idea of Greville's existence. You don't want to tow him down there, endanger Aunt Isolde – especially after what happened back then with Dahlberg – or risk Brannic finding out about Greville . . .'

'Which he's not likely to . . .'

'Unless someone lets him know. As no one's going to . . . you're taking me back to Berlin to keep his focus there. Which, in a way, makes sense . . .'

'In a way?'

'It's only part of it, Müller. You can't keep me locked up in your apartment.'

'You'll be very comfortable. Plenty there to keep you occupied.'

'I'll go stir crazy hiding in there day after day, no matter how much of a palace it is. You've got to force Brannic to do what *you* want him to do . . . not the other way round. You've got to outflank him.' She paused. 'You've got to let him take me.'

'No!'

'Müller, you're doing nearly two hundred and sixty goddamn kilometres an hour. Keep your eyes on the goddamned road!'

'It's still no.'

'It makes sense! Brannic wants to force you to tell him what he thinks you know. What does he believe are your weak flanks? People you care about. Right now he believes his prime leverage will come from having me as hostage. He knows that as Dering is dead – and I believe the asshole *has* killed him – I might decide to go against orders. He's already got me tagged for my attempt – against orders – to rescue my brother, and holds that against me. Unless he's the most dumb asshole on the planet, he also knows I don't like or respect him. He's many things, but dumb isn't one of them. Are you with me so far?'

'I'm listening . . . which means just that.'

'He's also accused me of getting too close to you. In his eyes, that marks me down as being unsound. He *expects* me to disobey. Snatching me makes tactical sense to him.'

'It's still no.'

'Goddamn it, Müller! You're playing against a man who plays hardball . . . every goddamn time . . .'

'As you said, we're travelling very fast. Arguments in cars are folly at the best of times. This is the worst of times.'

'Jeezus!'

'What are you doing?'

He had glanced down. Both her hands were wrapped around the stubby gear lever.

'You listen to me, mister, or I'm going to haul this damned shift stick right through the gears!'

'Are you mad? Have you any idea what this gearbox costs? Not to mention what might happen to the car at this speed?'

She did not let go of the lever. 'As you said, arguing in a car is a no-no, arguing at speed . . .' She shrugged. 'And as I know how much you love this car.'

'You can kill us both. You're mad!'

'You can fool Brannic, and be a step ahead. You know deep down I'm right.'

He had begun to slow down rapidly, moving from the fast to the slow lane. 'Let go of the stick. I need to change down.'

'This car is so powerful, you can slow right down in sixth gear, and it will still pull strongly. I have driven it, remember?'

'I do remember. Must have been mad to let you.'

'Do we have a deal?'

'What deal?'

The car was now cruising in the slow lane, untroubled by being in sixth gear.

'You let Brannic snatch me. Only, he must *not* suspect that it's a set-up . . . or I'll sure as hell end up dead like Dering. This means people he cannot associate with your unit must keep watch. They must not look like cops, either. So non-cops, or cops who look like anything but cops.'

She was still holding on to the gear lever.

'Are you permanently attached to that?' he asked.

'Until you agree.'

'At this speed, we'll not make Berlin before midday tomorrow.'

'Don't exaggerate. Deal, Müller?'

'Something like this is no deal at all.'

'Come on, Müller! I've been in tougher situations . . .'

'Kidnapped by a psychopathic general? I don't think so. Besides, I promised Greville I would look after you.'

'You'd better. If you let him kill me, I'll come back to get you. Do you know even that cute, eccentric English gentleman would kill me if he thought I would betray you?'

Müller shot her a disbelieving glance. 'What?'

'Oh, yes. See, Müller? That's the difference between someone like you, and people like Greville and me . . . or Brannic. We follow through for the mission, if we decide to do so. Greville would kill even me, to prevent anyone getting their hands on the DNA weapon. I would kill . . . well, you've seen me do it. You on the other hand . . .'

'Are a policeman. One of those who prefers not to fire his weapon if he can possibly help it.'

'But there are circumstances when you can be as hard as someone like Greville. We both know that. You're going to have to deal with Brannic, and you've got to stop him. You know he does not negotiate. You've got just the one way to stop him.'

After a long while, Müller said, 'Are you asking me to let you willingly become his hostage?'

'I'm not asking, Müller. I'm telling you it's our only option. And no, I'm not doing this willingly.' She let go of the stick.

There was silence between them for the rest of the journey.

During the night, twelve people arrived in Berlin from different points of the compass. Some knew each other. Some did not; but all were linked.

Friedrichstrasse, Berlin. Monday, 0745 local

Three men were sitting in a small café that had recently opened for the day's business. They were the only customers so far. One, in glasses, looked like a student. His companions were slightly older, and did not look like students. The 'student' was American, as was one of the other men. The third was German. They were in low-voiced conversation, and all spoke English. The Americans had arrived from Frankfurt by car. The German was one of Sternbach's men.

The café, though not directly opposite, had a perfect view of the police building, particularly of the main entrance, and of the entrance to the garage.

'We must not remain here long,' the German cautioned. 'Some police use this place.'

'We won't be long,' the one who looked like a student said. 'We've been in here for what . . . fifteen minutes. Let's stay just long enough to have our coffees. If I see no one, we leave, and try again another time. How's that?'

The other two nodded. 'OK,' the German said.

'How the hell can you spot a hacker just by looking?' the second American asked. 'We've seen people coming and going. Anyone could have been a hacker to me.'

'To you. Not to me. I'll know him when I see him.'

'Oh, give me a break.'

The German smiled in disbelief, and said nothing.

'Nearly there now,' Berger said.

'Thank God!' Reimer heaved a sigh of relief. 'She drives just as you would expect. In her own dream world.'

'Reimer,' Berger warned as they followed the goth's black VW Beetle at a safe distance.

'Well,' he said in protest. But he did not push it.

The black Volkswagen passed the café, then stopped for traffic.

'Hey,' the apparent student said, 'will you look at that beauty?'

'The woman? Or the car,' the American asked. He looked at it with interest. 'One of the real old ones, in great condition.'

'The car, of course. She looks after it well.'

'She looks good, too,' the American said with approval. 'Doesn't look like a cop to me though, Blake.'

But Blake, the apparent student was frowning, staring at the goth as if he'd found gold. 'Nah,' he said eventually.

'What are you talking about?'

'Just a crazy idea. Your saying she doesn't look like a cop made me wonder.'

'I know that one,' the German said.

They stared at him.

'How?' Blake asked.

'She's the one who killed Sharon Wilson. She's a cop.'

144

The other American was surprised. 'That gothic looking thing's a cop?'

'Who can shoot well enough to beat Sharon Wilson. We know, because someone told General Sternbach. I think the person who gave the information said she looked like a goth. We'll get her one day . . .'

But Blake was still staring at the Beetle, and still frowning. 'It just could be . . .'

The American stared at him. 'You think she's . . . oh, come on!'

'Just because I've been thinking it's a man, doesn't mean it has to be, Arnold. You didn't think she looked like a cop . . . she is, and a good shooter at that. But look at her. She's a goth, and a cop. Unconventional, in a very conservative profession. Why couldn't *she* be the hacker?'

Blake stood up.

'What are you doing?' Arnold demanded in a sharp, low voice.

'Going for a closer look.'

'Are you *nuts*? What if . . . ?'

'Chill out, Arnold. What am I doing? Looking at a car. Take a look at those people walking by. Look how many are staring. And see that woman with a kid. They're both staring. She's probably seen all the movies when *she* was a kid, and he's looking like he wants it for Christmas.'

Before either of them could object further, Blake went out.

'He's nuts,' Arnold said.

Bruch said nothing.

They watched as Blake strolled past the Beetle, pretending to be uninterested. Then he glanced at the goth's car more than once, feigning indifference. The goth never looked at him. He returned as the Beetle moved on.

'She's in her own dreamworld,' Blake said. 'She's the one.'

'I still don't buy it,' Arnold said.

Blake turned to the German. 'You said you had a score to settle. Why not start now? If she's the hacker, we'll find out. If she isn't, you can still settle your score.'

'The problem with you, Blake,' Arnold said, 'is that you're in *your* own computer world. Things just don't work like that. Unless you're a hundred per cent sure, I'm not going to recommend doing something that will have the cops all over us, for nothing. The big boys will sanction things that have a pay-off in our favour. This will have shit all over us.'

'While you think about that,' Blake said, 'think about how many monitoring centres they're prepared to lose.'

'I still don't buy she's the one. She doesn't look it.'

Blake rolled his eyes in resignation.

'She's gone in,' Berger said.

'The goth's safe,' Reimer said. 'Hallelujah . . .'

'Shut it. Coffee?'

'I could do with one,' he admitted. 'But why . . .' He paused, staring at her as she began to slow down. 'What are you doing?'

'What's it look like? Slowing down.'

'I can see you're slowing down. But why?'

'Did you see that man?'

'What man?'

'You're not very observant for a cop who's supposed to be good!'

'Don't start on me. Too early in the day.'

Berger let that ride as she turned into the next corner, and parked at the side of the road.

'I thought we were going in.'

'We are,' Berger said. 'After the coffee.'

'All right. What have I done now?'

'Why so guilty? I am only buying you a coffee.'

Reimer looked at her with wary eyes. 'Why?'

'I want to check something.'

Berger, in a medium weight T-shirt and jeans, got out of the car, taking with her the bag in which she currently carried her gun.

Reimer, in jeans, T-shirt and full-length denim jacket, carried his own gun rear holster. The weapon was not visible to the casual observer.

146

He climbed out, and looked at Berger. 'Now what?'

'Put an arm about me and don't get any funny ideas.'

At first looking at her as if someone had told him to put his hand in a snake pit, Reimer hesitantly did so. His hand strayed too low and touched her bottom lightly.

'If you want to be able to use that hand'when you go to the toilet, take it off!'

Reimer moved his hand as if scalded.

'God, Reimer! How did you hold your Nina?'

'I . . . I always had my hand down there.'

'You mean she's actually got a bottom?'

Reimer took his arm away. 'Look. If you're going to . . .'

'OK, OK. Sorry. Put the arm on my shoulder. That way you won't lose it. Now we're just a couple going for a first coffee on this nice morning.'

'Why this place, anyway? Because some colleagues use it?'

'No, Reimer. And anyway, it's a bit too early for the regulars. Have you ever noticed, Reimer,' Berger went on, 'what a good view of our building you can have from here?'

He glanced at her. 'You don't think . . . ?'

'I saw a man checking out the goth's car. He seemed a little too interested in it, while trying hard to pretend he wasn't. Other people looked at it. They did not hide their interest. He, on the other hand, came out of the café, just to check it out. Then he pretends not to be interested. He's gone back in. Just testing a hunch, Reimer. Hope Klemp doesn't turn up and spoil everything. He sometimes rushes in for a quick coffee. I don't think I'd like to hear his comments if he saw us.'

They entered the café, and took a table well away from the three men they saw sitting at the large window.

'Look at those men,' Berger whispered, as they sat down. 'They glanced at us, then continued with what they were doing. And don't stare!'

'What?'

'Taking an interest in our building.'

'They'll have seen the goth . . . if they were here when she passed.'

'They were. The man who came out is with them.'

At that moment, the café owner, whom they knew, turned up. He was wise enough to keep it neutral.

'Nice morning,' he said.

'It is,' Berger said.

'Coffee for two?'

'Please.'

The owner went off to prepare the order.

'Cops,' Stefan Bruch, the German, said, keeping his voice low.

'How do you know?' Blake asked. 'They look like lovers after the night before, grabbing a coffee before going off to work.'

'How do you know a hacker?' Bruch countered. 'And work could be in this building we're watching.'

'He's got you there,' Arnold said.

'Even if they are not,' Bruch said, 'I think we should leave. It was not a good idea to stop here.'

'You brought us here,' Blake reminded him.

'I was ordered to show you the closest place that was not too obvious. I did so. My opinion was not requested.'

'I think we should stay,' Blake said. 'If they are cops and we just up and leave, it will look suspicious. If they're not cops and just a couple having coffee, we're leaving for nothing.'

'I'll buy that,' Arnold said.

Bruch looked from one to the other. 'OK,' he said. But he was not happy about it. 'There is a way to find out exactly what the woman who looks like a goth does,' he went on to Blake. 'Ask your people to ask General Sternbach to find out what her job is. Whoever gave him the information before should know, or be able to find out.'

'I'll definitely buy that,' Arnold said.

Berger and Reimer finished their coffees, and got up to leave. The men were still there as they paid, and they left the café.

As they walked back to the car, Reimer said, 'Well?'

'I've still got that feeling.'

'So what now?'

'We go in to work, get the goth to work her magic with a photofit from descriptions we give her. If we ever see them again, we'll remember.'

'See?' Blake said to Bruch. 'Just a couple for coffee.'

'Perhaps,' Bruch said.

Berger turned the car round and drove into Friedrichstrasse.

As they came up to the café, traffic halted them for a few moments. With deliberation, she turned to look . . . and found her eyes squarely held by Bruch's. She gave him her most penetrating, hawk-eyed stare in return, holding it long enough to leave him in no doubt that she knew what they were.

The traffic began to move again.

'What did I tell you?' Bruch said. 'Cops. And see where they came from.'

Berger was turning to enter the police garage.

All three watched the car.

'They'll be doing a photofit as soon as they get in,' Bruch continued. 'It was foolish to come here.'

Arnold looked at Blake, expression neutral. 'I'll buy that.'

'No, it wasn't,' Blake insisted. 'When we know what that goth really does in there, we can take action.'

'You are making a mistake,' Bruch said to him. 'I will not recommend it.'

'And I will,' Blake retaliated.

The two men looked at each other, no love lost.

'We should leave before you two start fighting,' Arnold advised. 'Cool it, Blake.'

Berger knocked on Pappenheim's door.

'In!'

She coughed as she entered.

'Don't overdo it,' Pappenheim said. 'It's not that bad.'

'How would you know?' she countered.

'And good morning to you, too.'

'Have you been home?'

'What does it look like?'

'You slept in your clothes.'

'I always look as if I've slept in my clothes. So how's the goth?'

'Safe.'

'But? You wouldn't be in here without a "but" to come.'

'Three men in Lino's. They were watching this building. I'm certain.'

Pappenheim removed the cigarette that had been between his lips throughout. 'Ah,' he said.

She told him about Blake, and of the pantomime she had played with Reimer.

'Bet that gave Reimer a thrill . . .'

'Don't you start, Chief.'

Pappenheim grinned at her, unrepentant. 'Speak to the goth. See what she comes up with. Then we can see if we can find matches.'

'Exactly what I was thinking.'

'Good thinking, and good work. Let me know how it goes.'

'Storm's coming,' she said.

'Definitely.'

In Hermann Spyros' department, Berger and Reimer gave Hedi Meyer's descriptions of the men they had seen. It did not take her long to come up with virtually exact likenesses.

'Yep,' Berger confirmed. 'That's them. A genius as usual, Hedi. See if you can find matches, then let the chief know.'

'OK.'

'And Hedi, if you ever see any of those men anywhere in your vicinity, expect trouble, call us, and get out of the way . . . fast.'

The changeling eyes looked up from the screen and at her. 'OK. But I keep my gun.'

'You keep your gun. Who knows? You might surprise them

as you did Sharon Wilson.' Berger patted the goth's shoulder. 'Thanks, Hedi.'

'Anytime,' the goth said, watching them leave.

Then she began to hunt out matches.

Three of the people who had arrived in Berlin during the night were in a big, powerful saloon with darkened windows, parked some distance from Müller's building, but with a clear view of the entrance to his apartment, and the garage.

'Shouldn't they be leaving by now?' one said.

'Give them time for their morning exercises,' another said with heavy meaning.

'So you think the colonel's fucking him?' the third asked.

'Does it give you a charge to think about it?' the first goaded.

A rear door opened, startling them. 'I could have shot you all,' Rachel Worth said to them, cold eyes raking. 'Keep your minds on the job!'

She slammed the door, and went back to where she had parked her own car, a sports coupe, a good fifty metres away.

'She couldn't have heard,' one of the men said. 'You can't hear anything from outside this car.'

'She's got weird instincts.'

'And crazy with it.'

Traffic was normal for that time of day in the area; people going about their business. Between where the saloon was parked and Rachel Worth's car was a pumped-up white Golf, with two young men in calf-length shorts, football shirts, and baseball caps worn back to front. Something seemed to have happened to their car, and they were trying to fix it.

The Golf had been there already when the saloon and the sports coupe had arrived.

In the apartment, Müller said to Carey Bloomfield, 'Ready for this?'

'No. But there's no choice.'

'I still don't like it.'

'Think I do? You'd better come get me, Müller.'

'Nothing will stop me.'

They looked at each other for long moments. 'No good-byes,' he said.

'No.'

He went out, leaving her staring after him.

'Garage door's opening,' the driver of the big saloon said in an urgent whisper.

'Why are you whispering?' another asked. 'They can't hear you.'

'Fuck you, Pastius!' the driver snapped.

'Hey, you two! Can it. Better warn Miss High and Mighty, Pastius.'

All were American.

Pastius warned Rachel Worth by radio. 'They're coming out.'

'I'm ready,' she said.

They watched as the snout of the Turbo emerged, like a ferocious beast emerging from its lair.

'That is some car,' the driver enthused. 'They pay German cops well.'

'He's got his own money,' Pastius informed him sniffily.

'Do you always have to be such a smart asshole, Pastius?'

'Hey! Zinno, Pastius, can it, I said. The general's not going to like it if you two piss around and fuck this mission!'

'Shit!' Zinno said.

'What? What?'

'He's alone! Goddamn it!'

Pastius was already warning Rachel Worth. 'Target *not* in sight.'

'Got it.'

They watched as the Porsche rumbled unhurriedly past.

'What the hell's he done?' Zinno asked. 'Where is she?'

'You're asking me?'

'Pastius!'

'All right, all right, Penton. Keep your shirt on. So what do you think? She's not there?'

'I think she is in there,' Penton said. 'We can't get into that place. In his place, that's where I'd put her.'

'We can't hang around here forever. It's got to be done before he gets back.'

'Don't you think I know that?'

'Perhaps he thought we'd follow him,' Zinno suggested.

No one responded.

Fifteen minutes later, he said, 'Hey . . . lookee here. Cab stopping.'

They looked at the taxi, then at the building. No one came out. The taxi drove off.

'Just a cabbie stopping to check his cash,' Penton suggested.

Another fifteen minutes went by.

This time it was Pastius who spoke. 'Look! The same damned cab. And it's stopping again . . . same spot.'

'A cop in the cab?' Zinno suggested. 'And he made a round to check all was clear?'

'You could have a point,' Penton said. 'If so, he hasn't seen us. If she comes, we'll have to do this fast. *Don't* kill the cop . . . or the cabbie, if he really is one.'

'All heart, Penton.'

'General's orders. You obey them. Warn the lady we may have action.'

Pastius did so.

'We've got action!' Zinno announced sharply. 'She's out!'

He started the car, while Pastius alerted Rachel Worth even as the car shot forward.

Carey Bloomfield had just touched the door of the cab when the saloon pulled in front of it and stopped. Before she had fully taken that in, Rachel Worth's coupe pulled up behind the taxi. It was a neat sandwich.

Rachel Worth got rapidly out of her car and placed herself before Carey Bloomfield, barring her way.

'Why don't you let us give you a ride, sweetie?' she offered. 'I'm not pointing a gun at you, but don't let that fool you. My friends in that car over there have many pointed at you. I suggest you get into it before people come to look. OK?' She smiled at Carey Bloomfield, predator eyes unblinking.

Carey Bloomfield looked from her to the taxi to the dark saloon.

'You don't have a choice, sweetie,' Rachel Worth said. She glanced at the cab driver. 'If he's a cop, we don't want his blood all over the cab, do we? And if not a cop, same thing. Your choice, sweetie. The only one you have. You can get in, or we'll do it for you. Time's flying, and someone you know is waiting to see you. Move!'

Carey Bloomfield's eyes were murderous.

'Aah . . .' Rachel Worth breathed. 'I think you'll be fun.'

Carey Bloomfield walked over to the saloon, and climbed in.

As she did so, Rachel Worth opened the front passenger door of the cab and leaned in. 'Hello, sweetie.'

She hit the driver with a fist that had far more force than expected.

The driver went out like a light.

'Hmm,' she said, pulling back and shutting the door. 'Sometimes, I don't know my own strength.'

The football fans with the Golf watched the two cars drive away.

One spoke into a radio. 'Snatch done.'

A motorcyclist went past, caught up, and passed the small convoy. He spoke into his helmet mike, giving the direction of travel.

Five minutes later, an ordinary saloon pulled into the normal traffic behind them.

Rachel Worth's car peeled off.

'The coupe's turned off,' the passenger said into a radio. He gave the direction.

The pursuers were changed frequently to avoid suspicion, never losing sight of the saloon, or the coupe.

'Any tails as yet?' Penton asked Zinno.

Zinno glanced in his mirrors. 'Nothing I can spot.'

'It doesn't mean we're not being followed,' Pastius said.

'We've got some of our own people shadowing,' Penton said .'They would have reported by now.' He was sitting next to Carey Bloomfield, playing with her gun. 'Nice weapon, Colonel. Good balance. Neat harness. Present from the boyfriend?'

She gave him a cutting look, and turned away.

'You won't be so huffy when we get to the general. He's *very* disappointed in you. Wilful disobedience of orders, treason, going AWOL . . . oh, he's got a nice package to throw at you. I reckon we're looking at many, many years behind bars. Think the boyfriend will miss you? All those nice *frauleins . . .*'

Carey Bloomfield maintained a stony silence. But her thoughts were racing. They hadn't blindfolded her. That could only mean they did not intend that she would live to tell anyone where she had been taken.

In the Rogues Gallery, Müller and Pappenheim were standing behind the goth, watching as she inserted the information which came in through her headphones into a program she had long devised. This translated itself into real-time updates on both the saloon, and Rachel Worth's car. Each was marked by a small transparent disk on a moving map. The saloon was blue, the coupe red. Despite their different routes, each car so far seemed to be heading towards the same destination.

Every now and then, Pappenheim would glance at Müller, knowing that Müller was hating himself for agreeing to Carey Bloomfield's suggestion.

'They're well out of Berlin, now,' Pappenheim said, more to make conversation than to impart information.

Müller watched as the disks headed first westwards, then south-west. The coupe seemed to be closing in.

'They must be nearing wherever they're headed,' Pappenheim said. 'The coupe's closing the separation.'

Both cars had taken tortuous routes, clearly intending to shake off any pursuit, whether they spotted one or not.

On the way back from the Schlosshotel, Müller had stopped off to inform Pappenheim of Carey Bloomfield's plan, which he had still considered insane; but Pappenheim had surprised him by agreeing with her. However, Pappenheim had also devised the pursuit strategy, using police colleagues in unmarked vehicles, from other units. The football fans with the Golf had been the eager patrolmen, only too happy to be included in the action.

'It's going to be very hard to avoid their request for transfer after this,' Pappenheim had commented with a long-suffering air.

Now he watched as the coupe got ever closer to the saloon. Fifteen minutes later, both cars were on the same road. A bare ten minutes later, both had stopped.

Pappenheim touched the goth's shoulder. 'Tell all pursuit teams to clear the area.'

She nodded, and did so.

He looked at Müller. 'Now what?'

Müller's expression gave nothing away. 'We wait for the call. I'll be in my office.'

He went out.

The goth turned round to look up at Pappenheim. 'Is he going to be all right?'

'I'm not sure. If it's any consolation, he'd be just as worried about you.'

'I know,' she said, looking at the door.

'Can you give me a close-up of where the cars have stopped, in high definition?'

The goth turned back to the computer. 'I can do better. I can give you up to less than a square metre, including topography. Not in real time, of course; but wherever they are will not have changed since the last time I updated this map.'

'Then let's see.'

She brought up the local area, zooming in, until a small, factory-like building came into view.

'Stop there for a moment. Pan around.'

She did so, while Pappenheim studied the layout of the buildings, and any high ground close by.

'Go out slightly – about a kilometre.'

She zoomed out, and several areas of high ground appeared.

Pappenheim tapped at the screen. 'Give me a close-up on that area.'

It was a wooded section with what seemed like a clear field of fire to the factory.

'Mark that for a print out, as well as the one-kilometre image. OK. Now go back to that factory. Close-up shot of the whole site, then selected shots. I'll point out which.'

When she was done, he had a very clear idea of what he planned to do.

Müller sat at his desk, reading through the file on Brannic.

This was the third time he was doing so. He had picked it up when he had stopped to talk with Pappenheim to discuss Carey Bloomfield's plan, and had taken it home. She had also read it. He had insisted that she do so, so that she would have some insight into the kind of person she would have to deal with.

He was on the section about Brannic's mortality rate with hostages, when the phone rang.

He picked it up. 'Müller.'

'Ah, Mr Müller,' came the hard American voice speaking English. 'Your fame precedes you.'

'Who are you? And what do you want?'

'Let's not treat each other as fools, shall we? I think you are well aware of who I am. You must know by now that I have got the colonel.'

'I know someone has kidnapped her. The colleague driving the cab was knocked out . . .'

'So he was a policeman, after all.'

'Unfortunately, he was hit too hard. It took him a while

to wake up. He gave only a vague description of the car. There are many dark saloons in Berlin.'

'I could commiserate, but why lie? I am not sorry. What did the colonel tell you?'

'What could she have told me? She is not exactly forth-coming . . .'

'Come now, Mr Müller.'

'She does not trust me, and I don't trust her. Whatever your quarrel happens to be, it does not concern me.'

There was a silence, as if Brannic had been caught off balance.

'Then why have a police officer masquerading as a cab driver?'

'Why do you think?'

Again, there was the uncertain silence. Then the line went dead.

Müller slowly put the phone down. He looked at his hand, checking to see whether it shook, even slightly. It did not.

The phone rang again.

'Do not take me for a fool, Mr Müller.'

'Why should I take you for anything? You call me to tell me you have taken an American officer – an official guest – hostage. Every effort will of course be made to find her. It is our responsibility. However, if our efforts fail, we will inform the American military, our military, the diplomatic—'

'That, Mr Müller, would be a very foolish thing to do . . . unless you want the colonel's death on your hands.'

'So you now threaten to kill her?'

'If you try to trace this call – though we have taken pre-cautions – this will also mean her death.'

'No attempt is being made to trace your call.'

'Can I believe that?'

'Yes. You are clearly going to give me instructions. Why bother tracing the call?'

There was another pause. 'You are an unusual man, Mr Müller. I can see you will make a worthy opponent.'

'I am not your opponent. You have – according to you –

kidnapped a guest of ours. I have no idea why you have done so. Therefore, I await your instructions to learn what you require in exchange for her.'

'A very direct man. I respect that. Very well, Mr Müller. What I want is information. Information you may have, even if you may not at the moment know it. In order for me to decide whether you do have that information, we must meet, at a place of my choosing. You will, of course, come alone.'

'Naturally.'

'You will receive your instructions.'

The line went dead once more.

Back in his own office, Pappenheim called the goth, who was still in the Rogues Gallery.

'Hedi, do you remember the Dragunov sight I asked you to work on some time ago? How is it coming?'

'Do you want it now?'

'Er . . . yes. Is that difficult?'

'I'm not finished with it. It will still take some time; but I've got something temporary as a working prototype. It might not be too reliable.'

'Does it work?'

'After a fashion . . .'

'Which means?'

'I don't know when it might decide to stop working.'

'I'll take my chances.'

'I'll go and get it. Give me a few minutes.'

'You've got them.'

She was as good as her word and returned to the room with the doctored sight, to hand it over to the waiting Pappenheim.

He had already taken out one of the Dragunov sniper rifles that had been taken off dead Semper killers. It had come with a silencer.

He mounted the sight, as she watched.

'So what's different?' he asked, turning it on.

'It still has all its normal functions. I'm just trying to add something more . . . user friendly. Look through. What do you see?'

'The normal sighting symbology.'

She walked to the far end of the room. 'Sight on me.'

He did so, and the powerful scope showed a part of her cheek in sharp focus.

'Ignore my spots,' she said.

'You have no spots. Your cheek is as smooth as—'

'Thank you, sir,' she interrupted. 'Now, what do you see?'

'I'll be . . .' Pappenheim said in astonishment.

Four transparent red bars had appeared from each side of an imaginary square, slowly coming together to form an open cross, as targeting solution was confirmed.

'What's it doing now?'

'The cross is pulsing.'

'You have the shot. It will do that every time the target is secured, irrespective of range.'

Pappenheim relaxed from his stance, and switched off the sight. 'Miss Meyer, you're a wonder.'

'Don't be too happy,' she cautioned. 'It can choose to malfunction at any time. I haven't stabilized it as yet. If it does decide to go on strike, the standard sight will still work, but you'll miss my user-friendly little cross.'

'Well, let's hope it behaves.'

'So you're going to back him?'

'Of course,' Pappenheim said.

'That's why you were looking for high ground at a distance. Does he know?'

'Not yet. But I'll tell him in time. I'll be taking the BMW . . .'

'Don't forget to turn on the locator in the nav system, so that I can track you. Persuade him to do the same in his car, sir.'

'Don't worry, Hedi. I'll look after him.'

She gave a quick little nod, and went back to the computer. 'I'll stay here till you're all back,' she said.

Pappenheim went up to her, and stood next to her chair for a moment. 'Everything will work out well,' he said.

Then he went out.

He ambled over to Müller's office, knocked, and entered.

Müller stared at the Dragunov. 'What are you doing with that?'

'Backup. You're going to need it.'

'Pappi . . .'

'You're going to need it. Any contact?'

Müller nodded. 'I'm waiting for instructions.'

'You've read the file. I've read the file. We know his peculiarities. That gives us a big edge he does not realize we have. He's going to ask you to come alone. He will have people looking to make certain you *are* alone. As he has no idea we already know where he is, I'm setting off immediately to be in position long before you get there. Me, and my trusty Dragunov. Let them know I'm there when you think it right. I might also announce myself if I believe it will give you an extra edge. Do you have difficulties with that?'

Müller gave a tired smile. 'None.'

'Good. And don't worry. We'll get her back . . . alive. Even if it means killing the lot of these bastards. Brannic included.'

They looked at each other.

'No goodbyes,' Müller said. 'No handshakes.'

Pappenheim grinned. 'Not really my style, anyway. You'll be OK. See you later.'

He turned, paused at the door without looking back, then left.

He made his way to the lift, went down to the garage, where he headed for the big BMW coupe. He placed the Dragunov in the boot. He had already put plenty of ammunition, a pair of binoculars, a pump shotgun with several reloads, an H&K submachine gun, and two extra pistols into a large, slinged sports bag. The shotgun had a folding stock for ease of storage. With them were full-body, camouflaged overalls. He had also put the photographs of the area in the front of the car.

'That should do it,' he said to himself as he shut the boot.

He got into the car, and drove up the ramp.

Eight

Pappenheim had been gone for over an hour, when the phone rang in Müller's office.

He picked it up without haste. 'Müller.'

'Your instructions, Mr Müller. Listen carefully because they will not be repeated. If you make any mistake getting here, Colonel Bloomfield might pay the consequences.'

'Then all this is pointless. You want to talk to me. Threatening the colonel is not the best way to go about it.'

Brannic pondered upon this. 'Don't push your luck . . .'

'I'm not pushing anything. You are threatening me with the colonel's life. I am in no position to push anything.'

'You're good. I'll give you that. Now, your instructions . . .' Brannic gave them. 'And Mr Müller . . . no need to tell you not to bring any of your buddies with you.'

'No need.'

'Then we understand each other. You have one hour. You've got a fast car. You'll make it in plenty of time.'

Carey Bloomfield looked about her for about the fifth time since she had been brought into the room without a ceiling. She was tied hand and foot to an upright chair. It was the only item of furniture in the entire room. Throughout, she had neither been gagged, nor blindfolded.

Since being brought to the room, she had been left alone. She had not seen the general.

She decided she had been brought to some kind of long-disused factory. It was not one of those big, labyrinthine buildings, but small: compact for a factory. She wondered what used to be made there. It was in the middle of nowhere, with virtually open ground all around, and as it was still in what used to be the former East Germany, she assumed it was yet another factory that failed to survive the realities of Western commerce. They would see Müller coming for miles, she decided. Not a good omen.

There was just a single metal door, the only access into the room, except from above. It was so far to where the ceiling used to be, climbing, even if she were free, would be very difficult, if not impossible. There were few protrusions that could be used as handholds.

She looked up. High above her, were huge gaping holes in the roof of the building, as if some giant had peeled it open. From where she sat, she could just about see a girdered catwalk, framing the rectangle of the room where she sat. There was no one up there, keeping guard.

They did not expect her to attempt an escape. No doubt they were all in other parts of the complex, strategically positioned to stop her, were she foolish enough to try.

She heard the sound of rubber heels hitting the floor hard. As the footsteps approached, she looked to her front, eyes going blank.

A key was turned in a lock, and the metal door was flung open. Brannic, in combat fatigues and boots, was framed in the doorway. There were no badges of rank, or emblems of identification upon the fatigues.

He entered the room. The door was shut behind him.

'Well, Colonel,' he began as he came closer, 'I did not expect it would be like this when we next saw each other.'

She did not look at him. 'And I did not expect that the general who gave me an order would kidnap me . . . *sir*.'

'Let us not use such terms, Colonel. Kidnap is a harsh word. Let us use the word lever. It is much more appropriate.'

Brannic planted himself before her, directly in the line of her gaze.

'You disappoint me, Colonel.'

'Why, sir?'

'You disappeared, without letting anyone know where you were going.'

'With respect, sir, you gave me a mission. How I carried out that mission was up to me. What matters are results.'

Brannic appeared to think about that.

'And do you have results, Colonel?'

'No, sir. One day into the mission, and I have been kidnapped . . . by the general who gave me the mission. *You*, sir.'

Again, Brannic appeared to ponder upon her words. His next question took a different tack.

'When did you last see General Dering?'

'Friday, sir. In his office.'

'Why did you go to Manassas?'

'I always take a little drive, sir, before leaving. I like driving my car – which my father gave to me – and it's a routine with me that before I leave on a mission, I go for a drive. I once had a friend who always went fishing before a mission. The relaxation prepared him mentally. A drive does the same for me, sir.'

'You expect me to believe that?'

'It's the truth, sir. The person in question was Major George Roland, a Ranger, sir. He died in combat two years ago.'

Brannic stared at her. 'I've heard of Roland. I know about that fishing thing of his.'

'There you go, sir.'

Brannic continued to stare at her in silence for several seconds, then he turned abruptly and left the room, closing the door firmly behind him.

The key turned in the lock.

Pappenheim drove the BMW off the road and on to a short track which appeared to end in a thick clump of bushes. He stopped, got out, and checked. It was possible to drive the car through. He got back in and did so, emerging into a small clearing about a hundred metres from the road, beneath a canopy of trees. The clearing ended at the base of high ground. He stopped the car again, and switched off the engine.

He had come from a direction least expected, the last few kilometres being over narrow roads that crossed farmland. It was his way of entering through the back door.

He climbed out, and made his way back to the road. It was impossible to see the car, or where it had gone in, even if someone came to look. There were no tyre marks on the hard ground. Just to be safe, he picked up a small, dried branch and used it as a makeshift broom to brush at the ground. Satisfied, he dropped the branch, and went back to the car.

He opened the boot, and removing his jacket and tie placed them in the boot, then put on the camouflaged overalls. He then loaded all the weapons, checked them, attached the silencer to the Dragunov, returned all weapons except the Dragunov to the bag, then slung the bag over a shoulder. Taking out the Dragunov, he closed the boot and locked the car. Carrying the rifle and the bag, he began making his way across to the wood he had picked out, staying in cover as much as possible. He had chosen a route that would give him sufficient cover for the half kilometre, indirect walk to the woods.

He arrived without incident and immediately went deep into the woods until he found a hollow that formed a perfect hide. There was a lip of rising ground around it. It was a natural foxhole.

Pappenheim put down the bag and the rifle. He leaned against the slope of the depression, peered over the rim, and saw that he had a clear view of the factory, while remaining well in cover.

He lowered himself and began to get the weapons ready, then he used the Dragunov to scan the immediate area near the factory buildings. He spotted one man behind a small building that was more like a shed. Another was positioned near the wide and low, now dilapidated wooden gate that once barred a long unpaved drive to an open square in front of the main building. A single chimney rose from the side of that building.

Pappenheim checked along the chimney. A man was up there.

'That's three,' he murmured.

In the end, he counted seven men outside. In a few cases, he had to wait until they moved, before spotting them. He knew there'd be more inside. He did not see the general, or Rachel Worth, although her car was among the five vehicles in the wide square. In addition to the coupe and the saloon in which Carey Bloomfield had been taken, there were three other big saloons.

Dragunov ready, he leaned against the low rampart to wait.

Brannic entered the room again.

Carey Bloomfield looked at him, expression blank.

'He'll be here soon, Colonel. In that fast car of his, he should make it within the deadline. The knight coming to the rescue of fair damsel. Then the fun will begin.'

'You consider this to be *fun*, General?'

'Only in a manner of speaking. Müller has information I want. He gets you back in exchange.'

'May I say something?'

'Let's hear it.'

'I've been on this for a long time. If Müller knew anything we could use . . .'

Brannic gave her a hard stare. 'Do you take me for some kind of fool, Colonel?'

'No, sir. I do not. But Müller lost the Hargreaves *before* he could get to them. They were supposed to have the answers he was looking for. Someone killed them first. He is still searching for answers. I honestly can't see what he can tell you at this point in time. My job is to tag him until he finds those answers. If he can't tell you what you want to know and you kill me because of it, everyone loses . . . including you.'

'Why should I want to kill you?'

'Now don't you take *me* for a fool, General. You've come this far. There's no turning back. You can't let me live. You'll have to kill Müller too. Problem is, you might not make it out of Germany. Losers all round, General.'

'And, of course, you have a suggestion.'

'Let me continue my mission. Müller's colleagues will do nothing if you don't touch him. I continue to shadow him until he finds what he's looking for . . .'

'The DNA weapon . . .'

'General!' someone shouted from beyond the room.

'I believe your knight is on his way in,' Brannic said. 'I'll consider what you have just said,' he went on. 'But I make no promises.'

Brannic went out, again shutting and locking the door behind him.

'Sure you'll consider,' she muttered to herself. 'Then renege. I wasn't born yesterday.'

In the scope, Pappenheim saw a flurry of activity. Guessing what might have caused it, he panned the scope to his left until he had the approach road in his sights.

The Porsche, at high speed.

And here comes the pressure cooker at last, he thought. *About time you started to let your anger loose, Jens.* He swung the scope back towards the buildings. *I wouldn't like to be in your shoes in there. Müller is on his way and you're not going to like meeting him . . .*

He sighted on the man positioned on the chimney. The arms of the goth's red cross appeared, merged, and pulsed. Target acquired.

'You'll be the first to go,' he said softly. He did not fire. 'When the time comes.'

He swapped the rifle for the binoculars, and did a full sweep of the general area, looking for point men. Brannic might well have others on the lookout for possible backup teams coming with Müller.

He could spot nothing to betray their presence. Then he

167

saw slight movement, about half a kilometre from his position, to his left.

He waited. Perhaps some animal. He switched to the Porsche. It still had some distance to go. He swung back to where he had seen movement, and waited again.

A head moved. The man also had binoculars. He was following the Porsche, then sweeping behind it to check if there were others following.

Change of plan, Pappenheim decided. And targeted that man to be first.

A systematic check showed no further lookouts this far from the buildings.

Then on the periphery of vision through the binoculars, he spotted movement near the main building. A tall, bare-headed man in combat fatigues had appeared.

Pappenheim focussed on him and he recognized Brannic. Then a familiar figure joined Brannic. The sexual apple of Waldron's eye, Rachel Worth, appeared.

Pappenheim swept his view back to the racing Porsche wondering how Jens was going to play this one.

He put the binoculars away, and picked up the Dragunov.

In his office, Sternbach picked up his phone and called a number. 'You know who this is.'

'I do,' came the reply.

'Not long ago, you told me of the person who killed Sharon Wilson. What is her specific job with Müller's team?'

'I'll find out. Call you back.'

'Thank you.'

Blake and Arnold were admiring the huge grounds of Sternbach's mansion.

'This is some place,' Arnold remarked.

'I've seen better in Connecticut,' Blake said dismissively.

Arnold's retort was cut short by the appearance of Bruch, coming out of the building.

'And here comes our favourite German,' Blake commented.

168

'It may be news to you, Blake, but we all belong to the same organization.'

'Sure.' Blake gave Bruch a false smile as Sternbach's man approached.

Bruch rewarded Blake with a neutral stare. 'The woman we saw – the goth – is called Hedi Meyer. Her specialty with the police unit is electronics. Computers especially. They call her a genius.'

Blake grinned. 'Yes!' He looked at Arnold. 'Do you buy that now, eh?' He walked away from them, cackling.

Bruch looked at Arnold. 'How can you stand him?'

'One day, I hope I get the word to kill that little bastard.'

Bruch smiled. 'If you need help . . .' Bruch went on, 'Some advice . . . if you want it.'

'I'm listening.'

'The woman, Hedi Meyer . . . it is a mistake to go after her at this time. I believe those two cops in the café are her bodyguards.'

'How can you be sure?'

'Call it . . . what do you Americans like to say . . .'

'A hunch?'

Bruch nodded. 'Hunch, gut feeling. Whatever. Müller's unit are not fools. They have already caused us plenty of damage. Going after the woman could backfire, very badly. We need less profile. Not more.'

'I buy that,' Arnold said after a while.

'So what do you do about Blake?'

'Leave the little shit to me.'

Bruch smiled again.

Müller brought the Porsche to a halt, mere feet from where Brannic and Rachel Worth were standing.

He climbed out, eyes cold.

'At last we meet, Mr Müller,' Brannic began. He glanced at the Turbo. 'Nice car.'

Müller was short. 'And you are?'

'Brannic, General.'

'Do American generals normally kidnap American colonels?'

'There's that word again. Colonel Bloomfield used it too. I tried to explain that perhaps seeing it as a lever would be more appropriate.'

'Where is she?'

Brannic actually gave a tiny smile. 'To the point. Does not waste time. I like that. The colonel's quite safe, and unharmed . . . so far. Her continuing state of health will, of course, depend on you. But first, a few formalities – your gun, and your police radio or phone. We would not like to excite the neighbourhood cops now, would we?'

'You don't get my gun until I see Colonel Bloomfield, unharmed, out here.'

'Let me remind you of the rules, Mr Müller. You are in *no* position to give me orders. My men are all over this place. They can and will cut you down in a heartbeat if I order it; after which Colonel Bloomfield will be dog meat. After they have finished with her—'

'Spare me the lecture, Brannic. You kill me, you get nothing, and all this effort you've gone into is wasted . . .'

'Goddamn. You do speak English like a Limey.'

Knowing Brannic's tactics, the deliberate interruption did not throw Müller off balance.

'The colonel for my gun.'

Brannic took a deep breath, then said, 'Just to show I am not unreasonable. Keep the gun . . . for now. Hand over the radio.'

Müller remained unmoving for long enough to show resistance. 'It's in the car.'

'Get it. Careful now! Don't excite my men. They have been known to be trigger happy.'

Rachel Worth had been looking at Müller with her head cocked, a raptor surveying prey, a strange little smile about her mouth. The predator eyes were slightly narrowed.

'He's pretty,' she said moving forward. 'Nice car. Can I drive it?' she asked Müller.

He reached in to get his phone, then straightened. The coldness in his own eyes stopped her in her tracks, leaving her confused; an unaccustomed sensation.

'No!' he snapped.

She recoiled from the sudden fierceness of it, involuntarily moving backwards to where she had been standing. The dark eyes surveyed Müller with a new wariness: that of one predator to another.

Watching this with interest, Brannic said, 'I don't think he likes people driving his car, Miss Worth.' He held out his hand for the phone.

Müller gave it to him.

Brannic studied it briefly. 'Very interesting piece of equipment. Not seen one like it before.'

'Don't think of keeping it. If you open it, it will die on you.'

'Interesting,' Brannic repeated. He took out his own radio. 'Harmon, any movement out there?'

The man that Pappenheim had spotted in the bushes answered immediately. 'Quiet as a duck pond without ducks, General. Nothing for miles. Reckon he did come alone.'

'OK, Harmon. Stay out for another twenty minutes then come on in. We're not going to hang around here all day.'

'You got it, sir.'

'Well, Mr Müller,' Brannic said, 'it seems as if you are a man of your word. Because of this, I will have the colonel brought out. Then you hand over your gun.'

Müller nodded.

Watching this through the scope, Pappenheim wondered what was going on as he saw Müller hand over his phone, and noticed his interaction with Rachel Worth.

Don't lose it, Jens, he warned silently. *Attend to her later . . .*

He paused as he saw Müller brush something from his nose.

Flies? he wondered. No one else seemed affected. Then

he remembered when they were younger policemen they had used various signals. What was this one?

'God,' he muttered. 'I need a cigarette.'

But he knew he would not smoke until this had been attended to.

What the hell was that signal? Ah!

Memory came flooding back. Müller was telling him not to shoot yet.

He continued to scan with the scope.

Müller kept his expression neutral as Carey Bloomfield, hands tied behind her back, was pushed none too gently out of the building, and towards them.

She stumbled, but succeeded in regaining her balance.

Brannic had turned to look. 'Be careful there with the colonel, Höde. We don't want to bruise her. Mr Müller might not like that.'

Höde gave Müller a humourless grin.

Looking at Höde, Müller realized that Brannic was possibly the only one in military attire.

'A German citizen?' Müller asked Brannic.

'We're one big, global family, Mr Müller.'

Carey Bloomfield was positioned between Rachel Worth and Brannic.

'And now, Mr Müller,' Brannic said. 'Your gun, please. Then we commence with the proceedings. And be careful.' He pointed with a reminding finger at various locations around the buildings. 'Trigger happy.'

With a very careful hand, Müller drew his gun out of his shoulder holster. He passed it butt-first to Brannic.

Brannic gave it an appraising look. 'A beauty. 92R, well looked after. You're a serious shooter, Mr Müller. You have something in common with the colonel.'

Müller looked at her. 'Are you all right, Colonel Bloomfield?'

'I'm good.'

Brannic spoke into his radio again. 'Still nothing, Harmon?'

'Quieter than a strip joint without strippers. No metal birds in the sky, either. The cavalry's not riding in for this one, General.'

'OK. A few more minutes, then get your ass over here. You've got ground to cover.'

'You got it, General.'

Brannic turned back to Müller. 'And now, Mr Müller, some questions.'

Müller sneezed.

Watching through the scope, Pappenheim caught the mime of the sneeze.

'Showtime.'

Müller had signalled that he was free to fire as he saw fit.

Pappenheim had made a slight groove in the lip of the hollow, within which he now positioned the rifle. It gave good support for firing, and held the weapon as effectively as a bipod.

He sighted on the man Brannic had addressed as Harmon, who seemed no longer bothered about concealment. The four arms of the cross floated into the scope, merged, and pulsed. The shot could be taken. The Dragunov had a killing range of 3.8 kilometres though, effectively, this was at its very extreme end. Even silenced, Harmon and the buildings were no troublesome distance away for the weapon.

The left side of Harmon's head filled the scope. The central square of the cross was zeroed just above the left ear.

Pappenheim fired.

The rifle made a *pheeew* sound, and even as he watched, Harmon's head turned into a bloom of red. The body dropped like a stone and could no longer be seen in the screen of bushes.

Pappenheim swiftly sighted on Brannic, moved to Rachel Worth to Carey Bloomfield, to Müller.

All was as before. No one knew that one of Brannic's men had just died.

Pappenheim selected the man up the chimney as his next target, and waited.

* * *

'Sorry,' Müller said to Brannic. 'Summer cold coming on, perhaps. Or some small insect might have got into my nose. Or it could be the air-conditioning in the car . . .'

'That happens to me sometimes,' Rachel Worth said. 'The air conditioning.'

Brannic glanced at her, as if wondering what she was on about.

Müller hoped Pappenheim had read his signal correctly. He saw that Carey Bloomfield's eyes had a question in them, but he ignored her. The situation was still far too dangerous. There was no window of opportunity as yet.

'Careful with those sneezes,' Brannic said, watching him closely. 'My men might not understand. May we continue?'

'Please.'

'Your father, Mr Müller, successfully infiltrated an organization for a great number of years . . .'

'The Semper. Yes.'

An expression of approval came upon Brannic's face. 'I like this. Straight. To the point. No pretence about not knowing. We can do business, Mr Müller.'

'I hope so. Even if I do not trust the colonel as far as I can throw her, her safety is my responsibility.'

Brannic's eyes opened briefly, and he shot a glance at Carey Bloomfield whose facial reaction to what Müller had just said was eloquent.

She looked shocked.

Even Rachel Worth said, 'He doesn't trust you, sweetie. Fancy that!'

Brannic turned back to Müller with a slight frown. 'Your father may have left you something that might indicate the whereabouts of an item this particular organization lost, many years ago.'

'My father took it?'

'No. He never had it in his possession, but there is a strong suspicion that he knew of its whereabouts.'

'Excuse me, General. I'm a policeman. Suspicions are not facts.'

'And frequently, police act on suspicion when investigating a case. This is merely a similar situation.'

'So what is this item, General?'

'A weapon. A DNA weapon.'

Müller stared at him. 'And you believe that I know where this . . . this DNA weapon happens to be? This is insane.'

Brannic's expression clouded over. 'Now this is where I stop liking what I hear.'

'General, my father – my *parents* – died when I was twelve. How do you expect me to know of something that may or may not have happened when I was a boy?'

'Your father left you the Semper rings . . . yes. I know about them. I cannot believe that is all he left you.' Staring hard at Müller, Brannic grabbed his radio. 'Harmon! We're going to be done here soon. Get your butt moving!'

There was no response.

'Harmon! If you're sleeping out there, goddamn it, I'll have your butt. Move out!'

There was still no reply.

Müller sneezed again.

Pappenheim saw it in the scope and realized things were moving fast. There had been no need for a second sneeze before, so he concluded some quick shooting was needed now.

He had loaded the ten-round box magazine of the semi-automatic rifle with a mix of normal, and incendiary ammunition. The first four were non-incendiary.

He shot the man on the chimney.

The choking cry high above startled everyone except Müller, who was already moving towards his car as Brannic, Rachel Worth, and Höde could not prevent themselves from turning in the direction of the cry. They stared at the falling body of the man who had been positioned at the top of the disused chimney.

Carey Bloomfield took the opportunity to begin moving towards Müller.

Pappenheim's next shot tore into Höde's chest, doing terminal damage to it. Höde slammed to the ground, dead before he hit it.

Brannic was recovering fast, and despite suspecting he could be next, turned with a roar of anger and frustration towards Carey Bloomfield, the gun he had taken from Müller rising, pointing squarely at her.

'Noooo!' he bellowed. He squeezed the trigger.

Carey Bloomfield flinched, but kept desperately moving towards Müller.

Brannic pulled the trigger several times before it dawned upon him that the gun was empty.

Despite his mounting rage, and by now certain he could be the next target of the unseen shooter, Brannic displayed something of what had made him such an effective combat sergeant.

Still on the move, he threw Müller's useless gun away, and drew his own, determined to cut Carey Bloomfield off. It must have been his swiftness that spoiled Pappenheim's aim. Even so, the next shot hit Brannic in the ankle.

And it must have hurt fiercely because Brannic gave the howl of a monstrous animal in pain. The blow threw him off his stride. He fell heavily, rolling to get out of the line of fire, and taking him further away from Carey Bloomfield who was now taking cover behind the car.

Müller had reached into the car to get his second Beretta, this one fully loaded.

Pappenheim's next round was incendiary and it exploded into one of the saloons. The explosion set off another that engulfed a second of the big cars.

Two men were dragging the wounded Brannic into cover. Rachel Worth was nowhere to be seen.

'We can't stay here,' Müller said to Carey Bloomfield quickly. 'They're in shock, but that won't last.'

'You finessed Brannic,' she said in wonder, peering from behind the car at where the men had dragged Brannic from view. 'Untie me before we move.'

'No time. I stopped the car here to bunch them so that Pappi . . .'

'Pappi's doing this?' She ducked as another round hit another car.

'He'd better not hit my car . . .'

'We're about to get killed by a mad general and you worry about your car?'

'Over there,' he said. 'That small building to the right. Next shot from Pappi and we move . . .'

'I'll need a gun.'

'Grab one from the dead when we get to one of them.'

A third incendiary slammed into what looked like a big old rubbish container. It exploded, and spewed dark smoke into the air.

'Hope Pappi has not just caused a chemical discharge. All right. Move!'

Together, they hurried for the cover of the small building. Unfortunately, one of Brannic's men was already there. He had ducked into cover to avoid being seen by Pappenheim, and was startled by the arrival of Müller and Carey Bloomfield. It slowed him down, robbing him of all advantage. Müller was already zeroed on him by the time his weapon, an Ingram, was coming up.

The Beretta barked twice as Müller fired. The man fell backwards, weapon spinning out of his dying hand.

'There's your gun,' Müller said to her.

'It would help if my hands were untied.'

'All right. Let's do this quickly. Turn round. Pappi will keep them under cover. Ah,' he continued as she did so.

'What?'

'They used the kind of binding tape that needs to be cut. Nothing to untie. They used a commercial binding tool.'

'You mean the stuff they use for heavy packages?'

'Yes.'

'Shit! Were you a boy scout, Müller? Don't you have a scouting knife or one of those Swiss things?'

'I was never a scout.'

'That figures. So you grew up into one . . . no. Sorry. That was a cheap shot. I am just mad at you.'

He stared at her, astonished. 'Why? I came for you, didn't I?'

'You said you didn't trust me. I want to whack you for that, and my goddamned hands are tied.'

'Sounds safe to me.'

'I'm really going to hit you, Müller!'

He smiled at her, then moved over to the man he had shot. 'Perhaps he's a boy scout.'

He began searching the body. 'No. Nothing. Ah. Well, this is no scouting knife, but it will do.' He drew out a big flick knife.

She gave an expressive shudder. 'They could have used that on me.'

'The general planned to give you to them first.'

Her eyes grew hard. '*Did* he?'

Müller began to cut at her bonds.

'First him,' she said, 'for this, and for Dering. Then Miss Sweetie . . .'

'Miss Sweetie is mine.'

The way he said that made her ask, 'Why?'

'She was the one who blew up my parents' plane. There. You are a free woman again.'

'Sorry, Müller.' Carey Bloomfield massaged her wrists, getting the flow back into them.

'I want her alive. Now what's this about hitting me?'

She looked at him for a long moment.

Another incendiary hit somewhere.

She smiled at him. 'Shall we help Pappi in his one-man war?'

'Go get your gun.'

She picked up the Ingram, and looked at it critically. 'These things shoot all over the place and can be pigs to hold down. But I love them.' A car could be heard racing. 'Müller! Your car!'

He took his key out of his pocket. 'Not mine.'

'Then . . .'

'Rachel Worth!' they said together.

They inched round the shed-like building, until they could see the approach road, and Rachel Worth's coupe racing away.

'Perhaps Pappi will get her with an incendiary,' she said, hoping.

'No. He will concentrate on forcing the general and the rest of his men to keep their heads down.'

'One less for the general,' Carey Bloomfield said. 'Sorry, Müller.'

'I'll find her. Ready?'

'No.'

'Then let's find the general.'

Pappenheim saw Müller and Carey Bloomfield move out of cover.

Go get them, he willed them. The odds are better now, I can watch your backs.

He saw a head poke from a gaping window above them. A round from the Dragunov toppled the owner of the head off his perch.

How many's that now? Pappenheim wondered.

He loaded a fresh magazine.

Very carefully, Müller and Carey Bloomfield made their way into the main building where she had been held. They moved in quick bursts, using the shadows as cover, waiting and listening for the slightest noise. Every so often, the building itself seemed to moan.

They did not speak, communicating with each other by sign. They checked each room they came to, approaching from opposite sides of gaping doorways.

Outside, the sound of rounds striking somewhere from Pappenheim's shooting came at irregular intervals. It kept the heads of the general's remaining forces down.

They came upon a body with most of its head missing. This

had been the man near the window, hit by Pappenheim. He too had carried an Ingram. Carey Bloomfield picked it up.

Müller looked at her.

She held a gun in each hand, and grinned at him.

Then they heard a sound that was not a bullet from the Dragunov striking somewhere.

They froze.

Carey Bloomfield knew where it had come from. Someone was above them, on the catwalk. Without looking up, she pointed a thumb upwards.

Müller acknowledged with the barest of nods.

They kept moving slowly forwards, as if unaware. Then suddenly, moving quickly, they split left and right. The person above them had to decide who to shoot first, and took too long about it.

Carey Bloomfield whirled, Ingrams rising. She sprayed the catwalk, going for quantity rather than quality. In the emptiness of the building, the frenzied chatter of the guns echoed like a heavy shower on a galvanized roof.

Someone screamed, tumbled, and slammed to the factory floor.

They ducked back into cover.

'You're dangerous,' Müller said.

'Oh, yeah. So how many's that, counting Pappi's hits?'

'No idea.'

'Great, Müller.'

'I'm the last one left.' They heard a savage voice rage from somewhere to their right. 'Damn you!'

They dived away as bullets from an automatic spattered close to where they had been standing. The noise the shots made bounced off the bare walls.

'It's over, General!' Carey Bloomfield called. 'I know you killed my boss!'

She changed position just in time. More shots came in her previous direction.

Orientating on Brannic's voice, Müller moved to flank him.

'You can't move properly, Brannic,' Carey Bloomfield said. 'You got hit by a Dragunov. That ankle is shattered. Give it up!'

'And then what, Colonel? You take me back?'

'That's up to the *Hauptkommissar*. You're in his territory. No diplomatic immunity, General.'

'Mr Müller! You played the game well. I have the feeling you were pulling my chain. You were somehow one step ahead. How did you manage that?'

Müller did not reply, continuing to move in the gloom.

'Ah, I get it. The flanking movement. From which direction, Mr Müller? The front? The back? The sides?'

Müller still did not reply.

'General!'

'Ah, yes. Now the good colonel, doing her part well. Keeping . . . keeping my attention focused on her.'

The muzzle of the gun against his cheek made Brannic's voice fade.

'That's it, Brannic,' Müller said.

'Noooo!'

Brannic's move was sudden enough to take Müller off guard, and just long enough to perhaps give the general an edge. But the movement caused Brannic to be framed by the door to the room in which he'd been hiding.

And Carey Bloomfield had been waiting.

The Ingrams chattered, spewing their frantic burst of rounds into Brannic. He was pushed back into the room, as if pulled from behind. He fell heavily on to his back, the darkness of his blood leaking out of him.

The powerful life force that had seen Brannic through several dangerous missions in numerous parts of the world, refused to let him die just yet. In the better light of the room, he lay like a beached turtle upon his back, head turning from side to side as he looked in turn at Carey Bloomfield and Müller.

His breath becoming shallower, he studied them.

'Mr . . . Mr Müller, you have won. How?'

'I've got a file on you, General. I know your weaknesses, and your strengths.'

Brannic's eyes closed for a few moments. He gave a fading nod. 'Of . . . of course. Clever. Know . . . thine enemy. You studied me and you . . . used that . . . against me. Having that sniper was smart. He came in . . . ahead. Right?'

'He was on his way before you called me. We already knew where you were. You were tagged.'

'You set me up. You deliberately let me take her.'

'It was her idea.'

Brannic nodded again, as if understanding. He looked at Carey Bloomfield, eyes showing an unnatural intensity. 'You got Dixon. Years with me. Almost last man standing.'

'Why did you kill General Dering?' she asked in a hard voice.

'So you don't know about him? What he did to us?'

'I know nothing, General,' she replied, lying. 'What did he do?'

'He infiltrated us!' Despite his wounds, Brannic sounded outraged, and almost tried to get up. 'Didn't intend to kill him, not then. Not yet. Needed information. He deliberately made a . . . sudden . . . sudden . . . move. Made us kill him. Men too quick, on the trigger . . .'

'How many of the men here today did the killing?'

'Four here . . . not including Dixon. All dead now.'

'Can't say I'm sorry, General. The bastards deserved it. My only regret is that it won't bring Dering back. You're all alone now. Even Rachel Worth ran out on you. Some people will clean up this mess, and you'll vanish . . . just like Dering.'

As she spoke, something pocked with a powerful slam against a wall.

'She . . . did not . . . run.' Brannic gasped in pain. 'I allowed her to leave. She has another mission.'

'What mission?' Müller demanded.

Brannic did not reply. His breathing seemed to have become more urgent. Müller looked down at the wounds.

Brannic saw the look. 'I've . . . had worse . . .'

'Not this time, General.'

'So, tell me,' Brannic said through his shallow breathing. 'Do you . . . do you know where the weapon is?'

'Sorry, Brannic,' Müller replied, doing his own lying. 'That's the point. I don't know of any weapon. My father left nothing to indicate such a thing exists.'

'God . . . damn it!' Brannic swore weakly. 'I was . . . so . . . sure.'

Then Carey Bloomfield saw that Brannic's right hand was slowly beginning to move off the floor. 'Hold it right there, General! Or I'll blow that hand away.'

But Brannic continued to move the hand, struggling to do so.

'General!'

Brannic chose not to listen.

She fired into the hand, turning it into a mess.

Brannic screamed weakly, the hand now useless.

'I warned you!' She moved the aim over to the left hand. 'Move it, and it gets the same.'

Müller stared at her as if anew.

After several seconds of shallow breathing, Brannic said in a voice almost too weak to hear, 'Can't . . . can't move it . . . anyway. Damn you! God . . . damned . . . *bitch*!'

'Life's a bitch, General.' Carey Bloomfield was implacable. 'What mission is Rachel Worth on?'

'They should have let . . . let me . . . into West Point. When I first joined.'

'What is this to do with West Point?' Müller asked, turning away. He looked at Carey Bloomfield. 'You continue to amaze me. Do you know what he's talking about?'

'He's dead now, Müller. He had a thing about not being a West Pointer.'

Another pock sounded.

'Better call Pappi off.'

Müller looked down and saw his phone, which Brannic had taken earlier, falling partially out of one of the general's pockets. He picked it up and walked out, indicating that she should follow. He did not call Pappenheim until they were outside the building.

'All over, Pappi. You can call off the artillery.'

'Got you in my sights. Artillery off.'

'Brannic's dead. Thanks for the diversion. Excellent shooting. Great job.'

'Anytime. We aim to please. So I might as well pack up?'

'Unless you feel there are more of them out there.'

'Nope. I think we've cleaned them out. How's the colonel?'

'In perfect health.'

'Good to hear. Though I can see she is myself.'

'I thought you came too close to my car at times.'

'He worries about his car,' Carey Bloomfield muttered under her breath.

'I didn't go *near* your car,' Pappenheim said, chuckling. 'And, speaking of cars, I had to let Rachel Worth go.'

'We saw. You had no other choice. We'll find her. But Brannic said she was on a mission. He died before he could tell us, even if he would have. Just in case, the goth—'

'Is being covered by Berger and Reimer. I'll head straight back. See you there.'

'Yes.'

'And I'll have a clean-up team sent in.'

'Thanks, Pappi.'

Müller and Carey Bloomfield walked on, leaving Brannic and his men where they lay.

'Ah,' Müller said, spotting something as they approached his car. 'My gun.' He went over to where it had fallen after the irate Brannic had tossed it away. He picked it up, checked it. 'Dusty, but otherwise perfect.'

'That was a neat trick, Müller,' she said as he joined her. 'But what if he had checked it first?'

'But he did not. That's what matters. You read the same file that I have. Brannic's need to do everything quickly worked against him. His quick-or-dead methods work well in combat. Not so in situations like this.'

'Was it empty?'

'In a manner of speaking, not really. I was worried he might have felt the weight difference with an empty magazine, so I loaded it with inert rounds.'

'That was a good one, Müller.'

'It wasn't bad.'

She looked about her. 'I think I've lost the one you gave me. They took it.' She put the Ingrams down on the ground. 'They're nearly empty, anyway.'

'Do you want to check the bodies?'

'What if it was Harmon?'

'What if it wasn't? Let's find out.'

They did a quick search, even going back into the building. Nothing.

'Well, we've checked them all,' she said as they came back out again. 'Sorry, Müller. Looks like I've lost it for good.'

But Müller was looking at where the big cars had been parked. Three were smoking ruins, the fourth was barely scorched.

She saw his look. 'You don't think . . . ?'

'You never know.'

They hurried over to the car. It was unlocked. The gun and the harness were on the back seat.

'Yes!' she said, opening the door and grabbing them.

'Run!' Müller bawled.

She needed no second bidding.

They took off, desperate to put as much distance as possible between them and the car. Time appeared to stand still.

Then a cushion of air, soft and hard at the same time, pounded them, throwing them to the ground, and followed by a deafening roar. Müller grabbed her, rolling away into a screen of bushes.

Great lumps of metal hurtled past. Something from high up thudded into the ground bare feet away: a slice of car boot, spiking itself into the earth. Things could be heard whooshing earthwards all over the place, clanging madly as they hit. Some pieces fell on the burnt-out cars. A banner of dark smoke boiled into the air.

Then silence that seemed to fall like a blanket, broken only by the crackling licks of flame.

'Are you all right?' Müller asked.

She nodded. 'I'm good.' She looked at him. 'You're holding on to me, Müller. Kind of tight.'

'Sorry.' He let go.

'Hey, I didn't say . . .'

But he was on his feet, studying the scene. The flames were not as widespread as he expected, and were contained within a small area that did not reach the surrounding bushes.

'Brannic nearly won the last round.'

She stood up, brushing herself down. 'He *planned* this?'

'In case, for whatever reason, it all went wrong for him. We read his file. He also had instincts that served him well. He knew you would want your gun back, if he failed. He could not have expected that Pappi would be there to put incendiaries into the cars, nor that this one would survive if something like that did happen; but he still planned to have the last say.'

'What warned you?'

'Nothing I saw. It just did not feel right. I preferred to look foolish, in case the car was not rigged at all. I went on what I had read about Brannic. He always had one last trick to pull. I had been wondering what it was.' Müller stopped. 'My car!' He hurried off to check.

'His car!' Carey Bloomfield muttered as she followed him. 'Well?' she asked as she joined him. 'It looks fine to me.'

'It is.'

'There you go. Your car's got nine lives.'

He stared at her. 'What have I done now?'

She opened the passenger door and climbed in. 'Get into the car and drive, Müller.'

Müller got behind the wheel, started the car, and turned it round in silence.

As they drove off, she said, 'Now you're mad at me?'

'No.'

'You lied to Brannic. Why? He was dying, going nowhere.'

'You lied to him too. Why?'

'I didn't want to give the bastard the satisfaction.'

'That decision might have been a smart thing.'

'I don't follow . . .'

'All through what was happening, I was thinking about Brannic's penchant for last little tricks. The rigged car was one, as we now know.'

She looked at him in surprise. 'You think there were more?'

'I don't know. I simply decided to err on the side of caution. We did not check Brannic's body . . .'

'Booby trap?'

'I would not have put it past him, but I'm thinking of something else. A hidden microphone. From the moment I arrived, I had that in mind. I could not see it on him when we were outside, but that did not mean it wasn't there. In the bad light inside the building, it would have been even more difficult to spot. So when I spoke to him, even after you had shot him, I considered that we might have had an interested audience.'

'So that was why you walked out before calling Pappi. Jesus, Müller, do you ever sleep?'

'With one eye open. Of course, Brannic may not have been wired at all, but knowing what that file said about him, it would have been surprising if he had not pulled a stunt like that.'

'The file! You told him about his file.'

'Yes.' Müller was unperturbed. 'It could be any file. For all they know – if they were listening in – I could have had access to some of his service documents. They will never imagine where that information really came from. How could they? Saying you learned nothing from Dering was a good thing.'

'But I also said I knew Brannic killed him.'

'I think you can get away with that. You despised Brannic. That was clear enough to hear. They will know you shot him, *and* will have heard you shoot his hand. But they will also assume it was because of Dering.'

'It was, for the most part.'

'And that thing with the hand . . .'

'I'd have shot the bastard's left hand too.'

'You'll get no argument from me.'

'What do you think he was trying to do?'

'No idea,' Müller replied. 'But they should be leaving you alone . . .'

'For now, you mean.'

'There is that.'

'That makes me feel so relieved.'

He smiled at her caustic remark. 'Look at it this way, you're alive, and he's dead, and the whereabouts of the DNA weapon is still a mystery to them. As far as they are concerned, it no longer exists. That's a big plus.'

'And Rachel Worth?' she asked after a while.

'I'll get her.'

'Revenge?'

'It's a lot more than that.'

Nine

Waldron opened the door to Rachel Worth's knock.
She breezed into his hotel suite, glancing at his clothes as she entered. 'Going out?' She gave him a look that held a combination of sexual promise and danger.

He chose to ignore the danger signs in the dark eyes. 'Nothing that can't be postponed.'

'Then out of those clothes, lover.'

She sailed into the bedroom, leaving a trail of discarded clothing.

'Missed having you here last night,' he continued, removing his own clothes as he followed her.

She was fully naked on the bed as he entered, legs spread. 'Missed having me? Or missed having me here?'

'Both. So did you have that action you talked about?'

'Oh, yes. Now can you shut up and let's have the action I can see you want? And close all windows. I want to do some screaming.'

Waldron grinned and raced to close all the windows in the bedroom, and then the bedroom door itself.

'I love it when you scream,' he said.

'Then hurry, hurry, hurry . . . !' Her voice rose in a mewling crescendo as he entered her.

Her body began to give a very good impression of attacking Waldron's, slamming rhythmically against him.

'Jeez!' Waldron exclaimed between slams. 'Something's worked . . . you . . . up!'

'Don't you like it?'

'Ooooh, yes . . . jeez . . . jeez . . . my God!'

Half an hour of ferocious sex had them sweating and lying across the bed, gulping air.

'That,' she said, 'was one of your best.'

'One of *our* best,' he corrected. 'Jeez, girl. You emptied me.'

She licked her lips. 'More to come.'

She got up, and went into the bathroom. Waldron lay unmoving, enjoying the languid aftermath of their love-making.

He was still lying there, a blissful look upon his face when she returned, still naked. She came up to the bed and stood there, looking down at him.

The look of bliss vanished as he stared at the silenced gun pointing at him.

He propped himself up on his elbows. 'Jeezus, Rachel! Don't joke with guns!'

'I never joke with guns.'

'What the hell's this? We just had some of the best wild, crazy, screaming, all-over-the-bed sex we've ever had, and you *point* this thing at *me*?'

She cocked her head to one side, predator eyes surveying him. 'There was one man who made me scream louder. I was very sad when I had to shoot him. He really knew where my buttons were . . .'

'Jeezus! I'm not hearing this. What the hell's got into you, Rachel?'

'Müller.'

Waldron stared at her, for a moment forgetting the gun pointed at him. 'You *fucked* Müller?'

'I'd love to,' she said, so conversationally it was bizarre. 'But I don't think he likes me enough. Now if I were that colonel . . .' She paused. 'I'm not sure whether I should feel humiliated, or just annoyed. When men see me, they weigh up their chances of getting on top of me. You can see it in their eyes. Men can't hide that. When Müller saw me, it was as if he wanted to crush me, not in his arms, but under his heel, like a bug.

'It was shocking to see. It was not just a policeman

wanting to take down someone he considers a criminal. This was a *man* with a personal hate. It was all there in his eyes, and he didn't care if I saw it. He *wanted* me . . . he wanted me *dead*, as if I'd taken something from him. So I said to myself, I don't know this man. What does he think I've done to him, to make him look at me like that? Then I—'

'I still don't know what the hell you're going on about—'

'Shut up, Peter! I'm not finished! Then I said to myself there was something in his eyes that told me he *knew* I'd done something to him. The way your wife knows you're cheating on her. But I thought what could I have done? Then I had another thought: the Hargreaves. He wanted to get what was obviously very important information out of them, but thanks to you, we got the Hargreaves first . . .'

'Rachel—'

'Shut up! Shut up, shut up, shut up, shut . . . up!'

Waldron closed his mouth, looking even more anxious by the second.

'So I realized,' Rachel Worth continued, as if there had been no interruption. She was almost talking to herself. 'I thought . . . who knew what had happened, apart from those responsible for arranging the Hargreaves' exit? No one. So it had to be that one of those people talked. Now I am sure it wasn't me. I am also certain it was not any of the people who made the arrangements to get me to the place where I set the charges. They already knew it was me.' The dark eyes zeroed in on Waldron. 'The only person who didn't know, and whom I told myself, was you, sweetie. What did you do, my scream-making lover . . . tell your fat friend, the policeman?'

'No!' Waldron shouted, inching back on the bed. 'That's crazy! How could I . . . ?'

'How could you? I don't know. How *could* you?'

Without warning, she fired at his left kneecap.

'*Jeezzussss!*' Waldron screamed. He grabbed at the knee, trying to stem the blood and shattered bone. That hurt even more. 'Oh, Christ! You shot me!'

'Oh, look,' she said. 'You're bleeding all over the bed. Does it really hurt? Good thing we closed all the windows. People might have heard you screaming.' She shot the other kneecap.

Waldron screamed again, trying ineffectually to attend to both his ravaged knees. 'Gawwwd, Gawwwd, Gawwwd!' He was weeping and moaning at the same time. 'What did you do that for?'

'You betrayed me, sweetie, just as you did your wife, just as you did your friend the fat cop . . .'

'I didn't do anything!' Waldron insisted, crying with the pain of it. 'Why did you shoot me? *Why* . . . ?'

'All right,' she said. 'You didn't do it. But some people are very disappointed in you, Peter. I'm sorry.' She pointed the gun at his naked crotch. 'I don't believe you . . .'

'No! No, *no*. Jesus! All right, *all right*. Pappi found out about me. I don't know how. But he seems to know everything! He threatened to let our people know he knew about me . . .'

'So you were sent here to get information out of him, and he ended up getting it *out* of *you* through blackmail? And you betrayed *me* to him, you bastard?'

She shot Waldron twice through the heart. Then she turned away from the body, face completely expressionless.

She got dressed quickly, and left the suite.

Having already arranged for the clean-up team to head out to the factory while on the way from there, Pappenheim was back in his office when the phone rang.

He picked it up. 'Pappenheim.'

'*Herr Oberkommissar* . . .'

He shut his eyes briefly as he recognized the voice. It was one of the two patrolmen.

I'm going to be haunted forever by those two, he thought with a heavy weariness.

'Hello,' he greeted the patrolman with a cheeriness he did not feel. 'What can I do for you? And thanks for that job earlier in Wilmersdorf.'

'A pleasure, sir!'

'So where are you now?'

'By the hotel.'

Pappenheim shut his eyes again. *Give me strength*, he thought.

'Something's happened?' he asked.

'It's that woman, sir.'

Pappenheim perked up. 'Where, and when?'

'She came to the hotel about forty-five minutes ago, not in a limousine, but in a coupe . . . Er . . . sir? Are you there?'

'I'm here. Where is she now?'

'She just left.'

'All right. Thank you. You're doing a great job. I've got to make some calls. Thanks again.'

The patrolman barely managed to say 'Yes, sir' before Pappenheim hung up.

He immediately called Waldron's suite. There was no reply. He tried four times before deciding to call the hotel reception.

'This is Pappenheim. You may remember me?'

'Yes, sir. Mr Waldron's friend.'

'Is he in?'

There was a pause. 'I have just looked. He has his key . . .'

'So he's in his suite.'

'Or somewhere in the hotel.'

'I see. Thank you. I'll be over to see him.'

'Very well, sir.'

Pappenheim put down the phone, and smoked a cigarette while he thought through the latest events. *Rachel Wilson drives quickly away while we are having fun with Brannic. She goes straight to the hotel, then leaves again, a short time later. I call the suite several times. No reply. I call hotel reception. Waldron is definitely in, perhaps 'somewhere' in the hotel.*

He finished the cigarette, stubbed it out in the already full ashtray, and got to his feet. It was his fourth smoke since returning.

'Time to pay my friend Pete a visit.'

He was in the garage heading for the BMW, when the armoured door rolled upwards and the Porsche came down the ramp. He waited until Müller had parked next to the coupe.

'Just arrived?' Müller asked as he and Carey Bloomfield got out. 'Or just about to leave?'

'Colonel,' Pappenheim greeted Carey Bloomfield. 'Glad to see in person you're in one piece.'

'Glad to be. That was humongous shooting, Pappi. Thanks.'

'My pleasure. Glad I was able to help take Brannic.' To Müller, he continued, 'In answer to your question . . . going out. Coming? My car. I can't get into the back of yours.' He looked at them both.

'Should we?' Müller asked.

'I think we should.'

'Since you put it like that.'

They all got into the BMW, Müller getting into the back.

'So what's the story, Pappi?' Carey Bloomfield asked as they left the garage.

'Rachel Worth.'

She glanced back at Müller.

'Our Rachel came straight back to the hotel,' Pappenheim continued, 'then left again about forty-five minutes later. Alone. Waldron does not answer his phone.'

'Uh-oh.' Carey Bloomfield glanced at Müller again.

'That's the second time you've looked at him,' Pappenheim said. 'Something I should know?'

'Just before he died, Brannic said Rachel Worth was on a mission. That was why she left in such a hurry.'

'You think it could be Waldron?'

'I think Brannic was playing to the last, but you never know. I'm expecting unexpected things. Lessens the surprise. Saw you got the clean-up boys up and running quickly,' Müller continued. 'We met them on the way. I asked them to check Brannic, and the other bodies, for microphones.'

'Microphones?'

'One of my mad ideas.'

'Ah, one of those.'

'I also warned them not to talk while they were doing the search.'

'Just in case?'

'Just in case.'

Pappenheim looked at Carey Bloomfield, who was smiling. 'What?'

'Have you any idea how you guys sound? You've got your little routine so seamless, I don't think you're even aware anymore.'

'She's getting to know us too well,' Pappenheim said over his shoulder to Müller.

'You may be right.'

Carey Bloomfield gave a little snort, and shook her head slowly.

Some minutes later Pappenheim parked a little way from the hotel, and they continued on foot. The doormen politely let them in.

The receptionist recognized Pappenheim as they approached. He glanced at Müller and Carey Bloomfield.

'Friends,' Pappenheim said. 'May we go up?'

'Of course, sir.'

They found the door of the suite unlocked. Müller and Pappenheim drew their weapons.

'Mine is in your car!' Carey Bloomfield mouthed at Müller. 'Don't get me shot.'

He indicated that she should remain outside.

'No way!' her mouth signalled.

Carefully, they entered the suite. No one was waiting in ambush. They made for the bedroom.

'Oh, Jesus!' Carey Bloomfield exclaimed softly.

Putting their weapons away, Müller and Pappenheim stared at the body with hard expressions.

'She was either very angry,' Carey Bloomfield said, 'or very vicious . . .'

'Or both,' Pappenheim finished. 'I wanted to shoot him myself. But I did not want him to end up like this. Is that soft?'

'No, Pappi,' Müller said. 'He was once a good friend.'

'He got your parents killed.'

Müller's lips tightened as he looked at Waldron's body. 'I know. But the person who did this to him, actually did that killing. And I want her. And the people behind her.' Müller paused, staring at the mangled kneecaps. 'I think she enjoyed doing that.'

'After sex too,' Carey Bloomfield remarked. 'A real sweetie, Miss Sweetie.'

'He forgot about spiders,' Pappenheim said.

'Better get that receptionist to ask the manager or the assistant manager to come up here, Pappi,' Müller said. 'We've got to handle this discreetly.'

'Diplomat son of diplomat found shot in hotel,' Pappenheim said, predicting a possible banner headline. 'I can imagine the gory details, especially if they saw the way he was shot.'

'Not what we want, not what the hotel wants, and not what the Semper want.'

'Everyone wins,' Carey Bloomfield said drily. She looked at the body once more. 'At this rate, you'll run out of clean-up teams, if you're not careful.'

Friedrichstrasse, Berlin. 1730 hours

Carey Bloomfield, Pappenheim, and Müller entered Müller's office. The two men perched themselves on a corner of the desk, while Carey Bloomfield went over to the window to enjoy Müller's favourite view.

'Faces saved,' Müller said with a sigh of relief. 'Good idea getting the Blue Folder boys to handle it, Pappi.'

'Who better to handle a bit of diplomatic – what did one of them call it?'

'Awkwardness,' Müller supplied.

'Awkwardness,' Pappenheim repeated. 'Amazing how they can find these little words to describe something that's swimming in brown stuff. They've got to be good for something, I suppose.'

Despite Pappenheim's disparaging comments, the Blue Folder boys as he himself had dubbed them, were an invaluable set of helpers in the fight against the Semper. They frequently passed on normally embargoed, but unattributed information. Pappenheim, being Pappenheim, had not been slow to do certain individuals some favours, which he in turn used mercilessly to force them to do more than they really wanted to.

Both he and Müller suspected, however, that the establishment of the Friedrichstrasse unit had more than a passing connection with the Blue Folders.

As Pappenheim had once said, 'We're here to take the stink, when the shit really hits the fan, while they remain smelling sweet.'

While this may not have been an entirely correct appraisal, there was sufficient truth in Pappenheim's observation to make watching their own backs a prime requirement. The Blue Folder boys were so called because of their penchant for sending their information in blue files.

'Hey, Müller,' Carey Bloomfield called from the window, 'this view must make you sometimes feel like the king of the city.'

'The *Graf* of the city,' Pappenheim corrected with a tiny, sly smile. 'A king can only stand and watch, he can't really do much. A *Graf* on the other hand, gets in among the citizenry, and does things.'

'The king's pointman.'

'In a way, yes.'

'If you two are finished discussing me in the third person . . .'

He picked up his phone at the second ring. 'Müller . . . ah, Martin. Did you find anything?' He stopped, listening. 'Ah! I knew it. All right, bring the whole thing in. Give it to the goth. Tell her what it is, and to be *very* careful when she takes it apart. If she sees anything dangerous that she can't handle when she inspects it, she is to alert the bomb squad. Yes. Thanks, Martin.'

Müller hung up to stares from Pappenheim and Carey Bloomfield.

'Bomb squad?' she said.

'That was Martin Halsinger. Leader of the team that went out to the factory,' he explained to Carey Bloomfield. 'The one I talked to when we met them on the road. He found a mike. I would never have spotted it under those circumstances out there. It's a button . . . from the left breast pocket on Brannic's fatigues. A camouflaged button on a camouflaged background . . .'

'I'll be damned,' she said. 'You were right. So every word we spoke . . .'

'Was transmitted. To where or to whom is anyone's guess. But whoever listened – and where they listened – must belong to the Semper. Brannic seldom did anything without some deliberately planned reason behind it. He was not dressed that way just to play the mad general. It was the best way of hiding that mike, and it would have worked, had we not had that file on him to warn us. Lucky for you, you maintained ignorance of whatever he wanted to know. If possible, we must try to turn their mike against them.'

'But you mentioned a bomb . . .' Pappenheim said.

'Brannic being Brannic, I would expect him to leave another little surprise, just in case we did get that far. The goth will scan it first, and if she spots anything, she calls someone from our bomb squad team, if she can't disarm it herself.'

'Jesus,' Carey Bloomfield said. 'Brannic. That hand. He was trying to rip it off and blow us all to hell!'

'If it was also a bomb,' Müller said. 'He was a nasty piece of work, but he knew his jungle.' He picked up his phone and pressed an extension button. 'Hedi, Martin Halsinger is bringing something to you. He'll explain, but be very, very careful. Scan it first, before you even try to remove it. I don't want to hear an explosion. *What?*' He looked at the phone. The line was dead.

'Well?' Pappenheim asked as Müller put the phone down.

'She hung up on me.'

'I can see that. But what did she say?'

'After I warned her about an explosion, she said, "Serve you right," and hung up.'

Carey Bloomfield turned towards the city to hide a smile.

'Ah well,' Pappenheim said, getting off the desk, innocent blue eyes at their bluest. 'Something seems to have upset her. Me? I have no idea what it could be. And I need a cigarette. I'll keep an ear out for bangs,' he added as he went quickly out.

'Oh, thanks,' Müller said to the closed door. He looked at Carey Bloomfield, whose shoulders were shaking from suppressed giggles. 'I'm glad you're enjoying it so much.'

She turned to face him, wiping at her eyes. 'Blame it on a reaction to what happened today. Oh, Müller, Müller . . .' she went on, 'you really do get yourself into . . .' She stopped, looking at him with some amusement. 'And there's Kaltendorf's daughter too, Solange Dubois. Ever since you saved her butt from being blown in half.'

'The goth disarmed that bomb . . .'

'And became her shining knight,' Carey Bloomfield steamed on, ignoring his remark, 'that sweet lit'l thang has such a crush on you, if you were an orange, you'd be juice. You really must sort out your women.'

'*My* women?'

'They're not mine.'

The goth watched with an eloquent expression of disgust, as Halsinger carefully laid the bloodstained fatigues on the counter she had cleared for the purpose.

Hermann Spyros had come out of his office to look.

Halsinger put an urgent finger to his lips, and pointed at the button mike. Spyros nodded, understanding. When Halsinger had finished laying out the fatigues, Spyros indicated that he and the goth should follow him to his office.

They did so, and Spyros carefully closed the door.

'What do we have out there, Martin?' he asked in a low voice.

'A highly sensitive mike. I don't know if it can pick up anything through a door like this, but to be safe, we should keep our voices down.'

Spyros looked at the goth. 'Can you handle it?'

She nodded. 'I'll scan it first, to see if it's rigged to blow.'

'I remember how some time ago, you disarmed that explosive belt some bastard had put around the waist of *Direktor* Kaltendorf's daughter. Sure you can handle this one?'

'The boss said I should call the bomb squad if I can't.'

'OK. But *no* chances, Hedi. I'd never forgive myself.'

'I'm glad somebody cares,' she said and opening the door quietly, went out.

Halsinger stared at Spyros as he shut the door again. 'What was that about?'

'Don't ask.'

In Washington, the woman whose party Brannic had gate-crashed was sitting in the same room with the two men with whom she had the small conference with Brannic.

They were listening to a recording that a man had brought to them.

They listened in silence to the conversations, the sounds of gunfire, the explosions and, at the end, the death of Brannic.

'So Brannic failed,' the woman said. 'Müller knows nothing, the colonel knows nothing.'

'She's a tough one,' one of the men said. 'Shot his hand as cool as you please.'

The woman suddenly smacked her hand against the table. The portable minidisc player actually lifted a few millimetres with the force of the blow.

'We lost people out there!' she snarled. 'And for what? *Nothing!* And who the hell passed them a file with copies of Brannic's military documents?'

'Perhaps Dering?' one of her companions suggested. 'He was well placed.'

This man had no idea how close to the truth he was,

although what he was suggesting about the way it was passed was completely false.

'*Dering!*' It was a hiss. 'Perhaps. And his darling Colonel Bloomfield has not heard the last from us, whether she knows anything or not!' She calmed herself down. 'And why did he tell them about Rachel Worth having a mission?'

'He was dying, ma'am,' the man who had brought the recording said. 'He was losing it.'

She shook her head. 'A man like Brannic never "loses" it in that way. Other ways, yes. But to him, even the act of dying has a hidden purpose. He said that for a reason . . . possibly to distract them, making them focus on Worth, while something else happened.'

'But what?' the same companion asked.

'Am I in Brannic's head?' she retorted. 'Can you tell what's happening now?' she asked the man with the player.

'We're still monitoring. As far as we can tell, they have not yet found it; but there is no conversation to pick up. We heard them take the clothing off the body, but that's it for now. They've probably dumped it somewhere until they can dispose of it.'

'Is it rigged? That could be Brannic's hidden message.'

'Yes, Senator.'

'I hope it blows up in their fucking faces!'

The goth had placed the robust tripod legs of the shielded, enclosed scanner next to the counter. Sitting at a computer a safe distance from the scanner itself, she remotely lowered it until it was almost touching the button. It did so with uncanny silence.

She then started the scanner. It made no discernible noise.

An internal image of the button appeared. She expanded it until it filled the large screen. Its wiring was laid bare to her scrutiny. She inspected it closely for several minutes, tapping keys, clicking the mouse which made little noise, selecting sections of the image and blowing that up to screen size. She rotated the images, looking at every aspect of the button's construction. The entire procedure took her less than thirty minutes.

She stopped, left her seat, and went out.

In Spyros' office, Halsinger and Spyros stared at each other.

'What's she doing?' Halsinger asked.

Spyros gave a tiny shrug. 'Who knows? She has a world of her own. But she's a genius. To be honest, she's better than I am, by God knows how far. If they gave out rank based just on expertise, she'd be an *Oberkommissarin*. At least.'

'That's praise.'

'And well deserved.'

'She's coming back!'

They watched in consternation as the goth came to the office.

'I just went into another room to call the boss,' she began. 'I did not want to risk anything being picked up, even in here.'

'So?' Sypros asked.

'It's a bomb.'

Both men snapped their heads round to stare with apprehension at the counter where the fatigues lay.

'It's all right,' she told them with unnerving calm. 'It will do nothing, unless you try to detach it, or dismantle it. I certainly can't.'

'It beats *you*?' Spyros could not believe it.

'It's a one-way ticket. The person who wears this has two ways of getting rid of it: taking it off, or dying. Dying is self-explanatory . . .'

They stared at her.

'Or just take the whole thing off. It's perfectly safe if you leave it alone. The pocket is a false one. The flap is sewn down . . . probably to prevent anyone from trying to undo the button by mistake. But I'm certain there must have been at least one person who forgot, tried to open the flap, tugged at the button, and . . . boom.'

'Nice suit,' Halsinger said.

'The device has no trembler to trigger it . . . obviously, or you'd get just the one chance to try and put it on or pick it up . . .'

'Boom?' Halsinger asked.

'Boom.'

'Very nice suit.'

'Although,' she said, 'this could well be the only one like it. In which case, no one's died from it yet . . . except the person who was wearing it. But he got shot.'

Halsinger was staring at her, mesmerized.

'So what did Jens say?' Spyros asked.

'We cut around it . . .'

'We *keep* that thing?'

'Think I'm going to enjoy cutting into that blood-soaked thing? Did they have to turn him into a sieve? But it's completely safe,' the goth continued as if to children, 'as long as you don't try to remove it.' She looked at Halsinger. 'It's very robust. If not, you'd have been dead already.'

'Thanks!'

'Don't mention it. It's quite powerful too. A micro bomb. Some very special people made that. I've already told the boss. It could blow out . . . oh . . . the room out there, and here. Maybe more than that.'

She went out, and back to her work with the fatigues.

Halsinger stared after her as if she were some exotic animal, as she got a pair of scissors and began to cut out an area around the left breast pocket of the bloodied fatigues.

'She . . . she always like that?'

'This is nothing for our goth,' Spyros said, suspiciously proud. 'She's not really in full swing. Something on her mind, I think.' He did not elaborate.

'She's crazy!'

'That too.'

Müller arrived just as the goth finished cutting a circular patch out of Brannic's fatigues.

'So, what do you want me to do with this thing, sir?' the goth asked, making no attempt to lower her voice.

'Leave it for the forensic people to look at,' Müller replied, also in his normal voice. 'When they're done, dump it. Better yet, have it incinerated.'

'Yes, sir.'

'But don't forget. I don't want that thing lying around stinking the place out.'

Müller left, closing the door firmly.

In Spyros' office, the two men were staring in disbelief in the goth's direction.

'They were talking normally!' Halsinger said. 'What . . . ?'

Spyros had raised a hand to stop him. 'Look,' he said.

The goth was holding a finger to her lips.

'I think they just did some play-acting, for the benefit of whoever might be listening.'

The goth raised the patch she had cut out, and mimed that she was leaving. She took the piece of cloth, with its dangerous button, with her.

'Where's she going?' Halsinger asked, puzzled.

'Probably where Jens asked her to,' Spyros said. 'My worry is more about what to do with what's left.' He looked at the fatigues, with a large gaping hole where its fake pocket used to be.

The goth joined Müller, Pappenheim and Carey Bloomfield in a small room on the second floor. It had controlled atmosphere, and no windows. It was virtually a strong-room doubling as a spillover storage area for the unit's weaponry.

The room was itself barely used, and Müller had decided it would be a good place to leave the button-mike. As it was rarely visited, no conversation useful to the Semper would be heard, but the Semper could be fed whatever Müller chose. No one – apart from Müller and Pappenheim themselves – would have access to the room without first being authorized. If for any reason the button exploded, the room was strong enough to contain the explosion.

The goth entered, and looked at Carey Bloomfield. 'Good to see you back, Colonel, and with no holes in you.'

'Thank you.'

'Lucky for you they were bad shots . . .'

Not certain how to handle this, Carey Bloomfield said, 'I guess.'

Müller gave the goth a stern look.

'Just joking,' the goth said with a sweet smile to all.

She had made a small hole at the top of the patch. She now hung the material on one of the many empty hooks for weapon slings.

'The forensic colleagues are on their way, sir,' she said neutrally to Müller. 'When they're finished, we'll burn that thing.'

'Good,' Müller said.

'What do I do if they decide to keep it longer?'

'They can take responsibility for it.'

'That's a relief. I don't like looking at it.' This remark was not play-acting and everyone knew it.

Müller nodded at them to indicate it was time to leave. They filed out quietly into the corridor, closing the door loudly enough to be unmistakably picked up by the mike. The room was solid enough to prevent any conversation from outside being picked up from within.

'I've got work to do,' the goth said, and walked away.

As she watched her go, Carey Bloomfield said, 'Boy, oh, boy, does she hate my guts.'

Pappenheim glanced back. 'I don't think so. She's got a mood on . . . that's all.'

'You don't know women, Pappi,' she said. 'At least, not this one. You both don't.'

She was still looking as the goth walked to the end of the corridor and glanced directly back at her, before turning a corner.

'Guess not,' she said. She looked at Müller. 'That bastard *was* trying to blow us to kingdom come.'

'That was Brannic. Always one last trick. He *was* booby-trapped, but not the way we expected.'

In Washington, in the dedicated monitoring room where the transmissions from the button mike were picked up, the man who had brought the minidisc player to the senator and her companions was running a playback. He watched the frequency displays on his monitor screen, matching them to the sounds that had been picked up.

He looked about him to people who were themselves seated at other monitors.

'Hey, Jack,' he called to one. 'Take a look at this. Tell me what you think.'

The man called Jack went over to peer at the screen. 'What am I looking for?'

'Listen to this playback, and watch the displays. This is the latest stuff from the mike.' He ran the recording.

Neither spoke until it had run through.

'Right . . .' Jack began. 'First, there's some shuffling around. People moving . . . perhaps moving Brannic's fatigues.'

'They were moving it.'

'OK. Then more shuffling around. Then a door opens, closes, opens again a little later. More shuffling. Then conversation in German, asking her boss what to do. Boss goes out. More shuffling. Then . . . what the hell's that?'

'Ah, that's what I want you to really hear. I'll add some volume.' The man at the monitor glanced at his colleague with expectation.

'Sounds like something . . . crawling . . . Can I have more augmentation? Sounds like some insect eating. Perhaps there's a small animal in that thing. Something that crawled in while Brannic was lying there. It took a while for those clean-up guys to arrive. Plenty of time for something to crawl in there. The guy was dead, after all.'

'I thought exactly that. But listen some more.' He played

206

the section again, increasing volume and separating frequencies.

'Cutting!' Jack said. 'I hear cutting. But that could be the jaws of whatever it is in there. I've watched nature films. You'll never believe the sound an ant makes . . .'

'Again, I thought the same thing.'

'I don't get what you're getting at here . . .'

'Scissors.'

'*Scissors?*'

'Yup. You're right about cutting. You're hearing the cutting of cloth.'

'Aww, c'mon, Herb. That's stretching it till it squeals. So what are they cutting?'

'Maybe bandages, but I can't see why. Perhaps stuff to wipe the blood with. You heard her. She hates looking at the stuff. Kind of squeamish for a cop.'

'So what's the bee you've got buzzing around in there?'

'Perhaps they were cutting *into* the fatigues.'

'So what? They'll do some forensic work, then burn it when they're done.'

'Yeah, but if they keep cutting, sooner or later, they'll find the mike.'

'Well, we know what will happen.' The man called Jack grinned.

'The senator will love it.'

'Yeah. She will. Any more picked up?'

'Yup. Mike's still in place.'

Herb played the rest of the recording.

'English!' Jack exclaimed. 'And there's our errant colonel, alive and well. Boy . . . there's some needle going on between those two.'

'Yup. Wonder why. Could be of some use to us one day. You never know.'

'Could be.'

In General Sternbach's mansion, someone else had the goth in mind. Blake and Arnold were walking off a generous late lunch, in the general's vast grounds. Blake was still trying to press Arnold to act.

'We've got to get her, man!' he insisted. 'She can down our systems any time she fucking likes!'

'Why don't we wait and see what the big boys want? We can't do anything without their say so.'

Blake gave a sigh of impatience. 'Who's the hacker here? I found her! All we've got to do is take her out . . .'

'Blake, *not* until we have the authority!'

In Sternbach's study, the same subject, in a manner of speaking, was being discussed.

'I've heard from Rachel that Brannic is dead,' he was saying to Reinhardt. 'The entire thing is a mess.'

'Casualties?'

'Total.'

'Not *one* survived?'

'Rachel did. She believes they let her go. Müller had a sniper. He planned it well. According to Rachel, he was always one step ahead of Brannic. It was as if he *knew* what to expect, all along the line, and was able to counter. Rachel believes the kidnapping was allowed to happen. I have confirmation of that from our friends across the Atlantic. Brannic had a bug on him – a button – which transmitted everything. This seems to be the only thing Müller does not know about.'

Reinhardt's expression was grim. 'Where's the bug now?'

'With Müller's people. They have Brannic's fatigues. The bug is still transmitting, so they have obviously not found it as yet. Our friends across the water hope we may gain something from that. But all in all, an unmitigated disaster.'

'Where is Rachel now?'

'Upstairs. She has to remain here until we can get her out of the country. It must happen as soon as possible.'

'I can arrange that, but why, General?'

'Apart from the fact that Müller allowed her to run for a purpose we do not as yet know, she killed Waldron.'

'What?' Reinhardt was shocked.

'I did give him a friendly warning about her,' Sternbach said. 'Waldron betrayed us. Pappenheim was pumping him for information, instead of the other way round. So the idea of using his friendship with Pappenheim has also failed. We are not doing well today, Reinhardt.'

'Did she explain what led her to believe this about Waldron?'

'He told Pappenheim she blew up that plane.'

Reinhardt stared at Sternbach. 'My God!'

'Exactly, Reinhardt. Exactly. Pappenheim was *blackmailing* Waldron. He knew things that frightened Waldron into talking. From *where* could he have got such information?'

Reinhardt had no answer.

Seeing Reinhardt's expression, Sternbach continued drily. 'Neither have I. But this also explains Müller's ability to out-think Brannic. Prior knowledge. They know much more than we think they do. This puts us very much on the defensive. Müller has also kept the killing quiet. Nothing at all on the news. You can be certain he has his reasons, which will be of no benefit to us. But we are also relieved. The killing of a diplomat – one of ours – in a well-known hotel is not something we would like to see make the headlines. Rachel was excessive in this one. I believe there was an element of the personal about it.'

'Did you authorize her to . . . ?'

'No. It came from above me. This is a measure of how serious the situation is considered to be. For the same reason, we have been told that no move is to be made against that policewoman for now. Müller is on high alert, and will expect this. He would be waiting for any attempt. We can't keep losing people to this man!'

Sternbach's expression was one of impotent fury.

'If it's any consolation,' Reinhardt began with some caution, 'I happen to agree. Bruch is also against it.'

'Bruch's a good man. Solid. That other man, Blake, is barely out of his teens, and still behaves like it. But he's smart with computers. He's right when he says we'll keep losing monitoring centres if we do nothing, so, for now, monitoring Müller's unit is suspended until further notice. Blake will have to focus on something else. The Order has plenty of use for his considerable talents in other areas.'

'Bruch considers him unstable.'

'Of course he is. Most geniuses are. But he does not get his attack on that policewoman. See that he understands this . . . clearly.'

'Leave it to me.'

Blake was not happy about it, and he showed his displeasure.

'Whaaat? Oh, man. You've got to be *kidding* me! Arnold, are you hearing this?' He glared at Reinhardt, like a petulant child feeling put upon.

Arnold said nothing.

Reinhardt studied Blake with cold detachment. 'Mr Blake, do not make the mistake of believing that your excellent skills make you immune to censure.' Reinhardt's English was perfect.

'Are you *threatening* me, *Colonel* Reinhardt?'

'I never make pointless threats, Mr Blake. I am giving you some advice.'

'You can shove your advice! I am telling you people that unless you take out that woman, you'll keep losing centres.'

Reinhardt was patience itself. 'We are well aware of that, Mr Blake. However, it has been decided to take the current course of action. You would do well to accept it.' Reinhardt's eyes grew cold. 'And Mr Blake, don't you *ever* tell me to shove it again.'

'Or what?'

'It could be the last thing you ever do.'

Reinhardt turned and left.

Blake faced the silent Arnold. 'Do you believe this shit? How can they be so . . . so . . . dumb?'

'When you get high enough,' Arnold began, '*if* you ever make it that far, you can start throwing your weight around. Until then, you're just the PBI, so shut it.'

'Poor bloody infantry, am I? I'll show . . .'

'Remember what you yourself said back in Frankfurt, Blake. They *can* just shoot you if you piss them off. And to that I add . . . no matter how high, or how low you happen to be.' He mimed a shot at Blake.

But Blake, fixated upon eliminating the goth whom he saw as a professional rival who was roundly beating him at his own game, and who had to be taken down, refused to listen. He at once envied her, and hated her. It gnawed at him.

'You'll see,' he said to Arnold. 'You'll see.'

Arnold shook his head, giving up. 'Your damned funeral,' he muttered as he walked away. 'You'll deserve it, dumbass.'

Rachel Worth was no longer upstairs. Wearing a white, transparent linen top, and the cycling shorts, she was sitting by herself at a far corner of the gardens, reading. Her legs, drawn up and close together, were bare; as were her feet. She wore no bra.

She sensed someone walking towards her, but did not turn to look.

'Hi.'

She looked up from her book, dark eyes settling upon Blake.

'You're Rachel, right?' he continued.

'I'm Rachel.' The eyes probed at him.

'You're . . . er . . . the killer.'

'I am many things.' She opened her legs slightly, still looking at Blake.

Blake could not help himself. He looked at her legs.

'Like what you see?' she asked, still looking up at him.

His eyes snapped back to her. 'Er . . .'

'It's all right to say you do. I think they need shaving. But that's just me. Why don't you feel them, and tell me?'

'Er . . .' Blake said again, not sure how to handle the situation.

'You're Blake, aren't you?'

'Er . . . yes. Yes.'

'Sit down next to me, Blake.' She put down the book, and patted the ground close to her. 'Here. Then you can feel my legs and tell me what you came here for . . . if not for me.' The eyes looked deep into him.

Blake seemed to have some difficulty keeping his breathing steady.

'Come on, Blake. Don't be shy. Sit down.'

After some hesitation, he did so, cautiously.

'I won't bite, silly boy,' she chided him. She took his hand and placed it on her leg. 'Feel. Do they need shaving? Not like that. Stroke them . . . yes, like that. Well?'

'Er . . . no. They're as smooth as . . .'

'Silk?'

'Yes. That's it. Silk.'

'Do you like them?'

'They're beautiful!' Blake said in a rush before he could stop himself.

She smiled. Her eyes did not. 'There. Not so hard, was it?'

Blake fought to keep his eyes from her top. 'Yes . . . er . . . no. No. It . . . wasn't.'

'Now that's been settled, what can I do for you?' She moved her legs again.

Blake's eyes darted towards them, then back to the unsettling eyes.

'Apart from that,' she said, leaving no doubt about what she meant.

'Well . . .' he began, after some moments to get his thoughts back in order. 'Who authorizes you to . . . you know . . . ?'

'Do a killing?'

'Well, yes.' Blake was now fighting to keep his eyes from both her legs, and her breasts.

She studied his efforts with a tiny smile, head cocked to one side.

'That depends,' she replied. The reptile eyes were fixed upon him.

'Uh . . . on?'

'On who's giving it.'

'So, can someone like me . . . ?'

'No.' She paused. 'Do you want me to kill someone for you, Blake?'

He took some time thinking about it. Then, 'Yes.'

'Who?'

'A cop. Woman.'

'What has she done to you?'

'It's what she's doing to *us*. She's a hacker, and she's been killing our monitoring centres.'

'Is she better than you?' The dark eyes, unblinking, stayed upon him.

He did not like the question. 'No,' he lied.

'Then she isn't a worry.' Rachel Worth picked up her book.

'L . . . look, look,' Blake said quickly.

She put the book back down. 'Is she better?'

He was forced into admitting it. 'Yes.'

'Then we must do something about that, mustn't we, sweetie?' She stood up. 'Let's go upstairs and discuss what to do in more pleasant surroundings. My room.'

Blake got to his feet. 'Your *room*? The general . . .'

'Is not my father. I do as I please, unless you haven't the balls for it.'

Blake gave a sudden grin. 'I have the balls.' His eyes raked her up and down.

'That's my sweetie,' she said with approval, and took his hand. 'Go, shall we?'

As they walked back, they passed Bruch, who gave them a smile.

'See?' she said as they went by. 'Even old sourpuss, Bruch, smiles at us. The people here know me, and never interfere.'

Knowing how Bruch felt about him, Blake took that as a positive sign.

No one bothered them as they went up to Rachel Worth's room, which was baronial in dimensions.

'Wow!' Blake said. 'This is some room. And that bed!'

213

'We'll soon put it to good use.' She studied his expression. 'Cold feet, Blake?'

'No! No, of course not!'

'Then I'll just go into the bathroom for a bit. Won't be long.'

She gave his cheek a soft stroke, and left him staring at the bed in heated anticipation.

Some minutes passed, then he heard her call out, 'Blake! I need some help. The shorts seem to have . . . *stuck*. Urrgh! I hate when this happens, but I like them so much. Blake!'

'Coming!'

He hurried to the bathroom, eager to peel off the shorts himself. He barged in.

And stopped.

Rachel Worth was still fully dressed. A silenced gun was pointed at him; and behind the gun, the lifeless reptile eyes.

'You should have listened to good advice, Blake. You are not indispensable.'

His mouth opened to say something at the moment she shot him.

Gun still in hand, she stepped over the body to go into the room where she picked up the phone, and hit the general's extension.

'One hacker less,' she said to him.

'Pity,' Sternbach said. 'He was gifted, but a loose cannon. Had to be done. Bruch and Arnold will be coming up to take him off your hands.'

'Tell them to be quick. I need a bath. I don't want a corpse looking on.'

'They'll be quick.' Sternbach seemed to be smiling as he said that.

Ten

Müller and Carey Bloomfield were getting ready to leave. 'I'm looking forward to getting into that bath,' she said, 'after all the excitement of the day.'

'In a few minutes, you will be having it.'

The phone rang.

'Wanna bet?' she said, staring at the instrument.

He picked up. 'Müller.'

It was Berger. 'Boss, you should have a TV in your office.'

'As you know I do not, what's so enthralling?'

'They're reporting that a body was just pulled out of the Spree. No identification on it . . .'

'But?'

'If the pictures are correct, I know him.'

'Tell me.'

'Reimer and I saw him this morning. In the café opposite. He was checking out our building. In fact I believe he and his pals – two other men – were checking out the goth. I told the Chief, and he suggested we go to the goth to give her the descriptions. She made almost exact likenesses. It's definitely his body. The goth was supposed to look for matches in the database, but I expect she didn't find any.'

'Thanks, Lene. I'll talk with Pappi.'

'OK, boss.'

Müller put the phone down.

'No bath,' Carey Bloomfield said.

215

'Not just yet. But we won't be long.'

'Hah. You'll never guess how many times I've heard this before . . . and I'm not just talking about from you. So what's the story?'

'Man found dead in the Spree. It's on the news. Berger saw him this morning in the café on the other side of the road not far from here, with two other men, checking out this building. Berger believes they were actually checking on the goth. If true, my guess is that someone in the Semper might have found out that she's our electronics wizard. She has a high kill rate, taking out their systems. They would certainly like to stop her. We were already alert for possible kidnap attempts, so Pappi put Berger and Reimer on babysitting watch.'

'But weren't they taking a risk coming this close?'

'Not necessarily. They're desperate, but inserting unknown faces in a surveillance job would not arouse suspicion. They could not have known that we had a watch on the goth. Without that, they would not have been spotted.'

'And now one of them is dead. How come?'

'Your guess is as good as mine. The Semper took a beating today. Perhaps they called off whatever plan they had for the goth. Perhaps this man objected, and he paid the price. All guesswork. It may not be that at all. The goth was supposed to find matches from Berger's and Reimer's descriptions. She will have tried our normal police database, but she hasn't yet been able to search the one in the Rogues Gallery, given our own excitements today. I'll get Pappi to call her in.'

'Mind if I don't come?'

'Don't tell me you feel terrorized by the goth . . . ?'

'I'd just like to enjoy your view of the city, Müller.' She folded her arms.

'Be my guest,' he said, and called Pappenheim.

'No colonel?' the goth said as soon as she entered the Rogues Gallery.

Pappenheim ducked that one and said to Müller, 'Over to you.'

'She likes the view in my office,' Müller told the goth.

The goth made a sniffing sound. 'Hope she enjoys it.' She went across to the computer before either of them could say anything more, and powered up. 'There's nothing at all in the standard database. I was planning to hack into some intelligence systems, but some other things got in the way.'

Müller and Pappenheim exchanged glances.

'I saw that!' the goth said without turning round. 'All right, let's see what's in this database. The dead one first.'

She began to search the files from Woonnalla. The program raced through, trying to find a match for the image of Blake she had created.

'They may not have had information on this man . . .' Müller began.

'They have,' she said in triumph, as a photograph appeared next to the image she had created. 'Robert E. Blake,' she read aloud.

'Perhaps his parents were American Civil War enthusiasts,' Pappenheim quipped.

'Well, their little Robert E. is dead,' Müller said, 'probably killed by the people he worked for.'

'And here's the information on him, sir!' The goth sounded excited.

'Hacker!' Müller and Pappenheim said together.

'This man was your direct opponent, Hedi,' Müller went on. 'Perhaps you killed a system where he worked.'

'He took it personally?'

'Perhaps he considered himself the best, and did not like the competition.'

'Some people can get really worked up about it,' she admitted. 'But to go to such lengths . . .'

'He was not just "some" hacker,' Pappenheim told her. 'He was a Semper hacker. Big difference. You've been killing their systems. They had to try and stop you.'

'But now he's dead,' she said. 'Why kill their own?'

'If they did kill him,' Müller told her, 'we believe it could be because they called off whatever plans they had for you, probably because of what happened today. Who knows? If they did do it, I consider that a bonus. The more of each other they kill, the better I like it. See if you can find anything on the others.'

She did.

'James Arnold,' Müller read, 'Ludwig Bruch. Arnold's a surveillance expert, clearly no hacker, and Bruch is one of Sternbach's heavies. And look at this, Pappi. Arnold and Blake are – were, in the case of Blake now – based in Frankfurt. My God. These files are more up-to-date than we think.'

'So do we owe the general another visit? I love barging into his mansion. Perhaps I can knock down one of the suits of armour, drop ash on one of the expensive carpets, poison his koi . . .'

'Calm your enthusiasm, Pappi. We leave him alone for now. He's hurting, and I'm certain he's got Rachel Worth in there. They'll want to move her as fast as they can. Let's be ready for that.'

Pappenheim stared at him. 'You want her in the open.'

'Yes.'

Pappenheim glanced at the goth. 'Are you OK in here, Hedi?'

'Don't mind me.'

Pappenheim led Müller out of the room and into the corridor. 'Jens,' he began in a low voice, 'you can't just execute her. You're a policeman. Arrest her, if she resists . . .' He shrugged. 'Then that's her lookout. Let's go to the general's and take her for the murder of Waldron.'

Müller's eyes were cold. 'She murdered my parents!' he countered savagely. 'Sorry, Pappi.' He turned, and went back to his office.

Pappenheim stared at the door to Müller's office. 'I need a cigarette,' he said, and went back into his own.

As Müller entered his office, Carey Bloomfield looked at him closely.

'You OK, Müller?' she asked.

'I'm fine.'

'Any luck with that body?'

'Better than that. We have been able to identify all three men from the Woonnalla files.'

'All Semper, then.'

'Yes. The dead man was Robert E. Blake.'

'His parents must have been . . .'

'Pappi's been there . . .'

'Great minds.'

Müller gave a grim smile. 'The other two are James Arnold, and Ludwig Bruch. Arnold's a surveillance expert, and Bruch is one of Sternbach's men. Arnold and Blake were based in Frankfurt.'

'Wow!' she said. 'Those files really are on the ball. But now that Dering's gone, who's going to keep up the flow of information?'

'We know Dering's not the only infiltrator. Perhaps we'll be lucky and still get some info, if not as relatively easily.'

'You're the custodian now, Müller. You're going to have to take over from—'

The phone rang.

'Yep,' she added. 'There goes my bath.'

'Müller,' he said as he picked up.

It was Aunt Isolde. 'Jens, I'm so sorry to ask. I know how busy you are, but could you come down?'

'Now?'

'Yes. Sorry to do this, but I think . . .' She began to weep.

'Hang on, Aunt Isolde. I'm coming right now. Just hang on. Do you hear?'

'Yes, yes. Please hurry.'

Carey Bloomfield was looking at him wide-eyed as he hung up. 'What's wrong?'

'I think it's Greville. I think his nemesis has got him at last. She was crying.'

'Oh, dear God.'

'Do you mind if we go down there?'

'How can you ask me such a question, Müller?'

'But your bath . . .'

'Jesus! Skates on, Müller. That poor woman's waiting.'

On their way out, Müller knocked on Pappenheim's door and poked his head through. 'Sorry for that . . . um . . .'

Pappenheim blew a stream of smoke ceilingwards. 'What "um"?' He grinned.

'Thanks.'

'You look in a hurry.'

'We're going down to my aunt's. I think Greville's going. I just got a tearful call.'

Pappenheim stubbed out the cigarette and was on his feet. 'Need anything?'

'I need you to stay here, keep everything tight, and make sure the goth's safe.'

'All in hand.'

'See you . . . whenever.'

'And if Kaltendorf rears his curious head?'

'See you . . . whenever.'

Pappenheim nodded. 'I think I understand that.'

As Müller withdrew his head, Pappenheim went quickly to the door to whisper to Carey Bloomfield, 'Watch his back.'

'I'm a limpet,' she whispered in return.

At Sternbach's home, Reinhardt was talking to Rachel Worth.

'We're getting you to France tonight. Bruch will drive you as far as Baden-Baden. Someone else will take you on and across the border from there. You have two jobs to do. The first is here in Berlin. The second in France. After that job, you will be taken to the heliport in Monaco. The helicopter will take you from there to Cannes Mandelieu. One of our jets will be waiting. Are you clear on that?'

'Perfectly,' she replied.

She did not look at all like the woman the two patrolmen had so assiduously kept under surveillance; nor as Carey Bloomfield and Müller had last seen her, nor the unfortunate and overheated Blake, prior to his unfulfilled hope of an unexpected sexual liaison.

'Your targets.' Reinhardt showed her two photographs. One was of the goth. 'Memorize them. The photographs remain here. For France, this is where you'll find your target.' He showed her the other photograph. 'And the address. This remains here as well.'

Rachel Worth pointed to the first. 'The policewoman? I thought . . .'

'The general decided that Blake did have a point worth pursuing. That woman is inimical to our interests. She has to be stopped. People like her, of her calibre in that field of expertise, are very rare. She has more than talent. She has a sharp instinct, a *feel* for what she does that cannot be readily replaced, if at all. Without her skill, Müller will take a very severe blow. The general put this up to the Council. They immediately agreed that she should be eliminated *if* it can be done cleanly, and with a swift, unexpected suddenness. They consider you the best candidate to carry this out.'

She nodded.

'Ironically, the general considers that had she been one of ours, we would have had no such problems. An attempt was once made to recruit her. She turned down a very lucrative offer. She prefers to do what she is doing, for much less pay. People who can't be bought are dangerous individuals.'

'Did she know she would be working for us?'

Reinhardt shook his head. 'She was never meant to know. Blake's problem was not in his reading of what needed to be done, but in his instability. He was not a team player. Here's her address. Memorize it. She lives in Prenzlauer Berg. She's on the top floor. By the time you get there, she should be home. A key to the main door has been made. If you sense any trouble, abort. Do *not* press on. This is very important. We do not intend that you get yourself killed carrying this out.'

'Don't worry. I have a strong survival instinct.'

'You have total autonomy. Play it as you will. If you choose to abort, no blame will be attached to you. The Council were adamant about this. You are too valuable to lose.'

'Nice to know someone loves me.'

'Many people love you, Rachel. Now go with Bruch. Good luck, and safe journey.'

'See you sometime, Colonel, sweetie. You're a dear.'

She gave his cheek a stroke, before going out with Bruch.

'Look,' Reimer said. 'We've tailed her home. She's safe in her little eyrie. Can we go now?'

'Reimer,' Berger began in exasperation, 'the chief said stay with her tonight. He has his reasons.'

'Well, can't we at least go upstairs? We can have coffee . . .'

'And keep her awake all night? Coffee's in the flask. Help yourself. And stop whining.'

'You're a big help, you are. Hello . . . ?' Reimer had been gazing about him.

'What?'

'That car . . . it's slowing down, *stopping*, by the goth's building. That's not the kind of car you usually see around here, at the goth's building at this time of the evening, *stopping*. Golfs, Polos, Beetles, little Citroens . . . not big, dark saloons.' He began to get out of the unmarked car.

As he did so, the strange car suddenly accelerated, heading off at speed.

Berger was now out, staring after the speeding vehicle.

'Shouldn't we follow?' Reimer urged.

'Are you crazy? What if it's a decoy?'

Reimer got the message. 'My God. They were actually going to try.'

'What do you think of the chief's idea now?'

'That's why he's an *Oberkommissar*, and I'm not.'

'At least you know it.'

Berger called Pappenheim. 'They just tried it, Chief . . . just as you thought.' She explained what had happened. 'They must have either done some checking to know where the goth lives, or they may have tailed us. I'm certain I would have spotted them, but you never know . . .'

'I'm certain it was not a tail. They have their moles too. They could have got it that way. Good work, Lene. Stay with it. I'll put a fresh team on her tomorrow. Give you two some rest.'

'We're OK . . .'

'Who's got the rank?'

'You do. Fresh team.'

'I knew we'd agree.'

The big car was slowing down.

'They're not following,' Bruch said.

'Who?' Rachel asked.

'Cops.'

'The man who got out of that car?'

'Yes. I saw him, and his partner, this morning when we were with Blake. They came into the café. They left to go into the police building. The woman gave me a full-face look as they drove past, committing me to memory. She has a bitch of a stare. They've got their colleague under full protection. You would have been killed tonight, perhaps even me.'

'Your recommendation?'

'Do what Colonel Reinhardt said. Abort. It's the smart thing.'

'I think I agree with you.'

'I never liked this idea, anyway.'

'Even after what Reinhardt said about the Council?'

'The Council don't want you killed. I am obeying that. You have autonomy.'

'And I'm going to use it. Take me to Baden-Baden.'

'Wise choice.'

'Let's hope no one's watching the second target.'

Schlosshotel Derrenberg. 2200 hours

Müller drove the Porsche into the residential courtyard.

'Hey!' Carey Bloomfield exclaimed in surprise. 'He's full of beans!'

223

Which was certainly true enough, on the face of it. An apparently hale and hearty Greville was coming towards them. There was no sign of Aunt Isolde.

'There you are, dear boy,' Greville began as Müller stopped the car in a parking bay, and began to climb out. 'And you too, dear Carey. So good of you both to rush down.'

'Greville . . .' she began.

'Shh, dear girl. Be a good love and go in to Isolde, would you please, while I take your young man down to the stream.'

She gave Müller a puzzled glance.

'Sure,' she said to Greville.

'There's a love. Won't be too long. Come on, old boy.'

With a second glance at Müller, she made her way to the kitchen while Müller and Greville went back into the hotel grounds.

Greville did not speak until they were actually at the stream.

'This is it, old boy,' he began quietly. 'Time has finally come.'

Müller stared at him. 'I don't understand. You look perfectly—'

'Healthy. Yes. I know. That's the beauty with this thing. Kills you softly. No ghastly deterioration of the old cadaver, or the senses. Just one day . . . and you're gone. Not even the horrors of a heart attack, or the slow wasting from some wretched disease. No drooling dementia. More dignity this way, what?' Greville sighed heavily. 'This thing, quite unexpectedly, could be such a boon . . . yet, I cannot allow it to be turned loose. As with so many other great inventions before it, it would be abused for nefarious purposes. I'm not playing God, I just don't want to be the devil.'

'Are you telling me,' Müller said after a while, 'that you know the time has come? Definitely?'

'I am saying more than that. If you do not give me that last trip around the Nordschleife as we arranged ages ago, it will be too late after tomorrow.'

As he listened to Greville's words – despite knowing it had to happen one day – Müller was shocked.

'Greville, how can you be certain . . . ?'

'Could not be more certain, old boy. The bell is about to toll.'

'But we planned to do this in your old Healey.'

'Know we did. But Healey's in dear old Blighty, and we're here. Can't be helped. Improvise, what? Happy with that rocket of yours, if you've a mind to it.'

'Of course, I will. No question.'

'Thanks, old boy. Appreciate it. You will play "Stardust", won't you?'

'Ever since you told me, I've had it in the CD changer.'

'Be prepared, eh? Scouting motto. Good show.'

As he looked at Greville in the light of the hotel grounds, Müller thought he was already seeing a ghost. Yet a perfectly healthy-looking Greville stood before him.

'What happened?' he asked.

'Was standing here,' Greville said, 'just as we are now, enjoying the peace of the woods around me, the sound of the stream, letting the old mind wander. Then out like the proverbial light. No warning. Could have fallen into the water, floated away. Luckily, some instinct made me fall backwards. Lay there God knows how long. Never happened before. That's how I know. The warning gong, old son.'

'How . . . who found you?'

'One of your chappies came looking. For some reason, Isolde felt uneasy, asked him to look, after I'd been gone for about an hour. Look, I know she's going to take it badly when it happens. She's going to need you, old boy.'

Müller felt his eyes grow hot. 'She'll always have me.'

'Know it, old son. Know it. Thank you. Now let's go back to that gel of yours. Word of advice. Don't lose that gel. I went off. Look what happened. Don't be like me. Loyalty to duty is all well and good. Loyalty to oneself is also important.'

'It's a fine balance, Greville.'

'I did not say it was easy.'

Müller's phone rang.

'I'll go on, dear boy,' Greville said. 'See you in a bit.'

Müller nodded, then took out his phone as Greville walked on. 'Yes, Pappi.'

'Am I interrupting?'

'No, no. Go ahead.'

'They tried to get at the goth.'

'When?'

Pappenheim gave him the details of what had happened.

'Nice work,' he said, when Pappenheim had finished. 'They're getting desperate, but after this, I don't think they'll try again.'

'My feelings exactly . . . but I'll keep the cover on the goth for the time being. She's important, our goth.'

'Oh, yes.'

'So how is it down there?'

Müller was silent.

'That bad?' Pappenheim said.

'It's not good. He fell unconscious. Literally . . . for about an hour. One of the colleagues found him, out cold. He is convinced it's the warning gong, as he calls it.'

'How long before . . . ?'

'He believes it could be tomorrow, or the day after.'

This shook Pappenheim into a brief silence of his own. 'Jens, this is terrible. Your aunt . . .'

'Is not having a good time of it.'

'So sorry.'

'Nothing anyone can do. As Greville would say, it's taking its natural course.'

'Nothing natural about this.'

'In a strange way, it is.'

Müller opened the door to his room in answer to a soft knock. Carey Bloomfield stood there.

'I saw you come up,' she said. 'How are they?'

'Sitting holding hands in the kitchen. I thought it best to let them have whatever time is left to themselves. Please. Come in. Sit anywhere.'

She entered, and chose to sit on the edge of his bed. He leaned on a chest of drawers, facing her.

'Is it all right with you,' he began, 'remaining here with her while I take Greville to the Nürburgring?'

'Of course it is. What do you think, Müller?'

'I don't want to impose.'

'Jesus, Müller! I don't know which makes me want to grab you by the shoulders and shake you . . . when you're being British, like now, or when you're being German by being . . .'

'Correct?'

'No . . . not exactly correct . . . well, hell, yeah . . .'

'Imagine when both these traits get together . . .'

'Do I want a peek into hell?'

He gave a tiny smile.

'Müller, this is . . . shit. I don't want Greville to go. And poor old Aunt Isolde.'

'We can't change it.'

'No, damn it! That's what makes it such . . .'

'Shit. Yes.'

She stood up. 'Müller?'

'Yes . . .'

'Don't go killing yourself on that racetrack tomorrow.'

'Or?'

'I'll kill you. So help me.'

He watched as she stood up, ready to leave.

She paused, studying him for long moments, as if making her mind up about something.

'See you in the morning, Müller.'

'Yes. Goodnight.'

'Night.'

Schlosshotel Derrenberg. Tuesday, 0630 local

'Nice day for it,' Greville said as they walked towards the car. He was remarkably cheerful.

Aunt Isolde did not come to see them off, but Carey Bloomfield did.

'Make sure this guy does not drive too crazily on that track, Greville,' she said.

227

'Oh, I don't know. A little craziness in life is sometimes not too amiss.'

'You're nuts, Greville. You know that?'

'Of course I am, my dear.' He gave her a quick peck on the cheek. 'Thank you for caring.' He winked at her, and got into the passenger seat.

'Müller, you two get your butts back here later today.'

'Yes, Colonel.' He paused. 'Make sure she's all right.'

'I will.'

He climbed in behind the wheel.

She watched them leave, arms folded about herself.

'That gel's so crazy about you, dear boy,' Greville said as they drove through the gate, 'she does not quite know what to do with herself.'

Müller said nothing.

'I can see that went down like a lead balloon,' Greville said.

'Wha . . . what? Oh. Sorry, Greville. I was just thinking of the look on Aunt Isolde's face.'

'Ah yes. She does not think she's going to see me again. Alive, that is.'

'Nonsense. You'll be devouring one of her roasts this evening.'

'More like something devouring me.' Sudddenly, Greville shouted, 'But are we disheartened?'

'No, we are not!' they shouted together.

In that mood, they headed across country towards the Nürburgring, in the Eifel.

The normally four-and-a-half-hour journey in a standard car took them well under four hours, Müller making good use of the autobahn stretches of just over 300 kilometres.

They arrived at the Nürburgring at ten fifteen.

'That,' Greville began with relish, 'was *fast* driving. Remarkable time, considering the traffic.'

Müller smiled at that. 'I wanted to get you here before the rush. Would you like more than one run?' Müller continued as he parked the car in one of the many bays near the café.

'One will be sufficient, dear boy. Remember this will be my

second visit in your rocket. Last time we came to this track, it was police business . . . chasing my errant adopted son, who had become a hitman for the Semper. One of life's great ironies. I go to do my job in a Middle Eastern country, another man who was not supposed to be there turns up. We're both doing our jobs. He fires, I fire. He misses . . . not strictly true. *His* shot hits a vial containing some deadly stuff. He dies from my shot. I am contaminated by a long-delayed sentence of death. He leaves a son whom I secretly adopt, care for, and educate. Boy does not know, but grows up to become killer for the people you are fighting. We chase him here, where he dies. And here I am, decades after my contamination, finally about to confront my own nemesis.' Greville paused. 'Ironies.'

They got out of the car. 'We need to get a ticket for the track.'

'Where?'

'There's a hut round the back, at the track itself. As we did not stop on the way to eat, would you like a coffee and a snack of some sort?'

'I will, if you will.'

'I will.'

'Jolly good.'

'But first, we'll get the ticket.'

'Lead the way. I say, will you look that.' Greville went on smiling. 'Something to tease you, eh, dear boy?'

There were already several parked cars of varying types and manufacture, some decorated in racing colours. Their licence plates indicated they came from all over the EU and Scandinavia. Greville was looking at a bright yellow version of a racy model from a well-known manufacturer.

'Porsches for breakfast,' he read aloud, 'Ferraris for lunch.'

'Not this Porsche,' Müller said.

'Oh, ho! Challenge! Gauntlet dropped.' Greville sounded as eager as a schoolboy. Think we'll meet him on the track?' he added as they headed for the ticket office.

'I think we will pass him on the track.'

'That's the spirit!'

They got their ticket, then returned to the café to have a bite and a coffee.

'Ready?' Müller asked when they had finished.

'Absolutely.'

'One other thing . . . call of nature, if you need to. Toilets are underneath, access from outside.'

'Might be a good idea,' Greville said, as they went out.

Looking at him, Müller found it hard to believe Greville was really going to die. He looked far healthier than many of the people around him.

As he waited for Greville's return, Müller fought conflicting emotions within him. Part of him knew what Greville had told him about the DNA weapon; and had it not been for Greville's sudden blackout, there would have been no outside indication of what that thing was doing inside the major's body. Yet even so, Müller felt a sense of the surreal, still finding it difficult to look upon the cheerful Greville as a dying man.

Then Greville was back. 'Ready for the off?'

They got into the Porsche, and joined the queue for the 20.6 kilometre track.

'Do look at that, old boy,' Greville said, excitement in his voice. 'Jaguar D-type, British Racing Green. A beauty!'

It was a remarkably well-preserved example. The driver was even wearing a peaked helmet, more in keeping with the era of the Jaguar. It carried a Swedish licence plate.

'Thank God for the Swedes, eh? Preserving the old Blighty heritage.' Greville cranked his head round. 'No sign of the challenger.'

Müller gave a fleeting smile. 'You want a fight, don't you?'

'Want to see you eat *him* for breakfast, old boy.'

'You're incorrigible.'

'Nothing else to be at my age.'

Then the Jaguar took off. Its roar blasted back at them, even through the closed windows.

'My . . . *word*!' Greville enthused. 'That's a *sound*!'

The Jaguar sped away into the distance.

Then it was their turn. Müller floored the pedal. The Turbo

snarled its unmistakable boxer sound and hurtled after the rapidly diminishing Jaguar.

'Tell me when to put on the music,' Müller said. 'It will take us eight minutes to complete the circuit. I'll put it on repeat. Depending on when it goes on, this will give you two and a bit plays by the time we're ready to leave the track.'

Greville was relaxed in his seat, watching as the car hurled its way through the 'Green Hell' along the curves, bends, swoops, and switch-backs of the legendary track.

'Not just yet, old boy,' he said. 'Let me savour this.'

Müller fed the Porsche through the meanderings of the track, at one with the machine.

When they were passing the four-kilometre mark, Greville said, 'Music, maestro . . . please.' He had spoken softly, almost inaudible above the sound of the racing engine.

'I can slow down,' Müller said.

'No, old boy. This is absolutely fine.'

'Greville . . .'

'I'm all right, old son. Really. Couldn't be better.'

Müller nodded, and put on the music. Glenn Miller's wailing saxes flooded the car as they oozed out the first bars of 'Stardust'.

Greville began to sing the words softly, hesitantly at first, to the accompaniment of the swirling music. By the time the sax solo with the burping trombones in the background had come on, he was singing with more confidence.

Müller kept his eyes fixed upon the track, but he felt a suspicious heat behind them, as Greville began to ba-di-ba with the sax. Then he would drop a few words of the song into the music.

Greville stopped singing when it ended its first play. They were halfway through the replay when Greville spoke softly.

'Sunset,' he said.

'Greville?' Müller said, not looking at him.

There was no reply.

'Oh, God,' Müller said, voice choking.

He drove the rest of the way at a much reduced speed,

enough time for a second replay. He realized tears were trickling down his cheeks.

'Our challenger never appeared, Greville,' he said.

The dying notes of the second replay faded just as they came to the end of their run.

Müller drove off the track, and took Greville home to the Derrenberg.

They scattered Greville's ashes into a deep hole dug in the residential garden. The deliberately chosen wooden box in which they had been placed was burnt in the hole, which was then filled. Aunt Isolde planted a rose bush over it.

'Now he'll always be with me,' she said.

Cap Ferrat, France. Wednesday, 1100 local

Rachel Worth walked into the gardens of the pink Belle Epoque villa towards a bench where a young woman was sitting, reading. A tiny needle hidden in her hand, she moved swiftly. Music suddenly started, and a water display spouted upwards. The woman looked up from her book with a smile of appreciation.

As she walked past, Rachel Worth appeared to stumble. In the attempt to steady herself, she touched the girl briefly near the neck. The needle went in, in a smooth, quick movement, the force of her palm disguising the pinprick. The needle was withdrawn swiftly as she straightened.

'Sorry,' she said to the girl in accentless French. 'Clumsy today.'

The girl smiled at her. 'No problem.'

Rachel Worth walked on, made her way back out of the gardens to the sloping car park where a car was waiting to take her to Monaco.

By the time the car had left the car park, the young woman was slumped on the bench, already dead.

On the Friday morning following Nürburgring, Müller and

Carey Bloomfield returned to Berlin. They made their way straight to his office.

Pappenheim was waiting in the corridor. 'Sorry about Greville.'

Müller gave a helpless shrug. 'Right up to the moment, I hoped it would not happen. The really frightening thing was that he knew with such certainty.'

'And he took his secret with him. Brave man.'

'A remarkable man. No one will thank him for it.'

'We will,' Pappenheim said. 'We know what it cost him. How's your aunt taking it?'

'Better than I imagined. She never cried . . . at least, not when we could see her.'

'It will take her some time,' Carey Bloomfield said. 'Then she will let go and grieve.'

'Well, I've got a surprise for you,' Pappenheim said. 'Arrived yesterday.'

He looked at Pappenheim. 'Surprises worry me. What is it?'

'Why don't you look?'

All three went into the office.

Müller stared at the small padded envelope on his desk. 'Kaltendorf put in a show?'

'He popped in yesterday, popped out again. He didn't even ask for you.'

'Good sign? Or bad sign?' Müller picked up the envelope and began to inspect it.

'Who knows with that man? Haven't heard since. Hasn't been in as yet today. Well? Are you going to open it?'

But Müller was staring at the stamp. 'Australia,' he said in a low voice.

'That got my attention too.'

Müller slowly began to open the envelope. He took out a square, blue jewel box. He frowned at it.

'I can see a note,' Pappenheim prompted.

Müller took it out, and opened the single fold. It was from Graeme Wishart, of the Western Australian police.

*I thought long and hard about doing this. In the end, I felt
it was right to send it to you. One of our divers found it,
clutched in a hand. I am so very sorry, Jens.
Your friend always,*
  Graeme

Wordlessly, Müller handed the note to Carey Bloomfield,
who read it with Pappenheim.

Then they looked up from the note with stricken expressions.

Müller opened the box carefully. When he saw the little
blue shell, a low moan of deep pain came out of him.

Pappenheim grabbed Carey Bloomfield and dragged her,
silently protesting, out of the office.

Müller sat down heavily on the edge of his desk, gripping
the shell tightly in one hand.

In the corridor, Carey Bloomfield was saying in a sharp
whisper, 'I should be with him!'

Pappenheim's grip was firm. 'Not this time. He must do
this alone. You know that.'

They heard a rasping sound come faintly through the door.

'Come,' Pappenheim said in a gentle, shaky voice. 'I'll
buy you coffee.'

He saw that her eyes were as red as his felt.

Cape Leveque, Western Australia, two weeks later, close to sunset

Müller stopped the four-wheel-drive nose-on to the water,
on the same stretch of beach where he had last seen the
Hargreaves – his parents – alive. After a moment's hesitation, he climbed slowly out of the vehicle.

In the passenger seat, Carey Bloomfield made no attempt
to get out. She knew he had to do this alone.

'You OK, Müller?' she asked with some anxiety.

'I'm fine,' he answered, and shut the door softly on the
warmth of the coming night.

The cape was having one of its more spectacular sunsets. The red pindan cliffs at his back seemed to glow with an unearthly fire, brighter than he had ever seen it. The white of the beach gleamed. The cloudless sky, which had been a bright blue during the day, was slowly turning a darker shade; and the surreal green of the calm ocean had now morphed into an emerald of shadows, sometimes glinting in the vivid blaze of the setting sun.

Müller walked slowly, right up to the water's edge. Held tightly in his right hand was the little blue shell.

He stopped, looking out to sea, and listening to the sighing lap of the wavelets at his feet. The sun painted its fire upon the stillness of his face.

Only a few of us know the value of what you have done, he thought looking out across the water. *The sacrifice you made. Forgive me for not understanding; but I was a child then, needing his parents. I would not have understood, had I known at the time. The Semper are bloodied, but neither down, nor out. But they have been badly hurt; and we know enough about some of them to take them down. But there are still many in the shadows. Greville is gone, taking his terrible secret with him. He too paid a high price for his sacrifice.*

Müller was uncertain what to do next. He'd considered resigning, and staying at Woonnalla. But information on the Semper still had to be collated. And if he resigned, he knew he'd miss Berlin, Pappi, and the others. He wanted some kind of compromise.

He knew Carey Bloomfield was also thinking of resigning her commission. Like himself, she was not sure whether it was the best thing to do. He thought they should spend some time at Woonnalla, to think it through.

The Semper have struck where we least expected it, he reflected.

The murder of Kaltendorf's daughter had shocked them all. And Rachel Worth was still out there.

Somewhere.

With Brannic dead, another assassin, the thin man with

the croak, had been called off. Müller had been totally unaware of his existence. However, those who had called off their assassin decided to keep their options open.

Müller turned his hand upwards, and opened it. 'Go, little shell. Tell me what to do.'

The blue shell had travelled a long way, in time and space. He had found it on a beach in Germany, when a child of six. Its bright, unusual colour had captivated him. There had not been another one like it and he had never seen anything remotely similar since then. He had given it to his mother as a present, putting it in a flowerpot.

'It will help it to grow,' he had told her at the time. It had always remained there; until the day they had made the flight that had ended in their faked deaths. She had taken it with her.

When he had come to Woonnalla for the first time, looking for the people he'd known of only as the Hargreaves, he had felt a sense of déjà vu; and he had entered the house in their absence, the feeling had grown stronger. Then he had picked up the scent of a perfume he had not smelt since he was twelve. But the growing realization he had not wanted to accept could no longer be denied when he had spotted the little blue shell on the back terrace of the Outback house. In a flower pot.

He closed his fist again; then after holding the shell tightly, drew his hand back and threw it as far across the water as he could. The boy had finally let go.

It sailed across the fiery globe on the horizon, and curved downwards into the darkening ocean. It continued in a fluttering tumble towards the ocean floor. In the gloom, it fell into the grasp of a skeletal hand, which closed over it.

This reaction could simply have been in response to the gentle impact, or of a current drifting past.

Müller stayed where he was, until the sun was fully set.

'Your sunset, Greville,' he said.

Some months later, Aunt Isolde looked at her rosebush. She thought it had grown faster than any rosebush she had ever seen.